LIGHT | DARK

short stories

LIGHT | DARK

short stories

Published in Canada by Engen Books, St. John's, NL.

A CIP catalogue record for this book is available from Library and Archives Canada.

ISBN: 978-1-989473-28-3

Engen Books
www.engenbooks.com
submissions@engenbooks.com

First mass market paperback printing: April 2012
Second Edition mass market paperback printing: September 2016
Third Edition: October 2019

Cover Image: Shutterstock
Cover Design: Matthew LeDrew
Editing: Erin Vance

CONTENTS

A NOTE FROM
THE PUBLISHER

A note to you, dear reader.

This is a collection of short fiction from within the fictional setting known as the Engen Universe, a world much like our own where strange and wonderful things can happen. The setting is currently explored over nearly twenty novels and short stories, in genres ranging from science-fiction, fantasy, and horror.

The stories included in this anthology exist in that shared universe but are intended to be able to be read on their own. The title 'light| dark' comes from the fact that these stories, like the universe they were inspired by, encompasses a broad range of tones and themes.

We hope you enjoy.

PREFACE

"Working late?" Matthew smiled, looking up from the soft glow of his computer screen.

The man did not respond, carrying his briefcase as though it weighed a hundred pounds as he walked past the clerk and into his office.

He was old, at least sixty, his silvery hair receding noticeably at the front. His nose seemed a little too big for the rest of his face, but his eyes were a kind and gentle shade of blue, no matter how he tried to hide it.

His office was large, taking up nearly the entire top floor of the building. The carpets were plush and soft against the soles of his shoes, usually putting him in a good mood, but not today.

There were three folders sitting on his desk at the far end of the office, his lamp shining down on them like a spotlight.

He let out a long sigh as he sat down, staring at them sternly. He opened the drawer next to him and withdrew a bottle of Chateau Lafite marked as 1787 and a glass. He popped its cork and poured himself a healthy sampling before he reached into the breast pocket of his blazer, withdrew a cigarette, brought it to his lips and lit it. There was a brief pause right after he took that first drag when there was no stress in him.

Allowing himself a smile, he turned toward the first folder and opened it.

THE THEOGONY

- MATTHEW LeDREW -

He lay alone on his cot with his legs curled up near his waist like he was cold, but he'd kicked all the covers off. They laid on the floor in a crumpled mess that looked like a used tissue: pure white except for the dark pits of shadow that the folds created and the subtle remains of yellow piss stains that were somewhere on every sheet.

It was a single room and the walls were cushioned. All the hearers got cushioned rooms, whether or not they'd ever been violent or shown themselves to be violent. There was nothing in the room except his cot, pressed up against the wall, and the empty space alongside it where Dr. Brakman's chair went.

He'd been lying there for days, it felt like. Sometimes they would leave him there for longer. Once he would have sworn he'd been left there for weeks: the light from the window hadn't changed, and it was too high up for him to look out through. The light could have been coming from anywhere. It could have been a spotlight that they'd pushed up to the window to try and fool him. Or they could have moved the Clinic to the Arctic Circle. It could be daylight for months there.

Sometimes these thoughts occurred to him and it was almost impossible to get them out. Most of the time he knew that they weren't right, but other times they latched in deep. Sometimes, lying there in bed, he thought he could almost feel the concrete base of the Clinic as it slid along the snowy field of the Northwest Territories and up toward the North Pole. Sometimes he could hear the little Inuit boys that the Orderlies paid three bucks an hour to pull it along, each with their own chain strapped to their arms and hauling with all their might. Of course, the Orderlies did this for nothing more than their own amusement. There was a switch in the fuse box that turned on treads that ran below the Clinic like a tank. The Orderlies would grin out the windows and flip the switch, then watch as the Clinic lurched to life and started down across the snow, the little Inuit boys running and jumping to get out of the way.

"Theo?" Dr. Brakman said, leaning in with a smile full of teeth and getting his attention.

Theo blinked twice. His eyes hadn't been closed, yet somehow Brakman had just appeared in front of him. He was sitting on the chair that was usually left just outside his room. It was only brought in for Brakman. Anyone else who came in to talk to him had to stand or lean against the far wall.

Brakman was a short man with a large nose that came out of his face and tried to stab you when he spoke to you. He would always inch closer and closer when he talked, until there was nothing of your personal space left and your chest felt itchy and claustrophobic from it. He said his name like brac-MAN out loud and when people asked him how it was pronounced, but in his head, it was BREAK-man. It was on the billboard he rolled in with him now, standing up behind him with spotlights shining up at it from every conceivable direction, blue letters on a bright green background: BREAK MAN.

Theo fidgeted, then squinted his eyes and turned away from the lights. His pillow had been pushed up against the wall next to him and he grabbed it, pulling it close until his face was buried in it.

Brakman frowned, then nodded and got up. He took the chair with him as he left. No sooner was he gone than one of the Nurses came in. She was holding a syringe up in the air, its tip long and dripping as she flicked it twice and pushed on the plunger. The liquid came out in sporadic little spurts that reminded him of squeezing juice boxes too hard as a child. She bent over and shoved the metal end into the meat of his buttocks and the world went fuzzy around the edges again, slowly working its way in until all he could see was the glowing white gauze that was his world.

They may have left him like that for days, he wasn't sure. The light outside was always on.

The Group Meeting room, like most every other room in Black Springs Clinic, was painted the same greyish white on all four walls. The far wall was almost completely made up of tall windows that stretched from just a foot off from the floor to the top of the ceiling, the glass covered by a thick wire mesh on either side. Outside, it was bright. The sun glistened off the sand that they were always told was at a beach, but you could never see any water past it, no matter what window you looked out of how hard you craned your neck. Many suspected that it wasn't actually there, that it was a cruel joke they'd made up to try and get some of the Closers to escape. They'd get it into their head to escape, and make it out in a laundry trolley and get out only to discover that there was nothing but sand and a few patches of crabgrass for as far as the eye could see. Some would just go back inside. Others would be caught within hours by the Orderlies. A few would actually die out there in the hot desert sun.

The room was one of two common areas in the Clinic, which were attached to one another by two doors on the Eastern wall. The Public Room (as it was often called by both the Residents and the Orderlies) was large and bright and always clean, with tables and games and a TV that could be turned, it seemed, to any channel in existence, though Brakman seemed to only tune it to the news stations. The Group Room was dark and grey and always seemed cold. While the Public Room only had one purpose, the Group Room served as a multi-function room. There were easels stacked against the far wall that were used for what the Pretty Nurse called Art Therapy. There was clay beneath a sink in the corner, too. But mostly it was used for the meetings, when the Pretty Nurse and Dr. Brakman would sit at one end of a circle with all the Closers and Hearers around them, and they'd talk. Everyone would talk. Sometimes they would talk about themselves, sometimes they'd talk about each other, sometimes Brakman would give a person or topic for them to talk about, but they always talked and nobody ever told the truth.

Theo sat on the far left, his chair pushed back just slightly so that he could see past Johnny's head and out the window. There was sand out there all right, mounds of it. It seemed to go on forever. He wondered how long they'd left him in his room. Long enough to make it from the North Pole all the way down to the desert. He squinted at what he saw through the windows, watching the way the light reflected off the fine grains and made it look white. It could have been snow, he thought. It might still be. They could have done something to the window to make it look like sand when really it was snow. Or it might not be real at all. They could have ordered one of the pull-down backdrops that they used to use all the time in movies before they started using computers for everything. It could have been the sand from Ben-Hur he was looking at. The more he stared at it, the more it was.

"Theo?" Dr. Brakman said, scribbling something down on the clipboard he held against his knee.

Theo's head snapped forward and he rolled onto his knees without a word, looking from patient to patient to see who was talking and then pretending to make eye contact with them to make it seem like he was listening. He'd discovered some time ago that if you stared at the spot in between a person's eyebrows, you could fool everyone that you were looking right at them, even the person doing the talking.

It was Jerry talking right now, one of the older Closers. He'd been here almost as long as anyone had; at least that was what he said. He was a thin old man with white hair that straggled down behind each ear, and a pointy nose and mouth that made him look like he had a beak that was always open. His eyes were sunken and dark under his forehead, only lighting up from time to time.

Paul Pike was next to him, a stutterer who couldn't even say his own name. The rest of the Closers were on him about it constantly, especially when they went around introducing new patients on the Ward. "That's Davey, and that's Fred, and this over here is Pill Poke."

"P-P-P-P-Paul P-P-P-P-Pike."

"T-T-T-T-Tall T-T-T-T-Tyke?"

"P-P-P-P-Paul P-P-P-P-Pike."

"M-M-M-M-Mall M-M-M-M-Mike?"

This would continue until Paul finally got sick of the game and found a spot on the floor and stared at it until they went away. Most times he'd stay that way until the Pretty Nurse came back to him and took him off to bed.

Carl was fidgeting with the sleeves of his shirt, trying to fix it so that people couldn't see his scars. Nobody ever could, but he always thought they could. He'd tried to kill himself twice the year before he'd come to Black Springs, and now all he wanted was to be out. He'd tried only once since he'd been inside, and Theo couldn't completely say that he blamed him. He never spoke except in the group meeting, and even then only when he was asked to.

Lindsey complained about his wife, always. He'd been in the Clinic for ten years and his wife had died after five waiting for him to get out, but he could still do nothing except bitch about The Wife.

Danny Cliff sat backward in his chair toward the group and thought he looked cool. He'd been convicted of six counts of sexual assault (four on women and two on a man) and had been sent to Black Springs as a sex addict. He'd been here three years and was no better than the day they'd brought him in. He was always smiling, always happy, and loved playing Monopoly and Gin. He also loved masturbating in the corner when he thought nobody was looking, or had until Brakman had found the right combination of drugs. Now he could rarely get it up, but sometimes he still grabbed hold of himself in the corner, even when it was nothing more than a limp noodle.

There was a guy named Pedro that everyone called Ruffles. He talked all the time, but didn't make any sense. He'd go on about Russia and The Bomb for hours, no matter how many times you tried to tell him that the war was over and that it was all good. Once Danny Cliff had told him that the Russians had finally got The Bomb into Cuba and Ruffles lost his mind so badly that the orderlies had to give him two helpings of Haldol to calm him down.

Rob was a Bruins fan that could not stop shitting himself in public. He never once did it on the Ward, but they'd let him out five times now, and every time he'd be back in a week later to tell them all the places he'd shit.

There were others that didn't talk, usually twenty (give or take) on the Ward at any given time. Some never shared, some only shared. Some never talked, some never stopped talking. The only thing that was true of all of them was that they all brought their own signs.

Each of them had billboards that sat behind them like giant TV sets all tuned to different channels. There was a different volume control for each one, but someone had set all of them to blast at all times. Sometimes if he tried, Theo could make a particularly annoying one (like a song playing on repeat) fade into the background, but it always seemed like the others would get louder to compensate. It almost wasn't worth it.

Rob was thinking about the last Bruins game he was at. The game was in 3D and almost came off the billboard at them every time someone shot or passed the puck down the ice. The crowd cheering droned into a white noise that was almost blissful, except that every time the Bruins scored (which they did often in Rob's memory, more often then Theo suspected was likely), a loud buzzer went off that cut through the cheers and made him want to cover his ears.

Ruffles' billboard looked like something out of science-fiction theatre, with a bunch of men wearing white coats all standing around a device that Theo could not recognize, but he assumed was Ruffles' twisted nightmare vision of what a nuke looked like. There were wires that looked like claws coming out of it everywhere. All the men were looking down at it and writing onto their clipboards. It wasn't a video; Ruffles' billboard never was. It looked like one of those slide shows that the General used to brief his men in the old spy movies, all shaky and sepia-toned. There was a flag with a sickle and hammer on it in the background.

"The Bomb," Ruffles said, looking intently at a line in the palm of his hand as though he were reading from some secret document in it. "They've got the Bomb."

Danny Cliff's billboard was replaying an old episode

of Gilligan's Island. It stopped and strayed to a different thought whenever Mary-Anne came onto the screen, though. He'd somehow managed to rescue her from the island and she was back in his bed and he was towering over her. She still had her hair in her pigtails and her eyes were closed, her face drawn out in an expression of simultaneous disdain and ecstasy. These only lasted a second before jumping back to the main plot of the Professor making a radio out of a coconut shell. It was as if someone had inserted single frames of pornography into an otherwise wholesome movie reel.

Lindsey seemed to be actually listening to Jerry. His billboard was of his mother. He was looking up at her as she cut potatoes at the kitchen table. Judging from his height, he was no more than four. Her lips were red, and her dress was blue with a white apron in front, and there was just a little grey catching along her hair at the temples. She looked absolutely beautiful.

Theo hung on that one for a moment, watching out of the corner of his eye (so that Brakman wouldn't notice) as Lindsey's mother picked him up and hoisted him into the air, laughing. He could smell her perfume. It smelled like lilies.

Carl's billboard was a still picture of the album *Dude Ranch*, the bull on its cover looking back at Theo from over its bulbous backside. *Dammit* was playing loudly from speakers on either side of the sign, and Carl was bobbing his head along with the beat. If the music hadn't been there, he would have just looked twitchy, but while it was playing he looked like he was ready to start singing along at any point.

Paul's was filled with static. Every so often there would be a flash of something, like a clown or a star-filled sky, but it would be gone again before Theo could really see what it was. It was like his sign was a television that some inept child was trying to adjust the rabbit ears on and failing miserably.

Everyone had a sign it seemed, except Theo. He wondered sometimes if they'd forgotten to give him one upon admission, but then he remembered that it wasn't just people in Black Springs that had the signs. If he tried hard, he could dimly recall that people out in the World had them too. It was harder to see them out there though. The lighting was better in here.

He shifted uncomfortably.

Even Dr. Brakman and the Pretty Nurse had billboards. Right now Dr. Brakman's was just the Group Room from his point of view, as though his eyes were cameras that projected the image out a lens in the back of his head and onto the screen. There was music though, a rendition of Beethoven's Fifth with pianos and oboes that seemed to keep his blood pressure down. The Pretty Nurse was thinking of her son, a young man named Christopher. He was two, and the image of him made Theo smile.

She saw Theo smiling at her, and it made her shift uncomfortably.

Jerry's billboard was dark, like a house at night after the lights have been turned off and your eyes haven't gotten a chance to adjust yet. Even now, there were bits of blue coming in from the moonlight, touching the edges of a dresser and a nightstand, as though someone were painting in the scene as they went.

"It was always my mother, you know," Jerry said, fumbling with his hands. He was looking down, but there was a sparkle in his eyes hidden deep within the shadow of those bushy eyebrows. "She could be so nice sometimes, but she didn't understand how being so horrid made all that go away. She could erase the nice by being horrid, but she couldn't erase the horrid by being nice."

The scene moved back and forth, as though the camera were on some kind of rocker that never seemed to stop. The wall was visible now, the moonlight reflecting off it and giving light to the other items in the room.

"She would always punish me. Most of it I didn't even know what for. Made me take a bath in ice water once, I thought my nuts were going to come off. I think it was because I had a wet dream."

The camera shifted focus rapidly, skewing down to look away from the wall. It was on a bed, not a rocking chair, and now there was enough light bouncing off of the wall that a girl could be seen wedged uncomfortably between the camera and the bed, the blue moonlight making her features soft. She was saying something, but the sound had been muted on her. Not everything had been muted though; Theo could still hear the squeaking. Could hear it even above the blare of the Bruins's latest goal.

"One time when I cut my hands chopping wood, she made me put them in bleach," he said, running his fingers over a deep scar on the back of his hand. "Another time she locked me in the cellar for a whole week, only fed me twice. It was dark and cold, and I hardly got any sleep on account of the rats. I don't even know why she did that."

"It was because you took your little sister to bed with you," Theo said, his voice monotonous and far away. He was meeting Jerry's gaze for real now, and Jerry returned it with a stare that could have frozen fire. He was snarling, but there was still that twinkle in his eye. The movie on the screen continued, but it was flickering now, as though about to change reels into a different picture.

Brakman looked up from his pad at Theo, his eyebrows stretching to reach where his hairline should have been. "Theo?"

"I never did no such thing," Jerry said, staring across the circle at Theo. "I loved my sister. She was an angel."

"Yes, you did," Theo nodded, motioning to the billboard behind him as though everyone could and should be able to see it. He tilted his head to one side. The incestuous film was playing again now, but this time with more light. It was still flickering though. "You went into her room sometimes after your parents went to sleep. You told yourself not to and that you'd never do it again and that she wouldn't remember, but you always kept doing it. It was like someone else took over you, like you couldn't control what you were doing when you did it."

"Shut up. That never happened."

"Theo --" Brakman started to object, but did it low enough that he knew Theo would not stop.

Danny Cliff's billboard had changed now, Theo could see out of the corner of his eye. It was a twisted imaginary version of the scene on Jerry's board, with Jerry the same age as he was now and the girl slightly older than she had been in Jerry's memory. The girl was blonde in Danny's version and brunette in the real one, but otherwise they were about the same. The cameras moved back and forth at different speeds and made Theo so motion sick that he thought he might get nauseous.

"You never even found out how your mother found out," Theo continued, "You came home one day and she started screaming at you and hitting you with her shoe and telling you all the things you'd done. You hadn't thought about it in weeks... it was always a few weeks between times, and for a while after each one you didn't think about it at all. Didn't even remember doing it. She hit you with her shoe and pushed you down over the stairs and left you there for weeks."

"Shut up!" Jerry yelled, and Theo snapped out of his trace and blushed.

Jerry's billboard had finally fully changed. It was like Brakman's now, his eyes turned into cameras that showed Theo himself from Jerry's point of view. After a second, the camera rose and came across the circle at him, arms reaching out from behind the fourth wall and gripping Theo around the neck, forcing him off the chair.

Theo almost had to look around and assure himself that it wasn't really happening.

Jerry was still burrowing holes into Theo's head with his eyes, with the sparkle back there again now, as (on the billboard behind him) Theo gasped for air through purple lips.

"I think we should move on," Brakman said, and the Pretty Nurse nodded in agreement and flipped to the next page in her chart and showed it to him. "Paul, we were talking last day about an incident between you and another boy when you were eleven."

∞

Everyone showered at once. All twenty-something residents on the Ward, at least the ones who could stand, crowded into a shower room that looked like a gas chamber out of a World War II biopic. It got Ruffles going every time, kicking and screaming and saying that they were going to gas him. Every day they tried to get him in, and every day they wound up giving him a shot and scrubbing him down themselves with the Vegetables while he was out.

There was one door and there was one Orderly at it at all times to make sure nobody got out and snuck off into the desert nude. They didn't like tanned Closers. He was supposed to be watching them to make sure that Danny Cliff or someone like him didn't try to sodomize the others, but most of the Orderlies were too liberal to spend fifteen minutes every day looking at twenty-something dicks flapping in and out of the stream in the room.

Theo loved the shower. The water was always hot (the entire building was heated by hot water), and it was the only time he felt clean and sane while he was here.

He leaned forward and pushed his head under the spray, letting it wet down his hair. He closed his eyes and felt it run down over him. There were dozens of songs in his head, and the few times he'd tried to sing, he'd ended up stuttering worse than Paul.

Jerry punched him in the face while he had his eyes closed, sending him crashing to the floor.

The fist had connected with both his left cheek and eye, and he could already feel the skin bruising as blood rushed to the surface. Redness streamed down his nose into his mouth and dripped from his chin, cleaned away almost instantly by the hot water and making deep pink swirls as they travelled down the tile and into the drain in the center of the room.

Jerry looked down at him, rage twinkling in those horrible sunken eyes of his. His fists were clenched tight at his sides as he waited to see if Theo would get up, prepared to smack him down again if he did.

Theo didn't say anything, just stared up into Jerry as blood seeped down from his face.

Jerry just breathed harder and harder until he finally turned and stepped away without a word.

Theo stayed on the floor until the Orderly turned off the faucets.

∞

The Public Room was called so because it was the only room that anyone from the outside could regularly see. Once a week (although it seemed like much longer sometimes; in fact Theo was sure there had been a year between visits once), friends and relatives would come in and sit at long tables to chat, visit, and play board games.

It was easily the largest room in Black Springs, fitting ten long tables from the front of the room to the back. There were windows looking out at the beach again, although they didn't go as far down the wall here, leaving room for shelves that held books, magazines, videos and games. There was a ping-pong table in the back with no net next to some armchairs and a television (which was too high up for anyone to reach, even Danny Cliff, who was well over six and a half feet when he wasn't slouched over).

The time when the visitors came was the only time when all twenty of the patients at Black Springs were there at the same time. Of the twenty patients, there were three groups, though they were not equally divided.

There were two Vegetables who lay in their beds by the windows with tubes coming out of them everywhere. These fed in IVs and heart monitors that were carted around with them everywhere. They couldn't move or eat or talk, but the Orderlies carted them around to all the group meetings and public visits anyway as though they were a part of it somehow. Theo didn't know their names, but one had been named Carrot because his Mexican heritage gave his skin an orange complexion. The other had been named Turnip, just for virtue of consistency.

There were fifteen Closers, named for being 'closer' to getting released than any of the other groups. They comprised the majority of most mental institutions. They were self-committed or committed on behalf of family or, in rare cases such as Danny Cliff, here by some mercy of the state in lieu of a prison sentence.

Theo was a member of an elite class of clinic patient called Hearer (or Listener, alternatively, though they'd stopped using this moniker as it implied that the patients were hearing something that was actually there). They were the true schizophrenics, according to Brakman. They heard the voices that told them to do things. Caught somewhere between the lucid Closers and the catatonic Vegetables, they were unfortunate enough to likely be permanent occupants of Black Springs and unlucky enough to be aware of that fact. There were two others at the Ward at the moment, Ruffles and Rob, although there had been a fourth named Terry when Theo had arrived. He'd tried to kill Paul with a fork during Theo's first week. The next week he'd pushed the same fork so far into his own eye that he'd bled out before the Orderlies could do anything about it.

Jerry's wife came every week to visit him. Most days they'd talk at 'their' table closest to the door, but sometimes they'd play Gin or Bridge. A few times they'd laugh, and if they managed that, then Jerry was pleasant for days afterward. His billboard would be turned to her smile until something would be said in Group to make it flicker out, and he'd be back to mean Jerry again.

The Vegetables had what seemed to be a nearly endless supply of family that took turns coming in and taking care of them. The two clans seemed to know each other, and know of each other very well, and would talk for hours over tea while Carrot and Turnip lay there staring out the window, oblivious to what was going on around them. It was as though the families had formed their own little club: Vegans of the Psychiatric Ward.

Paul's parents would sit with him and he didn't stutter nearly so much then, only on his M sounds, which he could try to avoid. Lindsey's son visited every second week, and Carl's wife seemed to be the first one in every time. Sometimes it seemed like she camped out in front the night before just to get in as early as she could.

There were three people visiting with Danny Cliff alone. Two were older and clearly his parents, while the third was a young blonde girl that looked about nineteen. She might have been his girlfriend, or possibly a much younger sister. There was a pink stripe in her hair and she wore metal hoop earrings so big they almost touched her bare shoulders. She wore a top with horizontal black and white stripes under a brown leather jacket with no zipper and jeans. Her navel was showing, and it was pierced as well. She was leaning against the wall a few feet from where Danny and his parents spoke, eyes moving freely around the room from one patient to another. She looked like she should have been smoking.

Everyone had somebody.

Theo sat alone at a long table in the middle to the room, caught between the Vegetables and the Closers. There was a bag of potato chips in front of him that was opened and pointing at him, though he did not remember how they had gotten there, and he hadn't eaten a single one. They smelled disgusting, like old cheese.

He sat alone until the Orderlies told him it was time to go.

∞

It was dark in Theo's room when he went back to it. He could not remember the last time it had been dark. Had they turned off the light? Or was it time for the six months of darkness now? He hoped not.

His pillows and sheets smelled fresh and new, so he curled up in them instead of tossing them away as he usually did, even though he knew that by midway through the night, he would hate the stench of them and they would be a gaggled mess on his floor.

His head hit the pillow and he closed his eyes, and for one blissful moment there was silence and darkness, and he felt sleep take the first tentative tugs at his eyelids. His mouth was still numb from the pill the Pretty Nurse had given him before closing the door, but it was fading fast. Soon he wouldn't even remember it.

There was a small sparkle in the darkness that made his eyelids flutter. It looked like the twinkle of Jerry's eyes, or maybe even the headlight of some far-off train. It glimmered in the distance for a moment, then came at him at warp speed. Suddenly the darkness was gone and his padded walls turned into flat-screens, all of them turned to their own channel and bawling at them at their highest volume. His bed was gone, even though he could still feel it beneath him, and the screens started to close in on him as they did every night, the sphere of his personal space becoming smaller and smaller. His heart beat faster and faster as the glowing, yelling images descended upon him until finally he was inside the screens. All of them. At once.

The Pretty Nurse was on his bed and was about to fold the sheets when Danny came up behind her. He bent her over the bed and she fought at first, but only at first, and after a minute she turned over and let him climb on. Her breasts were bigger here then they were in the Group Meets, enlarged to an almost comedic size as Danny settled himself down between them.

Jerry punched him in the cheek and he went down. There was so much water falling down on him that he thought he was going to drown.

There was a field then. The walls all collapsed away as though the Ward was actually a house of cards that just got a good easterly gust. Danny was still fucking the Nurse on Theo's bed and they hadn't even noticed that they were in a field even though the tall grass was tickling their bare skin. Jerry was still standing above him. Carl sat on a log near them and was laughing wildly, slapping his knee repeatedly as he did. His wrists were clean and there were tears coming down his face, he was laughing so hard. His kids were behind him, and for a moment, Theo thought he was laughing at him.

"Don't be silly now, boy," Carl said, motioning Theo to turn around. "You're missing the show."

Theo turned and saw that there was a Circus Tent behind Jerry, with clowns running in one side in all sorts of silly matters. Carl's kids ran out from behind him to go and play, all thirteen of them, and they ran right through Jerry and made him disappear.

Theo breathed a sigh of relief.

"That's better now, ain't it?" Carl smirked, offering Theo a hand up.

There was a monster hanging back in the shadows. It was large and purple and looked like it was made of slime. It wouldn't come into the tall grass, but it swiped at it with its long talons and cut it down with each pass. Theo hoped he wouldn't be smart enough to use this method to cut a path toward them.

Lindey's mother stood next to Theo's bed holding a plate of cookies in her hand and looking for all the world like Barbara Billingsley. She smiled that unflappable smile down at Danny as the Nurse again tried to push him off with that face like Mary-Anne had had, wanting but not wanting what was happening.

"Well, that's not very nice now, is it?" Barbara said, taking one of the cookies off the tray and having a bite.

Jerry punched him in the cheek and he went down.

There was so much water falling down on him that he thought he was going to drown. Jerry bent over and grabbed him around the throat, squeezing the wet flesh until it was impossible for him to get air.

The Purple People Eater started mowing the lawn with huge swipes of his claws.

Paul's brother was yelling at him and he was running away from it. He went over to his girlfriend's house, but she was eating zebra and working a pedal with her foot. It looked like the pedal of a sewing machine, but it wasn't, it was a pump for poison gas that started to come in through the vents even now.

The poison did not affect the monster.

Carl laughed and laughed. The gas was Nitrous Oxide, at least partly. Paul's girlfriend was pumping the Nitrous Oxide that she'd stolen from the Russians who were trying to find a way to mix it with Mustard Gas and send it to every Dentist in Amerika, a fiendish plot if ever the Commie Bastards had ever had one. They would have stopped her too, but they were too busy dealing with Ruffles. He'd found their secret plans for The Bomb, and he wasn't going to give them back until they gave him thirty-six Twizzlers and a Cherry Coke.

"Oh, Danny. You feel so good," the Pretty Nurse moaned; and for a moment, Theo forgot where he was and when he turned around the Greased Lightning was there and Danny was screwing Sandra Dee in the back seat in some weird never-before-seen outtake. He blinked and the car was still there, but now it was Danny Cliff and the Pretty Nurse in the back seat, still dressed like their fifties counterparts, Danny with his hair greased back and his leather jacket on.

Carl laughed so hard that he pissed himself.

Paul's girlfriend kept pumping Nitro into the air, feeding her pet poodle a few scraps of zebra under the table.

Jerry punched him in the cheek and he went down. There was so much water falling down on him that he thought he was going to drown. Jerry bent over and grabbed him around the throat, squeezing the wet flesh until it was impossible for him to get air. Theo's lips turned blue as he fought for air, but Jerry seemed unaffected by anything he did.

"Stop it," he said weakly though bloated lips. The blood vessels in his cheeks were bursting. "Stop... stop it."

He closed his eyes as they rolled back into his head.

When he opened them again, there was light bathing in through the windows and getting caught in the stream of sweat he'd made. Had they only turned the lights off long enough to fool him? Had they ever been off at all?

The pads on the wall were ripped and torn in long, winding patches as though something had dug its claws in deep at the top and dragged them right down to the baseboards. At first he'd thought it had been the People-Eater, but then he'd noticed the scrapes of white fabric still underneath his nails.

There was a knocking sound from beyond the wall, and when he looked, he could see that the billboards were still there. Carl was still on his log and Danny was still fucking the Pretty Nurse to high heaven even though he'd came three times over already. He didn't seem to be losing his drive any. The billboards weren't on top of or inside of him now; they were floating away as if he were driving past them on the highway.

A new billboard that looked like Snow White singing about whistling while she worked was there too. It belonged to the Pretty Nurse, and Theo could hear her whistling along with the movie as it played in her head. She knocked on the next door in line and the billboard of Carl laughing fizzled out into nothing before becoming static for a half second, then turning into the Pretty Nurse. It was like his eyes were cameras again, looking out at her as she peeped in through the window in the door to make sure Carl was getting up.

There was a knock at the next door and the image of her on her back in the Greased Lightning vanished, replaced by her soft face peering in through Danny's bedroom window again. It wasn't long before it was replaced by the same movie-reel porno though.

She came to Theo's door and looked in, noticing the fabric that had been ripped from the walls immediately.

He sat on his knees in the middle of the room and looked like he was in prayer, hunched over so that his shoulders looked huge and glaring out at her through wisps of hair.

She shook her head.

The easels had been pulled out from the wall and arranged around the Group Room in symmetrical, evenly spaced little cubicles so that everyone could have their space.

They were all there. Jerry was one seat behind Theo

and one to the left, enough that Theo kept seeing him move out of the corner of his eye.

The billboards were nice now, like watching psychedelic colours move to music, each stroke making something magnificent.

"That's good," the Pretty Nurse said. She walked between the easels with her hands clasped behind her, and looked more like a Nun in a Seminary than a Nurse in an Institution. She might as well have traded in that purity-white uniform for a Habit and Whipple.

She walked behind Paul and looked over his shoulder. He was painting a bust of a fox with the night sky behind it. The moon was bisected by the beast's ear and the stars behind it seemed to twinkle in the dark blue mat he'd made for them.

"That's very nice, Paul," she said.

He smiled, then went back to his painting.

Lindsey was painting something in light blue that looked like one of the Rorschach tests that Brakman used on them from time to time, but on his billboard it was clear that it was the dress he remembered his mother best in. He'd left the white from the apron unpainted, and it faded into the background and looked like something a real artist might have done.

"That's wonderful."

Ruffles had made a few marks on his canvas with his brush, but had quickly moved to using his hands. Despite the mess he'd made on himself and the floor around him, the resulting cacophony of blues and yellows and reds did look stunning, if random.

"That's good."

She walked behind Theo and threw a glance toward his canvas.

It was blank, the rivets in the white paper staring back at him. The paintbrush was in his hand with bright orange paint on the top that had dried on it had been there so long. It had dribbled down the wood of the brush and down across his knuckles.

She sighed and looked away.

"That's very good, Robert."

The Public Room seemed larger today.

Doctor Brakman said that there was something wrong with the Air Conditioner and that he'd already called the electrician, but when they piled all the Closers and Hearers and Vegetables into the room again to wait for their families to filter in, the heat and humidity ratcheted up with every warm body that came into the room until it was like an oven. The walls sweated with the immensity of it, and every inmate had beads rolling down into their eyes. The walls seemed to expand and contract with the heat, as though they were breathing.

Carl's wife was the first one in again, slinging her arms around him as though she hadn't seen him in months. It made Theo wonder if maybe it *had* been months. Maybe the lights had been out in his room for six whole months of darkness and he had been too far gone to realize it. He twitched out the corner of his mouth and brought his hand up to examine the level of scruff on his face. Was it more or less than the day before? Or the same?

Danny Cliff's father was back today, but not his

mother. They were sitting over in their usual spot and playing chess while talking about her now that she wasn't there. When the Pretty Nurse walked by, the father looked her up and down and asked his son if he'd tapped her yet. Danny only smiled in response and moved his knight to king seven.

Theo sat alone at the long table between the Vegetables and the Closers with a Snickers bar unwrapped in front of him that he had yet to take a bite out of. The plastic wrap that still covered its lower half had started to curl from the heat and the humidity in the room.

"Well, don't you look happy," a blonde girl said, flopping down on the chair opposite Theo in such a way that she was laying down across several, her entire weight supported on the crook of her elbow and the meager swell of her lip. Her hair bounced on her shoulders with the impact and she smiled at him, a perfect row of white between two thin slivers of crimson.

She was the one who'd been visiting Danny the day before. That pink stripe was still in her hair and came down on either side of her earrings, getting caught in them and wrapped up in them. Her shoulders looked as white as milk as she brought one colourfully painted fingernail up onto the table and used it to spin the chocolate bar around to face her.

"Mind if I take a bite?"

He didn't say anything, just shrugged.

She laughed a little. "I said: Mind if I take a bite?"

"Nn," he said at first, as though it took great effort to speak. "No. No, go ahead."

She nodded politely and picked up the bar between

her thumb and forefinger. It entered her mouth without touching her lips and she bit off the tip, bits of caramel running out of it and staining that picturesque smile of hers. "Heaven."

She held it back out to him as though it hadn't been his to begin with. "Want some?"

"No," he said again, and it came out much easier this time.

"Why not? You don't eat? Is that what they got you in here for; you anorexic?"

"No. It just all tastes bad. Like feet. Really bad, smelly feet."

She looked at him without a smile for a moment, a kind of understanding buzzing behind her eyes as she mulled that over. She wrapped her hand around the bar and grabbed it fully now, taking a tearing bite of it. A chunk of peanut fell to the floor.

He was silent again then, listening to the drone of voices all around him and the TV behind him until it all became white noise. He stared past her until his vision focused on the row of chairs behind her and she became soft and blurry until it was like she wasn't there at all.

"So what're you in here for if you ain't anorexic, anyway?" she said. She had a drawl as though she was from the street even though she didn't look like it. Her clothes, her accent, her hair... it was all fake, he thought. There was something wrong that he could't quite put his finger on.

He didn't answer her.

"And where're your folks? You can't be the only guy in here without visitors every day. Young stud like you, I would've thought you'd've had a different girl here every day of the week... tell the redhead that visiting day is Tuesday and tell the brunette that it's Wednesday."

He didn't answer her, but she was in focus now. Everything was in focus now.

"And what about your parents? One of them has got to still be kicking around. Why aren't they camping out and waiting to come in like poor old Carl's wife?"

An Orderly walked by and she sat up in her chair as though she were about to get scolded. She leaned in close to Theo as though they were having an in-depth conversation about the answer to life, the universe, and everything.

Their hands touched for a moment and she bit her lip, looking from their hands to his eyes and then back again quickly.

"I --" he started, his mouth drenched with saliva and yet somehow dry at the same time.

"No, wait. Don't tell me." She smiled, peeling back his fingers until his palm was open on the table in front of her. "I'm psychic."

He smiled a little at that.

"Hey, worked already," she said, smiling back wider and wagging her head from side to side. Her earrings bounced. "Let's see what else we can get."

She bent over and began to study his palm, the tips of her hair tickling it and making him jerk away reflexively. She held on as though she'd done this a million times and was used to this response. His hands were rough and dry with yellowed nails that had been broken and split by the previous night's escapade. There was a line of blood blisters along the base of his fingers that he'd never even noticed until now. Each knuckle was like a tiny, dry, swirling bit of dessert sand. Her fingers were smooth and quick, running over the rough hewn lines of his palm and studying each one, tracing them all from start to finish and then using her nails to measure the distance between each.

"Interesting..." she said, humming contemplatively.

"What?" Theo asked, leaning forward to try and see what she was talking about.

"This is very interesting."

"What is it?"

"Well, you've got a fate line. Not many people do."

"Fate line?"

"Mm. See this one here that runs straight down from the middle finger to your wrist?" she said, tracing it gently as she did so and sending shivers up and down his spine. "That's your fate line."

"What does it mean?"

"It would seem, Mr..."

"Theo."

"It would seem, Mr. Theo, that you are the unlikely wielder of a destiny. You have a deep fate line, and are strongly controlled by fate."

Her eyebrows jostled from side to side as she spoke with a fake Scandinavian accent like some mystical palm reader at a county fair.

"What else is there?" he asked, leaning in closer now.

"Well, your head line is curved, so you're creative."

"I'm not."

"Yes, you are," she corrected, poking her nail into the

line as though she were pointing out a certainty in a signed contract. "But there's a cross in it here. You, my friend, are in some sort of emotional crisis."

He met her eye and said nothing, then looked back at his own palm as though it were some foreign object.

"Your life line tells me you're often tired, but you have more than one here so there's a chance to change that. You have extra vitality in you and... oh." She smiled.

"What?"

She gave him a coy look.

"What?"

"Your heart line, Mr. Theo... I never would have pegged you for the romantic type."

He stared at her with a puzzled expression on his face.

"It starts here at the middle finger and reaches down to touch the life line here and here. And there are little circles and smaller lines cutting into it... you fall in love easily, Mr. Theo, but I think you've had your heart broken."

He took his hand away, and this time she let him. "I haven't."

"Maybe you will," she shrugged, popping the last of the candy bar past her lips.

He shifted uncomfortably. His stomach rumbled, loud enough that he could hear it above everyone talking and the TV and the sound of the Air Conditioner trying to cut back in.

She squinted at him, feeling bad about the empty wrapper between them.

"That's a not a very nice thing to tell someone," he said finally, his hands darting under the table and away from her.

"Everyone gets their heart broke from time to time," she smirked. "There's no shame in it."

He shuffled uncomfortably.

"So why don't you eat anything anyway? You holding out for some good home-style cooking like your Mama used to make, or are you just picky?"

He did not respond to that.

"Or do you like your meals simpler? Maybe waiting for some good-old meat and potatoes like the one's your dad used to fire up on the grill on hot summer days."

The side of his mouth twitched again, and he found a small black stain on the table to stare at and avoid her eye.

She smiled, then nodded. "Well, if you ever get out of here, there's a little restaurant about a half mile off the highway that I think you'd like. The Olympic it's called, and it lives up to the name. Best steaks you ever had..." She paused. "Better even than the ones your daddy fried up."

He let out a short, frustrated sigh. "Why're you even here?" he asked the table, skulking. "Shouldn't you be over there with Danny?"

"Oh, I'm not here to see Danny, Mr. Theo," she smiled.

For the first time he realized she had no billboard behind her head. That he couldn't see any more to her than just her, all blonde hair and green eyes and white, smooth skin. He looked around for it for a moment, as though she might have somehow left it leaned against the wall on the far side of the room, then turned back to her.

She was still smiling at him and hadn't moved a muscle.

"I'd like to be left alone, please."

She exhaled through her nose and let her hands fall down by her sides. "Of course you would," she said, as though they'd had this argument a thousand times or more. "I mean, why wouldn't you? A man learns he has a destiny and all... it'd take the fun out of anyone, I guess."

"Please," he said, finding his spot on the table again and letting everything become blurry. He might not have been able to see her thoughts, but there were still plenty around. They screamed at him now, like fifty television sets all turned to different channels blaring information at him at the same time. "I just want to be left alone."

"Yeah," she said, standing up and straightening her shirt. "Too bad they don't have a line on a palm for Daddy issues. I bet that one'd run real deep."

He blinked, then looked up at her. She towered above him now. He hadn't realized how tall she was. "What?"

"Old man Theo, whoever he is... I bet he must be a real piece of work to have messed you up this bad. Did he put you in here, is that it?"

"My last name's not Theo."

"I know. That's not the damn point I was making."

"It's Flaherty."

She stopped speaking with her finger in the air like a cartoon character, frozen for a moment. "Flaherty?"

He nodded.

"Flaherty? Eff El Ey Hurty?"

He nodded again.

She brought her nail to her mouth and started to chew it, finding her own spot on the table to stare at and sat back down.

"What is it?" he asked, wishing she had a billboard so that he could just see whatever she was thinking all on his own.

"Nothing, it's... Nothing," she mumbled, waving the question away and then putting her hand right back into her mouth. She was picking at her nail with the minuscule gap between her two front teeth that he wouldn't have said was there a moment ago. "*Flaherty.*"

They sat there in silence until there was a full strip of paint gone from her nail.

"Did you..." he frowned, then stopped. He sighed, then forced himself to look up again. It was the first time he'd made himself do something consciously in months. He'd spent most of his time moving from white room to white room on the Orderly's commands. "Do you know my father?"

Her eyes moved to meet his and she studied his face, *really* studied it, just as she had his hand. His eyelids were shadowy and dark from lack of sleep, and there were deep torrents slicing down his face coming from either nostril, as if they had to be there to keep his frown from stretching clean off his face. He was white and his hair fell down into his eyes constantly, like the boys on the covers of pop singer albums. The lobes of his ears connected to his head. His eyelashes were long.

"Maybe," she whispered finally, reaching out and pushing his hair out of his face and squinting. Her touch sent shivers through him again. "Do you have any uncles? Brothers?"

He shook his head for each.

"There's this guy named Flaherty that I've seen on the road once or twice. Sharp dresser, always looks like he's to the nines."

His face perked up.

"I'm on the road a lot. I've seen him in a few different places, always with that briefcase and looking at things on his phone... I get the impression he travels for work a lot. He's got hair like yours, but he wears it different. Slicked straight back."

"That's him," Theo said, his voice almost a gasp. "That's my dad."

"Wow, look at that," she said. His hands were back on the table now and she clasped them. "Will wonders never cease?"

"Did you talk to him? Did he say anything to you?"

She tilted her head at him, a slow smile growing out one side of her mouth. "No. I mean, do I look like the type of girl your daddy would talk to?"

He looked her up and down. "Actually... yes."

"Hey!" she laughed, slapping him playfully on the arm. "I caught that. Watch your mouth."

He laughed, and the sensation was strange to him. Like a spasm in his throat he couldn't control. It died down after a moment, and he got quiet again. "So you never spoke to him?"

"Naw," she sighed. "Sorry. Caught his name from the truckers."

He nodded. His stomach growled ravenously. "Well, if you see him... just... make sure he knows when visiting hours are, okay? Take a pamphlet. He forgets stuff like that easy."

She smiled again, a real smile that showed off her teeth. "Why don't you tell him yourself? It's Wednesday, I bet he'll be there tonight."

He looked around the Public Room, as if she'd forgotten where they were.

"Come on," she said, waving his objection away again. "It'll be fun. Just you and me. We'll slip out of port via cover of darkness." The Scandinavian accent had returned, and he thought maybe she thought it was Russian. She smiled playfully at him. "We have ways of making you talk," she laughed, then hit him again. "I can have you out and back before light. That is, if you even want to come back."

Theo thought for a moment. He debated for an instant telling her that it was no use waiting until dark. That dark here never came, there was always the same light coming in through his window and that they never turned it off and they'd use it to catch them.

He opened his mouth to speak, then shut it again.

"Come on," she pleaded, running her thumbs along the edges of his hands. "You're not going to let me go out there all alone, are you?"

He met her eye, then smiled.

It was still light when the Orderlies tucked him in that night, using the sheets to tie him down to the mattress so tight he couldn't move. The padding on the wall had been replaced, the new pads a slightly brighter shade of white than the rest and glowing in the light from the window as though they were radioactive. It looked like the secret passages you'd see in old eighties animation, when the animators always coloured the part of the wall that would move a different colour than the rest so that everyone would know which one was supposed to move.

He didn't close his eyes for quite some time, and wondered if he even still had the ability to blink. The light from the window started to come in a slightly deeper shade of orange, then deeper again, and again, until it was always red and he wondered if someone was playing with the dimmer switch out in the hall. Before he knew it, it was dark in the room for the first time that he could remember.

All around him, billboards began to switch on to different channels, each one glowing in the dark and broadcasting in 5.1 stereophonic surround sound certified by George Lucas and the whole THX crowd personally. Danny was ploughing the Nurse again, this time in an awkward manoeuver that Theo didn't even have a name for and wasn't sure he wanted.

He raised his arm until his shoulder bulged up out of the sheet like an erection, until it hurt against the strain of the tightly-woven sheets. It didn't take much. He wondered if he'd been sewn in like they used to do to men staying at their fiancées' houses back in the old days, but he didn't remember the Orderly having a needle. His fingers *may* have been needles, they were long and pointed.

"Stop talking crazy," he told himself, trying to ignore the billboards that were coming on.

He raised his other shoulder the same way, straining until he couldn't any more and gritting his teeth so hard that his bite slipped and sent a loud crack ringing throughout his skull. He relaxed back onto the bed, feeling that the sheet was a little looser from the effort. He started rocking back and forth, making the bed squeak in a way that seemed to fuel Danny's fantasies, pushing one arm up and then the other until they were loose enough that he could reach his arm out and into freedom.

He gave a satisfied sigh and smiled.

He pulled the covers off of him and sat on the edge of his bed to make sure he didn't fall asleep. They'd given him the pills before they'd tucked him into his bed, but they never worked. They never seemed to work. Still, it was better to be safe than sorry. He looked up at the window in his door and expected her face to be there already, floating there from the second he'd gotten out of bed and ready to open the door for him.

Of course it wasn't.

He sat with his arms propped up on his legs and waited, staring at the chicken-wire covered window. Time seemed to draw out like a blade, and eventually he turned and found a spot on the floor (a sister to the one on the table, identical in almost every way) and lost himself in it.

Lindsey was dreaming about painting.

Theo focused until his billboard came closer and closer, like he was approaching it on the highway at top speed, until it took up his whole wall. Colours would start out of nowhere and fade in from the blackness, soft and warm, and in tones and shades that Theo couldn't name. He didn't think there was a name for them, that these were colours that couldn't exist in real life. There was a red so soft and warm that it was like the sky, and a brown like the tint inside a tree when you first cut into it that only lasted a second. Less than a second. Each stroke happened on its own and then disappeared. The paint faded back into the canvas so that Theo couldn't see what Lindsey was painting, but he knew it was beautiful. There was a long, blue, quivering horizontal line across the entire canvas that he was sure was the top of a water's edge. Was it the ocean perhaps? Or maybe a cabin on the lake? That would certainly explain the brown. There was green now, making little lines up and then out, out, out... up and then out, out, out... they were trees, he thought. Evergreens, the type that you didn't see much in California, but may well have been frequent wherever Lindsey was from. He thought he knew where Lindsey was from, but couldn't remember.

-*Knock Knock*-

His head turned back to the window and she was there, the pink highlights in her hair just visible in the frame of the window.

"Come on!" she mouthed, as though she were scolding him for still being in bed.

He got up and brought his face to the window, his heart beating furiously in his chest. Was it really happening? He didn't think so. He thought maybe this was Danny's dream. He turned to eye Danny's billboard to see, but found him to still have the Pretty Nurse bent over the desk that used to be in his old high school library.

Their faces, Theo's and hers, were both pressed so close to the glass that it fogged. It was almost like they were kissing.

"I can't get the door open," she said, just loud enough to hear. Her voice was muffled through the glass. "You have to."

He ran a hand through his hair and then looked around. There were long staples holding in the new pieces of mattress. He pried one out (hooking it under his fingernail and making it bleed, leaving a small smear on the otherwise pristine white pad) and inserted it into the small hole under the knob. His tongue poked curiously out of the corner of his mouth and he wriggled it around until finally it clicked.

He pulled down on the lever and it swung itself forward, revealing her standing on the other side clapping silently.

"My hero," she said, taking her chin in his hand and giving him a kiss on the forehead while he was still down on one knee. "Come on."

He got up and stepped out into the hall after her.

The hallway was long and dark, the lights having been turned off hours ago to let some of the more fidgety Closers sleep. There was a light at the end off the hallway that was so bright and white that it shimmered and reflected off the metal walls, floors, and ceiling, and cast bending, monstrous shadows everywhere.

She trolled along the highway two doors up, just a black silhouette against the cold metal of the hospital. "Come on!"

Theo started after her.

When the doors opened, he saw that Black Springs didn't exist in the Arctic right now, if it ever had. It wasn't on a beach either, although Theo thought he could hear waves crashing somewhere far in the distance.

It was in the desert.

The moon was high and red overhead. The road that led from the front entrance of Black Springs out to the highway was the same compacted dirt and sand as the rest of the grounds, as hard as concrete and yet light enough that a good gust of air could send it spiraling in mini twisters toward a person's eyes. The only thing to distinguish the trail from the rest of the barren land was its colour. It was a sort of light orange. The rest of the ground was the hard brown of true grit.

The highway was a thin gray line on the horizon, marking the edge of a long line of hills that looked like they'd been drawn on. The brown of them was layered, getting darker as it went down, as though somebody had shaded it lazily in Photoshop.

She was a few paces in front of him and still jogging, when she stopped, the dirt she'd kicked up by running still continuing forward for a moment before fading into the night air. She leaned over onto her knees for a moment to catch her breath, then spun around to look at him over her shoulder. The night was hot, and her golden hair clung to her cheeks and her breasts with glimmering sweat as she took deep, gasping breath after breath.

Theo was standing in front of Black Springs, looking up at it. His back was turned to her.

It was smaller than he'd thought it would be. He'd pictured it as a massive prison with a stone-and-wire fence that went up the whole way around. He'd pictured towers on either corner that rose up story after story until they ended at points that pierced they sky and caught stray bolts of lightning on stormy nights. The truth was that it was small. All of it one story, a rectangular white building with very few windows and a black slit for a door in the middle. It looked like one of the bunkers people used to use in the forties, only bigger. Dirt clung stubbornly to one side and yellow, powdery roofing dust tumbled over one corner onto the ground. Beyond it there was pitch black that he couldn't see, but he could hear and smell. It was the salt of the sea. It was there, after all, but it hid from him even now.

"You're not having second thoughts, are you?" she asked, turning toward Theo and the Clinic.

"No," he said, still staring at it. "No, not at all."

She didn't have a car, and the ground was hard against his feet.

Black Springs was far behind them. Its narrow, thin frame had sunk into the distance quickly, becoming just a slit on the horizon. No cars had passed them in the hour they'd been walking, and sometimes it felt as though they were walking in place. The monotony of the sand seemed to never end, though sometimes he thought he saw the lights of the city far in the background.

Their shoes were covered in dust almost immediately. Within ten minutes, it had worked its way up to their knees where it stayed now, flirting with rising only to retreat again every few minutes.

He twitched and turned around, then back to her. The night was hot and she was sweating. The striped shirt she wore clung to her body tightly.

Taking a deep breath, he closed his eyes and listened.

There was only silence. Silence and darkness. No screaming voices, no videos, no loud annoying billboards assaulting him and entering him and raping him... just the peace of the windless night, the air hanging thick around him as he walked through it.

"You okay?" she asked, stepping in tune with him as they made their way around a long, curvy bend. She looked the way he pictured hippies looking, all blonde and young and beautiful and hitchhiking safely through warm summer nights.

"Yeah," he said, and smiled the first real smile he had in months. He turned around again to make sure Black Springs wasn't following him somehow, even though he knew it wasn't. Knew it. It seemed that it had been forever since he'd known something, even longer since he'd known something comforting. "Yes."

∞

"So, what's your father like?" Theo asked, when he realized that neither of them had spoken in an hour. The backs of his legs hurt, a sharp ache travelling from his ankle up to the back of his knee with every step he took.

"My dad?" she laughed, throwing her head back and smiling wonderfully. Her teeth were bright even in the dark of the night. "I bet you think a girl like me must have a real piece of work for a father, huh?"

He smiled at her. "No."

Her head came back down, hair tumbling over each shoulder stringy and damp. It hid her face for her when she spoke next, her pace slowing just a little when she spoke. "My dad's a bit of a scoundrel. Has what Mom used to call The Sickness. Said it was in his genes, that his father was like it, too."

"Were they married?"

She snorted. "He put the ring on, but he never married. Not one day in his life was that man ever married. Made my mom frightfully jealous."

Theo nodded slowly, turning his eyes forward.

The moon was in front of them, and sometimes it seemed like they were walking toward it instead of some unseen spot along the highway.

"He used to run around with women half his age, sometimes younger. Always cheating, always whoring... he never stopped." She sneered a little. It looked odd on her pretty face. "I told myself I'd never be that uncivilized."

"You're not uncivilized."

She did not respond.

"What did your mother think of it?"

"Other than the jealous bouts, she never really used to mind. At least not until a few girls started showing up pregnant."

Theo winced.

She laughed. "You'd think the man was setting up franchises, the way he went at it. Sometimes I think he had a different girl in every town across America. The first time I hit out onto the road was for one of those kids."

"You been there ever since?"

"No," she smiled, finally making eye contact with him again. "This isn't one of those stories. I make it back whenever I can. Dad's still the way he is, but he's gotten old enough now that no lady but Mom'll have him, and I think it learned him a thing or two. Or maybe one of his conquests got a hold to his heart and showed him how it felt... maybe it was just time."

They were silent again then.

∞

"Can I turn around yet?" Theo asked, calling out into the air around him from where he sat.

"You can't turn around, period," she called back from where she squat behind him, trying to pee. "When I'm done, I'll come around to you."

He sighed and smiled, looking at the open land around him. The desert was timeless. It stretched on forever as it had when the first settlers had come here and the way it had been when the first natives passed through before that. The only difference was the sand, the way the rocks were striped and coloured darker the further you went down them... The rings had been less tanned then, their depth the only thing to show the passage of time.

There was a cactus off to his left that had blossomed bright pink flowers from the top of each of its four spires. They looked bright even now, their yellow centres beaming with enough light to rival the moon above. The spikes of the plant caught the moonlight and sent it glimmering in all directions, turning the green of the cactus into a dull gray.

A coyote stepped out into Theo's field of vision, and he felt his breath catch in his throat.

It was big, easily as tall as the smooth rock that Theo had found to sit upon. Its coat was reddish brown and its eyes were solid black marbles in a soft pinkish bed. They got no rest there, darting about quickly through the desert night for other signs of life.

Its eyes fell upon Theo, and it let out a low hum of a growl from deep within its throat. Air puffed out from its long snout and kicked up dirt that had scattered across the desert's surface, and it seemed not to have to blink as it stared Theo down.

Theo stared back at it, paralyzed with fear and unable to move or blink or call out to her for help.

It snorted again, then licked its lips and turned away. It looked back after a moment, but made no sound, then turned and ran back to the highway. When it got to the road it began to trot tranquilly back down the road the way they'd come, its great paws kicking up grit as it went and its bushy tail swerving from side to side behind it.

Theo told her nothing about it.

The desert seemed to go forever, until, some hours after they had left, the two of them came across a light that glowed from around a turn in a highway creating a halo around a large striped rock formation. It made her face light up, her smile stretching until the pink of her lips pushed the rise of her cheeks up and her ears wiggled.

"Is that it?" Theo asked, the backs of his legs burning by now.

"That's it," she laughed, taking his wrist in her hand and breaking into a jog until they were around the corner.

It looked like something out of a Phillip K. Dick adaptation. It sat in the midst of a vast wasteland of sand

and gravel and grit, and was the only thing bright enough to compete with the bright white light of the moon above it. While everything around it was earthy and muted (the gray pavement, the caffeinated-brown sand, the maroon hillsides), this was bright and pink and neon.

The Olympic was one story that stretched so far back into the sand that the lights of the entrance could not penetrate the darkness, making it seem like the area behind it simply ceased to be. In reality, it skewed down on a steep angle and met with the desert floor so that anyone who wished to could simply step from the ground behind it onto the ceiling and walk their way up without any effort at all. There was no roofing dust on it, just regular brown sand from the desert that had blown up over time and had never been dusted off. The front-facing wall was painted a bright blueish green that seemed out of place here, as though someone had taken the ocean and brought it in to the middle of the dessert. There was a hot pink oblong with one rounded corner sitting at the top of the building and the rest of it jutting out over like a blob, a flowing tube of pink neon light travelling all around its edge. It buzzed constantly, the tube flickering near the top just enough for Theo's eye to register that something was wrong.

Written across the oblong in a glowing cursive script was the name, *The Olympic*.

There was a series of connected windows that took up the entire middle front of the diner, and even though it was early in the morning, there were still people inside.

Theo slowed down until her hand was tugging against his arm, then stopped.

She turned around and squinted at him, smiling. "You don't need to be scared."

"I'm not scared, I'm just..." he paused, trying hard to find the right words and coming up with nothing. "I'm not scared."

"Okay," she nodded, as though she were now completely in agreement.

He looked past her to the diner. The parking lot was unpaved and crowded with vehicles. Most were semi-trucks. Beyond that there were some old beater cars with wooden panels along the sides, but there were one or two nicer cars that a businessman might have driven, especially if he were driving a secondary car... something he used to get from place to place.

There were large plastic crates tracing the light on either side of it, the type that looked like they'd need a forklift to move. He didn't see a forklift anywhere. It was like all of the gray and gloom and bad from the rest of the world was captured by the light of the sign and compressed itself into cubes at its edge, frozen there forever.

He closed his eyes and took a deep breath, in through his nose and out through his mouth.

There was still a glow in the darkness, one that had nothing to do with the buzzing neon he could still hear. Within the diner's walls were small billboards of the same type that he'd always found in Black Springs among the Closers, small television screens that belted out their insanity in non-stop commercial free continuous coverage of the mind behind it. There was a man in the corner reading *The Bluest Eye* to himself, turning the pages every few moments. His billboard was an odd form of black that did not quite fit in with the black around it, the words on the page echoing through the dry heat in a British accent not his own, like some never-before-seen audio book only available in his mind. Another screen showed the psychedelic greens and red of an Alanis Morissette cover, one face in the foreground staring up into the vampire moon and another looking to the right, seemingly interested in what Toni Morrison was writing about. The lyrics radiated through the confined space, and Theo was surprised that everyone else in the diner wasn't bobbing their heads. *And I'm here to remind you of the mess you left when you went away. It's not fair to deny me of the cross I bear that you gave to me.*

He winced and opened his eyes. She was standing in front of him, her face and bust taking up the entirety of his vision. He hadn't realized that her hands had been on his shoulders, but they were. He could still see the screens though, shining through the supple skin of her breast as though she were partially transparent. The notion sent a shiver down his spine.

"Is something wrong?" she asked, biting the corner of her lip.

"I think so," he said, furrowing his brow and shaking his head. "I think... I think I just got used to the dark."

She nodded, then backed off from him a pace. "I'm going in now... I'd really like it if you came with me."

He nodded again, walking just a step or two behind her as they crossed the street into the parking lot.

The light from the sign hit the toe of his shoe and sent jolts of Electric Mirror Sundance up his leg and out through the back of his head.

There was a rustling sound in the darkness just to the right of them and they stopped frozen in their tracks. Theo's face grew taut with worry as his eyes bulged and searched the shadows of the gray boxes.

She smiled, even as the disheveled man came into view.

He looked old even though he wasn't, his neck and forehead were loose and full of wrinkles, but his cheeks were still high and smooth. They glowed in the pink light when he smiled his large smile out from over a battered novelty sombrero. A gray mustache the shape of handlebars came down from either side of a large nose filled with blood blisters that perfectly framed his swollen lips. He wore layers of clothing despite the heat, and the stench of sweat that came off of him was wretched. There were patterns in the clothes, but no colour, any colour having been drawn out of it after hours spent in the desert sun. Now there was just the gray of the dust that clung to it.

At first, Theo thought he didn't have a screen either like her, but then he saw it. It wasn't a song or a movie or a memory, just a feeling of deep, deep need. It scared him, and he backed off a pace into the light as the man got closer. "Watch out," he said, holding a hand out to her and motioning for her to step closer to him.

She rolled her eyes and tisked him, stepping closer to the man and bending down a little to match his height. Theo hadn't even noticed now short he was or how tall she was until this happened.

"Do you have any change?" the man said, looking from her to Theo and then back again. His lips barely moved when he spoke, and it sounded like his throat were almost completely devoid of moisture. "I need a... a cup of coffee."

He motioned toward the diner as though there were some choice as to where he would buy it.

She smiled at him, her hair coming down around either side of her face and looking like the colour of spun gold. Her mouth remained tightly wound, but she smiled with her eyes. Their noses were less than a foot apart, but they weren't touching yet. "How much do you need?"

"Ffffffffffffffffffffffffty is all," he replied, the word getting stuck against his lip. "Fifty cents."

She nodded knowingly. She laid one hand down on his shoulder and looked him straight in the eye. "You don't need it."

A tear escaped his eye. His mouth was slack slightly, and he did not seem to be able to tear his gaze from her.

She smiled, bringing her other hand up and stroking his youthful cheek lovingly. "Whatever it really is, you don't need it."

He nodded slowly.

She released him and took a step back, then reached into the pocket of her jeans and pulled out a bill. She handed it to him, her arm stretched out as far as it would go. "Here."

He reached up and took it, clutching it as tightly as he would a life preserver. He turned from her and made his way into the desert one shuffling step at a time.

"What was that?" Theo asked, stepping up beside her to watch that man as he walked away.

She smirked, her arms crossed in front of her midriff,

then turned and walked into The Olympic. He watched for a moment longer, then followed her.

The diner looked as though it had been ripped straight from a movie about the 1950s. There was a real bell hanging above the door that chimed happily as the two of them entered, not one of those robotic sensors that beeped angrily whenever someone stepped near them.

The setup was simple enough, with pink and red booths lined against the front window and far wall to form an upper-case L and the bar taking up the majority of the rest with stools in front and the kitchen in back. There was a large man standing behind the counter wearing a big smile and a bright apron, his palms both leaning flat against the blue counter and his sleeves rolled up to his elbows.

"Hey, Girl!" he yelled happily as they entered, coming around the counter.

She twirled her arms through the air and he picked her up, spinning her around so that her shoes almost hit the walls and stools around them. They both laughed like madmen until he finally put her down. "How have you been, Darryl? Keeping that wife of yours happy?" she asked.

"You know it," he smiled, winking mischievously at her. His hands were still on her hips. Her hands were still on his shoulders. "What about you? What've you been up to?"

She shrugged. "Making my way along, like I always do."

"You two... know each other?" Theo asked, shifting from one foot to the other.

Darryl turned to him and smiled. His mouth was comically small for the size of his face, but still showed that he was missing at least two teeth. His cheeks were bulbous and full of stubble. "Hell yeah, this girl here is the reason I own this place!" He hugged her close to his side and shook her joyfully one final time, then let her go. She seemed to shrink when he released her, as though he'd been holding her up that whole time.

"Really?"

"Oh yeah! Never would've been able to make something of myself if Little Miss here hadn't come along and civilized me! Was just around here, too!"

Theo looked from Darryl to her and smiled. "You don't say?"

Behind Darryl's head was a picture that showed a slightly younger version of the girl he was standing next to. It radiated joy and sadness all at the same time.

"He's exaggerating," she beamed, stepping away from him politely.

"Sure I am," he snickered. "Whole cities of men like me got lot to owe you."

Again she smiled respectfully.

"So what'll it be?" he asked, moving slowly back around to his side of the bar. "The usual?"

"Oh --" Theo said, laughing. "We're not here to --"

"Two usuals will be fine. Mash his," she interrupted. She turned to him with one eyebrow raised. "While we're here."

He relented, and the both of them stepped over to the

nearest open booth alongside the window.

There was a man in the back wearing all black, from his tee-shirt to his jeans. His hair was combed to one side, he had a pencil-thin mustache and chin-beard and he looked like an art student. He was reading a book that he was too engrossed in to look up, the coffee in front of him having gone cold while it waited for him. His hand covered the front cover, but Theo knew that it was *The Bluest Eye*.

There were three large men squat into the booth behind Theo's companion, each of them wearing baseball caps with plastic mesh on the backs. One wore black and red checkered button-up shirt, the buttons on it pulled as tightly as the strings behind them would allow and sections of his chest visible between them. One man was sitting alone at the counter, his head bobbing along to the music streaming into his brain through his headphones. The track had moved on from *Oughta Know* to *In Bloom*, and the album cover hovering above his head had changed suitably. Four men sat symmetrically in a booth a few rows behind Theo, each of them wearing straight black ties except one who wore a tie with a Tasmanian Devil on it. The desert behind the character looked much as Theo imagined the desert he'd just crossed would have looked in the light.

Theo craned his head around and examined them all. She watched him with her hands clasped together and her chin resting on them, her eyes following his head wherever it went until he turned back and met her gaze.

"He's not here, is he?" he sighed, running his hands through his hair.

She frowned. "Doesn't look like it. Give it a chance

though. He might show up."

He shook his head, then pressed the heels of his hands against his eyes hard enough that he saw spots. "This was a stupid idea," he said between gritted teeth. "I knew it the second I stepped into the parking lot that this was a stupid idea."

"Hey," she soothed, leaning in and touching the palm of his hand with her index finger. Her touch was light and feathery and made him feel warm, even though he didn't want to feel that way right now. "It'll all work out. You'll see. I can tell the future, remember."

He smiled despite himself as Darryl walked over to them carrying a graceful golden pitcher of water. He placed a small silver-plated basin between the both of them. They watched in silence as tipped the water over the basin so that his guests might rinse their hands, then nodded and stepped away wiping the excess water from the jug with his apron.

Theo dipped one hand gently into the basin and watched as the water surrounded it and distorted its proportions. It ran into the cup of his palm and made a small lake there, so clear and perfect that he could see the rough hem of his heart line within it.

After a moment, she took his hand gently in both of hers, her touch little more than a sensation running across his skin. The water poured from his hand and she began to massage it without rhyme or reason, rubbing the muscles and tendons of his fingers.

A moment later Darryl emerged at the table again, this time carrying two steaming hot plates. The smell filled the air as he laid them down, one in front of Theo and the other in front of the girl, and Theo wondered how he hadn't smelled it long before he'd done so. The sweet hickory scent of meat cooked just right. It was a porterhouse steak cooked to a perfect medium-rare. There was a half-cob of corn resting beside it and mashed potatoes brimming with volcanic butter. Hers was much the same, except instead of the mashed potatoes there were fries.

She dug in immediately, picking up her fork and impaling several fries on it with a few short stabs, and then shoveling them into her mouth all at once. As she chewed, she picked up her knife and started to cut her steak into small, bite-sized sections.

Theo looked down at his plate. His mouth was salivating and his stomach was rumbling, turning over upon itself with excitement as it got the signals from the rest of his senses somehow about what was in front of him. The steam rose up from the plate and fogged his vision. Even the aroma of it was better than any food he'd had in him in months.

She looked at him for a moment, her cheeks filled with steak and french fries. "Well?"

He smiled at her meekly, then turned back toward the plate as though it were an enemy. He brought his hand to rest on his fork, but did not pick it up. He stared at it like that for what seemed like a long time while she chewed. When she swallowed, she opened her mouth to speak (something sarcastic, he was sure of it); he spoke first.

"You don't know what it's like not to know your name," he said, looking away from the pile of rapidly melting butter and into her eyes, then back again. "I mean, I know my name. But it's like I don't know who I am...

because I don't know who *he* is. All my life I grew up never knowing who he was. I could read his mind backwards and forwards and still have no idea who he was. And it just... I mean, the son of a big snake is a big snake, right? And the son of a big bear is a big bear too. But if you don't know where you came from, how're you rightly supposed to know--"

He trailed off, his eyes becoming damp. He picked up his fork and used it to saw off the end of his steak and pushed it into his mouth. It was warm and juicy and good, and it filled his whole being with flavour. He smiled, then laughed as he chewed, scooping up a heap of potato and eating it all. The need to cry was gone again now, but the few tears he'd made dribbled down over his cheeks nonetheless. He sniffed back hard, laughed, and took another bite of his steak. It was even more delicious than the first. And before he knew it, it was half gone.

She watched him and smiled at him, eating her own dish more conservatively now. When he was almost done, she reached out and laid her hand across his the same way that paper covered rock, gently cupping it. His eyes rose to meet hers.

"You, are Theo Flaherty," she said, her voice hushed and serious. "Nobody ever needed to be anything else."

He smiled.

Behind her, the large man with the red-and-black shirt's ears perked. He turned around and kneeled his arm over their booth (much to the surprise of the men he was with) and poked his head over until his nose was almost in her hair. His baseball cap had a large jewel-encrusted cartoon crown on it with a small pickup truck in all four corners. "Excuse me," he said, in voice that was almost too eloquent. "Did you say Flaherty?"

She smiled happily, turned from the man to Theo and then back again. "Why yes we did, good sir. Do you know someone by that name?" When she spoke, she was trying not to laugh from happiness, milking every moment out of it that she could.

"Don't call me sir, I work for a living," he chuckled, inching his way out of his booth and coming around to stand next to their table. His eyes locked onto Theo's face, and he seemed to study every inch of it. The long slope of his nose, the prominence of his chin. "The name's Nathaniel. Nathaniel Esther. Folks around here call me the King." He motioned to his cap, as if to illustrate.

Theo was looking past him at the billboard there. There was an image of him on it, wearing clothes he'd never worn and doing things he'd never done. And he was older, though not by much. He extended his hand. "I'm --"

"Theo Flaherty," Nathaniel said, taking his hand and pumping it heartily. "I've heard a lot about you."

The girl moved over so he could sit down, and he did.

"You knew my father?" Theo whispered, ducking his head down low.

"I know your father," Nathaniel laughed, an action that shook the table and most of the row. "Helped me out of a jam once. Me and my wife, Donna, we'd got in a little deep with the debt collectors. Seemed like everyone was coming after us, her especially. Almost drove us apart. Your daddy hired me on at a ridiculous salary... hell, you can probably tell I'm not worth it. He didn't keep me longer than I needed... said he didn't like better men than him working for him. Made him nervous. Don't know what I would've done that Christmas without him."

Theo listened with awe and intensity to every word, as though he'd found some heretofore-lost book of the Bible that mentioned him by name.

"It all worked out, but I wouldn't be where I am without him," Nathaniel said, getting up again so that he could fish out his wallet. He took out a hundred dollars in twenties and laid it on the table between them. "Your meal's on me, it's the least I could do."

He turned to leave, and Theo reached out and grabbed his arm. He turned around just enough to meet Theo's eye.

"Wait..." Theo said, holding his sleeve for a moment and trying to gather his thoughts. "What was my father like?"

Nathaniel stopped for a moment and thought, his face taking on a comical expression with his lower lip jutting out moist pick flesh. "He'd rarely give a man ten dollars when he only needed five, but he would *never* give a man five dollars if they really needed ten."

Theo smiled. "What's that supposed to mean?"

"How'm I supposed to know?" Nathaniel winked at him. "He's your father."

He turned and left the diner then and Theo let him, watching until he disappeared out the front door into the desert night.

She smiled at him from ear to ear as he stared at the place where Nathaniel had been, her hands laced in front of her.

"Come on," she said, tapping his arm. "It's time to go."

"Thank you," Theo said, when they reached the edge of the light The Olympic provided just at the edge of the highway.

"You don't need to thank me. Ever," she replied, rubbing her arms. A breeze had started in from the west, and even though it was warm it made her flesh dance. "It was fun."

He turned and looked at her over his shoulder and smiled at her, then turned back toward the highway. It stretched off to the left and right from where he stood seemingly forever... the left road taking him back to Black Springs, the right taking him... somewhere else.

He held up his hand to the light behind him, examining the deep trench of what she had called his heart line. Slowly, he brought his opposite index finger over and traced its edge from his middle finger to the edge of his palm.

"Hey," he said. "Do you think-"

He turned around to smile at her.

But she was gone.

∞

When dawn with the rose red fingers crept her way over the horizon in the morning, Theo was back in his bed in Black Springs.

∞

The easels had been pulled out from the wall and arranged around the Group Room in symmetrical little cubicles so that everyone could have their space.

"That's good," the Pretty Nurse said. She walked between the easels with her hands clasped behind her and looked more like a Nun in a Seminary than a Nurse in an Institution. She walked behind Paul and looked over his shoulder. He was painting a basket of fruit with a bright red cloth behind it. "That's very nice, Paul," she said.

He smiled, then went back to his painting.

Lindsey was painting another of his Rorschach tests.

"That's wonderful."

Ruffles had made a few marks on his canvas with his brush, but had quickly moved to using his hands. Despite the mess he'd made on himself and the floor around him, the resulting cacophony of blues and yellows and reds did look stunning, if random.

"That's good."

She walked behind Theo and threw a glance toward his canvas.

There was a beach on it with a roaring sea made up of blues and greens and reds and browns and every colour imaginable. It crashed and swirled out in the harbor, yet was calm by the time it reached the land, cresting in small laps against the golden grains of sand. There were a few rocks, but they'd all been worn smooth by the waves. There were two sets of footprints leading from the foreground up along the beach until they disappeared over the horizon, one slightly bigger than the other.

"Theo!" the Pretty Nurse gasped, smiling as she came around behind him. She laid a hand on his shoulder proudly. "That's absolutely beautiful!"

She beamed to herself, then continued walking over toward Robert.

He stared at the picture he'd painted for a long moment, the oil on it still wet. On the easel tray below it were the colours he'd used, small pails of red and brown and a bright, vibrant blue. It stared at him for a moment, then he picked it up and walked over to the solid gray wall of the Group Room.

He drew back and splashed it against the wall with all the force he could muster, the thick blue paint arching up from the pail and looking solid for a moment as though it were suspended in midair and then crashing against the wall in a great splash.

All the Closers jumped in their seats and turned to him, startled. He began to spread the paint around with his fingers, covering as much of the wall as he could.

"Theo!" the Pretty Nurse shrieked even as the Orderlies entered the room.

He kept painting, running his fingers along the dry, rough surface in spastic swirls and jaunts.

An Orderly took him by either shoulder and pulled him off, his feet dragging along the floor as he was pulled laughing from the Group Room.

There, on the west wall of Black Springs Clinic, was his ocean.

GRISTLE WHILE YOU WORK

- JAY PAULIN -

A siren pierced the calm air.

Alicia Bond rolled over slowly in her bed, rubbed her eyes, and stared blearily at the black box on her dresser. Through her rapidly correcting vision, she saw the red digits of her alarm clock stating the time – 11:00 – and knew she couldn't dawdle. Her brother, Tyler, had a job for her at noon, and she knew better than to disappoint him. He brought her aboard his business because of her knack for cleaning. "Leave nothing behind," he would remind her, although she did not need to be told.

Before heading down the stairs, Alicia kissed her left index finger and tapped the adjacent photo of her parents. They passed away five years ago during a business trip to Maine, leaving the family home in Tyler's fresh-out-of-medical-school hands. The insurance policy, Tyler's income, and the siblings' side jobs had allowed her to live quite comfortably; a fact she had never taken for granted.

The moment Alicia stepped out onto the front porch and felt the warm breeze upon her face, she knew it would be a good day. She loved working with Tyler as it gave her an opportunity to use her skills more than her weekend mall position ever could. As she approached her destination, her parents' credo ran through her mind: "Be proud of yourself and your abilities – they'll carry you far." The words filled her heart with confidence and her eyes with tears.

"C'mon, Alicia. What are you waiting for?"

At the sound of her brother's slightly agitated question, she wiped her face with her sleeve and jogged toward the direction of the voice. The house was almost as large as her own and immaculately landscaped. Alicia pegged the owners to be quite wealthy, which isn't surprising; she wouldn't have been called to work otherwise.

Tyler bored her with the same details as always, so Alicia took the opportunity to look around. The usual cast of goons was there, lifting valuables off of shelves and passing them to a sack-holder like a perverted assembly line. Tyler and his friends had been doing this for years. Alicia didn't like the thievery but it gave her an opportunity to use her skills, so she disapproved in silence.

Once Tyler's spiel ended, the siblings arrived in the basement where she found her task waiting. A middle-aged couple and their teenage children were bound together, choked to death with double-braided nylon rope.

"You gonna be fine down here?" asked Tyler.

Alicia was already salivating at the prospect. "Oh, yeah. Thanks, bro."

The elder Bond hastened upstairs. A few years ago, he made the mistake of sticking around while his sister did her thing. He was in therapy for two years and continued to get night sweats.

Alicia approached the lifeless bodies; her eyes glimmered and her smile became a crooked gnarl of sharpened teeth. She chose her first target and opened wide. The initial soft, juicy sound gave way to a bone-chilling snap. Flesh was vacuumed off the bone, blood swallowed like water, and marrow sucked dry. Like a ravenous, cartoon pack of piranhas, she made the teenagers disappear. Within moments of completing her appetizer, she moved on to the main course.

Stepping away, Alicia inspected her handiwork. The only thing left was the rope, which she balled up to give to Tyler. He always marveled at her ability to clean a crime scene, even though she could tell it disgusted him. She brushed it off – a growing girl's gotta eat, right?

Back on the main floor, Alicia looked around for her brother. Most of his friends had already left. She never asked where they hocked the goods and didn't really care. The only thing she cared about was that Tyler kept her secret safe from those outside the gang and she kept his equally guarded. Wandering from room to room, she finally caught his voice carrying from the back of the house. Tyler sounded aggressive, which was strange, so Alicia made her way toward him.

"Look, man, I got nothin' against you, but some of the new guys don't feel comfortable with that freak around.

I know she helped us good back in the day, but we don't need that shit. If we get caught, I'd rather it be..." The voice was cut short by a more familiar one.

"We've known each other a long time, Ryan, and you know we'll never get caught. We put too much work into each job. I don't give a damn what the new guys think. If they don't want a piece of what we pull, let them walk – more for us." Tyler grabbed Ryan by the collar and slammed him into the house's brickwork. "If you ever say something about my sister again, you're gone. Not from the group – just *gone*."

Letting go of the smaller man's collar, Tyler stepped back and glared. Ryan adjusted his shirt, uttered a curse under his breath, and slunk away.

Tyler rubbed the bridge of his nose between thumb and forefinger. "I know you're there, Alicia. Sorry you had to hear that."

She stepped outside onto the patio and reached into her pocket. "Here's the . . ." She gasped and cut herself short. "Look out!"

Tyler spun around just in time to avoid a two-handed hammer swing by Ryan. He obviously didn't take his lesson to heart. The forward momentum brought Ryan crashing to the ground. To add injury to insult, Tyler repeatedly kicked him in the ribs before reaching for the hammer and cracking his former associate in the middle of the forehead. Normally calm, collected, and passive, Alicia's brother looked panicked for the first time since their parents died.

"Oh, God! What did I do? Alicia, you've gotta . . ."

She pressed her finger up to his lips. "I'm way ahead

of you, bro. Remember what you always tell me? 'Leave nothing behind.'"

Tyler paced around frantically, looking about for signs of witnesses. Every bird chirp caused his heart to stop as he mistook it for a police siren. "Hurry!" The last sickening slurp chilled him to the bone and he shuddered.

"Done," Alicia uttered a tad too cheerily for his liking.

"Good, then let's go!" Tyler grabbed her by the arm and tugged.

"No. We can't. Not like this," Alicia said. She rubbed her left forearm and pivoted her right foot, almost as if she was squashing a cigarette.

Tyler turned around and felt as if he was moving through water; the events seemed hazy and in slow motion. The last thing he ever saw was the gaping, toothy maw of his sweet little sister. In his mind, he chuckled at his ludicrous final thought: "So much for my life flashing before my eyes."

Alicia Bond crunched the last of her brother's bones, then gleefully bounded home. Suddenly she stopped: a siren pierced the calm air.

She smirked and continued on her way.

SCARLETT
- ANDREA HACKETT -

It smiled as it looked down at its latest victim. The teenage girl remained still among the ferns on the forest floor. The damp leaves beneath her were quickly becoming moistened with the crimson blood that flowed freely from the gashes all over her youthful body.

It knelt down beside her and brushed a strand of blood-soaked blonde hair off her pale face. It caressed her cheek with almost parental tenderness and shushed her as if she were a child slumbering.

It opened the filthy jean jacket she wore and unbuttoned her blouse, exposing the pink bra she wore over her under-developed chest. Its nails extended into long pointed claws and burrowed deep into her soft skin. Drops of blood formed around the nails as they dug deeper and deeper into the flesh. There was a loud crack as its hand broke its way through her ribcage. Finally the fingers reached their destination, clenched shut around its prize, and pulled.

It licked the fresh blood, still warm, that dripped from the torn veins and arteries hanging from the girl's heart. It opened its mouth wide, exposed its pointed teeth, then sunk them into the heart and fed greedily.

Scarlett sat in a quiet café beside the highway eating homemade pancakes drenched in maple syrup. It was early morning and the only other customers in the café were a couple truckers looking strung out and dirty from the road.

She never took her eyes off her laptop as she shoved the last forkful of pancakes into her mouth. She had been searching the local newspapers of towns and cities all over Maine until one finally caught her eye. It was a newspaper called the *Pearlview Times*. Jodi Levi, a fourteen-year-old girl who had been missing for five days, had been found in the forest behind her home. They were calling the incident a "vicious animal attack" stating that her body had been badly mutilated.

Scarlett continued to search the blogs and online journals of local residents until she found one that confirmed what she had already suspected. It was rumored that Jodi Levi's heart was missing.

"Gotcha!" she whispered triumphantly. She gulped down the remains of her glass of orange juice, packed her laptop into her backpack, threw a twenty on the table, and hurried out of the restaurant. She jumped into her black Honda coupe waiting in the parking lot and sped away, flicking dirt out from behind her.

"Hey! Joseph! Wait up!"

Joseph turned to see his teammate running to catch up to him. His blonde hair blew back from his face as he ran, exposing his long forehead and prominent nose. He was still wearing his basketball uniform, navy blue with yellow trim and "The Eagles" plastered across the front under a muscular, cartoon eagle. It didn't take long for him to catch up with his long legged strides. He was the typical tall, lanky basketball player.

Joseph continued to walk.

"What's up, Tony?"

Tony wiped the sweat from his forehead with his bare arm and slowed his pace to walk alongside his friend.

"Why didn't you wait for me after practice?"

"Didn't know I was supposed to."

Joseph ran his hand through his short, dirty-blonde hair and put his Adidas baseball cap back on. His features were softer than Tony's. He was very good looking (in a boyish way) with a small nose and lips and high cheekbones lightly sprinkled with freckles. To make himself look older, he had grown a short goatee. He was much shorter than Tony, but was still the best player on the school's basketball team.

Tony eyed his friend suspiciously. They rounded the street corner and he grinned.

Up ahead of them was Beth Parker. She was wearing a pair of snug-fitting jeans and a red hoodie. Her wavy, long brown hair was blowing wildly around her head.

"Why don't you just talk to her, man?"

"'Cause I'm a wimp."

"You're captain of the basketball team. You could probably have the head cheerleader and you're afraid to talk to the hottest geek I've ever seen? Pussy."

Beth was captain of the Chess club. She had no

interest whatsoever in sports, but she was far from being considered a geek, if only because of her looks. She had a fit and curvy body. She had high cheekbones and a healthy, sun-kissed complexion with long dark eyelashes that emphasized her beautiful emerald eyes and soft, pink lips.

She hung out with the most popular groups, but her very best friend was Susan. Susan was the cliché geek. She had dull, dirty blonde hair, glasses, and braces. Her body was skinny and boyish; she got straight A's and was also on the chess club. None of the popular girls paid any attention to her and that was the way she liked it.

"The geek must be sick today, she's walking home alone. Here's your chance!" Tony urged.

"That was the idea…"

"Then quit bein' a pussy and do it! I'll take the long way home." He crossed the street. Before rounding the next corner, he turned around and yelled (much louder than necessary): "See ya' tomorrow!"

Beth turned slightly as if on cue and glanced at Joseph.

He took a deep breath.

"Hey, Beth!"

She stopped and waited for him to catch up.

"Um, hi," she said, timidly.

"Do you mind if … well, we live on the same street so…"

"Sure."

They walked a couple blocks in awkward silence until she finally spoke, "So, how's the team looking this year?"

"Good. I mean, I guess. How about the chess club?"

Beth laughed in her unique and playful way. "Same old."

He turned a light crimson and smiled at her stupidly. When Beth laughed, her mouth opened, her eyes closed, and her nose scrunched up cutely. She had beautiful, white, straight teeth. Her father was a dentist.

He walked her as far as her front gate and they stopped.

Her house was a tan split entry with dark brown trim and shutters. The yard was landscaped and surrounded by a picturesque white picket fence. She and her father lived there alone. Her mother had died when she was young and her father had never remarried.

"Well, see ya' tomorrow," she said. She waited a moment, but when Joseph replied with a simple "See ya'!" she turned and walked through her gate, across her yard and into her front door.

"Fuck!" he said. He shoved his hands in his pockets and stormed down the street.

Beth could hear the TV blaring some cartoon as she entered the house. Her father always left the TV on for their cat, Fluffy. Fluffy was a shorthaired calico cat with an unusually long and skinny tail. She had been a stray Beth had brought home and fed on the front porch until finally her dad, the cat hater, had let her inside. Beth had called her Fluffy for reasons unknown.

Fluffy grew on them, especially on her dad. He had read in a magazine that it was comforting to leave the TV on for animals while they were home alone, so now he insisted that they turn on cartoons for her to watch while he and Beth were gone.

Every day when Beth returned from school, Fluffy was always asleep on her dad's recliner. She joked that while they were gone, Fluffy actually channel surfed and watched soap operas, but changed the channel back to cartoons and pretended to be asleep when Beth got home. Her father told her she had a wild imagination, just like her mother.

Beth barely remembered her mother. She had died when Beth was only three. Her relatives loved to tell her how much she looked and acted like her. There was a huge family portrait of the three of them hanging over the fireplace in the living room, taken when Beth was only two. Her mother's warm smile watched over them every day.

Beth blew a kiss to the picture and scratched Fluffy behind the ear. She turned the TV to a music station, cranked up the volume, then headed to the adjoining kitchen to start supper. Tonight she was making Chinese: chicken balls with rice, wontons, and egg rolls.

By the time her father got home from work, supper was ready, the table was set, and the local news channel was turned on. When the door opened, Fluffy jumped off the recliner to greet her owner. She rubbed against his ankles affectionately and he bent over to scratch her behind the ear.

"Beth! I'm home!" he called as he walked into the kitchen and took in a deep breath through his nose. "Oh, my Lord, Elizabeth! Supper smells delicious!"

Beth walked to her dad to embrace him in a warm

hug, followed by a kiss on the cheek.

"How was work today, Daddy?"

"Same old dirty teeth," he said, and his eyes twinkled. "Chinese?"

"I wanted to try something different. I hope you like it."

"You know I will!" He gave her a kiss on the forehead and sat down at their round, oak table. Beth had all the food strategically placed on different serving plates in the middle of the table and a candle lit in the middle. She loved to go all out. She joined her father and they began to eat in silence.

In the background, the reporter on the evening news recounted the day's events in his monotone voice.

"Tonight on the evening news hour: Fourteen year old Jodi Levi's body has been found in the wooded area behind her home. The police suspect that a wild animal attacked Levi not far from her home, but are awaiting autopsy results before making any confirmations. No foul play is suspected. In the meantime, police are urging residents to refrain from going into the woods, especially after dark, as a precaution."

"Did you know her?" he asked, holding a spoonful of rice in front of his face.

"No, but I remember seeing her at school. Scary."

"Her poor parents." He cleared his throat. "You make sure you tell me whenever you leave the house, okay?"

Beth wanted to roll her eyes, but refrained and just nodded. She was able to forgive her father for his overprotectiveness. After all, they only had each other now.

"Don't worry, Dad, I'm smarter than you give me credit for."

He smiled, and when he did, his smile reached his eyes.

They changed the channel and continued to eat in silence.

◐

Scarlett shoved her foot hard on the clutch and jammed the gearshift into third. The RPM's revved higher as she sped past a sign that read *Welcome to Pearlview*.

The sun had recently set, leaving behind a rainbow of red, pink, and orange on the horizon. A scatter of houses along the highway finally led to an intersection at the top of a hill. She drove straight through and down a hill to the houses at the bottom of the valley. Stores and streetlights dotted the way.

Pearlview was a town of approximately fifteen thousand people. The business district was located along the main road. The rest of the town consisted of houses, subdivisions, gas stations, and convenience stores.

Scarlett knew it would be hard to keep a low profile in a small town, so she turned into the first and only hotel she saw.

"The Pearlview Hotel... Original," she said as she stepped out into the badly paved parking lot, removed her suitcase from the back seat, and headed to the front door. Her heels clicked on the pavement and echoed off the walls. She entered through a glass door and stepped up to the registration desk where a middle-aged woman sat. She smiled brightly, her wrinkles reaching from her cheeks to her eyes.

"Hi, darlin'! Lookin' for a room for the night?"

Scarlett brushed her hair out of her face and lay down the small suitcase she had in tow.

"I'll need a room for an indisposed amount of time."

"Not a problem, do you have family here?"

"Nope."

The woman paused, expecting Scarlett to elaborate. When she didn't, she asked, "Credit card?"

"I'll give you one week in cash, upfront."

Scarlett threw her bag onto the double bed. It was covered in a plain beige comforter. She unlocked the unusually large lock on the zipper and opened the case. She took out the black yoga pants, spandex t-shirts, and tank tops it contained and threw them into the dresser drawer.

Underneath the few outfits, she took out a second bag, this one thin and black. She opened it carefully and began to remove its contents: a silver dagger with a ruby gem on the bone-shaped handle, a pair of sai, and, finally, a 9mm gun and a box of pure silver bullets. She loaded the bullets into the gun, cocked it, and smiled.

That night, Joseph couldn't sleep. He had arrived home after school to be greeted by his mom and little sister, Gayle. Usually this would have made him happy, however today he had just wanted to be left alone.

Gayle adored Joseph and there was no way he was going to get any time to himself. She immediately took him by the hand and led him to the family room to play with her Barbie dolls in their dollhouse. Gayle was four, and for the most part they got along.

Joseph's mom was the stay-at-home type, or a "domestic engineer" as she jokingly called herself. His dad worked away three weeks and spent one week home so Joseph was pretty much the man of the house.

Gayle had finally fallen asleep at eight, giving Joseph enough time to help his mom clean up the kitchen and the toys scattered about the house before he went to his room and checked his email and Facebook.

He was greeted by numerous pictures in memorial of Jodi Levi. He hadn't heard the whole story, but the entire school was in an uproar with rumors flying around about her death. A lot of the kids were scared, but most were too upset to be scared. There was a lineup outside of the guidance counselors' office all day long and even the police had been to the school to speak with the teachers. Joseph and Jodi hadn't been friends, but she had been in his Math class and he had talked to her a couple times. He tried not to think about that empty seat in the classroom again tomorrow. He had been avoiding it since she went missing, but now, knowing her fate, he dreaded it even more.

His thoughts then turned to Beth. He had made a complete fool of himself today after school and he already regretted walking home with her. He was sure she thought he was a total tool by now. Only one more day until the weekend and he could set his mind on other things, like the big basketball tournament on Saturday. Their rival town was coming to play against them, the Delon Tornadoes.

What a dumb name for a team.

A light tapping on his second story window interrupted his thoughts.

He sat up and looked out, but didn't see anything except the reflection of his lamp light from next to his bed. The tapping came again, but louder this time. He got up, went to his window, and opened it to look outside. The cool fall air blew in, sending a chill down his spine. He stuck his head out to look down on the ground and, without warning, was grabbed around the neck by strong hands.

"What the..!?" Joseph struggled to catch himself from falling out the window and quickly pulled his head back inside.

"Hey, man! Did I scare you?"

Tony slipped in through the window and buckled over with laughter, holding his stomach.

"You're an asshole!"

"Did you think it was the boogie man?" Tony asked, still laughing.

"What the fuck are you doing here?"

"Nothing. Was sitting home bored and got sick of my parents screaming at each other so I decided to go for a walk. What's up?"

"It's ten o'clock. I was just chillin' here in my room."

"How did it go with Beth today?"

"I don't want to talk about it. I'm a total tool."

Tony laughed. "Hey! Let's go get her!"

"What do you mean? It's a Thursday night and you know how uptight her dad is! He probably has surveillance cameras all over her yard and house."

Tony sighed. "You're such a pussy."

"Am not. She won't want to see me after today anyway."

"Yeah, whatever, if you won't come with me, I'll go myself. Maybe she'll invite me into her room." He winked at Joseph mischievously, then went back to the window and climbed back down, hanging for a moment on the eaves trough before letting himself fall the last couple feet to the ground.

Joseph sighed, locked his bedroom door, and headed out the window after Tony.

They snuck through the dark backyards, running when the motion sensors popped on. Finally they got to Beth's backyard.

"Which one is her room?"

"How the hell do I know? I'm not a peeping tom!" Joseph exclaimed.

They circled around to the side of the house where one single window illuminated the alley between the houses. The curtains were purple and slightly open, showing the green walls inside.

Tony shushed Joseph and picked up a couple pebbles. He tossed them gently at her window.

After a couple minutes of this, Joseph started to get uneasy. "Come on, she's probably asleep."

Tony shushed him again and threw another couple pebbles, harder this time.

Finally there was movement inside and a figure appeared at the window, shielding its hands around its face to peer outside into the darkness.

Tony waved ecstatically. He jabbed Joseph in the ribs

with his elbow.

"Wave, man!"

Joseph waved reluctantly.

Beth opened the window and stuck her head outside.

"Who is that? Is that you, Joseph?" she called, in a loud whisper.

"Yeah, um…."

"Come out for a walk with us!" Tony interrupted.

"Now!?"

"Sorry, to bother you…"

"Shut up!" Tony whispered. "Yeah, now!"

Joseph continued, "Yeah, just come out for a walk with us; it's nice out."

Beth was silent for a minute, then she said, "Okay. I have to make sure my dad is asleep, then I'll be out. I'll come out the back door, so wait in the backyard."

She ducked inside and closed the window.

Joseph and Tony headed to the backyard and slipped into the darkness behind the tree line. A couple minutes later, a figure crept out the back door and silently ran to the woods.

"What's up?"

"Not much. Was just watching TV. Dad is sound asleep. What's going on?

"Nothin', just out for a walk and Joseph suggested we'd see if you wanted to come out too."

Joseph could feel his face flush and he silently thanked God that it was too dark for Beth to notice. He wanted to punch Tony for putting him on the spot.

"Yeah. Um…. Just 'cause you live close by."

"Oh. Okay. So what are we going to do?"

"I know!" Tony declared, snapping his fingers. "Let's go look at where they found Jodi's body!"

"Gross!" Beth said, scrunching up her nose. "No way!"

"Yeah, Tony, that's a bit much. Don't forget the police advised everyone to stay out of the woods," Joseph agreed.

"Oh, come on! Don't be so wimpy! There's three of us and one of whatever it was that killed Jodi!"

"Don't talk about her, please. It's weird," Beth pleaded.

"Yeah, come on, Tony. Don't be such a dick."

"Sorrryy," Tony answered, probably rolling his eyes.

"I bet the police have it all wrapped up in that yellow tape like in CSI."

"Come on, now we've got to check it out. I don't think it's far from here."

Reluctantly, Beth agreed, then looked to Joseph.

He nodded as well, if only because he knew they would be walking together in the dark woods. He fantasized about her getting scared and holding his arm for safety.

They walked deeper into the woods to the footpath that travelled parallel to the houses. They could still see the lights of the yards through the trees, but they themselves were out of sight of anyone. Beth began to shiver.

"Do you want my sweater?" Joseph offered.

"What about you? You'll get cold then."

"Not at all." He unzipped his hoodie and slipped it off his shoulders and onto hers.

"Thanks." Her eyes glistened in the moonlight as she gazed up at Joseph's face shyly.

Tony purposely travelled a little farther ahead of them.

They walked in silence for what seemed like forever until Tony exclaimed, "Look! There's yellow tape!"

They sped up and headed to the yellow plastic that was blowing in the wind, loosely wrapped around the surrounding trees. The forest was eerily silent, as if even the animals and insects knew what had transpired here.

They each ducked under the tape and into the small clearing. The ferns and grass that carpeted the forest floor were flattened by the unusual amount of traffic that had recently been here. A shiver ran up Joseph's spine and he shuddered.

"This is creepy, I don't like this. Let's go home," Beth requested.

"I wonder if there is any blood around," Tony said, mostly to himself.

"Yeah, Beth is right," Joseph said. "This isn't right. We knew this girl."

There was a loud rustle in the woods nearby.

Beth jumped and held Joseph's arm to her. He would have been excited if the sudden movement hadn't also startled him.

"Okay. Maybe we should go," Tony agreed.

Suddenly, out of nowhere a dark figure jumped out of the nearby brush and landed in front of Tony. The seven-foot inhuman figure loomed between the friends and an ear-piercing screech erupted from it. Beth screamed, and she and Joseph both fell to the ground on their backs.

Tony froze and stared up at the figure. Its body and face were silhouetted against the moonlit sky. A long extremity with gnarled fingers and inch-long, pointed nails swiped down and slashed at Tony's chest. Tony leapt back in time to avoid his stomach being completely slashed open and cried out in pain when the nails scratched across his front, slicing through his shirt. He fell back onto the ground as blood started to seep through his shirt.

The figure advanced on Tony to continue his attack when it suddenly fell backward, clutching at its neck.

A small human figure appeared out of the darkness from behind Tony and leapt at the large figure with a pointed object in hand. She jabbed at the creature's stomach, nearly missing it as it hissed at her and removed the weapon that pierced its neck and threw it to the ground.

"Run!" the small figure yelled, revealing her sex.

Beth and Joseph ran to Tony's side and helped him up. They ran in the direction they came from without looking back.

They burst out of the trees and into the backyard of Beth's neighbor.

"I've got to go home!" Beth cried shrilly. "Don't tell anyone I was with you guys! My dad would kill me!"

"Why would we tell anyone?"

"You've got to bring Tony to the hospital!"

"What? No way!" Tony protested.

"Come on, let's go to my place," Joseph suggested. "We'll take a look at you." With Tony's arm still around his shoulder, he turned to Beth. "Sorry."

"It's okay. I'll talk to you guys tomorrow." She turned and headed toward her house and slipped silently in the back door.

"Come on," Joseph said as he helped Tony through the backyards until they got to his house. The back door was locked and all the lights were out except the one in his bedroom.

"I'll climb the tree and let you in the back door, ok?"

Tony nodded and sat in the grass in the shadow of the house.

Joseph scaled the tree, then tiptoed across the roof, and slid in his window. When he got to his bedroom, he changed into his pajama pants and slipped out into the hallway. He could hear the light snores of his mother in the next room. He crept down the stairs and to the back porch to open the back door.

"Tony!" he whispered, loudly.

Tony walked slowly around the corner and into the back door. Joseph locked it behind him and they headed up the stairs to his room.

When they were both safely inside his bedroom with the curtains closed, Joseph helped Tony take off his shirt so they could see the extent of his wounds. The shirt was soaked with blood and completely ruined. Joseph put it in a plastic bag he found under his desk and tied it shut, then stuffed it into his garbage. He would dispose of it tomorrow.

Tony had five six-inch long gashes on his chest running diagonally from his left nipple to the right of his abdomen. Blood oozed from each slash. When he looked down at his chest, his head went fuzzy and he fell to the floor. Joseph checked to make sure he was breathing. After coming to the conclusion that his friend had just fainted, he went to the bathroom to get a few old towels that wouldn't be missed and a bowl of hot water. He dipped the towel in the water and began washing the wounds. They were not as deep as he thought they would be. They were more like deep scratches. After they were cleaned, he got some bandages from the first aid kit his mom kept in the bathroom, and put them over the injuries.

The next morning, Joseph woke up to the sound of his mother knocking on his door.

"Joseph! Unlock this door this instant!"

He groaned and rolled out of bed. Tony was asleep on his floor with a pair of Joseph's pajamas on. He had woken up an hour after passing out and had gotten dressed. Shaken up from the ordeal, he had decided to stay the night on Joseph's floor.

Joseph opened the door to see his mom standing there with a cordless phone in her hand.

"Why is this door locked?" she asked, sternly.

Joseph rubbed his eyes. "I didn't realize it was."

"Tony! Your mother just called worried sick about you! I suggest you get home right away! I'll call and let her know you're on your way."

Tony sat up and mumbled something about being surprised his parents even noticed him gone, then left saying, "See ya'."

After the front door closed, she turned to Joseph again. "No sleepovers on school nights! Especially when Tony's parents' don't even know that he's here. Now, get up and get ready for school before I decide to ground you."

Joseph picked out some clean clothes and headed to

the bathroom to shower. His head was still groggy.

After Tony had regained consciousness, they'd stayed up and talked about what had happened. Neither could conclude what the thing was that attacked them or who the girl was that saved them.

He wondered what would happen with Beth today at school. He decided that he would skip the baseball cap today and actually gel his hair and wear cologne, just in case.

Tony was late for school. He arrived halfway through first period. Joseph was struggling to stay awake as their half-senile teacher read from their Biology book in his steady, monotonous voice.

Joesph's eyes closed and his head dropped but popped back up before hitting his desk.

A white piece of paper landed on his desk in front of him from the girl across from him, Jayme. She didn't even look at him.

He opened the neatly folded piece of paper and read the contents.

Sit with me at lunch -- Beth.

He looked to his right and nodded at Beth, who was sitting on the other side of Jayme.

When the bell rang, Joseph and Tony continued to their next class while Beth went to hers. The next two periods passed in a very slow blur. Joseph couldn't have concentrated even if he'd wanted to. He silently thanked God it was Friday.

He sat, watching the clock, waiting for the long hand to move to the nine indicating eleven forty-five, lunchtime.

He watched the hand hit eleven forty-four and it seemed to take an eternity for it to move the last notch to the nine. The bell rang immediately and Joseph jumped out of his desk, hastily throwing his books into his book bag. Tony followed.

They went to their adjacent lockers, threw their bags in, and headed through the crowded hallway to the lunchroom.

"Hey, man, what's the hurry?' Tony asked, fighting to keep up with Joseph. He wore both a baggy T-shirt and sweater to both hide the already scabbed wounds and to prevent the cloth from rubbing them.

"Beth wants me to sit with her at lunchtime."

"What about me?"

"You sit with us too, just in case we run out of things to say. It will be less awkward with you there."

He slapped Joseph on the back. "No prob, man!"

They got in the line-up for food and after ordering, they turned to see Beth sitting at the table farthest back in the corner away from everyone. She wasn't alone.

Susan sat at the table next to her at the table stuffing her face with a gooey sandwich from a paper bag. Tony and Joseph headed toward them and sat down. Susan gave them a look of distaste and continued to eat. She brushed her dirty blonde hair out of her face, but not before getting a bit of mayo in it.

They sat down and began to eat in silence until Beth finally spoke.

"So, about last night," she began. Both boys looked at

her in awe and motioned toward Susan. "Oh, she knows all about it. She's been trying to research mythical creatures for what it could be."

"Any luck?" Joseph asked her.

She swallowed what was left of her sandwich and shook her head with wide eyes. "It could be anything! It could be a demon! Imagine if it was the devil itself!" she exclaimed excitedly.

"Sorry, Susan, but I'm not as excited as you are about this. You weren't there. It was scary."

"You know what we need to do," Susan began. "We need to find that kung-fu chick who saved your asses! I bet she can help us! She's got to know what it is and how to kill it!"

"That's actually not too bad of an idea," Joseph agreed. "This town isn't that big, she shouldn't be too hard to find. There's only one hotel, maybe we'll luck out and she'll be there."

"Okay! It's settled then. I'll get my dad's car tonight, pick you guys up at Joseph's and we'll stake out the hotel to see if we see the woman we saw last night," Beth said.

They all nodded and continued to eat in silence. As Joseph ate, he glanced up at Beth. She was delicately eating an apple, the desert to her lunch. A small strand of hair fell out from her ponytail and into her face. She gently tucked it behind her ear and took a bite of her apple. As she did, her eyes met Joseph`s and he looked away quickly. She blushed slightly and continued her lunch.

After lunch they all parted for their individual classes. Beth told them to be ready at eight and she and Susan would be there to pick them up.

Tony went to Joseph's straight after school. He called to let his parents know he would be staying there for the night and would see them tomorrow. Joseph's mother stood within earshot while he phoned his parents. They went upstairs into Joseph's room and closed the door behind them.

"Take off your shirt. I want to make sure your cuts aren't infected," Joseph ordered.

"Yes, doctor," he teased as he lifted his t-shirt up over his head, revealing his bandages. Joseph carefully removed them and gasped.

Tony looked down at his stomach. "Ohhh, man."

The cuts were completely open; they hadn't closed up at all and there was a greenish-brownish pus oozing out of them. With the bandage removed, the pus began to run down his stomach, threatening to soak into the waist of his pants.

"Lie down so it doesn't run down, I'll get some Polysporin," Joseph ordered. He got up and left Tony lying on his bed, his head still spinning and swallowing hard to prevent the inevitable spew of vomit about to be released from his mouth.

Joseph came back and rubbed a large amount of the Polysporin on the wounds, then dressed them with new bandages. Tony closed his eyes and breathed deeply as this was done.

``You need to see a doctor."

"What? No way! What would we tell a doctor? A big monster attacked me!?"

"Well, we have got to do something. It's infected." When Tony just glared at him, Joseph sighed. "Maybe that missus will know. Hopefully we can find her," Joseph said, relenting.

At five after eight, a car pulled up outside Joseph's house and honked its horn. Tony peeked out the window and saw that it was Beth. They pulled their jackets on and headed out of Joseph's bedroom and down the stairs to the front door.

"I'm going out for a bit, mom!" he called, opening the door and letting Tony out through.

"Be home by eleven!" she called from the kitchen.

"Okay!"

He closed the door behind him and walked across the front lawn to the car. He and Tony jumped in the back seat of the four-door sedan and put on their seat belts.

"So, what's the plan?" Beth asked as she put the car in gear and pulled out into the street.

"We have to get something to eat first," Tony said. "I'm starving and got a craving for a nice greasy burger."

Susan cringed. "Yuck. I could go for a salad though."

"Okay. Let's go to McDonalds, my treat," Joseph suggested.

They picked up their food at the drive-thru and headed to the hotel to park in the parking lot and wait. There was a lot of traffic coming and going through the hotel and the parking lot, but they did not see the woman.

"I'm friggin' bored," Tony announced after a few minutes.

"Yeah, me too," Susan agreed. "Why don't we go

inside and check it out?"

"I don't know…" Beth protested weakly.

"Come on, don't be such a wimp!"

"Shut up, man. I'm not sure either. How are we going to find her?" Joseph said.

Beth smiled at him.

"I don't know. I'm sure we can roam around the hotel. Maybe we'll see her inside. She could be in the restaurant or at the bar." Tony opened the door and started to get out. Susan followed. Reluctantly, Beth and Joseph followed as well.

They walked up to the front doors. The old lady who worked the front desk was sitting down working at the computer.

"How are we going to get past her?" Beth said, quietly.

Just then, the telephone inside rang and the lady turned back to the door to answer it.

"Let's go!"

Tony silently ran in through the door and the rest of them followed him. They darted through the door and past the front desk into the nearest hallway.

"There's like, one hundred rooms here. How are we supposed to find her?" Joseph asked.

"I don't know. How about we split up?"

"No!" Susan and Beth said in unison.

"Okay, okay. We won't split up."

They walked through the dimly lit hallway with its beige walls and numerous grey doors. The right side of the corridor was marked with all the even numbers from 100 to 130 and on the left side was all the odd numbers from 101 to 129.

At the end of the hallway, they exited into the stairway and went up two flights of stairs to the second floor. The second floor was exactly like the first except that the numbers on the doors went from 200 to 230. They didn't see or hear any movement from either of the rooms.

After making a complete circle around the hotel, they had not seen or heard anyone and they were back to the first corridor.

"This is ridiculous. We're never going to find her!" Tony exclaimed, his voice echoing through the empty hall. He suddenly swayed to the side and had to grab the wall to keep himself upright.

"What's wrong with you?" Beth asked, concerned. She gently touched Tony's shoulder. He looked up at her and she gasped. His eyes were glassy, his cheeks were red, and his face was wet with perspiration.

"Oh my God! Are you okay, Tony?" Joseph opened Tony's hoodie and looked down at his stomach. His shirt was soaked with the greenish-grey goo that was oozing from his cuts earlier that day.

"What the hell!?" Susan exclaimed.

"We've got to get him to a doctor!" Beth said. She took Tony under the arm and Joseph did the same on the other side. Suddenly, Tony fell forward onto the floor unconscious.

"What are we going to do!?" Beth shrilled.

"Call an ambulance!" Susan demanded.

"A doctor can't help him now," said a raspy voice said from behind them. They all turned to see a woman standing in the doorway to room 101.

It was the woman from the night before.

"It's you!" Joseph exclaimed. "Can you help him? We need your help!"

"Not much of a thank you if you ask me," she drawled. "Maybe next time I'll let you die in the woods."

The group of teens stared at her in disbelief until she sighed and left the doorway. She knelt down to grab Tony by the arm and stood him on his feet. Joseph grabbed the opposite side and helped. She led them into the room and laid him on the floor.

"Close the door," she barked at the girls.

"Shouldn't we put him on the bed?"

The woman looked at Joseph, her green eyes piercing through him.

"No. He's better on the floor. It's sturdier."

"Can you help him?" Beth whispered.

"Sure. But it's not gonna be pretty. Think you can handle it, sugar?"

Susan and Beth both nodded.

"Stand back, out of my way."

She walked over to her suitcase on the bed and opened it. Joseph gasped at the contents. The entire top layer was filled with different weapons. He thought he even saw a set of nunchuks. She flipped the first layer over and exposed the bottom layer. A strong stench reached his nostrils from the suitcase.

She pulled out a few bottles of mysterious elixirs. One was green, another was bright red, and a third was dark red, the color of blood. She laid the elixirs on the bed next to her and continued to take out a few bandages, a bottle of white powder, and a dagger. She brought them over to the floor beside Tony whose breathing was coming in short rasps. His chest heaved quickly along with his breathing.

"Stand back and don't say a thing," she ordered.

Joseph stood up and went over to the Susan and Beth, who still stood just inside the door.

"Before you start, can you tell us your name?" Beth pleaded.

She eyed Beth skeptically and answered: "Scarlett." Then she turned her back to the group and began to work on Tony.

First things first, she removed his hoodie. Then she sliced through his T-shirt and the bandages below it with her dagger in one quick movement. The cuts were worse than they had been earlier. They were completely open and the skin was peeling away from the middle of the gashes. Inside them, deep green goo flowed slowly out from the inside.

Susan urged and she ran to the bathroom where they could hear her heave as her McDonalds spewed into the toilet. Beth turned away and Joseph watched in awe.

"Shit. This is worse than I thought," Scarlett said, more to herself than anyone else.

She picked up the bottle containing the green elixir and dropped two drops into each of the cuts. They did not seem to make a difference. She then picked up the bottle containing the deep red elixir. It oozed out into each of the cuts, from beginning to end, and sizzled. White foam bubbled from the cuts and spilled out onto the greyish colored skin that was now Tony's abdomen.

She took the last bottle, containing the bright red

substance, and poured it over the dagger. The knife gleamed in the lamplight as the red stuff dripped off it. It looked like something out of a cheesy Hammer horror movie.

She gently forced the dagger down into one of the cuts and cut off the loose skin around the wound. Tony began to moan, but remained unconscious.

"I may need you to hold him down for this."

Beth and Joseph knelt down on the floor next to Tony's head and held his arms up. Susan was still in the bathroom. Her heaves had halted, but she did not dare to reappear in the room. Scarlett positioned herself so that her body had Tony's legs pinned to the floor.

Taking a deep breath, she began peeling off the skin from each horizontal slash. Then she dug the dagger in to the middle of the cut where most of the green goo was oozing. Tony cried out in pain and struggled to free himself. Joseph and Beth held his arms as tight as they could as he continued to cry out and swear.

Finally, instead of green pus coming out of the cuts, they began to ooze red blood. Scarlett put away the knife and splashed the green elixir onto the cuts again then she cleaned around the areas and bandaged them over.

Tony was still unconscious and his face still burned from the fever. Scarlett went to her bag and got a bottle of pills. She tossed them to Joseph.

"Give him one of these. Make sure he swallows it."

"What is it?"

"Oxys. They'll ease the pain for the night. And don't get any ideas, I'll notice if you take any for yourself."

Beth huffed. "We aren't drug addicts and we are *not*

going to steal any of your pills."

Scarlett smirked at her.

Joseph opened Tony's mouth and put a pill in.

"Chew this up and swallow it," he instructed.

Tony's eyes remained closed but he did as he was told.

Beth and Joseph helped him up and put him on the double bed to rest. They put a comforter over him to keep him warm and called out to Susan to get them a cool facecloth.

"Is it safe to come out now?" she asked timidly, peeking out from behind the bathroom door.

"It's all over, soldier," Scarlett remarked.

Susan crept out and looked at Tony lying on the bed. She handed the cool face cloth to Beth, who placed it gently on Tony's head. The room was quiet until finally Joseph spoke up.

"Okay, so what the hell are we dealing with? And is Tony going to be okay?"

"Well, it's not human so I guess you could call it an animal," Scarlett answered. "The truth is, I'm not really sure what it is. I just know it lives a long time and it's hard to kill. I've researched happenings much like the ones that are happening now, and they've dated back way back to ancient times. I guess the only real description of it is Demon."

"Demon? Like the devil?" Susan asked.

"Well, not really. Demons aren't all necessarily linked to the devil, if a devil does exist. Demon or Daemon is actually Latin for spirit. You know as much as I do now, and I don't really give a shit what the thing is, I just want to know how to kill it."

"Have you found out?" Joseph asked.

"Nope. I've tried everything but beheading it, which I am pretty sure will stop it. Of course, I can never get close enough to it to actually try that theory."

"So, what about Tony?" Beth asked, looking over to his still form in the bed. His breathing was steady and less laboured.

"Oh, he's screwed."

"What?" Beth and Joseph exclaimed in unison.

"Well, the potions I gave him will make him better, but the demon isn't going to stop until he's dead. He doesn't leave anyone behind. And those cuts of his draw him to his prey. He can smell the wounds, the gangrene, the pus, the scent of Tony himself."

"Well, we've got to stop it," Joseph protested. "We can't just wait around for it to come get him!"

"I don't plan to. We've got to get him out of here, when he's stronger of course. The potion will keep the creature at bay for now, but it won't last long."

"So that's it? We just wait around? No way."

"No, I didn't say that. We can use this to our advantage." She smiled coyly. "He will be feeling a lot better by tomorrow. Then we have all day to come up with a plan."

"A plan to do what?" Susan shrieked.

"Well, we aren't going to have tea with it now are we? We need to think of a way to kill it. Before it kills us of course."

"I thought you said you thought you knew how to kill it," Joseph said.

"Well, I'm pretty sure that will kill it but I just need to figure out a way to get close enough to it to actually take its head off. That's where you and Tony come in." She smiled.

"You mean you're going to use us as bait."

"Well, not you, just your friend over there. When it smells him in the forest, it won't be long before it comes to finish what it started."

"No way. No way in hell."

"Okay. Well say goodbye to your friend now because unless you do what I say, he's going to die and whoever is with him will probably die too."

The room was silent as the truth dawned upon the three teenagers. They could not figure out another way to save Tony on their own, and each silently concluded that Scarlett was their only choice.

Beth was first to speak: "Okay. What's the plan?"

They stayed at the hotel with Scarlett for about an hour as she told them her plan. When she was done, she opened her suitcase and started showing them the different weapons she had.

"Pick one and I'll show you how to use it. I can't bring you out there without any protection at all."

Inside the suitcase was a pair of sai, shuriken, daggers, knives, and finally a long case containing a katana.

Joseph reached for the katana immediately.

Scarlett slapped his hands away from it. "No way, that's mine. You wouldn't be able to use it anyway."

He gave her a dirty look, then reached in for the

longest dagger inside. It gleamed silver in the dim hotel lamplight. He eyed the handle. It was wooden and carved with images of strange demonic beings, angels, and thorny bushes. One particular carving was of a human-like creature with wings like those of an angel. The face was that of a young boy smiling, but he had long jagged teeth. His eyes were two ruby red gems.

Beth picked out the pair of sai. They were pure silver with smooth silver handles, plain but beautiful. She positioned them in both her hands and somehow looked comfortable with them. Scarlett smiled at her reassuringly.

"Those are my favourite."

Finally, it was Susan's turn. She eyed the weapons with disdain. She wanted nothing to do with this hunt, and her face and eyes showed it. She picked up small pistol. It lay heavy in her hands and looked very old fashioned. Instead of being silver, it was coal black with a brown handle.

"That won't do much damage but it will slow it down," Scarlett announced. "Are you sure you wouldn't want to use something else?"

"I'm sure. I don't want to be near whatever it is."

"Okay. School time."

Scarlett proceeded to show each of them how to use their weapon.

Except for Susan.

"We will have to practice tomorrow in the daylight," Scarlett explained. "I can't show you how to shoot a gun in a hotel, the cops would be here in no time."

Susan sat on the bed next to Tony and relaxed as she watched Scarlett show Beth to use the sai.

Beth caught on quickly and Scarlett was impressed. She held the sai tightly in her hands, jabbing at her imaginary opponent with more force than she looked capable of.

For a final test, Scarlett used her extra pair of sai and challenged Beth. She taught her how to defend herself and how to bestow killing jabs into her opponent. They practiced for an hour as Susan and Joseph watched silently in awe. Finally, Scarlett stopped.

"You're ready. Keep practicing." She smiled and Beth smiled back, breathing heavily and rubbing the sweat from her forehead.

"Your turn," Scarlett said, turning to Joseph. He stood up, holding the heavy dagger in his right hand.

She showed him how to properly hold the dagger and jab it at his imaginary opponent. She then picked up a dagger of her own and used it to mock fight with him, showing him different moves to defend himself from threats from any angle.

After about two hours, Scarlett called it a night.

"Good job, guys. Tomorrow afternoon I want to meet you girls in the forest where we first met. I'll show you how to use the pistol," she said, looking at Susan.

"What about us?"

"You two will meet us in the forest, the same area before it gets dark. Once Tony is there, it won't be long before it comes for him."

The teens glanced at Tony, who was still in the bed but starting to move and moan.

"Now, let's wake him up and get him home."

They did as Scarlett said. Tony's eyes opened slightly and he squinted when the light from the lamp entered his pupils.

"Where am I?"

"We're at Scarlett's hotel room. You passed out. Your cuts were infected badly," Joseph explained.

"She treated them to make them better," Beth continued.

"We're going to take you to my place, okay? Call your parents and tell them you're staying at my place for the night."

Tony nodded and they helped his weak frame out of the bed. Susan and Joseph got under each of his arms to support him.

"Take the back entrance, just down the hall," Scarlett instructed. "It opens to the alley."

"I'll drive my car around back and meet you there," Beth suggested. She headed out the door and left Joseph and Susan to assist Tony out of the hotel room and down the hall. They both silently thanked God they were on the first floor and that there were no stairs.

Scarlett said nothing and closed the door behind them leaving the three of them alone in the hallway. Tony tried to walk on his own but his legs were still too weak to support his weight.

"I feel like shit," Tony announced.

"You look better, how are the gashes?" Joseph asked, nodding toward Tony's abdomen.

Tony lifted his shirt and looked under the bandages. The wounds seemed almost healed. They had closed over and were no longer bleeding or leaking pus. He poked at them gently.

"They don't hurt as much anymore either."

"Okay. I'll fill you in on the plan while Beth brings the car around."

The next morning, Joseph and Tony woke up at 8 a.m. Neither had slept well in anticipation of the day ahead. Tony was less than impressed with the fact that he would be used as bait to lure the creature to their trap and more stirred into action with the realization that if the plan did not work, he would be killed viciously and violently.

"I need a shower," he said to Joseph. Joseph passed him a change of clothes, and he headed to the bathroom and started the water.

While Tony showered, Joseph went downstairs to where his mother and sister were already sat at the table. Gayle was having heart-shaped pancakes and his mother was sipping on a steaming cup of coffee.

"You're up early," she greeted him.

"Joseph!" Gayle exclaimed. "Try Mom's love pancakes! They're awesome! Mom told me they are made with love!"

Joseph smiled and sat at the table next to his sister. She jabbed her fork into a piece of pancake and held it out for Joseph to try.

"Mmmmmhhh. There must be a lot of love in these! They are awesome!"

Gayle beamed.

"Would you like some?" his mother asked.

"Maybe later. I'm not hungry yet. Thanks."

"What's wrong with you today? Do you feel okay?"

"I didn't sleep well, that's all," he assured her. "Tony stayed over last night. He called and left a message for his parents."

"Okay, good. I was wondering who was in the shower," she answered, more to herself than to Joseph.

"Can I have a cup of coffee?"

"Yuck!" Abby exclaimed.

"You? Coffee?"

"Yeah. I told you I'm tired," he smiled weakly at his mom as she got up from the table and made him a fresh cup. She put the sugar and creamer on the table with his coffee and gave him a kiss on his cheek.

"My little boy is growing up," she said teasingly.

Joseph smiled. Usually he would grumble and wipe off the kiss, but today he didn't. He couldn't help wondering what today would bring, if he would ever see his family again.

Tony came down the stairs in Joseph's clothes, the jeans just reached the floor. On Joseph, they were bunched up on the bottom.

"Good morning, Tony," Joseph's mother greeted him. "Would you like a cup of coffee also?"

"Yes, please."

"What were you boys doing last night to make you so tired? I hope you didn't sneak out after curfew." She eyed them suspiciously.

"No, just didn't sleep well. You know boys, up late talking about girls," Tony said with a chuckle.

"Tony! Have some love pancakes!" Gayle insisted.

"Sure." Tony stood up to help himself but Joseph's mom told him to sit down.

"Would you like yours cut in hearts too?" she laughed.

"Of course!"

Gayle smiled at Tony and Tony returned her smile, affectionately mussing up her hair.

He sat down and ate all the pancakes that were piled onto his plate, after soaking them with syrup of course.

"These are delicious," he said, stuffing the last pancake into his mouth whole. "I feel like I haven't eaten in days."

When he had finished eating, they took their coffee upstairs to finish. Joseph got in the shower and got dressed for the day. Tony was very quiet as he finished his coffee.

"Everything will be okay tonight, ya' know," Joseph said as he put on his shirt.

"Yeah," Tony nodded. He didn't sound convinced.

"Scarlett is really talented. She just needs us to distract it so she can do her thing. We won't let anything happen to you or anyone else."

Tony grunted.

"I promise. Everything is going to be alright."

Tony was quiet for a minute and then he said, "Don't make promises you can't keep. I'm going home to spend some time with my parents."

After Tony left, Joseph sat quiet for a minute in his bedroom and silently prayed to God that they would all make it through the night. Then he went downstairs with his mom and sister.

"Let's watch a movie," he suggested. "Your pick, Gayle."

They sat down together, munched on popcorn and watched a Barbie movie. It was not the most interesting movie for Joseph or his mother, but Gayle had a ball. She laughed and looked up to her big brother to see if he was laughing too. He smiled at her affectionately.

By the time the movie was over, Gayle was sound asleep on Joseph's lap and his mother had gone to the kitchen to make them a lunch. Joseph stroked Gayle's hair and she snuggled closer to him, reaching her little arm over his leg to hold him in place. Before his mother had finished making lunch, he had fallen asleep himself.

He woke up to the sound of the phone ringing. It was an hour later. Gayle had quietly awakened earlier and went to her room to play while he slept.

"Joseph! You're wanted on the phone!" His mom called from the kitchen.

He reached to the table next to him and picked up the cordless phone.

"Hello?"

"It's Beth. We were thinking of meeting here at my place after dinner. Maybe six or seven?"

"Sounds good," he said. "All of us?"

"Yeah, but you can come over a little earlier, I mean, if you would like to."

"Sure."

They said goodbye and hung up their phones. The butterflies in Joseph's stomach fluttered worse than ever. He immediately went upstairs to pick out something different to wear.

He gave his mother and Gayle a hug and a kiss before leaving to go to Beth's house. He held them tightly and a little longer than normally.

He stepped out his front door, wondering if he would ever step foot in his house again. He choked back a rush of emotion, swallowed hard, then continued to Beth's house just a few minutes down the street.

He knocked on the door to be greeted by her father. It wasn't a warm greeting; Beth had never had a boy over to her house before. He led Joseph into the living room and told him he could take a seat on the couch.

"Beth is upstairs getting dressed. She'll be down in a minute. Would you like something to drink?"

Joseph's throat was parched and his forehead had broken out into a cold sweat. Beth's dad was his dentist but he had never been as nervous to see him as he was today. He knew how protective her father was over her.

"No, thank you," he said, his tongue sticking to the top of his mouth as he struggled to talk.

Her father left and went into the kitchen. It seemed like eternity before Beth actually walked into the room and joined Joseph on the couch.

"Hi! I'm glad you came over," she said, softly.

"No problem."

She looked deep into his eyes. He was captivated by their jade lenses surrounded by beautiful, long, dark lashes.

"I'm really scared about tonight. I hardly slept at all last night. I spent the entire day with my dad, worrying that this would be the last day we would ever spend together." She choked back a sob and continued, "I also worried about something else."

"What's that?" Joseph asked. He too felt overwhelmed by the emotion that he himself had felt the entire day with his family.

"Well, it's why I wanted you to come over before the

others," she started.

Joseph wasn't sure where she was going with this.

She looked over his shoulder into the kitchen. Her father was back on to them at the stove cleaning up after supper. She was sure he was straining to hear everything she was saying and she was sure her voice was low enough that he couldn't.

"You can tell me anything," he assured her.

"Okay. I hope this doesn't backfire."

Before Joseph could ask any questions, she kissed him. He was stunned, and for a moment he didn't kiss back. Then he moved his lips and returned her kiss. Her soft lips caressed his ever so gently and tasted of the cherry lip-gloss she must have put on before she came downstairs.

The kiss only last a few moments and she pulled away. Joseph had never wanted it to end. Her face was flushed and she looked deep into his soul. Her eyes showed doubt. Joseph reached up his hand and caressed her cheek.

"I can't believe you just did that," he whispered. "I'd been trying to get up the courage to ask you out forever."

She smiled and breathed a sigh of relief. "Really?"

He nodded.

Her smile broadened and she kissed him again. This time the kiss was more intense and she gently caressed his tongue with hers. He put his arms around her head to pull her closer and kissed her hard. His fingers entwined in her hair and he twirled a strand around his finger and played with the beautiful locks gently.

There was a gruff sound from the kitchen of Beth's father clearing his throat. They pulled away from each other and Beth's face turned red. She looked down away from her father's glare. Joseph didn't dare turn around to se the look on his face. At that moment, the doorbell rang. Both Beth and Joseph jumped up to go to the front porch and greet their friends. Joseph could feel the eyes of her father burning into his back and the butterflies in his stomach returned.

Beth opened the door to see Tony and Susan on her front step.

"Come on in, guys!" she greeted. Susan walked on in, she had spent many days and nights at Beth's house. She headed straight for the family room in the back of the house adjacent to the kitchen.

Tony, Joseph and Beth followed.

"We're going in the family room to watch some TV before go out, okay, Dad?" she called.

"Sure." He watched the foursome disappear into the next room. He made sure to stay in the kitchen within eyesight of the teens.

In the family room, they turned the TV on loud enough that Beth's father could not overhear their conversation.

"So, Scarlett told us to meet her in the woods at nine. That gives us an hour." Joseph said, eyeing the clock on the wall.

"How did the shooting practice go today?" Beth asked.

Susan beamed. "Awesome! Who would have known I was such a good shot? Even Scarlett was impressed."

"Awesome!" Joseph exclaimed, giving Susan a high five.

"How are you feeling, Tony?" Beth said, shifting her

gaze to him.

"Well besides the fact that tonight I am being used as bait, pretty good. Mom, Dad and I had a good day. No fights, no drinking, we just watched movies, talked and had a nice supper together."

"That's good," Susan said, "And don't worry, I'll be in or behind one of the trees hiding and ready to shoot that thing, Beth was awesome with the sai and Joseph can stab the shit out of that bastard. We won't let it hurt you. Everything is going to be fine."

Tony nodded but was not convinced.

They left Beth's house at seven forty-five to go into the woods where the first attack occurred. They all remained close and listened for any strange sounds around them. They knew that the creature could sense Tony's presence, but they hoped it didn't show up before Scarlett arrived.

As they neared the clearing, still surrounded by police tape, they heard a loud crunch behind them. All four of them turned at the same time, drawing their weapons and ready to fight. Tony stayed behind the others.

A black figure emerged from the darkness. It was Scarlett. She was wearing a tight fitting long-sleeved Henley top and high-topped black hiker boots. Her hair was tied back in a long ponytail and held back with a band of cloth.

"Good! You guys are ready!" She strolled out of the darkness and into the moonlit clearing.

"I could have shot you!" Susan exclaimed, lowering her gun.

"Yeah, but I needed to test you. Make sure you were on your guard."

"Thanks a lot," Tony muttered sarcastically.

"I just scoped out the area again. We'll all split up around the clearing. Tony is going to stay in the middle, in the moonlight so that he can be clearly spotted, both by us and the creature."

Tony grunted.

"Susan, you have a long range weapon so I want you over there," she pointed all the way across the clearing to a big spruce tree. "You can hide on the lowest branch there. I hope you like to climb."

Susan muttered a complaint under her breath and headed to the spot Scarlett pointed out.

"Beth, I want you close by, but not seen. If you have to step in, you will need to be a lot closer than Susan. Tony and Joseph, I want you two in the clearing together." She passed Tony a long dagger, much like the one Joseph held.

"I know I haven't gotten a chance to train you like I did the others, but I want you to have a weapon. It's after you so you will need the most defense you can get."

"Where are you going to be?" Tony asked.

"I'll be just out of sight, waiting for my opportunity to strike. You guys are more or less the distraction. Your weapons will wound the bastard but won't take him down; they'll just slow him down and distract him long enough for me to strike."

"Great. We're all decoys," Beth said.

Scarlett turned to her. "No, you're helping me. I just hope this works." It was the first time they had heard any doubt in her voice and they didn't like it.

"Can we ask you something personal?" Beth asked,

timidly.

"Let me guess, why am I hunting it?"

They all nodded their heads.

She took a deep breath and began. "When I was ten, I remember my mother and father tucking me into bed one night. I can remember Mama singing Brahms' Lullaby to me as Daddy stroked my forehead. Almost every night this was how I fell asleep and this night was no different. Well, of course, except one thing."

She paused and in the darkness she sounded like she choked back a sob. "I don't know what time it was, but I woke up sometime during the night to a loud bang and my mama screaming. I could hear my dad shouting and I heard a gunshot. Then I heard an inhuman scream, or a growl, I'm not really sure what to call it. Of course, I'm sure you heard the sound yourselves. Anyway, I jumped out of bed to see what was going on and Mama met me in the doorway. She was crying and sweating and breathing heavily. I asked her what was happening. She couldn't tell me, she was hyperventilating. In between breaths, she told me to hide in the closet. I didn't ask any questions, I did what I was told. I begged her to come in with me but she kept saying it didn't see me and I remember wondering what she meant by it.

"I kicked my way through toys and shoes and sat back in the back corner of the closet. The door was left open just an inch and I could see the mirror on the dresser on the other side of the room. In the mirror I could see my mother climb under my bed and hide. Then, I heard a strange noise."

The clearing was quiet. Susan had come out to join the

group and listen.

"I don't want to get into details, even though I don't really remember. I think I must have closed my eyes or covered my head. Anyway, it didn't see me, it didn't smell me, it did what it did and left. I don't know how long I stayed in the closet, but I remember smelling their bodies starting to rot in the heat. I remember the phone ringing over and over. I remember the scream of my aunt when she came to check on us. I remember her pulling me from the closet, covering my face and bringing me to her house. She didn't cover my face well enough. I saw what was left of my mom. Her entire chest cavity was torn open and some of the insides were missing. I later found out her heart was missing. After that, I went to live with my aunt."

In the darkness she moved her hand to her face and Joseph wondered if she was wiping a tear from her cheek. Her voice remained nonchalant and matter-of-fact.

"Okay, enough talk. Get in positions," she demanded.

The foursome were stunned but listened without hesitation. Within minutes, they were all concealed in their hiding places with Joseph and Tony standing in the moonlight and completely at the mercy of whatever was coming to get them.

"You scared?" Joseph asked.

"Shitting my pants," Tony answered with half a grin.

Joseph grinned back.

There was a rustle in the trees nearby. Tony and Joseph stiffened and drew their weapons. They watched the brush in the direction the noise came from. The entire forest was quiet, not even a cricket or owl could be heard.

Suddenly, there was a gunshot and a scream. They ran to where Susan had been. She was no longer there, but the gun and a few drops of blood were on the ground next to the tree she was perched.

"Susan!" they hollered. There was a noise in the woods nearby and they ran towards it.

Susan was crouched on the ground with tears streaming down her face and shivering uncontrollably.

"Are you okay?" Tony asked.

Joseph looked at the hand she had clutched over her leg. He removed it gently and she cried out in pain. Her fibia was completely cracked and had torn through the skin and muscles of her legs to protrude out of her shin.

Tony turned and threw up; Joseph swallowed down the queasiness that he felt overcome him.

"Did it get you?"

"No," she whispered. "It just grabbed me and knocked me out of the tree."

"We have to get you out of here!"

"No! Just give me the gun!" she begged.

Joseph brought her gun to her and helped her bury herself in the bushes.

"I think I'm going to pass out," she muttered. She closed her eyes and clutched the gun in one hand and her leg in the other.

"We have to move away from her! It's after me!" Tony exclaimed.

Joseph nodded in agreement and they headed to the other side of the clearing. They looked around trying to see if they could see or hear the creature approach, but the forest was dead silent once again.

The crack of a branch echoed throughout the woods from above them and before they could look up, it jumped down from the tall trees and landed between Joseph and Tony. It turned its back to Joseph and advanced on Tony, who backed away but immediately tripped over an exposed tree root. The dagger fell from his grasp and landed just out of his reach. He looked at the creature that loomed over him with its long, dagger-like claws protruding from its oversized paws and long arms like those of a gorilla. Its breath came out in rasps and steam emanated from its nostrils.

Joseph lunged at the creature's back and thrust the sharp dagger into its back just below its shoulder blade. A loud screech erupted from the creature's mouth and it stood up straight, standing over seven feet. It turned to shake Joseph from its back, but was unsuccessful. Joseph held tight to the dagger and the greasy hair.

It reached behind itself and grabbed Joseph, then threw him against the ground in the clearing. The dagger remained in its back and it struggled to take it out but could not.

Beth decided to take advantage of this distraction to run from her hiding place in the trees and drive her sai into the stomach of the beast. It turned, and with one great swipe, it sent her flying across the clearing in the opposite direction of Joseph.

She lay unmoving on the ground, a low moan oozing from her.

Joseph jumped up, filled with adrenaline, and jumped on the monster again. He pulled out the dagger and thrust it into the creature's back again. At the same time, Tony got up off the ground, grabbed his knife and thrust it into the arm of the beast.

It swiped at both of the boys and sent them flying five feet or more away from it and advanced on them both.

Where the hell is Scarlett?

The boys jumped up, ignoring the pain they both felt and got in position to fight the beast that menaced towards their small forms. It stood to its full height and prepared to attack and no doubt kill the boys. They braced themselves, with both daggers in front of them.

The creature shrieked and turned around. Beth had gotten up and jabbed both her sai into his back and held on tight as it thrashed around trying to shake her off. The boys took this moment to thrust forward with their daggers and attack it from the front. A greenish brown blood-like substance leaked from its wounds but it still seemed unaffected by the wounds.

"Why won't this fucker die!?" Tony exclaimed.

It swiped Joseph away from Tony's side and tossed Beth off its back, leaving Tony completely exposed.

He closed his eyes and waited for what was to come.

The pain he expected didn't arrive. He opened his eyes to see the creature suddenly still with its black eyes wide. Its huge head fell to the ground with a sickening thud and landed in front of him. The greenish goo sprayed from the empty spot in its neck that used to hold its head. It soaked Tony's face and he stepped back to get out of range.

Scarlett jumped down from its shoulder as it fell to the ground in a great hairy heap.

"You okay?" she asked, holding out her hand to help

Tony up.

"I guess," he answered, shakily.

"How about you two?"

Beth and Joseph stood up and stumbled over to Tony's side to hug him.

He accepted their hugs and they embraced.

"Where's the other one?"

"She got hurt bad, she's over in the bushes there," Beth answered. She pointed in the direction of where they covered Susan with the bushes when she fell from the tree.

"Okay, go get her quick and get home, I'm going to burn this son-of-a-bitch and make sure he stays dead."

The threesome headed over to the bushes to get their fourth friend.

"Susan! It's dead! We did it!"

They uncovered her still body and shook her.

"Wake up, Susan! It's dead! Let's go home," Beth exclaimed again, happily.

Susan did not wake. They could hear Scarlett moving about behind them, piling dry wood and grass on top and below the beast's body.

"Susan?" she said, softly.

Joseph leaned down and moved close to her mouth to listen for her breathing.

"I don't think she's breathing," he said in a whisper.

"Susan!" Beth shrieked, shaking her friend. Susan's head nodded to the side and her hand flopped loosely from her broken leg to her side. She slowly fell sideways and her face hit the ground with a low thud.

An anguished groan came from Beth's throat and she

reached to her friend. She looked down, and both her pants the entire area around Susan's body was drenched in blood.

Joseph reached for Beth and put his arm around her as she sobbed loudly. Tony stepped back and sat on a nearby rock, covering his face with his hands.

Scarlett came over to them.

"What's wrong?" she asked.

Joseph motioned to Susan's body in the bushes.

Scarlett leaned down and examined the body.

"She bled to death," she said, quietly. She looked down at the young body lying motionless on the ground and brushed the hair from her juvenile face. She choked back a tear and turned to the others.

"Might as well leave her here. I'll burn the corpse and the smoke will attract the police. By the time they get here, the corpse will be destroyed but they will find her."

"No!" Beth protested.

"We can't just leave her here," Joseph agreed.

"Okay." Scarlett nodded. "I'll help you bring her home."

Tony and Scarlett lifted Susan's small body while Joseph held Beth and helped her walk out of the woods. They left the two of them in the woods outlining Beth's backyard then Tony, Joseph and Scarlett went back to burn the body of the monster that terrorized their small town and was responsible for too many premature deaths.

A month passed.

The town was far from back to normal but their lives had continued on as normally as they could.

Tony's physical scars had finally healed, leaving five long white marks along his chest. His emotional scars, however, would be carried with him for the rest of his life. He barely ever went out after dark since the night that Susan died.

Susan's parents took her death very hard. They no longer talked to Beth and blamed her for her death. Beth had told the police a margin of what had happened. She said they were out to try and kill the animal that killed Jodi, which was almost the truth. The police found the carcass of the animal but after many tests on the badly burned body, they were still unable to identify what it had been. They knew something more had happened in the woods that night but without any proof were unable to hold the teens accountable for anything that had transpired.

All three were placed on probation for two years.

Beth and Joseph were now an item, however their popularity has plummeted greatly. Everyone at school knew that the three of them were holding something back, they just didn't know what. Beth, Joseph, and Tony vowed to take it to their graves. The three of them hung out all the time, before dark. Tony spent every night home with his parents who, after what happened, had toned down their fighting and drinking.

Beth visited Susan's grave often, always bringing a flower or chess piece to place next to her headstone, which showed her name, date of birth, date of death and a picture of her taken last summer at the beach. Her long brown hair flowed in the wind and she had her glasses off so you could really see into her lively, brown eyes. It was a beautiful picture and always brought tears to Beth's eyes.

Today was a foggy, misty day and those days always made Beth extra sad. She usually went to the graveyard by herself, but today Joseph came to visit with her.

"I can't believe it's been a month. It seems so much longer," she said quietly.

"I know. Tony's not getting much better. I don't think he will ever be the same."

Beth nodded in agreement and wiped a tear off her cheek. Joseph put a comforting arm around her shoulder and held her close.

"I miss her," she cried, tears flowing freely down her cheeks and dripping off her perfectly sculpted jawline.

"I know."

"Hey, guys."

They turned to face the familiar voice. Scarlett was standing ten feet away. She was wearing jeans and a grey t-shirt, and those high-top black hiker boots. Her long red hair blew wildly around her face.

"What are you doing here?" Joseph asked. His immediate reaction was fear. "I thought you had left the night..."

"I did. But I figured I would come back and check on things. Not to mention I never got to properly thank you guys, or say goodbye."

Beth wiped the tears off her face with her sleeve.

"You're welcome, I guess."

Scarlett smiled a sad smile. "It will get better. I've still been searching the news for other happenings. I guess old habits die hard."

Both the teens waited for her to elaborate.

"Anyway, I've found a few more incidents like this

one, up in Canada. So I just wanted to let you guys know, keep an eye out for each other. And I also have gifts for you."

She shifted her shoulder revealing a backpack she carried on her back. She placed it on the ground and opened it up. Inside were two oak boxes. She handed one to Beth and one to Joseph.

"Just in case. Thanks again." She smiled and, throwing the backpack over her shoulder, walked to her car. They watched her get in and speed away, flicking rocks and dirt back at the headstones behind her.

Beth and Joseph waited until she was out of sight and looked down in their hands at the old oak boxes. They looked at each other and as if on cue, then opened their boxes at the same time.

Inside Joseph's was the dagger he had used the night of the attack. The red ruby eye glared at him through raindrops that had begun to fall onto it. In Beth's were the sai she had used. In both boxes was a note:

Use these well. See you after graduation.

They closed the boxes, looked at each other emotionless and started to leave the cemetery, both holding the boxes close to their chests.

RePTiLiA

- MATTHEW LeDREW -

"Rata-tat-tat-tat-tat-tata!" Tyler yelled at the top of his lungs, his tiny form vibrating as the invisible weapon he clasped tightly with both hands riddled the hot desert air with a hail of bullets.

"No!" Jamie cried, clutching her chest with one hand as she fell to the ground, kicking up mounds of dust as she did. Her fingers went slack and her tongue protruded from the corner of her mouth, then she was still.

The gun disappeared all at once, Tyler's hands falling to his sides. "That's not how you do it," he said, whining his frustration.

Jamie did not speak at first, lying in the sand with her mouth hanging open.

"Give it up!" he cried, kicking up dirt.

She looked up, her mouth drawn up in a bow as she watched him scuffle about. "What'd I do wrong?"

"You're so stupid."

"Mom says you're not allowed to use words like that anymore," she said, brushing the dust from her leggings as she did so.

"Mom's not here," he teased, shoving her shoulder

and sending her back into the sand.

"Quit it!" she huffed, her cheeks livid for a moment as she scrambled back to her feet. "Mom says - -"

He shot her a look, and she stopped the sentence dead in its tracks. He ran a hand though his shaggy blonde hair, smiling as he lost all interest in what he and his sister had been fighting about and instead turned toward the sea of chestnut sand that surrounded them. "Come on."

She paused, bringing the joint of her finger to her mouth thoughtfully as she turned back and looked the way they'd come.

The walls of Stapleton were already a quarter mile behind them, its grey stones reaching out of the dunes toward the bright orange sky. The buildings inside stretched out like concrete fingers, long and bony as they tried their best to grasp the sun but never could.

Jamie couldn't recall any point in her nine years on this planet ever seeing the town from this far away. She was sure she had, driving over the hills to Kingian for supplies or just going out over the dunes with her father, but right now all she could think was how small it looked from where she stood. "I think... I think maybe Momma might need us."

Tyler turned back toward her, frowning. "Why would Mom need us?"

"I... I don't know. I just think... I think maybe she does, that's all."

"You're just scared."

"I'm not scared."

"Little baby Jamie, gets scared on the daily!" he sang, wiggling his fingers at her mockingly.

"I'm *not scared*!" she insisted, turning away from Stapleton and marching forward with clenched fists, stomping her way past her brother.

He laughed, jogging until his stride matched her own.

They walked in silence for a moment, with only the sound of their footfalls and bouncing displaced pebbles between them.

"What're you scared of, anyway?" he asked after a moment, bending over to pick up a rock and then throwing it. It landed in a splash of dirt in a nearby mound of sand, soon disappearing as the grains flowed over it.

"I told you, I'm not scared."

"Puh," he snorted, rolling his eyes. He turned away for a moment, his eyes surveying the landscape, then looked back at her accusingly, a wry grin on his lips. "You're afraid of the Northies, aren't you?"

Her plump face turned white, all the colour draining from it as she stared vacantly forward for a second, then turned toward him. "Am not."

"You are so. You're afraid that a big, bad Norther is gonna come up from the sand and grab you and take you away to be his wife!" he laughed, poking her arm with his index finger to punctuate every word.

"Go away!" she whined, jolting her arm away from his jabs.

"No, Jamie! Be my bride!" he yelled in a fake Northern accent, holding out his hands toward her.

"Stop it!" she squealed, turning away from him. Her heel got caught in the sand and refused to move, though the rest of her body continued to. The joint twisted harshly before she fell face first into a sandbar, sending sharp bits of stone into her face. She started to sob, even as she brought her palms flat against the warm mineral on either side of her to brace herself as she got up. "I'm telling Momma!"

Tyler did not respond.

"Puh," she spat, trying desperately to get the dirt out of her mouth. Each tiny pebble was like a bit of glass bouncing around the inside her mouth, slicing away at every gum, tongue and soft surface it found while there.

When she was done spitting, she looked over her shoulder at him. Tyler was standing a few feet behind her, his face as white as first-morning's light as he stared off into the desert beyond where she lay. One of his arms lay dead with shock at his side, while the other had gone up to meet his face in the same fearful, thoughtful position she had been in a few minutes before, the joint of one finger clasped between his lips.

Jamie turned around, lifting her head to see over the dune she'd fallen into. She shivered, her lower lip quaking violently even though the heat was blistering.

Thirty feet beyond the dune, a man lay in the sand.

He was almost invisible in the tattered beige uniform he wore, hidden against the soft bronze hues of the sands. His face was red, its lower half splotched with blood that still oozed from his mouth in slow seeping, congealed glops.

He looked at her with eyes that barely acknowledged what they were seeing, the pupils having shrunk to mere pinpricks in the blazing sun long ago. The skin on the right side of his face had blistered and peeled, turned a deep brown by the suns rays. After what seemed like an eternity, his chest rose ever so slightly to take in a breath.

Jamie opened her mouth and screamed.

"Mom-*Ma*!"

"Clear the way!" EMT Mark Baxter cried, pushing along the gurney as fast as he dared.

The doors to the emergency operating room at Stapleton General burst open as the gurney was wheeled through feet first, slamming against the tile walls on either side.

"Private Terrence Baker, 1054th Regiment. Found out in the desert thirty minutes ago suffering from massive dehydration, asphyxia, as well as multiple contusions and burns along the face and upper torso!" Mark belted out, holding an oxygen mask to the soldier's face as he yelled. His short black hair stuck to him with sweat that poured off him in buckets, even now that they were out of the heat and inside in the air-conditioned and sterile hallways of the hospital.

He positioned the gurney such that it was right next to the operating table. Three nurses gathered around, each clasping their own side of the sheet that Private Baker had been laid upon, then hoisted him over onto the smooth stainless steel table.

Blood shot up like a fountain from Baker's mouth, splashing against the surgeon's apron and turning it a deep, wet red.

"Christ," the surgeon cursed, backing up a pace a watching the blood make its way between his gloved fingers.

"Heart rate is slow, but steady," Mark continued. "I think his lungs are filling with blood. There might be a bleed in his left--"

"Well, what was your first clue?" the doctor barked, motioning down at his apron. It was hard to gage the man's expression with his surgical mask and goggles on, but his tone was very clear.

"Dr. Sutton, I was merely suggesting that --"

"Get back to your car, Mark," Dr. Sutton interrupted again, already unbuttoning the patients shirt. "There are plenty of scraped knees and broken wrists out there that are in desperate need of your help."

Mark stared at him for a moment, then looked down at the man on the table. Blood spewed from his mouth again, almost hitting a nurse before splashing onto the floor in a great wave of crimson. He frowned, then shook his head and left the way he came in, closing the OR doors behind him as he went.

Dr. Sutton finished unbuttoning Baker's shirt, spreading the torn fabric wide to reveal the entire torso. The skin was loose and rubbery, as though it were two sizes too big for him. His chest was covered in patches of short, curly hair turned white by the sun's rays while lying out in the desert sand.

Just below his right nipple was a small round puncture wound, trickling blood slowly.

"You think that might be the source of the bleed?" Sutton called, winking at the nurse next to him.

She smiled back. He couldn't see her mouth below the mask, but the laugh lines under her eyes told him all he needed to know.

"I'm gonna need a number five blade and a clamp. Get ready for some sutures too, people. Lots and lots of sutures. This guy's lung seems to think it's his stomach, and last time I checked those two things weren't the same."

He glanced up into the observation deck.

There was an older man standing as straight as a pole looking back down at him. His gaze was unblinking and unmoving, his features withered by time and seeming to melt down into his collar. He wore a clean white suit with brass buttons polished to a starry gleam. Red epaulettes were the only spot of colour of the whole thing, standing out like gaping mouths. His hands were clasped firmly behind his back and the only sign of movement was the slight tap of his smooth, black shoes.

Dr. Sutton nodded once, then turned back down toward his patient.

The Officer nodded back as well, in a movement so slight it may not have happened at all.

Mark sat on the bench near the front entrance of the hospital, staring at the baseboards in front of him. The automatic doors were only a few feet to his left, and every time someone went in or out he was blasted with a wave of heat from outside, contrasting the almost biting cold of the hallway. The contrast played havoc with his body temperature, sweating when he was warm and then being drenched with it in the cold. His face was a low, deep purple around the cheeks as he let out a deep sigh, leaning forward onto his knees.

"He's like that with everybody."

He looked up to see Chauna Deeds standing a few feet to his left, her fists resting against her hips. One hand was clenching her surgical mask and cap tightly as she stood staring down at him, one leg cocked out in a relaxed, ready pose. Sweat lined the brim of her brow and soaked deep circles into the armpits and collar of her salmon coloured scrubs. "You look hot," he said.

She raised an eyebrow to him quizzically, then looked down at her sweat-drenched form and smiled, showing all of her teeth. "Oh, yeah," she laughed, taking down her ponytail and letting her curly brunette hair fall down onto her shoulders. "Air conditioner is broken in radiology. Been there all day taking scans."

"Hm."

She sat down next to him on the bench, looking up at the air conditioning vent on the ceiling above them and letting the cool breeze blow down onto her for a moment before turning toward Mark. "Like I was saying, don't be pissy about Sutton. He's like that with everybody. Man just doesn't have any people skills."

"You heard?"

She laughed. "It's a small hospital, Mark."

"It's a small settlement."

She nodded slowly. "True."

He brought both hands up to his face, stretching it downward and making a low, moaning sound in his throat. "Ugh. I gotta get outta here, Chauna."

She rolled her eyes. "Thought you liked it here. Allie does."

"Allie's an idiot."

The comment took her aback. Her mouth stayed open for a moment before she finally found the words with which to fill it, her brain catching up with the rest of her. "That's... okay, yeah. I thought you two were doing better?"

He snorted a laugh then turned to look at her. She was still warm from the hours spent in radiology, her breathing heavy and her chest heaving up and down with every breath she took. He mumbled something, then turned back to staring at the wall.

"What was that?"

"I said I wish you'd make up your damn mind," he spat, turning toward her again. The veins in his cheeks turned the deep purple they did whenever he got angry.

"Excuse me?"

"Excuse you. A month ago you didn't much care whether or not Allie and I worked it out, did you? Month ago you were sitting bare-breasted on my bed asking me to leave her. So which is it?"

"Neither... both," she huffed, shaking her head. "I thought we got past this. This snapping at each other."

He took a deep breath and closed his eyes.

Biting her lip, she reached out to lay her hand on his shoulder.

"What're you doing?" he barked the second contact was made, getting off the bench and glaring down at her.

"Whatever, Mark," she huffed, grabbing her mask from her lap and turning to walk away.

"Chauna," he called after her, his face softening.

She made a curt wave without even turning around, then went around the corner and disappeared from sight.

He sighed, placing the heel of his hand against his throbbing eye. He held it there for a minute, wishing for it to stop, before turning and punching the wall as hard as he could and turning toward the exit.

The automatic doors opened, surrounding him in the dry heat of the desert and sand blew by him, slicing at his skin.

Red streaks radiated out from the dent he'd left in the wall, seeping downward toward the floor.

"Jesus," Dr. Sutton cursed as another dollop of blood splashed onto his shoes. He stepped back, holding the scalpel in his steady grip as he looked toward Private Baker's mouth, still drooling blood. "Can somebody trach this guy before he chokes on his own blood, please?"

"I'm trying, sir," one of the nurses sighed, holding the tube in front of her in exasperation. "But he keeps--"

"You're useless," he shot, turning back to the large opening he'd sliced in the centre of the Private's abdomen. "Get Stein to do it. I think she actually went to medical school."

The nurse huffed, then passed the tube and laryngoscope to the person next to her.

"You can sponge," he said, nodding to her. He paused a moment, then added, "I do mean now."

She grabbed a cloth from the way station, brought it to his forehead and dabbed the moisture from it, careful not to interrupt his field of vision.

He took a deep breath, then moved Baker's gallbladder

aside and continued to manoeuver his blood-spattered, gloved hands further and further into the victim's chest.

Nurse Stein brought her own scalpel to Private Baker's trachea and made one clean slice. Redness gurgled out, spilling onto the table as though she'd turned on a faucet. "He's anemic!"

"Well, he can't be anemic," Sutton drawled, nodding his head toward his hands, both of which were submerged within Private Baker. "Because if he was, I'm fairly sure this would be a bit of a problem."

Nurse Stein cursed, washing the blood away and continuing with the tracheotomy.

Chauna flopped down into the soft suede chair that had stood against the wall of the surgeon's lounge ever since she'd been stationed there, smiling as its familiar grooves bent and flexed to the contours of her slender form.

Across the hall, Dr. Adrian Janes looked up from his paperwork at her and smiled. He was much older than her, in his mid-forties, but had managed to maintain a full head of dark, neatly styled hair. He even retained his boyish good looks, in Chauna's opinion, when he kept himself clean-shaven, which he was at the moment. He watched her reach into the mini-fridge next to the chair without even so much as glancing in its direction, pulling out a fruit cup and peeling off the vacuum sealed cover. She looked at it hungrily, then glared at the cutlery drawer all the way on the other side of the room. Weighing her options for a moment, she tilted her head back and drank the fruit from its container as if it had been juice. He laughed.

She brought her head back, wiping a dribble of pineapple juice from her chin. "What's so funny?"

"Nothing, just... nothing," he smirked, turning back toward the x-rays in his hand, holding one up to the light for a better look.

Her smile broadened, stretching from ear to ear. "What? Oh, you've got to tell me now."

He smiled, laying down the sheet. "Five years you've worked here. At least three times a week, I watch you get a fruit cup from that fridge; most of those times you end up eating it with your hands."

"And?" she chirped, picking a strawberry out of the cup with her thumb and forefinger and placing it gently between her lips.

"Does it never occur to you to get a spoon *before* you sit down?"

She paused as she chewed, reflecting on the question, then swallowed. "It has."

He looked at her, waiting for more.

"Priorities, Janes," she hummed, sinking even deeper into the chair. "Priorities."

He chuckled, shaking his head at her as he noticed a speck on the x-ray. He tried to wipe it away, discovered that it was indeed a part of the image, then scribbled something down in his file.

She ate the last piece of fruit from her cup, then tipped it back and drank the juice that remained in the bottom. The mix of all the different flavors made it taste like punch and reminded her of the boxes her mother used to pack in her lunch tin as a child.

"Did you see the guy they brought in from the desert?" he mumbled after a moment, still making notations.

"Yeah. Poor guy. Looked like a train wreck."

"You think it was the Northers?"

"What else could it have been?"

"Exposure. I've seen heat exposure do some weird things to the skin, things you wouldn't believe. If the guy was even a little allergic to sunlight or UV rays, the toxicity to his liver alone could account for the blood."

"Maybe," she sighed, laying her cup down on top of the fridge. "I dunno. I guess we'll find out if Sutton patches the guy up."

"Hmm," Janes hummed, tapping his chin as he examined another x-ray.

"What?"

"Nothing, just... you don't see many people like that pull through. I don't care who Sutton thinks he is."

Chauna watched him for a moment, then settled back down into her chair.

"Ow," Jamie whimpered, her lower lip sticking out as her mother dabbed a cotton swab soaked in peroxide against her face.

"Shh, sweaty," Karen Reynolds soothed, stroking her daughter's hair as she tried to be softer with the swab. "Its okay. It'll be over in a minute, don't cry."

"Yeah," Tyler spat from the corner, a handheld game covering the lower half of his face. "Stop being a baby."

Jamie's eyes began to tear up again as she waited for validation from her mother, her face stinging intensely.

"Jamie, that's not what I said," she assured her, taking a moment to smile at her daughter warmly before examining her face for more scrapes and cuts. Finding none, she turned toward Tyler. "And you'd best be good, mister, unless you want your father to hear about it when he gets home."

Tyler closed his mouth, then turned back toward his game.

Karen continued to watch him for a moment before turning her attention back to Jamie. "I heard the Officer say that you were the bravest little girl he'd ever seen," she said, straightening the collar of her dress.

Jamie sniffed once, her finger once again stuck in her mouth. There was a glob of red on it, almost hidden between her index and middle fingers.

Karen tisked as she grabbed her wrist gently and pulled it from her mouth, wiping the blood away with the cotton swab.

◐

"What the hell?"

Nurse Stein looked up from the ventilator she'd been preparing, her eyes traveling from Dr. Sutton to the patient and then back again in the span of a second. "What is it, Doctor?"

Sutton looked at her for a moment, then up toward the observation deck. The uniformed man was still there, in almost the same position he'd been in nearly two hours ago, leaning in only slightly to see what the doctor was talking about.

"It's the bullet," Sutton said finally, wiping the sweat off his own forehead into the shoulder of his pale blue scrubs. "I found the bullet, but it's nowhere near the lung. It's lodged in some fatty tissue a few inches shy of the liver. It's not really hurting anything."

"Then what's causing all that blood?" she asked, motioning toward Baker's mouth, which was still seeping blood around the corners.

"I don't know," Sutton sighed, reaching for his forceps. "But there's nothing wrong with this guy's lungs. Whatever's causing the blood is happening from someplace else."

Above them in the observation room, General Freemantle let out a long sigh as he watched Dr. Sutton remove the bullet.

Mark closed the door to his apartment, letting out a long sigh as he took off his shoes and laid them down next to the doormat.

"Honey?" came a voice from down the hall, followed closely by the sound of a faucet squeaking shut. "Honey, is that you?"

"Yeah, Allie," he called back, his voice strained and low. His face was still sweating from the heat outside as he peeled out of his burgundy EMT jacket. He held it out in front of him, staring at the closet just to his left, then dropped it onto the floor and left it there.

She came out from around the corner at the end of the hall, wiping her hands in a dishtowel before laying it on the kitchen counter and walking toward him. Her smile was big and bright, her thin lips pulling back and showing all her teeth. "You're home early," she chimed, wrapping her arms around his shoulders and squeezing him. "I can't remember the last time you came home early."

Mark grunted. Her hands smelled like cigarettes, and now that smell was all around him. He felt like it was choking him, killing every last strand of oxygen just as it reached his mouth. He reached up and placed both hands against her chest, calmly moving her away. "What's for dinner?"

She paused a moment, fixing her bun and straightening her left sleeve. "It's a roast. Your favorite."

He nodded, then made his way toward the kitchen.

She followed after only a moment's pause, walking past him as he sat down at the table. She stepped over to the counter and started to peel an onion, the skin coming off it large crackling husks.

The kitchen was small but serviceable. It had a stove with three burners, all of which were in use at the moment, as well as a fridge and a neat little table. The counter came out too far and there was an oddly vacant area at one end, but it did them just fine.

He grabbed the glass of water off the table in front of him and took a large gulp, watching her intently as she peeled the vegetable.

Her foot tapped aimlessly to whatever beat had been caught in her head, the sandals she wore to combat the heat flopping this way and that every couple of taps, trying to work their way off her feet but always failing to do so. Her legs were smooth and dark where they met her feet, her tan deeply ingrained into her flesh from many hours spent sunning on the back patio. She was wearing the jeans he'd bought her last year. They clung to her frame as if they were a part of her, moving with and spreading along her curves.

He got up from the table.

She felt his breath on her back before he touched her, hot against the nape of her neck. She tisked, letting both her hands fall to the counter, laying down the onion and knife. "What do you think you're doing?" she scolded playfully.

He did not respond. His tongue moved softly over the roof of his mouth, making a slow, barely audible clucking sound as he placed his hand on her hip, slowly moving inward.

"Not now," she cooed, squirming just a little. "I have to get these done, hun. The roast's already in. If I don't add these soon, it'll be too late."

He reached up with his other hand, placing it firmly on her chin and tilting it to one side, exposing the tender, moist flesh on her neck before he brought his lips to it.

She rolled her eyes, a smile beaming over her face. "Mark, seriously, not now," she shrugged.

He pushed her head forward, slamming it against the kitchen cabinet.

"Guh!" she shouted as she rocked back, hitting her shoulder off the table as she fell. Blood gushed from her nose and into her mouth, mixing with mucus and spit and becoming a mess on her blouse that was the same texture of tapioca pudding. "What the fuck is the matter with you?" she screamed, bringing one hand to her face as she looked up at him.

She squirmed back a pace when their eyes met, the burning and stinging sensations shooting from her nose ignored now.

The skin from his shoulders up had gone a deep shade of maroon, the blood rushing to it like she'd never seen. His cheeks were now royal purple, almost every vein in them clearly visible as they pumped even more blood into his face. He was sweating more than she had ever seen him, droplets the size of ball bearings falling off of him like rain. His teeth were barred, his upper lip quivering and shaking in a snarl. His skin split before her eyes along the creases of his forehead and cheeks, so dry and tight that it broke under the weight of its own movement. Blood ran down into his eyes even as the blood vessels there burst, making the whites a shallow pink but becoming a deep crimson with the blood from his face.

He was literally seeing red.

His tongue clacked against the roof of his mouth again for a second, his whole body rising and falling with each deep breath he took.

"Mark..."

"Raaagh!" he yelled, bringing both fists into the air and then crashing them down toward her.

She scrambled out of the way, knocking her head against the kitchen counter once more. She grabbed the handle of the cutlery drawer and pulled herself up even as he swung around again, drawing his fist back behind his head and plowing it forward toward her.

She grabbed the knife and spun it around, the cold steel meeting his hot flesh and jabbing into his palm.

"Argh!" he huffed, lurching forward as blood gushed from the open wound.

She grabbed the saucepan off the stove and flicked it at him, spraying hot gravy into his face. He howled in agony again, opening his eyes despite how they burned and staring at her with more rage and frustration than he'd ever felt toward anything. He charged at her again.

She ducked, swooping just barely under his arm and turning just in time to see him smash his face head-on into the fridge door.

He fell backward, slamming the back of his head against the table. He shook a little, at first looking as though he were going to get up and then like he was having a small seizure... and then he was still.

Her lower lip shaking, she reached for the phone.

"Sponge."

Sutton brought his hand up quickly, the needle that carried the wire he was threading throughout the Private's innards flitting about like a baton. In that moment he looked more like the conductor of a symphony orchestra than a surgeon, commanding the sutures of the patient's right lung to close shut. Instead of the soft radiance of harps and flutes, the only sound to react to his motion was the soft, moist sound flesh made as it was moved by some external force.

He paused with his hand in mid-air, the twine stopping its dance at once and hanging lifelessly at the end of the pin. "*Sponge*," he said again, casting a glance sideways.

Above them, General Freemantle leaned in and placed a hand against the glass.

One of the nurses stopped to stared at him, letting the oxygen mask fall from the patient's face. She was sweating too now, putrid liquid squeezing from her pores in bullets.

"For Christ sake!" Sutton yelled, letting go of both the needle and thread as he reached for the sponge that lay in a saucepan of water near him. They both fell into the patient's body cavity, the muscle twitching in reaction to their presence as they glistened and sparkled in the overhead lights. Sutton doused the sponge twice, slathering his face with it before squeezing it over his head and letting the water trickle down over him. "When I say I need a sponge, that means I need a sponge *now*, you idiots!"

He huffed and turned back to the patient. For a moment all he could see were millions of tiny black dots, dancing about his vision like a swarm of flies. When they went away, he saw the needle he'd dropped, resting comfortably against the patient's still-open lung. "Jesus," he cursed at himself, wiping brow again, this time simply using his sleeve. "Uh..."

The nurse still stared, even as the patient's oxygen saturation levels began to make the machines beside her howl.

Freemantle huffed, his hand reaching to the wall and pressing a large red button he found there with his thumb.

There was a soft, almost inaudible clucking sound in the air that sounded like the air conditioners cutting either in or out.

Sutton looked up from the open cavity, finally noticing the nurse. His forehead had split open, the blood on it watery and diluted from the sponge, and when he saw the dumbfounded expression on her face his own contorted with rage. "What the fuck are you looking at, you little twit?" he barked, reaching up and ripping off his surgical mask. He took several deep breaths though clenched teeth. "What is it?" he barked again, turning toward the sink to get another mask.

Nurse Stein lashed out, raking her nails across his face. Her surgical mask had been peeled away, revealing the same house-of-mirrors snarl that Dr. Sutton wore, her breathing heavy and labored as she hunched over him, her hands hanging poised and ready to strike at her sides. Her bun had been let down at some point, her previously permed hair sticking off in wild directions and making her appear ever more feral. Sweat drenched her face, dribbling off her chin and onto the floor like water from a leaky faucet. The whites of her eyes were gone; her blood pressure raging with such unrestricted animalism that reddish liquid seeped from her tear ducts and ear canals.

Sutton hit the floor as the other two nurses screamed, finally stopping their work altogether. There was a hunk of nail embedded in his cheek that spewed blood freely, smearing the left side of his face like war paint. Propping himself up against the table, he glared at her from under his massive brow, a series of clucks coming from somewhere deep in his throat and running together like a low growl.

They stared at each other, each of them swaying back and forth even though there was no breeze in the room, like cobras awaiting the opportunity to lash out.

The heat wafting off them made the air palatable, raging against the air conditioners and winning.

The nurses clamored against the far wall, as far away from the patient, Stein, and Sutton as they could be.

"D-doctor?" one of them stammered finally, reaching out her hand gingerly.

Sutton spun, foam and saliva spewing from his mouth and splattering against the wall as he did, letting out a long roar. His pupils were small and beady, engulfed in a sea of red as he pushed his way past the table, knocking Private Terrence Baker onto the floor. He lunged at the nurse, grabbing her by the neck as she opened her mouth to scream. The sound was quelled by his strong, clubbed fingers, coming out as nothing but a quick gasp of air.

The other nurse had no such problem screaming, a sound that erupted from her in shrill waves, using up one breath before taking another and then continuing. She fell to the floor, grabbing at a tray for balance as she went and only bringing it down with her, sending an array of scalpels and the infamous sponge onto the tile.

His fingers clamped down like vices, pressing in on the smooth, dry flesh of her already slender neck until he began to feel it give way beneath his grasp. Grunting, he jutted his face forward quickly, his neck craning about above the blood-slathered scrubs he wore. Opening his mouth wide, he engulfed it around her upper lip.

Her eyes grew wide as she felt the hot, wet surface of his tongue at first... then bulged as his teeth dug in, ripping through the flesh, their enamel scratching against her own.

This time she did scream.

The sound was muffled and stilted as blood gushed down her throat, its coppery tang filling her to the brim. The blood engorged her, filling her mouth so much that it ran out through her nose in massive spurts. She pushed hard against his wiry shoulders, trying to force him off as his hands finally left her throat and went to either side of her head. Bracing her, he pulled his head back, taking with it the flesh from her upper lip right up to the bridge of her nose.

She screamed as she fought for air, each of his thumbs riding her eye sockets and making it impossible to see anything but great burgundy blotches of pressure. Tears forced their way out painfully, the ducts closing off to make extra room for her eyes as they bulged and contorted under his grip.

The flesh slithered and sputtered about like a fish in his mouth. He fought with it for a moment, shaking his head as though he thought it were still alive, then sucked it back like a spaghetti noodle until it was all inside. He chewed it vigorously, blood and bile seeping out from between his lips.

Nurse Stein was on him at once, pouncing at him from the side. Her nails dug into his scalp and pulled, taking great chunks of hair and flesh with it as they crashed into the medicine chest, sending hundreds of syringes cascading down on top of them.

He grabbed her by the side of the head, slamming it into the stainless steel chest so hard that it left a blood-smeared dent.

She twisted her neck so far that he could hear the calcium in her neck pop. She opened her mouth and dug her teeth into his palm, hard. He pulled back, his mouth open in a silent howl as he wrenched his hand away from her mouth, taking one of her canines with it. Both his fists slammed down on her face, crushing her lower jaw. Clicking his tongue against the roof of his mouth, he leaned in again, digging his teeth into the taut flesh surrounding her eye and clamping down hard.

Nurse Sloan kicked away from the scene, backing up until her back arched against the stomach of Private Baker. The Private had stopped breathing, something she didn't consciously register but filed away nonetheless, somewhere in the back of her mind. She saw movement just to the right of where Doctor Sutton was sucking juice out of the open wound in Stein's head, her legs still kicking at him fiercely, and turned toward it.

The other nurse lay propped against the far wall, her neck and chest drenched with the blood that spewed out of her mouth more and more with every breath she took.

But she was still breathing.

Sloan crawled over to her, keeping one eye trained intently on Sutton, until she was hauled up next to her against the wall. "Beca?" she whispered, as loudly as she dared. "Beca, are you conscious?"

She stared straight ahead. The only sound she made was the soft whistle coming from her forever-open nostrils every time she exhaled.

Sloan sighed. Grabbing some gauze, she started to wipe the blood from Beca's chin.

From deep inside her throat, Beca let out a low, broken growl.

Sloan stopped, her face expressionless as her mind clicked over and realized what had happened.

Freemantle stared down at the bloody mess below. Shaking his head, he reached for the phone on the wall without turning away. He pressed the number one on its base and then brought it to his ear. He watched blood squirt up so high that it splashed against the glass, but did not flinch. "Get a team together in Observation One," he said calmly, in a voice that spoke of black lung from either cigarettes or the mines. He leaned over slightly to see the source of the blood, watching as Nurse Sloan's throat was opened up for the world to see. "We've got something of a situation."

"Jesus!" Allie hissed, jerking her head away as Chauna dabbed the gash on her upper lip with iodine.

Chauna frowned, giving her a look that was half concerned and half annoyed before she continued dabbing, albeit a little softer. "Sorry. Hard to gauge this with the gloves on."

"It's okay," she replied, moving back to the position on the couch she'd been in before. The doctor's lounge was empty now, Adrian having left long ago to tend to a patient. His papers were still scattered along the desk, next to a half-eaten tuna sandwich that caught her eye. Tuna, along with any other seafood, was a rarity here. Depleting fish stocks had led to a cut down in its production in the last twenty years and besides that, supplies were usually at a bare minimum by the time they reached the border colonies like Stapleton. She guessed that it had been sent to the good doctor in a care package from home, most likely accompanied by a homemade sweater that didn't fit right and a greeting card bought for two dollars at a local drug store. Still, she'd forgotten how much she missed tuna until she saw it.

Chauna turned, following her gaze for a moment. She smiled. "You can have it when we're done, if you want."

"I couldn't."

"No, really, it's fine. He gets them every few months. Doesn't have the heart to tell his mother he grew out of tuna around the same time he grew out of acne cream." Chauna laughed, reaching back onto the coffee table without looking and grabbing an adhesive strip. "This might sting."

"Thanks," she said, bracing herself. "And you can tell Dr. Janes that if he can't stomach the tuna anymore, there's a buyer right here in town."

"I'll pass that along," she smiled, pushing her hair back behind her ear as she hovered the strip just above Allie's lip, trying to make sure she got its placement right the first time. Applying pressure to a facial wound was torture enough, she didn't want to have to rip it off and then reapply it again. Her tongue sticking out of the corner of her mouth slightly, she pressed the strip down gently.

"Ow," Allie said without force, almost as a psychological reaction to the notion of pain rather than to pain itself.

"Sorry," Chauna said again, tisking to herself. She stood up and looked down at the top of her patient's head. She parted the hair there quickly, trying to get a good look at as much scalp as possible. "Doesn't look like there's any bruising... are you experiencing any blurred vision?"

"No."

"Sensitivity to light?"

"No."

"Vomiting?"

"Christ, no."

Chauna paused.

"A little, but it was the blood. I could taste that mentally taste all the way here."

She paused for a moment, waiting to see if there was more. "You should be fine. I don't think you have a concussion, thankfully." She stopped again, bending over to pick up some alcohol wipes from the table. "How about Mark?"

Allie shot her a look. "Are you asking because you care for him, or because you're a doctor?"

"Both," she replied honestly, unwrapping the swab and starting to clean the blood off Allie's forehead to make sure there was no bruising underneath. "But after today, I think I care for him a lot less than I thought I did."

Allie did not respond, barely even noticing the cool pad against her face.

"Hem," she huffed, clearing her throat. "I'm actually surprised you called me. Glad you still think of me in a time of crisis, even though --"

"I called you because you're the only one I can trust to keep this off the books," Allie snapped, looking up slightly to meet Chauna's eye.

Chauna stopped wiping and stepped back a pace so she could look at her patient properly. She sighed, dropped the pad to the table in a bundled up glob and then sat on it, bringing them both level. "You might have a concussion. You're definitely going to need x-rays, and I'd like to ultrasound to make sure you're not bleeding into your brain. Tests mean paperwork. Paperwork needs a place to be filed, and that place is your file."

"And putting it in my file means that it'll be seen by Freemantle. He'll take Mark off of active duty and you know it. You're keeping this off the books."

Chauna looked at her side on, shaking her head slightly. "Why're you protecting him? You can't seriously be staying with him after this."

Allie looked away, fixing her collar. After a moment, she grabbed the alcohol wipe from the table and started to apply it herself, meeting Chauna's gaze again. "He's done worse."

"Listen, I --"

The door to the lounge opened, Adrian's white coat flapping against it as he stuck one foot in. His eyes were wide, but they narrowed a bit in confusion as he looked from Chauna to Allie and then back again.

There was a moment of silence.

"Just cleaning up," Chauna said finally. "What is it?"

"Uh, emergency," he said finally, forcing his brain to snap to attention. "We're needed down in Observation One."

"I'll be there in a minute."

Adrian nodded, casting another glance toward Allie and then back to Chauna.

Chauna nodded, and he left.

She turned her back on Allie, grabbing her scrubs and surgical mask off the table. "Eat the sandwich and do whatever you need to," she said without looking at the other woman as she walking toward the door. "Call the police or don't, either way it's on your head at this point."

Allie curled her upper lip as she closed the door,

turning toward the mirror to see if she'd gotten all the blood. There was still a great glob of it there, just above her left eye.

Frowning, she brought the wipe up to it.

Sutton snapped the bone of Sloan's finger between his teeth, sucking hard at the stump that remained until the marrow was gone. He put the finger in his mouth then, biting down hard. His teeth gave way in some places, but the flesh and bone of the appendage finally broke and started to fall apart in his mouth, its sweet, salty taste filling him. He swallowed hungrily long before the pieces were small enough for him to do so safely, wanting to make room for more.

He was hunched over the table enjoying his meal. He was bleeding from his scalp and shoulder. His arm appeared to be dislocated, although that did not stop him from using it, and his foot had the remnants of a hypodermic needle tip sticking out of it.

Through the thick glass of the observation lounge, the scene looked staged and fake, the glass fading the colours and blocking their ability to hear and smell what was happening in the operating room.

Chauna brought her hand to her mouth but did not turn away, instead taking a step closer to the glass to try and see as much of the horror as she could.

"What the hell are we looking at?" Adrian asked in a hushed voice, standing firmly between Chauna and General Freemantle. Another doctor stood directly to Freemantle's right, a tall, portly man with a comb-over so poor that the slightest breeze rendered it useless.

"All due respect, Doctor, that's why I called you down here," Freemantle said, tapping the glass twice with his knuckle. "Diagnose this."

The other doctor, Drover, scoffed. "If you want a diagnosis for insanity, you're going to have to sedate him and get him over to the capital. We're physicians, not psychiatrists."

Freemantle and Adrian both turned to look at him.

"Oh, come on," he continued. "Sutton goes nuts and kills three nurses and you're looking for a medical excuse? The guy was an asshole. And a drunk. And Christ only knows what else. Trank him and let the police sort him out."

"He didn't kill three nurses," Freemantle corrected, motioning down toward the corner, which was mostly obscured from view. "That one killed Nurse Sloan while he was killing Stein. Then he killed her when she tried to eat a chunk of Stein's foot."

Drover's face went white as he turned back toward the scene, gulping back hard.

"I locked the door," he added, nodding to the button on the wall.

"Oxygen... depravation... has been known to cause hysteria," Adrian offered, taking his time to get the words out as he processed the information. "Have you checked the ventilation system?"

"Mmm," he nodded, taking off his cap and resting it under his arm, running his hand along the bristle-like hair on his head before putting it back on. "Once myself. Computer says it's okay. Got a couple of the boys from

R&D doing a manual check, but I doubt they'll find anything. Told them to strap on the hazmat gear just in case, though."

Adrian nodded.

"What about toxins?" Drover offered, stepping forward as he started to get some colour back into his cheeks. "Some sort of adrenalin injection or steroid."

"Never heard of this sort of affect before," Adrian sighed, sitting down.

"That doesn't mean it's not the case now."

"I wasn't trying to dismiss it. Just saying: never heard of it before now." He paused and leaned his elbows against his knees. Freemantle turned away from the window for the first time in hours, looking down at the boyish doctor. "It could be rabies."

"Came on far too quickly to be --"

"It looks like rabies."

"Had a dog with rabies once," Freemantle said finally. "That doesn't look like rabies to me. I'm no doctor, but it's not just the way they're acting... it's their eyes. Their eyes go red. Blood red, Doctor."

"Trauma can cause that, sir," he offered, getting up again and looking through the window, trying to get a good look at Sutton's eyes. They were mostly closed, eating the muscle off a rib now. "It might not be a symptom of--"

"Happened before the fight started, Doctor," Freemantle corrected gently, then pointed toward what remained of Nurses Sloan and Stein. "To both of them."

One palm pressed against the glass, Chauna cursed to herself finally.

Freemantle turned to look at her. "Something to add,

Nurse Deeds?"

"It's a contagion, sir," she said, turning away from the window. They all turned to look at her then, the sight of Dr. Sutton sucking on spinal fluid momentarily not interesting. She paused, organizing her words before she gulped back saliva and spoke again. "I don't know what kind. All I know is that it's blood born... and that it's already spread beyond the confines of the lab. We need to get a team out to the residences, sir."

Freemantle picked up the phone again without so much as turning to the two doctors for validation.

For their part they did not object. Drover stepped closer to the glass with a trembling right hand wavering in front of it as if afraid to make contact, while Adrian made his way to Chauna, touching her elbow softly.

"Freemantle," he said into the phone. "I need armed forces on the ground at Camp One ten minutes ago, you're looking for --" he paused, turning to Chauna.

"Mark Baxter," she said softly, wincing as if the words had physically harmed her.

"-- Mark Baxter. Restrain, use force if necessary. Do not make physical contact." He paused, then turned toward the glass one last time. "And cancel the R&D's examination of the vents. Have them torch the place instead. If there's anything but carbon left in that room by the time I get back, I'll have your head."

He hung up the phone and left the room through the south exit, followed quickly by Drover and Adrian.

Chauna moved to follow, then stopped. She turned quickly, pushing open the door to the north exit and running up the stairs.

Sutton gripped Sloan's liver between his fingers, squeezing it before taking half of it into his mouth and biting down hard.

Karen Reynolds picked up the dishes from the floor in front of the television, huffing audibly. She briefly considered scolding her children, who were now colouring at their table a few feet away, but decided to let it slide. They'd been through a lot for one day. She could stand to let the small things slide. She turned to look at them, watching as Jamie scribbled fiercely on her sheet with a red colouring pencil, going way outside the lines that the horse had presented her with.

She smiled.

Turning around to grab their glasses off the coffee table, she glanced out at the late afternoon light streaming in through the window.

There was a man outside staring intently at her mailbox.

He had a gash on his forehead about an inch long that looked a few hours old, the right half of his face covered with congealed blood so dark that it looked black. His fists were clenched tight at his sides and there was a sneer on his face that was filled with hate, as though the mailbox were the worst thing he'd ever seen in his life.

It was Mark Baxter.

All at once he swung a fist at it, his knuckles grating against the metal box. It wobbled on its base, moving backward for a moment before springing forward and connecting with his central plexus.

He looked to scream, though she couldn't hear it.

Then he lashed out again, this time with both fists, wailing on the offending object and ripping off the small red flag on its side.

Karen reached into the jeans pocket and pulled out her phone, holding down the number five and then bringing it to her ear. It rang three times before someone picked up.

"Rachel? It's Karen. Look out your window. You're not going to believe this."

Chauna opened the door to the lounge wide, her eyes doing a full sweep of the room as she tried in vain to catch her breath. Her scrubs were soaked with sweat by now, and it rolled down her face in barrels. She could barely hear anything above her heart and the sound of her gasped, labored breathing.

There was nobody in the room, just the same stack of papers Adrian had left out earlier.

Minus the tuna fish sandwich.

She cursed, took note of the blood-soaked gauze on the table, then turned and left the room again, running down the hall despite the objections her lungs were screaming at her.

Two floors down, Jim Keating was pushing his mop bucket along the main hallway on its wheels, humming softly to himself.

He stopped in front of the large automatic doors, grumbling when he noticed the amount of sand that had passed through them. Sometimes if the storms got bad enough the sand itself set off the motion detectors as it flew around, making the hallway a thousand times worse than it was now. In any event, mopping up sand was not his idea of a good time.

He stopped after one pass, grabbing a stick of gum from his front pocket and passing it through his cracked, dry lips. He let out a sigh as the minty cool filled his mouth, then smiled.

When he opened his eyes again, he saw the reddish dent on the wall.

He raised an eyebrow and dragged his finger along one of the red smears, the liquid coming off easily. He rubbed it between his thumb and forefinger, shrugged, took his rag out of his breast pocket and began to wipe it down.

The wind blew hard against the back entrance of the hospital, always did. It had started off the same eggshell white as the rest of the building, but the constant assault of sand had revealed the stainless steel underneath in less than three years.

Adrian pulled the collar of his lab coat up, trying to shield himself from the sand as it swirled around him like a million tiny razor blades. It only lasted for a few feet until he ducked into the backseat of the white limousine waiting for them right behind Drover and Freemantle. "What are we doing?" he asked, trying to catch his breath as he wiped dust from his lips.

"Getting the hell out of here," Freemantle said gruffly, taking off his dress uniform and tossing it to the other side of the cabin along with his cap. He looked infinitely more approachable in the sky blue shirt he had been wearing underneath, making the blue eyes that had seemed as cold as steel a moment ago appear warm and inviting. "There's a helicopter on the other side of the compound big enough for about twenty people. I've sent a message for police to meet us there with as many unaffected as we can."

Drover balked. "How can we be sure it's even spread beyond Baxter? Or that it's even contagious the way Deeds described? She's bright and all, but I'd rather a dumb doctor than a smart nurse any day."

Adrian shot him a look through the corner of his eye, then turned back to Freemantle. In the two years they'd lived on the same compound, he had never once seen the General without his dress uniform on. It had been a private joke between he and Chauna that the man even wore it in the bedroom. To see him without was disconcerting, no matter how pleasant he appeared. "What about the rest?"

"I'm calling in a team," he assured the doctor, nodding. "It'll be fine. It'll be dealt with. I just want to make sure the only people in the town to be hurt are other people with this... this whatever this is."

Adrian nodded, turning back out the tinted windows toward the back entrance.

Freemantle tapped the intercom panel just to his right. "Drive."

"No!" Adrian objected, turning back toward him with a shocked expression on his face. "You have to wait for Chauna!"

Freemantle raised an eyebrow. "I think you'll find I don't have to do much of anything anymore, Doctor."

Adrian huffed. "So much for never leave a man

behind."

"We're not leaving a *man* behind," Drover corrected, winking at the General.

Freemantle turned toward Drover, giving him a stern look. All three men were frozen there for a moment. He nodded, pressing his index finger to the intercom again. "Belay that, Reynolds."

There was only silence for a moment then, with the faint sound of static on the other end of the line and the wind howling outside.

Freemantle paused, touching the call button again. "Reynolds?"

The tinted window separating the driver from the rest of the cabin cracked, spider-webbing in all directions and letting them hear the low, clucking growl that it had blocked a moment before.

"Jesus!" Adrian yelped, pushing himself as far back against the seat as he could. Drover joined him, reaching for the door handle.

Freemantle dove for his uniform, fumbling with the pocket until he pulled out his service revolver. He turned it toward the window as a massive fist pounded on it again and let out three sharp blasts, shattering the window and sending shards of it cascading to the floor in all directions.

The driver hunched back against the wheel, struggling to draw breath as his eyes burned red with hatred. Duel bullet holes in his chest spewed blood, hissing slightly every time he inhaled. His hands were hauled up in distorted, bloody fists, the fingers curled back and spasming wildly.

"Hold on," Adrian gasped, reaching for the stethoscope in his pocket. "We might still be able to --"

"Do nothing," Freemantle finished, though it was not an order. He raised the barrel of the gun again, then fired one final shot into the forehead of Justin Reynolds. The body twitched twice more, let out a breath, then stopped moving altogether. He turned back to Adrian. "You'll get the blood on you."

Adrian nodded, grabbing the handle away from Drover and opened the door. "We can't drive this then, either. My car's out front, I'll drive."

Freemantle nodded, then followed him out.

Drover took one look back at the driver, shaking his head. "Monstrous," he breathed, stepping out into the sandstorm again.

He bumped into the chest of General Freemantle.

"I'm sorry, sir, I didn't--"

"That was not monstrous," Freemantle corrected, his glare making his look menacing even in the absence of his uniform. "That was a man. A good man who was never late for work, never sick and always made time for his children's softball games. And for mine, for that matter. You're going to be sending his family condolence cards every Christmas for the rest of your life." He paused, looked at Reynolds for a moment, then turned back. "And a check."

Drover tried to respond and even managed to sputter out a syllable or two before Freemantle turned on his heels as fluidly as though he were running drills.

Adrian nodded at him once, holding the door to the hospital open.

Chauna appeared in the doorway, her breathing labored as she bent over and rested on her knees. "I think we've got another patient," she huffed, bringing two fingers to her neck and feeling for her own pulse. She threw a glance toward the white limo and the blood spattered all over the inside of the windshield. "What the hell happened here?"

"Get back inside, Miss Deeds," Freemantle said by way of response, stepping past her. "Your friend Doctor Janes is going to be driving us today."

Drover followed Freemantle inside. Adrian and Chauna exchanged a look before he stepped inside to join her, closing the door behind him.

Sweat poured down Allie Meridian's face and neck as she leaned against the rack of chips, facing down toward the filthy tile floor as drool dripped from her open mouth. Her head was pounding, the beat rivaling that of the teenage pop-rock that played in the background.

"Guh," she grunted, reaching up a hand to wipe the moisture from her milky white face and knocking several bags to the floor as she did.

"Miss, are you okay?" called out the store clerk from behind the counter, craning his head to see what was going on. He was about sixteen with long blonde hair that looked like it had been straightened with an iron, the tips frayed and singed badly.

Allie turned to look at him, her eyes bulging. They were mostly white still, but the veins in them were bright red and looked ready to pop at any given moment. She opened her mouth to speak but found that no words would come, only a faint sound from the back of her throat that reminded her of a single popcorn kernel popping. Grunting in frustration, she turned her attention back to the shelf beside her.

Lined up in a row were hundreds of bottles of aspirin, each white bottle blurring together in her vision. She reached up to try and grab one, batting five to the floor instead. Groaning, she let go of the chip rack and let herself fall to her knees and grab one.

"You better not be making a mess back there!" the clerk called back, his voice annoyed and wavering either from fear or from hormones or both.

She crawled several steps before pulling herself to her feet, walking toward the counter with the pill bottle clenched awkwardly in one hand and the other contorted and misshapen so that it looked more like a paw than a hand. She started to fumble with the lid, her cheeks turning red with frustration as she bumped into the counter without even realizing it.

The boy looked at her a moment, her lips curling up as she stared at the pill bottle, her eyes open as wide as they could be and unblinking. After a moment the pupils moved, no longer aimed at the bottle but at the clerk's mouth.

She opened her mouth slightly, and several clucks came out even though her tongue did not move.

"Take it," he said finally, reaching into his back pocket and pulling out his wallet. "It's on me."

She stared at him a long moment, then shuffled herself sideways until her shoulder connected with the door and pushed it open. She stayed there for a moment with her hair caught in a gust of wind, still staring at him, as one of the blood vessels in her eye broke and starting leaking blood into the white cerca. She turned, running as quickly as she could.

"Junkies," the boy huffed, ringing in the bottle of pills and shaking his head.

Mark growled at the mailbox again as it rocked back and forth in the sand. It was hard to think, but he was sure of one thing: he knew he'd hurt it. It was covered in blood.

His knuckles were almost completely ripped down to the bone except for the slightest remnants of tissue and hair. His lower lip was a bloody maw that looked more like a used wad of chewing gum than a part of someone's face, and he sucked it in again and continued to chew on it.

He turned his head to one side and spit, the saliva light and foamy, making a tiny oasis in the sand a few feet from where he crouched.

He was missing hair. He had pulled it out of his own scalp in frustrated clumps when the enemy kept refusing to go down.

"Mark?" someone called from behind him.

His eyes grew wide with fear.

Rachel White took another step closer, her cordless phone still pressed tightly against her breast. She had shoulder-length dirty-blonde hair that caught the evening light fully, and lips such a dark red they might well have been already bleeding.

Back in the house, Karen held the phone to her ear. "Careful, Ray," she whispered, knowing full well her friend couldn't hear her.

"Mark?" she called again, reaching out a hand to touch his shoulder and then thinking better of it, noticing the state of the mailbox for the first time since exiting her home.

He turned his head slowly, almost further than he should have been able to. His eyes met with hers, the red of them such a dark crimson that they were almost indistinguishable from the pupils.

She stopped mid-step, her face dragging down in fear.

Before she could speak or move or even think he turned, thrusting himself at her and grabbing her by the hips.

She flopped down in the sand, the impact sending thousands of grains into her skin as she finally let out a scream.

He grabbed the right side of her head with one hand, pounding on the left with the other until he could feel his fist and his hand clapping together. When he opened his eyes, there was a red stain in the sand where her head had been a moment ago, dotted with chunks of enamel and white matter.

"Oh my God!" Karen yelled, dropping the phone and bringing both hands to her face as she watched in horror.

Mark turned toward the window, locking eyes with her.

Behind her, the children still coloured.

Adrian held the gas pedal of his jeep down as far as it would go, the treads of the large rubber tires kicking up dirt and dust in all directions as the hospital became smaller and smaller in the distance.

Freemantle sat next to him, loading his gun and taking the occasional glance up to make sure they were still in the clear and that they were headed in the right direction.

"You have enough ammo?" Adrian asked, never once taking his eyes off the road nor his hands away from the ten-and-two position.

"Should be."

"There's more in the trunk if you need."

He shot the doctor a glance, squinting as the sun glared off the red-tinted sand. "Whatever happened to do no harm? Thought they made you folks take an oath."

Adrian did not respond, gripping the steering wheel even harder.

Behind him, Drover rubbed the bridge of his nose. His eyes were closed and every few minutes he would let out a silent but horrendous fart that made the already humid cabin even more unbearable. He was mumbling something softly to himself that could only be recognized passingly as the Our Father. And he was crying.

Chauna sat behind Freemantle, staring out the porthole window of the jeep. "What are you doing with ammunition in your trunk?" she asked, not turning away from the window.

"Used to go out to the range when I lived in the city," he sighed. "Thought there might be time for it out here, but haven't found any yet."

"With any luck we won't need it," Freemantle said, sliding the last round into his gun and flicking it shut.

"Because luck is something we've been blessed with this far," Adrian said, making a sharp turn toward the township. The jeep's tire bounced quietly against a large boulder to just one side of the road, rocking its inhabitants for a moment before righting itself again.

Chauna gasped, placing her hand against the porthole. "I think I see Mr. Keating out there!"

"Is he --"

"I think he's carrying a boy under his arm," she finished, erasing Adrian's need to ask the question. She forced herself to turn away from the window. After a moment she ducked her head down between her knees and threw up.

"Alright, that's at least three confirmed infected and six or more dead," Freemantle said, clutching his gun. "That's one fifth of Stapleton's population. One third if you don't count the men down in the ore mines away from it all right now. We are officially calling this one. The four of us are getting to the copter and getting the hell out of Dodge."

"What?" Chauna exclaimed, looking up at the back of the General's chair in shock. There were still chunks of half-digested fruit stuck to her lips, but she unbuckled her safety belt and leaned forward into the front seat. "You can't do that! There are people here. Children! We have to get them out!"

"For all we know they could already be infected," he said, adjusting the side-view mirror so that he could see the hospital. There was a cloud of dark smoke rising from the wing that the operating room had been located in, and now, he assumed, no longer was. "We are getting out of here and getting a team together to stop this. Nearest base is two hours out."

"That could be enough time for this thing to kill everyone in town!"

"And what, prey tell, do you think our remaining here will do to dissuade that?" Freemantle barked, his cheeks growing livid for less than a second as he raised his voice.

Adrian took his eyes off the road for a moment and cocked an eyebrow at the General. This was another first, the raising of the voice. He glanced at the older man's eyes and discovered nothing but the pale blue that had been there a few minutes ago, then turned back toward the road.

The General calmed himself. "If we don't get out of here, then no help will come. This will continue until the entire town is overcome by this... this plague and then one of two things will happen: those infected will just kill one another like Sutton and the others... or they'll get out, and things will spread. One of those I can deal with. The other, I can't."

Chauna remained silent for a long moment, then leaned back into her seat. She nodded once.

Adrian's jeep sped toward the town's outer ring.

Karen slid the metal door of her hall closet closed, holding one of her children firmly to each breast. It was dark inside, except for the narrow bands of light that filtered in from the turrets of the metal. She could smell both the freshly cleaned coats that hung overhead and the old, damp sneakers that now rested in the arch between her buttocks and her feet, the mixture of both the pleasant and the pungent agitating her olfactory senses.

She remembered, briefly, a conversation she'd had with her husband when they'd moved in here. In choosing a location to live, he had mainly been concerned with square footage and yard space. She, on the other hand, had only two decided factors: neighbors and closet space. The latter was not important in Stapleton, however, as the houses here were of the cookie-cutter variety, with each one nearly identical in layout. Her decision to live here, then, had been made when she had met Rachel White.

At once, her mind shifted gears and she could almost see the scarlet stain in the sand outside her home where Rachel's head had been a few minutes before.

-Parr!-

The sudden sound of soft flesh against solid, sturdy wood reverberated through the boards and beams of her home. She felt the vibrations through the floorboards, making her yelp and jump a little.

"Mom?" Tyler called, turning to look up at her.

"Shh," she soothed, holding him closer and bending down to kiss his head. His hair got caught on the hot, sticky tears that had started to roll down her face. Her chin had become wrinkled and shook as her eyelids continued to fill again and again.

-Parr!-

Came the sound again, louder this time.

"Ah!" she said, despite her own efforts to bite her tongue.

Jamie did not speak, her index finger held in the cusp of her lips and her eyes wide.

-Parr!-

-Tuh!-

-tin, tin, tink.-

She'd never heard that sound before, and yet knew exactly what it was. It was the solid wooden door of her home hitting the scratched hardwood floor, the tiny bolts that used to make it swing so gracefully bouncing along behind it.

And then there was nothing.

She sat in the closet, her knees bent up into the fetal position and her children held to each breast as though she were feeding them.

Her neck itched wildly as beads of nervous, fearful sweat rolled down it in odd, winding paths. She tried so hard not to make a sound but her body simply would not comply, her breathing quickening into short, loud gasps and her blood pumping so loud that she was convinced anyone could have heard it, let alone Mark Baxter.

Tyler shifted at her side, squirming to get comfortable in the confined space. His heel knocked against the baseboard, creating a dull thump and an accompanying vibration that she felt but wasn't sure if it was enough to filter through to the rest of the house. She dared not shush him, squeezing his shoulder firmly but gently to try and make him be still. She debating using her nails for a moment, though she never had before, but decided that the risk of his hissing or crying out in pain or surprise was too great.

He moved once more without a sound, then settled back in.

Still, there were no more sounds from beyond the closet.

She strained her ears, trying hard to hear any sign of the intruder. She could hear the wind outside through the now open doorway, howling like a dingo baying at the moon. She could hear the sound of sand and dirt as it got kicked up into small cyclones, spinning about and scratching against the wall of the house as well as the children's play-sets with a series of light, metallic clinks. There was even the hum of the electronics that made life easier in the desert: the fridge cutting in and the steady, surreal clambering of the air conditioner.

For seven agonizing minutes there was nothing.

Karen leaned forward, peering out through the divides in the metal door that was all that separated her and her children from the rest of the house.

The cappuccino-coloured couch sat in the center of her field of vision, catching the light that streamed in from the bay windows in front of it. The coffee tables, freshly dusted, glimmered and gleaned. There were crayons scattered all over the floor, and she couldn't help but take note of a yellow one that was under her husband's recliner and would have been obscured from view at any other time. The floors were dusty but clean and, most importantly, devoid of any shadows. They didn't bend, creek or volley in response to a person walking on them.

Biting her lip and taking one last glance around the room, she slowly reached up and laid her hand on the door handle.

Mark Baxter stepped into view.

She jumped back, clutching her children's heads so tightly that for a moment they could not breathe. She bit her lip so hard that it bled, closing her eyes the way Jamie did when she was convinced that there was something under her bed and just willing it to go away.

When she opened her eyes again, she could see the backs of two long legs through the openings in the door. He was seven feet away from her, just to the left of the couch.

A drop of blood fell to the floor next to him, splashing up and crowning into several smaller droplets that cascaded down around it.

He stood straight, his entire body moving with each of his wet, heavy breaths. Even the back of his legs seemed to be a part of the motion, tightening and relaxing with every hackneyed sound.

Karen's teeth started to chatter despite her every attempt to grind them down and gooseflesh waved over her body. She brought her hand to her mouth and squeezed, so tightly that her nails left for small half-moon indentations in her cheek.

He stopped moving, standing rod straight for a moment. Then he turned, slowly bending over until he was sitting on the couch, hunched over and craning his neck backward like an animal watching out for fellow predators. She could see him through the spaces in the closet door now, his typically full-bodies hair whetted down against his skull with blood and sweat and bile. His face was the hued pink of boiled lobster and he took his breaths through clenched, grinding teeth. His eyes were what she noticed most, though. The white had ruptured and ripped, leaving only great swells of red, gelatinous goop behind. Rosy tears streamed down his face, so hot that they might have evaporated instead of falling from his cheeks and onto the floor.

There was a can clasped between both his hands, held so tight that his knuckles turned white. He cradled it against his chest for a moment, his eyes still glued to the hallway he had come from, before turning toward the coffee table and raising his hand high.

-BARM!-

"Mf," Karen mewed, stifling the yelp that had wanted to erupt from her lips as the edge of the can bashed off the corner of her coffee table.

He stared down at it, squeezing it as though it were a neck he was ringing and let out a long, vengeful grunt before raising his hand and bringing it down again.

-BARM!-

This time the top cracked, sending juice and pulp gushing onto the table in a bright orange wave.

He laughed, though it sounded strange and forced, as he poked the tip of his finger through the gouge in the metal. It sliced at his finger though he didn't seem to notice or care, worming it about until he got a good grip and pulled. The tin peeled back slowly, opening enough that he could see the sweet treasure inside. It also ripped at the calloused flesh of his forefinger, turning those contents vermilion in the process.

When he reached in again, he produced a juicy, if slightly discoloured, peach and placed it between his lips, slurping it back and sending it down his throat without so much as biting it. The instant it was gone he went searching for another one, his lips smacking together wildly as that constant low cluck in the back of his throat continued.

Karen sighed.

He stopped. His finger stopped rooting around the can and he even appeared to stop breathing for a moment.

She stopped, clamping her fingers down across her lips again as she felt Tyler squirm beside her.

Mark's head spun around like an owl's, his eyelids braced open so far that she could see the curvature of his eyes as they locked onto the closet door. His cheeks turned a dark, vein-drenched red again as that angry bird sound started to sound from his throat, his adam's apple bobbing up and down with every hark.

His eyes seemed to be staring directly at hers, though she knew that wasn't possible. Couldn't be possible. There was no way he could see in through the tiny spaces between the metal into the darkness of the closet, let alone lock eyes with her. Her eyes would be nothing but slivers of shadow to him. Yet he did lock onto her, his nearly invisible pupils focuses intently on her.

Slowly, he laid the can of peaches down onto the coffee table, his blood dribbling from the gouge he'd made in it as though it had gotten stabbed. The muscles in his legs tensed considerably as he rose to full standing position and she could hear his stomach growling from where she and her children sat huddled in a mangy closet, not wanting to think about what it that might mean. Hot blood was raging through him again now, if it had ever truly stopped. When he finished rising, the grate she had been looking out through held an almost perfect frame of his pelvis, demonstrating that indeed the blood was running rampant through his entire body. His pants throbbed and pulsed as though there were something inside that wanted desperately to get out and she watched his fists clench to either side of it, the veins on their backs popping out nearly a quarter centimeter and looking ready to burst. His abdomen mounted and relented so quickly that it almost resembled a seizure, the muscles around his portly stomach dancing and moving about with a mind of their own.

He took one lumbering step forward, his body slanting comically to one side before he righted himself and looked almost normal, but only because she couldn't see his face. She was infinitely thankful that she couldn't see his face in fact, yet still wanted to know if he was still staring at her.

His steps became lighter now, almost soundless. Every one seemed planned and well-thought out, something that seemed to be very much the antitheses of the way he'd acted only moments ago in opening the can of peaches. His left foot stepped out in front of the right in a smooth, graceful arch, not ruffling a single article of clothing or making any sound. When he brought it down to the tile floor, he laid the outside arch of his foot down first, then slowly rolled it down until it was flat. Again, there was not a sound, even as the metal toe of the boot touched down. The right foot came around from behind and repeated the moment almost identically, and before she could even remind herself to breathe, Mark Baxter's feet were less than and inch in front of her closet door.

Tyler stared at it wide-eyed as Jamie just turned away

into her mother's breast again.

For her part, Karen laid her head back against the wall as quietly as she could and closed her eyes despite her body screaming at her not to and whispered a prayer to herself, one she used to recite as a child and hadn't even thought of in twenty years until that moment. She opened them again when she heard a dog bark outside.

Mark's right heel turned, pivoting slightly at its base in the direction of the door, which she could only imagine was irreparably off its hinges. The clucking from his throat got louder and quicker and before she knew it, he was running toward the door. Allowing herself a rueful, desperate laugh as tears flew down her cheeks, she listened as his heavy footfalls got further and further away, then heard the familiar -Pff!- sound as they made first contact with the sand outside and kept going.

Laughing and sobbing as mucus drooped down into her mouth and onto her chin, she turned toward Tyler and kissed him softly on the head, then to Jamie and did the same, squeezing her tightly. She hadn't realized how much pain her position had been causing her until she tried to move, bracing herself on either wall and letting out a heartfelt "Umph" as she pushed off them and started to rise to her feet, twisting her neck quickly to throw her hair back out of her face.

"Come on, Jamie," she tisked, hoisting her child under the arm. She forced a smile to let her know it was okay, turning back to the door and grasping the handle.

Mark Baxter glared at her through the metal grate with eyes that burned like hellfire.

She opened her mouth and let out the longest,

loudest scream she ever had as he grabbed each side of the closet door violently and began to shake, the metal frame clanging against itself until it's own squeal rivaled hers. The children began to cry as well as Mark opened his mouth hungrily, letting that same click spew out like venom from deep below his uvula.

He reached one hand high, clenching his fist tight before bringing it down onto the door.

-BAM!-

She jumped, her back slamming against the wall as her feet pushed off against the floor, instinctively getting her as far away from the brutal, snarling thing in front of her. But never once did she lose eye contact with it, much less take her eyes off of it.

Nostrils flaring, he reached back his fist again, knuckles ripped to pieces and staring at her like four infected eye sockets.

-BAM!-

The shamrock-green door buckled inward. He stared at her exclusively, barely even taking note of the children on either side of her. His teeth ground together so fiercely that she thought she saw flakes of enamel falling away from them like dandruff just beyond her peripheral vision. Eyelids twitching for moisture yet refusing to blink, he lifted him fist again.

-BAM!-

Blood spurted from the left side of his head as several large chunks of his skull separated themselves from the rest, falling to the floor a brief instant before the rest of him did.

For a moment that seemed like forever, she could not

process what had just happened. She kept staring into the space where Mark Baxter's eyes had been a second before, waiting for them to return but seeing only the final sputtering spasms of his left leg.

As if by will, eyes did appear, though they were not red or monstrous or even unkind. The soft, cobalt blue spheres were turned upward in pity, accented only by the worry-lines that had formed beneath them many years beforehand.

"Karen," Freemantle said, his voice possessing a quality of calm she'd never heard from him before. "You can come out."

She hesitated for a moment, clutching her children before lunging forward and thrusting the door open as quickly as she could, tossing herself into Freemantle's arms. Slowly he laid his hands on her back and for a moment she wasn't in Stapleton. She was at home and it was twenty years prior and she was as safe. Tears that she'd tried so well to hold back for what had seemed like hours came gushing out now, and for a brief time she even forgot about her children, skill clutching on either side of her blouse.

"It's okay," he said, some of the gruffness returning to his voice. He patted her back twice with the hand not holding his service revolver. "It's all right."

When she opened her eyes again, she saw the other three, standing in her hallway and partially obscured by Freemantle's shoulder.

Adrian stood close to the kitchen cabinets, playing with something absently and trying to avoid looking at her as she was caught in Freemantle's arms. He didn't appear uncomfortable by the display so much as respectful, his eyes darting over every now and again out of simple, human curiosity.

Chauna stood near him, her hands at her sides and sweat still pouring off her and onto her scrubs; she was breathing hard and wasn't turning away, though wasn't staring at her either. She was staring at the children, watching them as they grabbed at their mother with needing hands. Her eyes darted toward the body of Mark Baxter then, welling up slightly before forcing themselves away again.

Drover stood the furthest away from her, staring down at his feet and shuffling about uncomfortably.

"Come," Freemantle said finally, tapping her on the back again as he began to rise to his feet. "We haven't a lot of time, I'm afraid."

She nodded to herself, rising to her feet and bringing the children with her as she made the first, tenuous steps toward the door. Her legs almost buckled beneath her, the adrenalin rushing through her turning them to butter.

"Here," Chauna said, forcing a smile and she stepped to Karen's side. "Let me help."

Karen smiled, taking Chauna's hand as the both of them walked out the back entrance to the Reynolds home, the children and Adrian close behind them. Adrian picked up Jamie, letting her head rest on his shoulder.

Freemantle straightened his shirt with one swift tug on the bottom with both hands, then started for the door himself. When he reached the hallway, Drover lay a hand on his arm.

"Who is she?" the shorter man whispered, leaning in

close to the General. "Who is this woman that you'd risk all our lives to save her?"

Freemantle stared at him for a long moment, the muscles in his face retaining their stanched and stern form. He looked down at Drover's hand on the crook of his arm, then back again.

Drover released it quickly, then slowly let his arm fall back into place.

"She is Karen Reynolds," Freemantle answered crisply. "Daughter of Katherine and Michael Peachtree, mother to Tyler and Jamie Reynolds. Spouse to Justin Reynolds, my driver of many years."

Drover opened his mouth, saying nothing as he nodded.

Freemantle leaned in until his dry lips were almost touching Drover's ear. "Remember their names. You'll be addressing sympathy cards to them for many, many years."

Drover stiffened as Freemantle walked past him. He waited until he heard the General's feet hit the sand outside before he turned to follow, taking one last look at the body of Mark Baxter before he did, still bubbling hot blood onto the floor. "And checks," he added, exiting the home.

Allie sat on the sidewalk and fumbled with the bottle in her hands, the beveled edge of its stopper grating on her nails as she tried desperately to open it.

Blood ran down her cheeks in several waving streams now, fed every few moments at its source, as her vision became more and more alizarin.

Her mouth scrunched and twisted uncomfortably as she fought with the pills, writhing in all manner of shapes. Her nostrils even contorted as she let out several small, monosyllabic grunts that until today she had reserved only for when she was mid coitus.

Andrea Mercer poked her head around the corner at the sound, one of her carefully drawn-on eyebrows perched skyward quizzically.

Allie did not notice her, continuing to fight a losing battle against the plastic capsule as her hair swung about her head in a wild, sweaty mess.

She turned, biting her lip as she looked back toward the car, then took a step closer to Allie. "Is there something I can help you with?"

Allie looked up from behind her ragged bangs, her eyes so deeply red they approached purple. The pupils had long since disappeared, yet somehow Andrea knew that the girl was staring right at her. Her breath became short and heavy as she dropped the bottle, letting it roll along the ground between her feet in small concentric circles, finally coming to a stop against the curb.

Andrea took a step back, bringing her hands to her face.

Allie arose slowly, her back hunched and her arms hanging low. She opened her mouth, revealing chipped and missing teeth that ripped at her own gums every time she clamped down. She let out a low, menacing growl made up of a long series of short clicking sounds.

Karen lay her head down in her hands as she willed herself to stop crying, staring down at the checked teal carpet and rubber mats that made up the floor of Adrian's jeep. Her face and hands had taken on the complexion of sour milk, that chalky white mixed with the slightest hint of green. There was a layer of sweat on her forehead that had nothing to do with the heat of the desert, though they kept the air conditioner blasting air at her regardless.

"Water?" Freemantle offered, holding a clear plastic bottle just in front of her. Its contents looked almost crystalline in the sharp light off the sand.

"No," she said dryly, her lips making an audible sound as they parted. "Yes."

She took the bottle from him and brought it to her lips, letting the first few gulps wash their way down naturally before stopping. She took another sip and swished it around her mouth, making every cranny and vein feel human again before swallowing that too. She handed him back the bottle, which he took back into the front seat gently.

To her left, Drover reached out and placed a hand on her back. "How are you?" he managed to ask, every word feeling forced and unnatural.

Not responding, she looked out the window between Adrian and Freemantle. From this angle all she could see were electrical poles whizzing by and the dark blue cloudless sky beyond them. She turned toward her children, both of them coiled up in tight little balls on either side of Freemantle. Neither spoke, but they were both skill awake. Her thoughts swimming and dazed, she lolled her head to her right and met Chauna's gaze, who promptly turned away and looked out the small circular window of the jeep's backseat.

"What am I going to do?" she said to no one in particular, her head swinging back down and looking at the floor. "What am I going to- - Justin, he was - -"

"Karen," Freemantle said, laying a hand on Tyler's head.

She stopped, looking from the General to her child and then back again, then nodded. Licking her lips, she held her hand out for the water again and got it.

Chauna sighed, watching as the houses that zipped by got fewer and further between as they approached the outskirts of town. They looked peaceful enough. Happy even. But just beyond them to the next street over and the street after that she could see the signs of something more sinister. Billows of smoke too big to come from smoke stacks. The frames of people walking not quite right, their shoulders lurched or their legs limping. The sound of sirens both getting louder and further away simultaneously as the last few squad cars were dispatched to whatever residents still had the sense to call in.

Adrian spun the wheel quickly, making a wide turn that kicked up a cloud of gravel.

She steadied herself, turning to frown at him although he wasn't looking anywhere near her. When she turned back toward the window it was on the last arc of their spin and one house had come perfectly into focus.

Its siding was a deep full red that made it stand out amongst the greens and the whites that had dominated the majority of the street if not the settlement. The door was metal but had been painted a soft, woody colour and stood perfectly in the middle of two great bay windows, giving the house a 'face' of sorts. The tiles on its roof were the same auburn as her hair, the white trim acting as the perfect highlight for each colour.

There was artificial grass covering most of the front lawn. Real grass was nearly impossible to maintain here and most families chose to adorn their yards with cheap stone or, cheaper still, leave the natural sand. The thin plastic blades of green made the house look like a vibrant oasis amidst the dunes, a symbol of life and unity tapered in by a white-picket fence that looked like it had been taken out of a movie.

Just beyond the furthest post of the fence, a German Shepard and a Labrador Retriever fought over the tattered, mauled remains of a human arm.

Both dogs growled viciously, their throats incapable of making that click but trying nonetheless as blood seeped out of each dog's ears and eyes, matting their mangey fur into wet, slimy clumps. Their eyes were completely red, without even the slightest hint of anything else. Foam dripped from their jowls in massive froths. As the jeep sped by, the Retriever raised its paw and batted the Lab across the snout, getting a better grip on the supple pink flesh in its teeth.

Chauna gasped, turning away from the window as her eyes darted back and forth inside her skull.

Adrian took his eyes off the road for a second, gazing up into the rearview mirror at her. "Everything okay?"

She did not respond at first, bringing one hand up to her temple and using her nails like a comb to rake the hair away from her face.

"Chauna?"

"Hate," she said finally, looking up into the mirror.

His eyes appeared to just float there in the middle of the sky as he squinted at her from the front seat.

"Excuse me?"

Freemantle turned slightly to hear.

"It's a hate plague. A contagion that somehow it, it --"

"Makes us angry," Drover finished, nodding. "Yes. Raise the blood pressure, increased cranial pain: rage."

Freemantle nodded, turning back toward the road ahead.

"But it's preposterous," Drover continued, almost to himself. "There aren't any natural factors that would account for a blood born, communicable contagion that affects hormone levels this way and can be spread from man to animal this quickly."

Freemantle frowned, turning his head slightly to give him a look.

"It wasn't natural," Chauna said, speaking for him.

"Up ahead," Adrian said finally, bringing the jeep to an abrupt halt and making them all lurch forward.

The airstrip station lay before them, its flat grey surface stretching out over the desert to seemingly no end.

It was empty.

The helicopter was gone, and had been long enough that the telltale stench of diesel and clouds of black smog that it left behind weren't even present.

Freemantle got out of the jeep without a word, leaning one arm against the door as he surveyed the situation, moving his eyes slowly from one end of the horizon to the other.

Adrian got out a moment later, running his fingers

through his hair as the wind gusted about and displaced it once again. "I don't understand. It should be here."

"Could they have left?" Drover offered, leaning forward between the seats. "I mean, I know they could have left, but would they?"

Freemantle leaned down until his eyes were just a smidgen lower then the frame of the door. He did not answer, nor was there any expression on his face one way or the other.

Drover nodded, then sat back.

Standing again and straightening his shirt, he turned back toward the station. Adrian was a few feet in front of the jeep now, and he moved to join him.

"Is this seeming a little too coincidental to anyone else?" Adrian asked under his breath, turning back to watch as Chauna got out of the jeep.

Freemantle nodded. "Are you familiar with history, Doctor?"

"Moderately, sir. Took a few courses as electives while I was at University."

"War and science have always seemed to go hand in hand throughout our history. If necessity is the mother of invention, than violence is its father. Or grandmother. Or what have you. Either way, wars have always proven great boons for scientific breakthroughs... and breakthroughs, as I'm sure you're aware, require experiments."

Chauna raised an eyebrow, walking a few feet toward the right of the jeep. The mines were in sight now, the small cavernous entrance to its eastern tunnel just a few hundred yards away. Her head was tilted downward, the rest of her body following suit, as she examined something on the desert floor.

"And experiments require control groups," Adrian finished, turning back toward the empty fueling station. "Must make sure the rats don't leave the cage."

"We need to get out of here," Freemantle said. There was a gravitas in his voice that Adrian had never heard before, and if he hadn't known the man as well as he did, he might have described it as fear. "We need to get the tanks in here and blow this entire place back to Shangri-La, and I mean right now."

"Reptiles."

Freemantle and Adrian both turned toward the sound, as did the passengers still in the jeep. Chauna was still bent over, examining two small creatures in the sand.

They were two small salamanders, each no longer than a human hand, sitting calmly in the sun. One was inanimate except for the occasional blinking of its eyes, the other moved forward awkwardly on its webbed purple legs.

Both were covered in deep crimson, congealed blood.

Drover leaned forward. "Incredible."

"This plague, whatever it is, it's activating our reptile genes. The R Chromosome that we haven't used since Lord knows when, but it's in all of us. Each and every one of us. And this thing activates it somehow... but for them it's already active. That's why they don't --" she stood, turning back to Freemantle and Adrian.

They were staring in her direction, but at the same time were not looking at her. They were looking through her and past her, to the area beyond the jeep. She turned, following their line of sight even though she was certain she didn't want to.

Less than four hundred yards away, a large group of the infected stared at them with massive, unblinking red eyes as they lumbered forward on unsteady and broken legs.

"Get back in the jeep," Adrian said, stepping toward the vehicle and then running after his first footfall. "*Get back in the jeep!*"

Chauna turned and dove back into the door as Freemantle and Adrian clambered inside. Adrian shifted the stick to drive and pulled forward immediately and with no real direction in mind except away, spinning the tires and then tearing away from the station in a wide arc.

"Where are we going to go?" Drover yelled to nobody, his head pivoting between the front window and the back. "Where do you think we can go that they can't follow? There's too much desert out there and too many of them in here! We're dead! Dead!"

"Shut up!" Chauna said finally, giving him a look before turning back to Karen. "We're not dead. We are not dead until we're dead, and we're not dead."

Adrian glanced up into the rearview mirror at her, meeting her gaze all but briefly.

"We're not dead," she said again, in response to some phrase her colleague hadn't spoken.

They were almost to the mines and the infected were disappearing behind them again, though they were still coming. Even if they couldn't see them, they could *feel* them, the way you feel panic as it ebbs its way up from the lining of your stomach and becomes something ravenous.

"Here!" Freemantle yelled, grabbing the wheel and jolting it to the left. "Hold on!"

The jeep lurched to the side and spun until it was facing the entrance to the caves and then plunged forward, slamming into the solid rock mouth and sending all seven of them into the dashboard and seats in front of them.

For a moment, nobody moved or spoke.

"Everyone okay?" Freemantle asked, breaking the silence as the jeep's engine wound to a final halt.

"Fuck is wrong with you?" Drover asked, rubbing the back of his neck gingerly.

"No, look," Adrian smiled, craning his head too see as much of the windshield as he could. "We're plugging the hole. The entrance to the cave is sealed. They can't get in."

"But we can't get out."

"That doesn't matter," Freemantle interrupted harshly, clearly in pain as he checked to make sure the children had not been harmed. "There are twenty miners in these tunnels with enough supplies and rations to last eighteen months, should anything happen. We'll be fine in here until we find a way out or a way to contact the outside world." He leaned forward and slammed his elbow against the plate glass windshield. It popped out on the second strike, sailing three feet into the cavern before landing on the solid stone floor and shattering. "Come on."

The walls of the cave were magnificent simply in their continued existence. What at first appeared to be solid rock was actually compressed sand, pressed together to the point that any weight put upon it by the surface was evenly distributed amongst the grains. Navigating them by flashlight was like being shrunk down to the size of a doll and exploring a sand castle built as a child, its construction weaving and intricate.

The swirls and twists of multicolored flecks of sand left patterns and shapes in the walls. They formed long flowing faces stretched out in agony and horror, red-sanded eyes watching them wherever they went.

Two miles into the cave the tunnel became narrow with sharp stalactites jutting up from either side, and it became necessary to walk single file. Freemantle led the way with the flashlight, careful to test every rock and crevice that looked suspicious to make sure it was safe for those following. Karen walked behind him, holding Tyler in her arms. Then came Adrian holding Jamie, Chauna, and finally Drover.

Chauna mumbled to herself, some of her words audible and some not, as the counted off digits on her fingers.

Adrian glanced back once or twice and noticed her get to four or five, stop, then start again. "What's wrong?" he asked after a moment of trying to figure it out on his own.

"Trying to figure out the route the pathogen took."

He raised an eyebrow at her.

She frowned, stepping carefully to avoid a large boulder. "Infectious diseases are transmitted from one source to another. Respiratory, gastrointestinal, sexual... they all have to be transmitted from person to person."

"Of course."

"Well typically it's hard to tell what sequence it happened in... but a blood born disease, and a new one at that... it shouldn't be that hard to track its progress."

"And?"

"And I can't. No matter what I do or how I do it, I can't figure out how the disease moved. Somewhere, somehow, it jumped the tracks."

He frowned, turning to Jamie to make sure she wasn't paying attention. She appeared to be asleep despite everything that was happening, nuzzled into the nape of his neck. "Talk it out."

"It started with that Private, we're all clear on that."

"Baker, yes. That was definitely patient zero."

"Then Mark and Sutton, in that order."

"I'm following you so far."

"And after that the disease takes a fairly clear path through town, albeit unbelievably quickly. It spreads from person to person in a predictable fashion for a blood born infection."

"What's the problem then?"

She leaned in, whispering. "I can't for the life of me figure out how the General's driver got it. Karen's husband. No matter what way I think about it, I can't figure out how someone with the infection managed to infect --"

Adrian screamed, turned quickly, and fell to his knees. Sharp rocks dug into his kneecaps and out the other side in a glorious spurt of blood and he thrashed forward, slamming his head against the pact sand in the narrow cavern. He dropped Jamie to the ground as her mother and Freemantle turned around, the girl landing on her feet next to him, her head still buried in his neck.

She pulled back, taking a chunk of his neck the size of his fist with him as a fountain of blood splashed out onto her face and hair, almost obscuring the opaquely red eyes that turned toward the light just as Freemantle shone it upon her. She opened her mouth and screamed, the sound coming out a long squeal and clicks and clacks that echoed off the walls and came back in all directions.

She darted at Freemantle, too fast for him to see, and pushed him into the rock wall. He fell, letting go of the flashlight and letting it tumble to the ground to catch himself. She bellowed at him, opening her blood-drenched mouth wide and yelling so loud it shook the molars of the tiny round teeth.

Freemantle started to get up and reach for his gun as Jamie turned, leaping at Chauna and clawing at the older woman's chest.

"Fuck!" Chauna yelled , trying her best to hold the child at bay.

Jamie roared back, turning and biting at Chauna's wrist and coming back with a vein caught in the gap of her two front teeth, pulling back hard until it came clear like a boiled noodle.

Freemantle stood and aimed his weapon, taking one step forward to steady himself before firing.

His steel-toed boot came to ground on the base of Adrian's flashlight, and the steady beam went out, bathing them in darkness.

The jeep that pulled up to the cave was eerily quiet, its treads packing the sand beneath it into jagged rectangular patterns. It came to a stop in silence, the well cared for breaks never once squealing in defiance as it came to a halt. There was a moment when all was still, and for once there wasn't even a breeze to carry grains over the dunes. The main turret of the tank stared out upon the entrance to the cave, an unblinking eye watching mournfully over the tomb.

The door at the top opened, and an officer wearing a black uniform with duel rows of black buttons stepped out and jumped down onto the sand, sending waves of it cascading in all directions around him. He took off his cap and wiped the sweat from his brow with a small red handkerchief, then placed it carefully back into his pocket.

A younger officer poked his head out from the jeep after a moment, then finally allowed himself to fall to the ground as well. He made a grunt when he did, as though the feeling of dirt beneath his boots were foreign to him.

"Any sign, sir?" he asked, his voice wavering in a way it hadn't since puberty as his eyes darted across the horizon. The town lay in ruins, the only sign left that there had ever been anything there a smoldering building a mile to their west that reports claimed had once been a hospital, the embers burning so hot that the ground around it had turned to glass.

The senior officer chewed slowly, moving the toothpick in his mouth from side to side as his eyes passed over the cave. The sand at the entrance was tinted a crimson he knew had nothing to do with their planets tone. He let out a long sigh. "There's nothing here," he said finally, turning back to his second-in-command. "Get the old man on the line, direct contact. Let him know Reptillia is good for mass produ--"

There was a sound behind him, not unlike the rattle of a child's toy, slow and rhythmic. A soft, almost soothing cluck that under any other circumstances might have been hypnotically pleasing.

His withered eyes went wide for the first time in years as he turned around on his heels so fast he almost ripped a ligament in his hip.

They say screams can't echo off the dunes. That they absorb the sound and prevent it from continuing on.

If they're loud enough, they do.

OMEGA

- ELLEN CURTIS -

Rebecca pulled her thin shawl tight around her. It was still damp against her skin, and her hair still hung limply. She could feel the scent of tobacco clinging to her; as if the cold and the dank weather was not enough a manifestation of her failing, the scent of death clung to her too. She slipped her feet back into her damp leather sandals, and gingerly brought herself out into the downpour.

She took to the left side of the building, moving toward the thin line of trees separating the city from the large rock wall looming over the town. She followed it for a few moments, coming to a path leading back toward the center city, away from the abandoned factory she had come to think of as a second home.

Rebecca emerged from the path at the end of a cul-de-sac, and she followed it to its mouth. The rain seemed to be coming down harder now, away from the shelter of trees and rocks. She scuffed her feet as she walked, flicking rocks into the small puddles forming quickly around her.

She glanced up only briefly as she tried to avoid the rain hitting her full in the face. As she did so, her breath caught in her throat. Already she could see a dense blanket of fog rolling into the valley from the Northern Hills. Darkness was coming fast.

Rebecca quickened her pace, her shawl clinging to the dampest parts of her arms. Again, she pulled it close to keep it in check, her sandals flapping madly as she half-ran-half-walked toward the apartment she and Exie shared. The road seemed long when she was this anxious to get home.

There was a willow tree in front of the blue-grey row housing where their apartment was located. Its branches rapped against Exie's bedroom window firmly, often startling her from sleep. Its tall body was coming into Rebecca's view now, and she slowed her jilting movements marginally, her heartbeat relaxing.

She passed under the overpass hanging above Trumont Street and was briefly sheltered from the rain as she walked. Pigeons cooed, hiding from the weather in small crevices in the concrete support form of the overpass.

Making her way up the road, Rebecca sighed heavily. She hated the thought of what Exie would say, how she would react to Oliver's steadfast refusal to join them. Her friend hadn't been herself lately, and the implications were worrying, all things considered.

Rebecca neared the driveway and cut toward the steps. She took the stairs two at a time, pulling open the door as she reached the landing and dashing into the porch. She slammed the door behind her and swung two deadbolts into the locked position, then slid the chain into place across the top of the door.

She turned then toward the door to the apartment she and Exie shared, hauling on the handle and repeating the two-deadbolt-chain process once she was inside. A long, narrow staircase led up to a landing, and she quickly took to the stairs, bolting to the top. "Exie!" she yelled out. "I'm back now!" There was no response.

Rebecca's brow furrowed and she called out again "Ex, are you okay in there?" Still no response. She raced toward the door, colour draining from her face. "Exie?" she yelled, more frantic now and she tugged at the door handle.

She yanked it open, barreling into the room only to stop short of an overturned chair. Between where Exie sat perched at her window seat and where Rebecca stood, there was an array of debris. It ranged from the chair, which bore a crack along the left rear leg, to a shattered mirror, to a make-up case emptied across the floor, to sheets upon sheets of music and poetry.

Exie was leaning against the wall with her eyes closed. She opened them at the sound of Rebecca's entrance, but instead of turning toward her friend, she turned her gaze to the willow tree outside. Oliver was leaning against the opposite wall, arms folded, staring at her with his face blank.

"Exie, Oliver, what happened in here? Why didn't you answer when I called out to you?" Rebecca blurted, picking her way quickly through the mess. She clutched her wet shawl to her as she avoided the broken glass, placing her free hand on Exie's arm as she reached her friend.

"Nothing happened, Beck. I was just upset. And I have a headache, so I'd rather not talk right now," Exie said as she jerked her arm out from under Rebecca's palm.

Her face showed no emotion, and she did not turn to face Rebecca.

Oliver sighed, pushing off from the wall and running his right hand through his dark hair. The movement caught Rebecca's eye, and she saw a lacework of red cuts criss-crossing the bare skin on his face and hands. Their eyes met, and he briefly betrayed a look of despair.

"Exie, we need to talk. If something got you upset enough to completely demolish your room, it needs to be out in the open." Rebecca sat on what little room was left on the window seat and folded her arms across her chest as she said this. "Exie?"

Exie glanced up at Rebecca quickly, then back out the window again. "I'd like to be alone now, please. Thank you for checking in on me though."

Rebecca sighed, pushing up from the window seat. As delicately as she had picked her way through the rubble, she made her way back toward the door, pausing with her hand around the knob to glance back at Exie. Oliver followed her out. Her friend's vacant expression troubled her.

Rebecca walked arms folded toward her own room. Oliver joined her, shutting the door quietly behind him as he entered. "Mind letting me in on what happened this time?" Rebecca sighed.

"We were just talking about what we're going to be doing with the room and she snapped. I mentioned getting some new furniture for us rather than getting second hand crap and she went ballistic again. Tried scratching my face off when I tried to stop her from hurting herself and then got all quiet and just sat down on the bench."

"Did you specifically say 'second hand crap'?"

"No, and even if I had, I hardly think that would have elicited that sort of response from her normally." Oliver crossed his arms and sat on a chair next to Rebecca's vanity.

"You mean if she was still medicated?" Rebecca said, looking him in the eye pointedly.

"It's not like I signed on for this, Beck. I didn't even know she was taking any medication until she told me she needed to go off them." He bent his head into his hands and let out a heaving sigh.

Rebecca paused, leaning against her desk. "I know, honey. It won't be too long before she can go back on them though, and the episodes will quiet down. Just think how nice it will be for all of us," she responded.

"Yeah, but the next few weeks will be the worst, and you know it. I won't be surprised if she has a larger episode yet. Lord knows how she's reacting with the drugs they've got her on now, and all the hormones to boot. I'm just shocked we haven't woken up to her at our throats."

Rebecca looked him in the eye. "I doubt she'd manage to break through all the deadbolts. Every single door, Olli. Every one, and there is no way she can get in or out if she goes manic. I just wish they were able to put her on some bloody sedatives at least so it wouldn't need to be a worry."

Rebecca moved toward her rice paper screen, slipping out of her shawl and her skirt, stripping down to a wet, thin undershirt and equally wet underwear when she was safely out of sight. She shivered slightly at her state of near-nudity, reaching for a robe to wrap herself in and a towel she could use to wring out her hair.

She returned from behind the screen and propped herself up with pillows on her bed. Oliver still sat, far away look in his eye, just as he had looked in Exie's room: almost emotionless, as if his guard just kept going farther and farther up.

"Olli?"

"Yeah?"

"You want me to make up the couch for you tonight? Save you the trip of going back across town."

Oliver glanced at his watch, realizing how late it was. "Naw, that's fine. She seems calmer now, but I still don't want to be spending the night in with her if she's liable to wake up and slash me, so I'd rather go home, get some packing done and call it a night. Don't want to be a bother to you either."

He pushed up from his seat and quietly left. As she relaxed into the plush of her comforter, she could hear him sliding the deadbolts into place. She let her breath out, not realizing she had been holding it. It was calm and quiet, finally.

Rebecca let her eyes rest, laying in the sheets and appreciating the silence while it lasted. The stillness of the room was a relief after running around all day. She wondered if it had really been worth it.

Rolling onto her side, she sat up and pushed off the bed. She moved toward the rice paper divider, tiptoeing to where she had left her wet clothes. From the pile she pulled out a small, leather coin purse, carefully prying the clasp open and extracting a small sheet of paper.

She moved toward a small desk next to her bed,

reaching to open her laptop. It came to life quietly, the screen lighting up and demanding her password. She typed it quickly with one hand, dragging her chair close to the desk with another so she could be seated.

Rebecca moved quickly, hands dancing across the keyboard as she pulled up the employee login for Ten Rivers Hospital. She glanced at the paper in her hand, fingers selecting the keystrokes she had written on the sheet. A list of names appeared in front of her, next to them a corresponding 9-digit number, and subsequent to each name and number was another 9-digit number, with the prefix 'M' or 'F'. She held her breath and scrolled down, her eyes scanning for a name.

The pre-natal patient directory for Ten Rivers was subdivided into low-risk and high-risk pregnancies, with a separate section for those high-risk mothers who had opted into one of a number of pharmaceutical trials the hospital was currently operating. The pharmaceutical trials generally involved medication aimed at lowering an expectant mother's blood pressure, for treating diabetes while pregnant, or for improving a child's chance of being born without hereditary or environmentally contracted illness. By the time the trials got to Ten Rivers, they had passed preliminary tests, and were mostly tested as to their effectiveness in different stages of pregnancy.

Exie, upon learning she was pregnant, had also been sent for extensive testing to monitor her sugar levels, which had shown to be very high on her blood work. Sure enough, she had tested positive for insulin-dependent diabetes, and had been offered various treatments. After it was clear her diet and insulin injections were still leaving her with dangerous sugar levels, a doctor had suggested she join a promising trial group that had recently been made available at the hospital.

Rebecca found Exie's name on a list for OmegaGene Pharmaceuticals. Her number, 747250201, was followed by F747250264. Rebecca let out a sharp breath. She wondered if Exie or Oliver knew they were having a girl.

There were other women listed under OmegaGene as well. Rebecca did not recognize any names, but in place of a prefix of 'M' or 'F' on their accompanying infant id code, three of the forty-two had an 'X' prefix, denoting a stillbirth or necessary late-term abortion. Two of those three also listed the mother as deceased. She felt a chill go through her as her eyes lingered on those, trying to reassure herself that the medication meant to help them had come too late, that it had been less effective on these women than on others. Even as she assured herself that three infant deaths and two dead mothers still added up to a 94% success rate, she still felt a bubble of fear for Exie grow in her.

She pushed those thoughts out of her mind forcefully, scrolling back to Exie's name and clicking her link. As part of the agreement with Ten Rivers, pharmaceutical companies and their trial participants had to sign a waiver of transparency, allowing their first names, ages, and pertinent medical conditions to be available for study at the teaching hospital by doctors and interns, including expected due date. Exie's due date, the 26th of April, put her roughly two weeks from being due, though with next to no pregnancy weight on and a barely there bulge, she looked more as if she had just become bloated after eating a large meal.

When she had started taking the medication, Exie had been warned that there was a possibility the pills could cause women with a history of depression to relapse. It was an understatement in Exie's case, but one she had hidden from her doctors very well, and to some extent even from her friends.

Oliver had been concerned from the beginning. When her erratic change in behavior had startled him, he had confronted her, and finally she had admitted to switching out her anti-psychotics for trial medication. Being off the anti-psychotics was bad enough, but the trial drug only exacerbated her psychosis and manic episodes.

The fact that Exie had been on anti-psychotics in the first place blindsided Oliver, and it was only recently she had managed to regain most of his trust. He had been instrumental in keeping her stable, but as Exie's manic periods grew wilder and more severe, his presence was less and less effective and more and more detrimental to his own health.

Rebecca sighed, dragging her mouse to the little red 'x' at the top of the window and closing her Internet connection. She rubbed the towel roughly against her hair once before pulling it off her head and laying it over the back of her chair.

Getting up, she moved to get dressed, nimbly plucking a shirt and leggings from a drawer. She shrugged them on, the loose fabric falling gently over her drying underclothes. Her hair, falling around her shoulders, was almost dry as well, giving Rebecca a warmer feeling and a calmer sense of things.

Exie awoke in pain, spasms arcing across her back. She rolled from her back to her side, heaving herself off the bed and propelling herself toward the door. Her knees trembled and buckled, and she grasped at the walls for support.

She stumbled toward Rebecca's room only vaguely aware of what was going on. She grasped the handle loosely, fumbling with the knob and bracing herself against the frame. She could hear Rebecca on the other side undoing the latches to try and get to her. Finally she managed to pop it open, and as the door swung in, she fell to the floor.

Rebecca caught Exie as she went down, her friend dragging her down and falling into her lap. Exie's breathing was shallow as Rebecca moved her friend into her arms, kneeling lower and picking her up. Even nearing her due date, Exie was only 115 pounds, though at the moment it seemed like so much less.

Rebecca hoisted Exie through the hall toward the kitchen, sitting her friend on the chair closest to the phone and leaning Exie against her own shoulder as she dialed for an ambulance. Exie's head lolled back as the phone rang and Rebecca noticed a distinct pool forming around the crotch of Exie's nightshirt. "Shit."

"911, please state your emergency."

"Yeah, I've got my friend here who just collapsed on me and she either just pissed herself or her water broke. My bets are on the latter and I'd really like someone over here quickly."

Oliver pushed his hair out of his eyes, glancing over forms and sighing. He initialed near the middle and again at the bottom, including his full signature and date where it was required. Oliver placed the pen and notepad down carefully at the nurses' station, giving the woman behind the counter a curt nod to signify she could start processing the sheets. She took them, glancing long enough to confirm that everything was in order before returning Oliver's nod.

He circled around to the waiting area, sliding into a rigid chair next to Rebecca. She sat upright, one hand holding onto a small pocketsize digest that was common to waiting rooms while the other clutched at her hair. She looked anxious, eyes flicking up from whichever article she was reading to the doors marked "RESTRICTED" that Exie had gone through over an hour before.

"Olli, they're taking good care of her. Don't worry quite so much."

Oliver glanced her way quickly. "Who says I'm worrying?"

"I know you. You're tense. You're frightened. It's understandable, but you can't worry right now. It only makes you more stressed out, and for all we know she will be fine. They haven't said anything to the contrary." Rebecca slid the digest to the side table and turned her whole body to face him. "You've got to let them just do their work, okay? They probably see situations like this everyday. They're trained doctors."

"It honestly sounds like you're the more worried one."

Oliver sunk down in the chair a little and Rebecca shot him a nervous look.

"Are you Oliver Trenton?" A man dressed in sea foam green scrubs and a white lab coat had made his way over to where Oliver and Rebecca sat.

Oliver sat bolt upright. "Is Exie okay?"

"Mr. Trenton, I'm Doctor Lewis. I'm given to understand you are the father of the child she is carrying?" Rebecca's stomach flopped as the doctor avoided Oliver's question.

"Yes. For fuck sakes, what's going on? The nurses wouldn't tell us anything when they were admitting her."

"Mr. Trenton, there have been some complications with the pregnancy, I'm sure you're aware. The pregnancy is definitely at a stage we normally consider viable, but we're getting some rather troubling results on routine tests. You're listed as medical proxy for your girlfriend, so I have to ask you to authorize us to pursue saving either your girlfriend or your daughter if something goes awry in the next couple of hours. The likelihood of the both of them making it through this alive is slim, I should caution you."

Rebecca felt a lump form in her throat. The news seemed to knock the wind out of her chest. Oliver struggled too, hands clenching at the seat of his chair, unable to speak in the wake of the news.

"You've gotta save Exie," he said, seemingly shell shocked. "How did this happen?"

Doctor Lewis straightened up. "That's what we're trying to determine. Her condition could be due in part to the medical trial she was involved with, but given her medical history it's really too early to say one way or another. Right now though, her blood pressure has been dropping dramatically and then rising without much warning. Her sugars are within the normal range, yet she is showing signs of potentially slipping into a diabetic coma. The baby's heartbeat is very weak right now, and normally we would be moving to do an emergency caesarean section, but with Exie in her current condition it would be exceptionally dangerous. All of our efforts to this point have been to stabilize them both adequately to perform the operation."

Oliver paused and then stood. "I want to be in there when you perform the surgery. I should be able to see my daughter before…" he trailed off sadly.

"I'm afraid that won't be a good idea Mr. Trenton. It's going to be a very delicate operation, and at such a high risk having you in the room would be inadvisable. Under normal circumstances we would allow it, but these just aren't normal circumstances." Doctor Lewis put his hand on Oliver's shoulder and Oliver shrugged him off.

"Do the best you can for them."

"Push 10 milligrams of apoxasine stat. I don't want to risk her waking up. No need to fuck over the coma story."

"Apoxasine injected. Her BP is 40 over 30 but holding. You're to start the procedure."

"Scalpel, please."

Doctor Lewis drew a long line across Exie's lower

abdomen with the blade, blood marking her immediately as if he had drawn the line in ink. Another man dressed in the same surgical gown and mask pressed gauze to the line, soaking up the blood and allowing a better view of the exposed flesh.

"Clamp and scissors." Doctor Lewis cut deeper, exposing and opening the uterus in deft, quick cuts. Another large clamp went into place as yet another surgeon joined in an effort to open a wider hole to remove the baby through. Blood poured out over Exie's stomach and the surgeons' gloves as Lewis ruptured the amniotic sac and placed his gloved hands inside Exie's womb. A pair of hands quickly moved a suction tube into place, but it did little to stop the flow of blood.

Lewis removed his hands from Exie, cradling her newborn daughter. "Clean her up. I'll handle the girl." He moved away from the operating table as soon as the umbilical cord had been clamped and severed, heading toward a small table with blankets. He suctioned out the mucus from the baby's airways, wiped her eyes and gently rubbed away any remaining blood from her body before wrapping her tightly in a fresh towel. Doctor Lewis took her in his arms then, as she gave her first feeble cry, and slipped out of the operating room.

Rebecca slipped the dress over her head, taking care to avoid getting make-up on the material. She smoothed it out, the cut coming just above her knees. She removed a pair of earrings from her desk, placing the pearl studs in the lobes of her ears slowly.

She lifted a tube of lipstick off the desk, uncapping it and moving the red cylinder across her lips. Her hand shook as she did this. A knock came at the door.

"Are you ready?"

Rebecca turned to face Oliver. "As ready as I'm able to be." She placed the lipstick tube back on the desk and slipped her feet into black satin heels. She was much paler than usual. "Let's do this."

The pair walked to Oliver's car, his dark suit and her formal dress making them stand out against the dockyard environment that spilled onto their street from the harbor. Rebecca held her chin high, her jaw set firmly as she slid into the passenger seat. Her hair was set into thick curls spilling around her face.

Oliver shifted out of park, pulling out onto the road. His hands gripped tightly at the steering wheel, his knuckles stark and white against the black leather. His hair was slicked back, and the jacket of his pantsuit held him firmly upright. Everything about the drive seemed unnatural.

They did not talk as Oliver drove. The silence hung in the car and made the air thick. Rebecca felt choked, her dedication to the part she had to play fading.

Houses passed by; first small and neglected ones, but as they drove further they became grand Victorian houses with parapets and rap-around porches and wrought iron. Slowly, the houses became more and more intermixed with trees the further they drove into the older part of town.

They finally pulled up at a large brick building, high fences looming around the entire property. Oliver drove up to the gate and rolled down the window.

"Appointment or admissions?" a static voice barked through the intercom.

"Appointment with Doctor Manuel. 2:30 sharp."

The static voice paused for a moment, presumably confirming the statement. "Mr. Trenton on behalf of Ms. Exie Barter?"

"That's me."

"Doctor Manuel is running late due to an emergency consultation. The wait may be a little while, be advised."

"Thank you."

The large gates swung open and Oliver rolled up the driver's side window. "Nervous?" he asked Rebecca.

"Very."

The tires crackled over the pavement and the car moved toward the small lot in front of the building. Oliver moved the car into park and glanced down at his watch nervously before undoing his seatbelt.

Rebecca undid hers as well, hand gliding to the door handle and gently opening the door just enough to allow her to slink out. She stood next to her door, pulling at the hem of her skirt and smoothing the fabric over her legs. Oliver walked around the car to join her, and the pair walked to the heavy double doors together.

Oliver heaved the left door open and held it for Rebecca to pass through. She waited for him to enter the building before continuing down the hall. The door swung shut behind them ominously, the click of the lock finite and cold.

They walked together to the main nurse station to sign the usual waivers and collect visitor badges. An orderly emerged from behind the glass to escort them to Doctor Manuel's office, wordlessly motioning for them to follow.

A labyrinth of beige and mint green walls surrounded them as they went deeper and deeper into the building. The orderly finally stopped at a door with a gold-plated nameplate affixed to it. He tapped the door with his knuckles and turned the handle, opening the door just enough to poke his head inside. "He's not in yet, but you should be fine to wait for a few moments inside. He shouldn't be too long now."

The orderly opened the door wider for them and allowed them inside. Doctor Manuel's office had three chairs: a large wingback behind his desk and two armchairs in front of it. Rebecca and Oliver took their seats in the armchairs. As soon as they were seated, the orderly shut the door behind them, leaving the pair alone with more silence and the doctor's office. Rebecca let out a sigh.

"Did he say anything when he called you in?" she asked Oliver.

"Only that he wanted to see us as soon as we could come in. I have no idea if that's good or bad." Oliver ran a hand through his hair, forgetting about all the gel it had taken to tame it and not realizing the spiky mess that this simple action created.

Rebecca stared at the corner of the desk for a moment, as if trying to come up with the appropriate way to express how she was feeling. She held her tongue though, pushing off the chair and moving toward one of three large bookshelves lining Doctor Manuel's office.

The shelves held more than books; there were the

expected volumes about mental conditions, psychoanalysis and the like, but there were also sculptures and wooden carvings, as well as the constructed skeletons of a mouse, a sparrow and a bat. Rebecca grimaced and returned to her chair. "I hate it here," she hissed.

"I'm sure most sane people do, and probably most of the insane people here as well also," Oliver whispered back.

The door opened as he finished saying this and Doctor Manuel entered the room. A balding man in his late 40's, Manuel looked more tired than most men his age, his eyes devoid of any sparkle. He moved toward his wingback, giving Rebecca and Oliver each a tight smile. "Thank you for coming in on such short notice," he said, "There's been quite the commotion downstairs today and I do apologize for keeping you waiting. Now, shall we get down to business?"

Oliver nodded stiffly. "Of course, Doctor Manuel."

"Alright then. I'm afraid I don't have much in the way of good news to share with you both today, however we do have a few options to choose from for treatment." Doctor Manuel paused, gauging their reactions.

"Go on," Rebecca murmured, barely breathing.

Doctor Manuel continued. "Exie is not responding to the drugs she was used to taking, this you already know. Unfortunately, the loss of her child and the... circumstances... under which she lost the baby are exacerbating her condition. Her paranoid delusions are giving way to full fledged schizophrenic episodes and the normal course of medication we've upgraded her to seems to have little effect on her."

"I thought she was doing better though? She seemed calm the last time we saw her. Almost back to her old self." Oliver seemed as if he was pleading with the doctor for this to be the case.

"Unfortunately her improvements over the past month are not to the extent where we are comfortable releasing her from our long term care facility. This is the reason I've called you in. Our treatment options right now will include Exie remaining at our facility for the time being, with a gradual move from inpatient to outpatient care. As it stands, OmegaGene Pharmaceuticals will cover her treatment up until she can be released. After that it could become quite expensive to keep her on many of the medications she is currently required to be on. There are a few options we could look at that would be more cost effective, such as putting a heavier emphasis on therapeutic counseling rather than medication so that in the long run heavy drugs won't be necessary, but it will be a very long time before she can be released, especially if she continues at her current pace."

"What are you trying to say?" Oliver sighed.

"It may be best in the long run to allow her to remain in the facility until she is fully recovered, gradually transferring her treatment from medical to psychiatric. It will be tricky, but it is the best option if you have any hope of supporting her treatment once she is released. I need you to understand though that this is not the fastest method, which would be a potent cocktail of medicine continued long after her release, possibly for the rest of her life if we were unable to wean her off of it safely."

"We'll do whatever we can for her. I just want her to

be healthy again."

Doctor Manuel nodded and pushed a pile of papers across his desk to Oliver. "I'll need you to sign these then."

Exie shivered in her room, despite the heat being turned on quite warm. They had begun the day with the group therapy, but it had quickly spiraled out of control. One patient had tried to trigger another, and a friend of the second patient had begun mauling the first. Before the orderlies could subdue them, it had become an all out brawl. In the end, everyone had gotten an extra dose of whatever pill to keep them calm.

She lay on the bed and stared at a spot on the wall where the pale blue paint was peeling to reveal a layer of white underneath. She wanted to pick at it, but she couldn't bring herself to get up. She wanted to uncover the white like she wanted to uncover the truth about her baby, but the medication they used to keep her calm kept her in a fog.

Rebecca stared through the glass hole in the door at Exie and sighed, turning to Doctor Manuel. "Would it be okay if we went in and talked with her?"

"I can get an orderly up to accompany you if you like. She's been quite tense lately."

"I think that's quite alright, Doctor. We've handled her through worse," Oliver cut in.

Doctor Manuel nodded opened the door for them. "If you do need assistance just press this button." He shoved a small black rectangle with a smaller circular button on it into Oliver's hand. Oliver nodded and shut the door behind him.

Exie sat bolt upright as the door jumped open. She couldn't quite tell if Rebecca and Oliver were real, the way they were dressed. She shrunk back against the wall.

Rebecca took the only seat in the room and Oliver sat on the bed, taking Exie's hand in his own. He was gentle with her as always, and he drew her close to him. He had always been tender, but a sadness had crept into their embraces that pained Rebecca to see.

"How have you been, Sweetheart?" Oliver murmured, kissing the top of Exie's head.

"Are you real?" Exie whispered, cuddling tighter into Oliver's chest.

He sighed. "Yes, I'm real."

She seemed content with this. "Have you found my baby yet? Have you stopped OmegaGene?"

"Exie, we've gone over this," Rebecca said gently, "You were there at her funeral."

"Not my baby."

Rebecca sighed. "Where is your baby then, Ex?"

"OmegaGene took her. Doctor Lewis took her to them and now she's gone." Exie was sobbing as she said this.

Oliver moved to comfort her. "Exie, I agree it is quite a coincidence that Doctor Lewis turned up dead a few days after your surgery, but you can't draw the two together. It's just paranoia."

Exie heaved a great sigh. "The nurse after asked me if I wanted to see my baby. She said she had seen Doctor Lewis leave the operating room with my living, breathing baby. She said my little girl would be up in the neonatal unit. Not that my little girl was dead."

"It was one nurse, Exie. She made an unfortunate mistake," Rebecca said, placing a hand on Exie's knee. Exie withdrew from her touch.

"Is it such an unfortunate mistake that she 'killed' herself after they put her on administrative leave? Too many coincidences! All the loose ends taken care of! Mark me off as crazy; I'm crossed out too!" Exie screeched, tearing out of Oliver's hold. Oliver pushed the button.

Exie lunged at Rebecca, but Rebecca put her arms around Exie tightly, restricting her movement. Rebecca whispered into her ear, "If what you're saying is true, you need to stay calm so we can get you out." Exie went slack.

An orderly rushed in. "Is everything alright?"

"We're leaving now and we just wanted to make sure someone was here when we left her," Oliver said, getting up from where he was seated.

The orderly nodded. "Very good."

Rebecca released Exie from the hug-like position, and Oliver scooped her up in a very real hug, kissing her head again tenderly. "I love you very much, my darling."

Another orderly saw them back out through the maze of the hospital, leading them to the main desk where they turned in their visitor badges. They made their way then back to the car, Rebecca sliding into the passenger side and Oliver back into the driver's seat. He pulled the car to the gates, and this time they opened without hesitation.

Rebecca looked at him. "It's hard on you, isn't it? Having to lie to her."

Oliver nodded. "It's the part she needs to play for now though. If they know we think she's telling the truth, we're all as good as dead."

"What are we going to do?" Rebecca sighed, sinking into her seat.

"The only thing we can do, Becca. Don't stop looking until we find my daughter and take down OmegaGene."

ReMeRS

- SARAH THOMPSON -

"Hey, Chase! Go long!" a young boy shouted; and the muscle-bound teen obliged.

Chase Davies dropped his gym bag and pulled off his letterman jacket to reveal a pair of grease stained coveralls underneath. He threw his arms in the air as he ran down the sidewalk away from the boy.

"I'm open! Toss it here, kid!" Chase grinned as he watched the ball fly through the air. He had to backpedal to get to the ball as it headed for the ground.

The kid stood in awe as the 6'3", 240lb teen made the catch look dramatic and jogged back toward him. "Here you go. You going to be a quarterback someday or what?"

Chase was not your average seventeen-year-old with a part time job at the Stoneville gas station. He was the star quarterback of the Robert Kennedy High School Bulldogs football team and well on his way to a full athletic scholarship. Even from an early age, he'd taken pride in maintaining his body, choosing to spend his spare time at Building Bodies, his neighborhood gym.

The kid's face flushed with pride as he accepted the

football. "You bet! I'm going to grow up to be as good a player as you, I swear it." Chase ruffled his hair before picking up his bag and waving at the boy.

He was the envy of many other boys his age and the dream of many teenage girls. They swooned when he walked by and erupted in giggles when he flashed them just a tiny smile. But Chase had only one girl on his mind, and Shaun St. Croix only had eyes for him.

She wasn't the head cheerleader, or the most popular girl in school, but he knew he loved her from the first moment he set eyes on her on their first day of kindergarten. If everything went as planned that weekend, he was going to ask her to marry him. He had saved every penny from his job at the garage to buy her a ring. Chase couldn't imagine leaving Shaun behind when he went to college and he knew the only way she would go with him was if they were married.

Shaun was waiting for him when he arrived at the field. He was surprised; Shaun never came to see him before the game, only for the celebration afterward.

"Baby, what are you doing here? You're going to throw off my routine." Even though he was a little irritated at the interruption, he still smiled and hugged her.

Chase rested his chin on top of her light brown hair. She was almost a foot shorter than him and a mere 105lbs. He often joked that his gym bag was bigger than she was. Shaun was almost his complete opposite in every way, but he loved her all the more for it. She was obsessed with fashion and modeled her wardrobe after the weekly *People* magazine cover. It was the only thing about her that bothered Chase.

She reached up and ran her fingers through his short brown hair and felt her heart pick up speed as she looked into his eyes, so dark they were almost black. They were a stark contrast to her deep blue eyes.

"I'm sorry. I've had the worst feeling all day, like something was wrong." She pulled back to look in his eyes. "I had to see you, to make sure you were all right."

"Of course I'm all right. You know how big and strong I am. What could happen to me?" Chase chuckled.

"I knew I was worried for nothing. Please don't be mad, baby; I had to see you. I couldn't get past the feeling in my gut that it was my last chance."

Chase hugged her again. "Don't be silly, everything is fine. Now, I have to go... I have to get ready for the game."

They were just two weeks away from graduation and hours away from the biggest football game of his life, the state final. Scouts from every school on the west coast would be at the game and he knew he'd have his pick when they defeated the Martin Luther King High Wizards.

Shaun was reluctant to let him go, but smiled weakly and watched him head toward the locker room. He tossed her his jacket and she wrapped her arms around it, taking in the scent of his Axe cologne she had given him on his birthday the previous month.

Chase adjusted his gym bag on his shoulder and started to jog away, stopping on the sidewalk in front of the stadium to wave at her before disappearing from her sight. Shaun was more anxious then ever as she watched the glass door close behind him. She tried to shake off the feeling of dread and headed to meet the girls to find their seats for the next two hours.

With less than two minutes on the clock, Kennedy High was leading by three. The Wizards had the ball on the Bulldog's fifteen-yard line on third down and Chase knew everyone was depending on him to stop them in their tracks and carry his squad to the biggest victory of their lives. He heard the call and watched the snap as though everything was happening in slow motion, but when his feet started to move, they knew exactly what to do.

He pushed through the offensive linemen as though they were children and felt his feet leave the ground as he jumped for the quarterback. The ball came loose and Chase looked up as one of his teammates picked it up and headed back down the field, all the way to the end zone.

He scrambled to his feet and joined the rest of the Bulldogs as they rushed the field in triumph. They had done it! *He* had done it, and now the rest of his life was falling into place. Chase turned his focus towards the crowd in search of Shaun in her regular seat. He pointed to her as he and another teammate were lifted into the air and carried across the field.

There was supposed to be a blowout party after the game, but Chase couldn't bring himself to leave the locker room when the rest of the boys were heading out.

"I'll catch up with you guys. I just need a minute to pack things up here." He looked around the room, slowly placing his gear into his gym bag. He paused as he carefully folded his grass-stained jersey and zipped the bag shut.

This would be the last time he took off his high school uniform and walked out of this locker room and he wanted to remember every minute. Chase kept looking back over his shoulder at the posters on the wall as he exited the stadium and stepped onto the road. It was that moment that his life changed forever, but not in the way he expected it would.

It's funny how life can throw you a curveball sometimes. One minute, Chase was walking down the road, focused on his past and his memories; the next he was opening his eyes in a strange room.

When Chase opened his eyes, he was staring into a bright florescent ceiling light. He couldn't figure out where he was or how he had gotten there, but the last thing he remembered was his long look back at the doors of the stadium. He wanted to speak, to cry out, but it seemed he couldn't remember how. Chase tried to look down at his body, to see that he really was moving, that his mind wasn't playing tricks on him. He was immobilized, unable to even lift his head.

It was then he saw a shadow in the glare of the lights above him.

"Don't try to move. I'm Doctor Maxwell Steinberg, and you've had a terrible accident."

Chase saw the shadow move closer and suddenly he was moving – actually, the bed was moving – so he could see the man beside him. Dr. Steinberg looked like something out of a science fiction movie. Although his face appeared human, his arms seemed to be made of metal and rubber, and his neck was covered on one side by a series of flashing lights. He raised his hand to adjust the mechanism that was keeping the teen in place and Chase saw that he had only three regular fingers. The other two were covered in a thin metal, almost robotic.

Chase was starting to panic. Nothing made sense. Steinberg pressed a button on the device and Chase could suddenly speak.

"Where am I? What am I doing here? What happened to me?" The questions poured out of him like water.

"Slow down, son. One question at a time." Steinberg smiled.

"Wh-wh-where am I? Am I still in Stoneville?" Chase stammered.

"You are at the Walter Reed Army Medical Centre in Washington."

"What am I doing here?"

"Well, there was an accident. You were brought here after the doctors in New York told your father there was no hope. Do you remember anything about what happened?"

Chase stared blankly at the ceiling. "We won State and I was leaving for the celebration party. Then I woke up here, just now."

Steinberg's face fell. "And that's it? You don't remember anything about the past three weeks?"

Chase studied the man's face. He could see every blemish, every mark on his skin as though he was watching television in high definition. His stomach started to roll as he mulled over and tried to process what the doctor had said.

"Just walking out of the stadium and waking up here a few minutes ago."

"You don't remember anything about the accident? Or the surgeries that you've been through?" Steinberg brushed his fingers along his own jaw line, making the hair on the back of Chase's neck stand on end. "What about the times when you were awake before today?"

Chase's confusion was starting to turn into panic. "What do you mean three weeks? How long has it been since the night of the game?" Chase began to struggle against the device that was keeping his body still.

"Don't fight it or I will have to sedate you again, and we really don't want to do that."

Chase took several deep breaths. He could feel the tears starting to build in his eyes. "You have to tell me, Doc. Is there some reason that I can't move? What are you talking about, an accident?"

"The answers will come in time, Chase. But know that you're going to be fine. You will never be the boy you were again and things have changed for you, but you will walk out of here." Steinberg turned toward the door. "I will be back shortly and then we can talk about the accident."

Chase was exhausted. In spite of all his questions and all his confusion – or, perhaps, because of them – he found himself falling into sleep. He tried to fight it, but he couldn't keep his eyes from closing.

General Davies knew he had to move quickly if he was going to save his son while making sure others believe he'd been killed. He picked up the phone and dialed John

Hopkins Specialty Military Division directly.

"Jack, it's Davies. I need to make an arrangement. There's been an accident."

Chase awoke as someone approached the door. Even though he'd been asleep, he could hear the footsteps coming down the hall, and somehow recognized that they were coming towards him. As they neared, he could hear something he thought might be a second heartbeat above his own; he heard each of the stranger's breaths and felt their calm.

He wasn't surprised when Steinberg opened the door.

Steinberg studied Chase's reaction as he crossed the room. "I see it's starting to kick in, then."

Chase was still immobilized but instinctively tried to look to where the voice had come from. "What do you mean 'it's kicked in'?"

"In time, my boy. Everything will make sense in time. First, I promised you that we could talk about the accident." Steinberg pulled a chair in front of Chase and sat down. "Still no memories of what happened that night?"

Chase closed his eyes and concentrated. "I remember I was cold. There was a flash and I felt very cold."

"Good. Then things are starting to come back." Steinberg noted something on his chart.

"I need to know what happened. You need to tell me." Chase could hear every hair move as the doctor ran his hands along the scruff that had formed on his chin.

"It would be better if you could remember yourself,

but time is running short, so I'll tell you what we know." Steinberg adjusted Chase's bed and shifted his chair closer to the teen.

"There was an explosion. The police are still working on the details, but it appears there was a leak in the gas line and when the furnace ignited, it lit the gas. You're lucky to be alive, son. More than that, if you weren't brought here when you were, you wouldn't be."

"So, is that why I can't move, or see my body? Was I burned? What happened?" As the adrenaline pumped through his veins, Chase could almost feel his senses become more alert. The second heartbeat was louder now; the doctor's breathing a rhythmic sound that he was subconsciously counting.

"It was worse than that. Metal from the sign above the doors was propelled from the building, slicing off your legs just above the knees." Steinberg looked away as he recounted the incident.

"But I can feel my legs, I can move my toes. How is that possible?"

"There is more and I will explain everything. Be patient." Steinberg made another note on his chart. "Another piece of the metal hit your neck, and brick from the building shattered the bones in your arms. They rushed you to Johns Hopkins, but the doctors told your father there was nothing that could be done. If you lived, you may never wake up again. That is when he called us."

"Why did he send me to you? How is this place any different or better?"

"This is a military installation. We don't follow just the conventional idea of medicine here, which I imagine you have realized after your first impression of me." He rotated his hands to show where the metal joined the skin and revealed a plate that not only replaced his fingers, but also extended up his arm.

"We have technology that is not available to the public, things that can rebuild almost any man, and because of your background you were a prime candidate for the program. But now that you are here, you cannot return to your old life." Steinberg finally looked back up at Chase.

It took a few seconds for it to register, but slowly, Chase began to understand what Steinberg was saying. "But... my friends... my scholarship..." he stammered. And then: "Shaun! Oh God, Shaun! I was going to ask her to marry me! Will they even know that I'm still alive?" Tears started to stream down his face – an odd feeling considering he still couldn't move most of his body.

"Only your father knows that you survived the blast. The rest will be told that you died in hospital from your injuries. They will move on, and as time goes on, the changes that you are already feeling will allow you to put them out of your mind and move on with your new life, with REMERS."

"With who?" he questioned, feeling panicked. "I just want to go home, back to how things were before. I don't even care if I can't play football again. Please, just let me go home!" he begged, the helplessness of his situation becoming apparent.

"I'm sorry, I really am, Chase. But by saving your life, the decision has already been made. REMERS is the Robotically Enhanced Military Expert Recon Squad. You will be part of a team of eight that live together, and work together: a family. I know it will take time, but you will come to terms with everything."

"Robotically enhanced *what*!? I'm not any kind of enhanced!" Chase began to struggle against his restraint. "*Let me out of here!*" he screamed.

"I'm afraid you are. It was the only way to save you." Steinberg pulled a full-length mirror from the corner so Chase could, for the first time since the accident, see himself.

Chase slowly shifted his gaze up and down, taking the time to calm down. Where his knees once were had been replaced by two pieces of steel, each with a panel on the outside and a green flashing light above it. One side had another panel where it joined the thigh and the other had a series of buttons in the same place. His feet and thighs seemed to be his own, as did his hands. Above his hands, his right elbow was also wrapped in a kind of metal, but he could see the veins of his familiar bicep. There were three buttons along the forearm, one red, one green and one yellow. Chase couldn't help but flash to the traffic lights that were ahead of him just before the explosion.

On the left arm, the metal extended from his forearm to his neck and across his chest to the centre of his sternum. There were more panels and buttons on his one, and a place on the arm that seemed to take an attachment. His face was the same as it has always been. Same dark hair, same strong jaw but a new scar below his right eye and one just over his left ear, no doubt souvenirs of the blast.

"I'm not even a man anymore," he breathed. The longer he stared at his reflection, the higher his voice rose. "What have you people done to me? What am I supposed to be now? Robocop or some shit?" Chase watched his reflection as he wiggled his fingers and toes, flexed the muscles in his stomach, and rotated his wrists.

"No, but you are among the US Army elite. You have joined special ops. A job that will take you places that you never thought possible. Allow you to see things that you never would have dreamed. "

Chase sobbed a little under his breath. "But I'm not a soldier. I have no training. I don't know how to do any of this."

"Oh, but you do! You have already started to take in the programming and I must say you are quicker than the others." Steinberg moved toward the window and stared through the glass. "Yes, my boy, much quicker than the others. You can already hear my heartbeat. You are already determining how close I am based on my breathing. I believe you are going to be among the elite of the elite son."

Chase closed his eyes for a moment and breathed. He couldn't deny what Steinberg was saying; he could hear the doctor's heartbeat and breathing. If that was true, then the rest must have been as well. And if that was the case, then… "So, are you part of this team, these REMERS? I mean, you seem to be as robotic as I am…"

"I'm afraid not. Although I do have enhancements, I am only the doctor that works to save those that will become members of the squad. I am far too old to be effective in the field or to do the type of tasks that you will be asked to complete. You'll meet them all soon enough, but for now, get some sleep. When you wake, you'll be released from the restraint and taught about the robotics that have been used to save you."

"What about my father? When can I see him?"

"Once you are able to function with your new enhancements and it's deemed safe, General Davies will be brought to see you. Now rest. You are going to need it." Steinberg pressed a button on his chest and the room fell dark.

Chase's mind was racing. Everyone he had ever known thought he was dead, aside from his father, and everything he had ever wanted or dreamed about was now gone. How was he supposed to sleep after his whole life had been taken from him? The tears started to flow again, thick and fast, and before he knew it, Chase drifted to sleep, cheeks damp with tear-tracks.

General Davies did his best to appear as the grieving father while he made the arrangements. The funeral home was informed that the casket would arrive already sealed due to the amount of trauma the explosion had caused.

He had made arrangements for the body of a John Doe, burned beyond recognition in a gas fire, to be placed in the casket in case it should be accidentally opened. Everything was planned, down to the last detail, within the first twenty-four hours.

Davies made all the expected appearances during the wake and had even arranged for a number of military personnel to take part in the funeral. It wasn't standard practice to hold a military funeral for a civilian, but for the son of the General, an exception was made.

He had purposely avoided Shaun and the rest of the

St. Croix family throughout the week. He didn't need their sympathy and he couldn't bear to face Shaun. He had watched her grow up from a little girl and knew how attached she was to his son. The fact that his decision would cause her so much pain hurt him worst of all.

Davies shuddered thinking about it. There was only one gesture he could make, but if would have to wait until after the funeral.

Shaun spent the three days before the funeral in denial. She spoke about Chase as though he was simply gone away for the weekend. She spent her evenings at the wake, but acted like it was for a great uncle she had never met, rather than the boy she thought she would spend the rest of her life with.

She laughed and chatted with friends that came to pay their respects and could easily ignore the truth, as it was a closed casket. She also ignored the wall of photos of Chase that had been carefully selected by Shaun – who had pretended it was for the yearbook – and members of the football team hanging next to a towering display of flowers. She was terrified they would somehow make it real.

When the sun came up on the day of the funeral, Shaun was still lying awake. She had spent the entire night sitting on her bed with a framed photo of Chase in his football uniform. She could still see the twinkle of his eyes as he smiled, or at least she could imagine it.

Denis St. Croix knocked lightly on his daughter's door, stirring her back to reality. "Shaun, honey, you need to get ready. It's almost time to go to the church."

Shaun wiped a tear from her cheek and swallowed hard before she could manage a response. "Thanks, Dad. I'll be down in a few."

Shaun took several deep breaths before dutifully donning her funeral attire, slowly accepting that Chase's death was real. It took all of her energy just to walk down the aisle of the church behind the casket and take her seat. She was more zombie than person, barely hearing a word said during the service, instead staring blankly at the priest and repeating the words in tandem with the rest of the congregation without absorbing anything happening around her.

She didn't remember the drive to the cemetery and only became aware of the change in her surroundings when four men in full military uniform began to fire blank rounds into the sky. She vaguely remembered the same four men carrying the casket through the church.

Shaun noticed that General Davies didn't flinch like most of the crowd at the sound of the gunfire and wondered how he had been handling the loss of his son. He walked toward her once it was over and placed his arm around her shoulders.

"You don't have to be so strong, you know." The General pulled Shaun's head to his chest. He hated what this was doing to her. He hated even more that he could make all of her pain go away by telling her the truth. In some way, he decided, her knowing would actually be more painful. Davies knew that at least this way, she would eventually be able to get on with her life.

Shaun let the tears flow freely now. She pressed her

face into Davies' chest and took the first step to accepting that at just seventeen she had lost the love of her life. When she finally started to pull herself together, she realized there were the only two still standing at the grave. She vaguely wondered where her parents had gone and if the general had said anything to them.

She wiped her face with a tissue General Davies had pulled from his pocket. "Thank you..." Her voice trailed off as she looked into his face. He was an older, more distinguished version of Chase. She imagined he would have grown up to look a lot like his father. Shaun's words stuck in her throat at the idea. "I love him so much... I don't, I just don't know what I'm going to do now."

"It's going to be alright. I have something in the house for you. Something I know Chase would have wanted you to have." Davies brushed the hair out of her face and produced another tissue from the jacket pocket of his dress uniform. "When you're ready, drop by and see me."

It was the sound of crumpling paper that woke him, then footsteps moving down the hall. He could hear six – no, seven – distinct heartbeats coming toward his room. He couldn't turn to see them in the doorway, but Chase figured by the weight of the footsteps that the men coming into his room were members of the REMERS.

The door creaked open and one of the men approached his bed, pressed a button on the side of his neck and Chase knew that he'd been released from the restraint. He felt his body relax as he was finally able to move any way he pleased.

He looked up at the doctor who was making notes on his pad about Chase's reactions. "I take it I'm going to meet the other team members today?"

Dr. Steinberg stopped his scribbling and gave Chase a confused look. He had assumed the boy was asleep when he first entered the room. "That just might be in the game plan. We'll see after I complete a few tests."

"Oh, I just figured it must be the six guys outside in the hall. No one else has come in here since I was awake. It's been so quiet, but in some ways so loud at the same time." Chase was lost in thought about how he could explain what he meant.

"Like, I notice sounds that didn't before, but none of the things I hear sound quite familiar. Does that make sense?"

"I understand. Excellent. Absolutely perfect." Steinberg made one final note before moving back toward the door.

Chase took the opportunity to stretch each of his limbs individually and look out the window. When he turned back to the door, Dr. Steinberg was entering with six men, all with similar enhancements, and all with the same scar over their left ear.

"Get up, son. Today is the first day of the rest of your life." Two of the squad members approached the bed and lifted Chase to his feet.

He struggled to stay standing with the weight of the metal pressing down on his spine. The taller of the two men beside him stepped back and scratched his chin. "He's quicker than most. I bet he even knew how many of us were coming."

Chase nodded, still fighting to remain on his feet.

The man extended his hand to Chase. "I'm your squadron leader, Captain Bradley Daniels, but you can refer to me as Trip."

Trip was even taller than Chase, at least 6'5", and with his robotics he probably weighed at least twice as much as him. His entire upper body was a frame of metal, although his legs seemed to be completely human. The breastplate extended up through his neck and ended just below the base of his skull.

"How I came to be here is probably the stupidest of all stories. I dove off a waterfall on a dare. Something I had done a hundred times before near my hometown, but I had just signed up for basic training and on our first weekend leave the boys in my unit and I decided to go swimming." Trip hung his head.

"So, for a ten dollar bet I took the jump. I thought I had judged it right, but I was a few inches off, came straight down on a rock. Broke my neck and crushed the vertebrae in my back. I was already in the army, so I wound up here. Like I said, it was stupid..." he drifted off, his eyes staring into the distance for a moment before he forcefully closed them. "Anyway."

He motioned to the man standing beside him. "Lieutenant Andrew Vaders."

Vaders stepped toward Chase. "The boys around here just call me Rock."

Chase couldn't help but think that Rock was a very appropriate name. Vaders was the shortest of all the men on the team, but made up for his stature in sheer size and brute strength. When he folded his arms across his chest, he appeared as just a large black mass wearing silver shoulder pads. Rock also had a metal plate surrounding his mid-section and one of his legs had been replaced by a robotic limb.

"I was regular army too. Served three tours in Iraq, but as far as the world is concerned, I never made it back from the last one." Rock dropped his arms to his sides and pulled his shoulders back. "Got hit by an IED. My unit was patrolling an area outside of Kandahar when we ran into militants. We turned to retreat back toward the base and the next thing I knew, I woke up here."

Trip spoke up again. "Next to Rock is Sergeant Tom Delaney, we call him Stoic or Stow. He rarely speaks, or even does more than acknowledge your presence. Beside him is his brother, Sergeant William 'Tiny' Delaney."

The next man in line then stepped forward. Compared to the muscular physiques of the other men, he was quite thin. Chase almost laughed when the thought crossed his mind that he looked a little like a Starship Trooper. He wore a metal helmet, but it was obviously molded to his head. There were a number of what looked like disc drives on one side and red and green flashing lights on the other. His left forearm had been replaced, but the rest of his body was not enhanced.

"Lieutenant James Crocket, but the boys call me Jiminy Cricket, like the conscious in Pinocchio, you know? And the woman over here is Commander Rachel Tyrell."

"You can call me Ty, soldier. Another thing, although we all have a rank around here, the only difference that makes is our pay grade. In this unit, everyone is the same."

Chase was finally standing without a struggle and even managed to take a step forward to shake hands with his new family. "Hey, doc, I thought you told me there would be eight of us?"

Rock perked up. "Captain George Munro is in for retrofit. You'll meet him in a couple of days. Now, kid, let's teach you about your new equipment."

In the weeks after the funeral, Shaun slipped further away from the rest of the world. Her parents had to beg for her to pull herself out of bed in the morning, but some days were harder than others and she could barely roll over to face them.

On the days she did emerge from her room, her friends uttered empty words about moving on that bounced around in her head. 'You're young, you need to pull yourself together and start rebuilding your life.' 'I know you loved him, but in ten years he'll be a distant memory.'

Every time she walked past what remained of the stadium, the gas station where he had worked, or the park where he had kissed her for the first time, she thought about Chase. The last couple of weeks of school, she could almost see him smiling at her in front of her locker between classes, or sitting next to her, his tongue pushed out of the side of his mouth in concentration, taking notes during math.

The things that once gave her so much joy now made her stomach roll. She couldn't bring herself to open her guitar case, as she knew the photo of them, taken at the junior prom, would be staring her in the face: Chase, in the awful plaid jacket she had begged him not to wear, clashing badly with her striped dress.

To those around her, Shaun began to look like a ghost. She'd grown pale and her cheeks were slightly gaunt after weeks of barely eating. Her eyes had consistent black circles from a lack of sleep despite the eighteen hours a day she was spending in bed.

No matter what anyone said, Shaun just couldn't accept the fact that he was dead. One month to the day after the accident, Shaun stumbled her way through the Stoneville graveyard before collapsing in front of the newly erected headstone. She slowly traced her finger over the words... *Davies, Chase. Taken too soon. Forever loved.*

Shaun's anger, which had been overwhelmed by her grief, began to take over. It was as though she was watching from the outside as her hands tore at the grass that was now beginning to grow strong in from of the stone. She was almost shocked as she realized she was banging her fists against the ground and the loud wail echoing in her ears was actually coming from her mouth.

Her father finally found her. It was dark when he noticed the reflectors on her sneakers as she rocked back and forth, her knees pulled tight to her chest. When she hadn't come home for supper, her family had become concerned and started the search at sunset.

Dennis St. Croix wasn't a very big man, just a little more than 5'7 and a mere 120lbs, but he scooped his daughter up into his arms and carried her twelve blocks to the community hospital. She was immediately admitted under twenty-four-hour evaluation.

It was a grueling two weeks that Chase spent relearning to use his body, or what was left of it, and learning about the tools that came along with his new permanent outfit. Each of the compartments in his legs carried construction tools or bomb creation materials, while those in his arms were for ammunition and small arms. The attachment on his left arm would allow him to sync his mind to a computer or input device and retrieve or send data, just by thinking it.

It didn't take long before he had full control of the enhancements that allowed him to be one step above the average soldier.

He was even getting used to the sound of each individual heartbeat and learning to recognize who was coming based on its rhythm, and how fast they were moving based on their speed.

It wasn't only his hearing that had improved. Chase could see better than he imagined any normal person should be able to and he even had moments when it felt like his eyes were zooming in on particular details of a piece of clothing or a word on a page.

His thoughts moved quicker and he was able to process more information in a split second than he believed possible in a lifetime. He knew things that he couldn't explain, had goals he didn't understand, and a new image of his life. He still knew who he was, could still keep those dreams alive, but they were now secondary to the mission. It was as though he was, for the first time, truly awake and alive.

By the end of the two weeks, Chase understood his reflection in the mirror, and instead of the horror he'd first felt, he could look at himself with pride. This new man had a purpose that the old Chase could never have imagined, and it was a pure and right purpose.

The final phase of his training was a chance to learn why the REMERS were formed and what his job would be.

He felt a little like he was back in high school, sitting in a specially designed desk with Commander Tyrell standing in front of him, a blackboard behind her. There was a sense of familiarity about it that put Chase more at ease than he had been since he arrived at the hospital. Even with the weight of his body's new machinery, he felt comfortable in the learning environment.

Chase took a good look at Ty. She appeared to be of Hispanic background with long dark hair and a dark complexion. He didn't see many enhancements on her body aside from her replaced right bicep, but when she turned to the blackboard he could see lights on her back flashing through her white shirt.

"The REMERS were started in 2001 after the 9/11 attacks, but it soon became obvious there was a much bigger threat to the United States than any terrorist faction.

"The Russian government created their own version of the super soldier. They started work on the project shortly after World War II, but it got out of control and they weren't able to control the men. You see, they weren't just enhanced like we are, they were mutated to be incredibly strong, fast and intelligent." Ty tossed a picture on the desk in front of Chase.

The men were disfigured almost beyond recognition as human beings, with enlarged craniums jutting out at the forehead, protruding almost the length of the bib on a baseball cap. Their muscle structures were far too large for their bones, hiding the joints and making it seem as though the men had beer bellies, even though it was firm and ripped.

"Although they don't make for a pretty picture, the men decided they should be doing bigger things than protecting the Russian agenda and destroyed the military installation where they were being housed before fleeing to somewhere near the North Pole."

Ty pointed to the picture on the desk. "The man you are looking at is the leader of the group. He wants to find a way to destroy western society and turn every man, woman, and child into one of them, what he believes to be the next logical step in human evolution. So far, we have only been able to slow down their plan."

"So, what is it that we're supposed to do to stop them?" Chase asked as he continued to study the grizzly image before him.

"Now that the team is complete, we will be heading off to find their hideout, and destroy their facility before it can destroy us." Ty placed her hand on Chase's shoulder and pressed down. "So how does it feel, kid? To know that the weight of the world is now resting on your shoulders?"

"Well, I know one thing, Ty – if it's as heavy as you, we're going to have to take care of these guys in a hurry." Chase laughed. He hadn't really grasped the magnitude of what was happening. It was still a little like a dream.

"It's like she's gone. I look at her and talk to her, but she looks right through me," Dennis said, his voice conveying his helplessness. Since Shaun had been admitted, he'd spent most of his free time at the hospital. The lack of sleep was causing the normally well-put-together man to become increasingly disheveled. He was fidgeting in his chair and nervously picking at the button on his shirtsleeve as he spoke with Shaun's doctor.

"Mr. St. Croix, I really believe the best thing for your daughter is to get her regulated on medication and home with family." The doctor leaned back in his chair and folded his hands over his protruding belly. "Not everyone deals with grief in the same way. You need to be patient. It's going to take some time, but she will come around."

Dennis had always been a firm believer in the idea that anti-depressants and other drugs like the ones they wanted to give Shaun were a waste of time and that there were better ways to deal with being sad. He had refused to allow them to medicate her, aside from sleeping pills since she had been admitted, and she had only slipped further away.

He shifted nervously and bushed his hand through his hair. There was nothing more he could do. "Okay. Do whatever you need to. Just give me my little girl back."

The next morning, the team gathered on the airstrip for mission training. At the front of the plane, Chase saw a man he didn't recognize and heard a heartbeat that he had not heard before making its way toward him. Before he could even process the thought, the man was at his side with his hand extended.

"George Munro, but they call me Quick. It's a pleasure to finally meet you, Davies. I understand you're the first to know how many men were headed for your room before the training. Can't wait to see what you're capable of in the field." Chase shook his hand and the two moved to the back of the Squad as they boarded the plane.

When they stepped off the plane hours later, nothing but ice surrounded the eight members of the REMERS. For some reason, Chase couldn't stop thinking about Shaun. It might have been from the first silent and quiet time he'd really had since he'd woken up, as the other REMERS had decided to doze or drift off in thought on the flight over. Alone in his thoughts, Chase was finally able to rest and consider what he'd left behind... But instead of feeling bitter about his lost limbs or possibilities, all he could think about was Shaun. Her shy smile and the way it felt when she pressed her lips to his. He thought about their first time on the night of the junior prom. The way her body felt close to his, the nervousness he felt with every touch. He could still remember the way her breath had felt on his neck and chest as she drifted off to sleep. There had been many more nights like that one to follow.

He was brought back to reality by the sound of a single gunshot. "Listen up, folks. This is where it all begins. We have set up a course that will allow you to face anything that may get in your way when we head off on our mission." Quick dropped his weapon to use as a crutch.

His enhancements were all from the waist down, the

total replacement of both legs with several areas that could take on attachments on each side. By the way he moved, Chase would have thought there were springs in his feet. He seemed to bounce from one place to the next with little or no effort, and despite being at least ten years older than the other members of the team, he could run circles around them.

"I want you all to pair off and prepare for the first phase of our training." Quick turned his back to the group.

Trip jogged over to join the teen. "So, Chase, looks like you need a buddy."

"Yeah, I guess so." Chase was focused on Ty. "So, I never did find out about Ty. How did she come to be here?"

"She was special ops. They were on a classified mission that went horribly wrong and she was the only one that made it out alive. That's all anyone knows about it, but some of the guys think that it was the first action against the mutants. Now, kid, time to get focused on the job at hand." Trip picked up a pack and tossed it to Chase before grabbing one for himself.

"REMERS, make sure you're tuned into your auto communicators." Trip tapped at the scar above his left ear. "Everyone has a target, so head out."

With the order given, the teams headed off in four different directions, all toward a wooded area at the edge of their range of sight.

It took close to two days of training exercises, but by the end each team could complete any aspect of their mission, and Chase truly believed that no average man would be able to deal with what the mutants could throw at them. He was exhausted when the plane finally arrived to take them back to the base, but he also felt as though he was finally prepared for what the team would face.

When Chase woke the next morning, his father greeted him at the door to his barracks. Chase blinked, wondering for a moment if he was still asleep and dreaming, but his father's image didn't go away. When his father began to frown, the peace that Chase had reached yesterday shattered into a cacophony of emotions.

"I'm not sure if I even want to see you," he whispered, unable to raise his voice any higher. He turned to walk away, but his father grabbed him by the shoulder.

"Now, Chase, you know that's not true." General Davies set his shoulders and placed his cap under his arm. He was just a little shorter than his son, but just as well built. Chase noticed the bald spot on the crown of his head was just a little bigger than the last time he had seen his father and suddenly understood how much time had passed since he'd lost his life.

He was angry. Angry and hurt and betrayed. "What did you do to me, Dad?! Why did you decide that this was the right choice for me?" Chase could feel a single tear as it trickled down his cheek.

"I've lost everything! How am I going to live without Shaun? You knew how much she meant to me. I was going to ask her to marry me; did you know that?" He started to sob uncontrollably.

General Davies moved to put his arms around his son, but couldn't bring himself to hold him, flinching as he touched the robotics that now covered Chase's body. Chase noticed and it just made the hurt deeper. "I couldn't let you go," General Davies admitted. Tears now started to flow from his eyes as well. "I just couldn't stand the thought of outliving you, not when there was a way to save you."

"But I might as well be dead. I can't go back to my life – you're the only one who even knows I'm alive. How is this living?" Chase pushed his father away with his last statement.

"I'm not sure if I should apologize to you or even beg you for forgiveness, but there's nothing else that I can say." Davies turned away from Chase. "I suppose I never put much thought into what you would want... other than to be alive."

"Well, Dad, little good it does me if I'm forced to live out my life as a freak." Chase turned and walked away from his father, but stopped several feet from the door. He thought about his father, still crying behind him and the only link to his past life… and Shaun. He closed his eyes and choked out, "I forgive you."

He wasn't entirely sure it was the truth, but at least this way, maybe he could start to forgive him… Maybe by the time he returned from his mission, it would be true. He pushed open the door and headed to join the rest of the REMERS who were already gearing up to catch their flight to the North Pole.

It was a long couple of weeks for Shaun, sitting around her hospital room. Her friends took turns visiting in the afternoons to keep her company, but she felt it was more for their conscience than it was for her. She rarely felt like talking and even when one of the girls was making her best effort at keeping a discussion alive, Shaun couldn't keep up her end, often drifting off in her own thoughts. The once vibrant, fun-filled girl was a shadow of her former self.

When the doctors started giving her medication, things got a little better. She became more alert and even began asking to see certain people she had previously asked not to visit. Her father was relieved the day she requested coffee and a cheeseburger from the local diner, as Shaun had ordered the same thing every Thursday night since she was twelve (until recently, Dennis had made her have decaf). It was a weekly ritual between her and her father where they took some time to talk about their week. The evening always ended when Chase arrived to walk her home after work.

Dennis dropped her off at home before going to pick up their order. She'd been acting like her old self the entire day and he didn't want to ruin her mood with a memory of Chase. He had even avoided driving through the town square where they had played together as children for fear it would upset her.

After several days at home, Shaun decided she was ready to get things back to normal. The school had postponed the prom until August and she still had to make up some of her final exams if she wanted to graduate with her class.

She started attending tutoring sessions at the school with others in her grade that had also missed exams after the accident. It felt good to be back in the classroom with familiar faces. She was a little upset that most of her peers avoided conversations about anything other than school, but she tried to shrug it off. Shaun knew they would eventually come around and start acting like they always had around her. She also knew that some of these people were also suffering because they had lost Chase, but she didn't know how to bring it up to anyone. For now, it was as if Chase's missing presence was as physical as she was, with a bubble surrounding them like there had been when he was alive. She couldn't really blame the others for being afraid to pop it.

She was lost in thought on her walk home when she remembered that General Davies had asked her to stop by and see him. Shaun looked up to discover she had already absent-mindedly made her way to the Davies' house. She stood at the end of the driveway for a long time, just staring up at Chase's bedroom window. There were many fond memories there and despite how much better she had been feeling, she still wasn't sure that she was ready to go in.

She was about to walk away when General Davies pulled into the driveway beside her. Shaun bowed her head and took a deep breath as he ran up next to her and threw his arm around her shoulders. It was hard for her to look at him as Chase had looked so much like his father.

Davies guided her into the house and sat her down at the dining room table while he puttered around in the kitchen making coffee. He removed his coat and threw it over the back of his chair, loosening his tie before taking the seat across from her.

"How have you been? Your dad says you're coming around, but I told him I wouldn't believe it until I spoke to you myself"

"I'm alright, sir. Just trying to go on with the day to day. I know Chase would want me to." Shaun looked up as Davies stood quickly from the table.

"Speaking of things Chase would want, I know something he'd want you to have." Davies opened the hall closet and pulled out Chase's letterman jacket. He figured his son would be pissed that he gave it away, but it wasn't like he could ever fit into it again. Plus, she deserved to have something of his and he knew that once she accepted that he was gone, Shaun would be glad to have it.

She stood slowly, reaching out to take the coat from the General's outstretched hand. She pulled it to her chest and was immediately overwhelmed by his smell, still clinging to the material. She pressed her face to the crest on the back of the coat. "It's that mix of motor oil, grass, and sweaty gear he always had at the end of the day," she breathed.

She lifted her head and smiled at Davies despite herself. "Are you sure you want to part with this? He loved it more than anything."

"I'm sure. I don't think it should just sit in the closet and I know that it's going to be taken care of if it is with you."

Shaun finished her coffee and made her excuses to the General. She'd said she would be home right after school and she figured her father would be getting worried by this time. As she walked toward home, she pulled the jacket on and stuffed her hands in the pockets.

She felt a smooth box in one of the pockets and, thinking that maybe the Band-Aid solution would be best, quickly pulled it out and ripped the lid open. Immediately, she broke down into tears. It was an engagement ring… From its place in his pocket, it would seem he'd planned on asking her after the game. She'd had no idea that he planned to propose, but in some ways, it made it easier for her to make him a part of her memory. She had the one thing she always wanted from him, a symbol that her loved her more than anything.

It was blowing a gale when the aircraft carrying the team members arrived near the Pole. It could only hover near the ground and the REMERS were forced to jump about ten feet to the snow and ice below. They trekked about thirty kilometers in the storm before finding any sign of life, a shack that seemed out of place in the clear white of the surroundings. Stoic and Tiny, the Delaney brothers, were the first to make it to their designated shelter area.

Stoic was covered on most of his right side by robotics. His arm and leg had been replaced and a metal plate covered the right half of his head. A piece extended from the head plate and covered his eye, almost like a monocle, but also resembling the sight of a gun. Another extension surrounded his throat and jaw, with just a small opening at the front that was covered in what Chase thought might be coloured paper.

Tiny had similar enhancements on his left side, but lacked the eyepiece and his throat was bare. Both of his legs had been replaced below the knee and he had several compartments in his chest plate. He stood about six feet tall but hovered about an inch from the ground. Plumes of smoke were coming from his heels where the jet packs were located.

When they all reached the shack, Trip and Rock started pulling supplies out of the pack to settle the team in for the night.

"Hey, Tiny, can I ask you something?" Chase slid down the wall to sit beside him.

"Sure, kid. I don't see why not."

"Well, I was kinda wondering how you and your brother wound up here?"

"Well, we were just regular Joes like you before the accident. We were driving down the I-90 when a transport truck lost control. Stow did everything to avoid hitting the truck, even left the road a couple of times to miss the trailer as it swung around. When it finally came to a halt, we were over a bridge." Tiny looked over at his brother.

"Stow slammed on the breaks and we stopped just before riding under the truck, but unfortunately it was carrying a load of steel pipe. The pipes came loose and rammed through the centre of the car. Next thing I knew, we were waking up in an army medical facility. Stow's throat was severely damaged. The microchip you see in the centre of his plate allows him to speak. It's not his voice, though, so you won't hear it often."

Chase nodded. He was starting to realize that everyone here was like him. Not because they had been enhanced, but because while they may still be alive, they had lost their lives to the team. It was a hard pill for him to swallow but he was a little better off because at least he still had his father. He barely closed his eyes that night, waiting for the task of the day to come.

For most of the guys on the Squad, this was at least their fifth mission, but it was Chase's first. He could still hear the sound of the gunshots in his ears from the training the week before and he knew there was more to come. Chase listened to the other REMERS' breathing as they slept. He wanted to be sure he would recognize any of them, even as he knew there was no chance that he'd mistake them.

The sun was barely visible over the horizon when Trip woke the team. They quickly packed up their stuff and noted the location of the shelter in their built-in GPS before heading off in search of the facility. They were all at least a day away from the projected location of the facility. Chase was teamed with Jiminy on day two of their journey. The two men hadn't spent a lot of time together over the couple of months that Chase had been with the unit and had never been teamed up together before.

Chase wasn't sure why he'd been nicknamed after Pinocchio's conscious, but he figured a little insight into how he came to be on the team might fill in the blanks. They were making their way north what seemed like inches at a time to Chase, but he knew caution was the best way to survive to see another day.

Jiminy noticed that Chase continued to stare at him as they made their advance. "You're wondering how I got here, aren't you?"

"Maybe a little, but mostly I was wondering how you got your nickname."

"I had that long before I joined the REMERS," Jiminy laughed. "I was always the guy that said, 'I don't know fellas, we might get in trouble.' The one time that I didn't say it, I woke up half-man, half-robot. Weirdest feeling of my life. I wasn't much older that you when it happened. We had been out partying the day after everyone received their college acceptance letters and one of the boys was determined to drive us to the local tattoo parlor so we could all have our nicknames done before we headed our separate ways. A rite of passage, you know?" He paused as they moved to the forward position.

"It was one of those things. You spend the whole time you're in the car worried about the fact that the driver has been drinking. You make it to your destination alive, step off the curb and in front of an oncoming car." Jiminy shuffled his feet in the powder snow.

"I was the only one of my group of friends that wasn't going to college; I'd signed up for basic training the day before 'cause my mother wanted me to make something of my life. But one drunken step in the wrong direction and I was another dead and forgotten. The problem was, I wasn't dead, just a crumpled mass taken away by the army to the Walter Reid Medical Centre. That's it. I wish it was a better story."

"I guess we all got a second chance at life, whether we wanted it or not." Chase closed his eyes and remembered the way it felt the last time he took to the football field. Suddenly, he heard three unfamiliar heartbeats.

"Right you are... Whether we wanted it or not." Jiminy touched the side of his head where the communication chip was placed. "Get ready, kid. It looks like we have company."

Chase peeked over the snow bank they were huddled

behind and could see the three men, just average soldiers, standing together talking about fifty feet from their position. Trip motioned for the first team to move to a closer position and Chase saw the Delaney brother quickly shift nearer the soldiers. Chase ducked back behind the bank and held his breath in anticipation of what was to come. That was when he heard the explosion.

He immediately noticed the loss of one teammate's heartbeat, and the other became faint. Before he could lift his head to see what had happened, Jiminy pushed him down and gunfire erupted with flashes of black through the whiteness of the Pole. They remained very still and Chase listened intently as the faint heartbeat became non-existent.

This was it. They were headed into battle and after one wrong move they were already down two men. Chase was still lost in thought about his fallen teammates when he felt someone lift him to his feet.

"Come on, Chase. We have to move back. They called for reinforcements when the bomb went off and there're already a dozen men out there. We need to get to a better position." Chase stared open mouthed at Ty as she spoke. She glared when he didn't respond and shouted into his face, "MOVE, KID!"

Chase finally scrambled his feet in under him and followed the other REMERS as they moved to better cover. He had forgotten everything he was trained to do the moment he heard the explosion and could no longer focus on the heartbeats of Stoic and Tiny. Even though he'd only known them a short time, he felt closer to them, and the rest of the team members, than he'd ever felt to anyone but Shaun.

He supposed it had something to do with the fact that there were so few people that would ever be a part of his life again. It was kind of the way he had felt about her; that no one else would be part of his life the way that she was, that no one would ever understand him in that way, and that he would never give his heart away to another person in that fashion.

It wasn't quite the same, but he had given his heart to the members of the REMERS. They really had become his family in a way that he would have never believed possible before the explosion. He looked around at the soldiers and for the first time started to wonder if this was a suicide mission for them all. He knew that the loss of any of them would be a major blow, not only to the squad, but also to him personally.

Trip made a forward motion and whispered, "On my mark." He, Rock, and Ty attached rockets to their arm enhancements.

The wait was like an eternity for Chase. He still didn't have any idea what it would be like to actually fire his weapon at a living person and maybe even kill them, and he hadn't counted on having to take out regular men. He had somehow prepared himself to take out the mutants, but this was not in his game plan.

"And, fire salvo one." The three Squad members stood and fired the rockets, killing several of the soldiers and sending the others diving for cover. The rest of the REMERS then stood and started shooting at the sheltered locations with their automatic weapons.

Chase dropped back behind the cover when one of his

bullets penetrated a Russian soldier. His breathing was more rapid now and the adrenaline made it seem like the rest of the world moved in slow motion. He stood again and took another shot, killing another one of the soldiers. Suddenly Monroe was beside him and things were moving at a normal pace.

"I said I wanted to see what you were capable of, kid. I never could've imagined the way you move. It is almost like you're able to dodge the bullets and still pull off a kill shot. Truly amazing." Quick chuckled to himself as he stood and fired off an entire clip at the soldiers' position.

The Russian men were retreating to the northwest and the REMERS kept the pressure on, hoping to force them back toward the facility. Chase could see clear outlines of red in the snow, some surrounding the bodies of the soldiers they had already killed while the rest dotted the trails from wounded and escaping soldiers. It seemed to almost glow against the bright white of the terrain.

His heart was racing, but he could hear others' pounding at three times the speed of his. Chase could tell that the rhythms were not coming from his teammates and that there was more than one.

"The beats are so fast. How many of them are there?" An explosion broke through their line and they were forced to pull back to their previous position.

"It's okay. I can't tell how many of them are coming either." Beads of sweat were rolling down Ty's forehead. "We must be right on top of them."

"I've got at least three coming up the left flank and a few more making their way right." Trip motioned for Rock and Jiminy to move north to intercept the approaching squad, and he and Quick shifted to the west to protect the western flank, leaving Chase and Ty to keep them from coming up the middle.

Fortunately, the snow banks near the facility created a bottleneck. It was likely created to assist the soldiers if there was unexpected company, but in this case it was to the REMERS' advantage. They could use the enclosed area to disguise their position and get a better vantage point of where the mutants were located.

Gunfire erupted to Chase's left and he peered out from his cover to watch at least three of the mutants fall into the snow. Another round of shots from his right and he heard Trip's voice echoing in his head.

"We're clear. Chase, Ty, move into a forward position and await further instruction."

Chase tried to keep track of the heartbeats of the other four members of the squad as they continued to approach the facility. They were too far away for him to hear their breathing, and the now familiar beating was getting hard to make out.

"Okay, guys. We can see what is likely the main entrance to the facility. It's at least wide enough for a vehicle and seems to lead underground. Everyone meet at my current location, I'm transmitting coordinates." The whispered voice of his team leader brought a sense of reality to Chase and gave him a sick feeling in his stomach that this would be his grave.

As it was supposed to be the mutant's main facility, there were very few guards between the REMERS and the entrance. Chase forced himself to keep his eyes open to keep his thoughts on the task at hand and away from his home, away from Shaun. He knew he had to stay focused on the mission if he wanted to stay alive, but most of the time he only wanted to be dead, the way almost everyone else in his life already thought he was.

He wondered then if they had buried an empty coffin and if there'd been a funeral. He wondered if she had cried when they told her, if she had someone to lean on, someone to take care of her without him there. He wanted to know that Shaun was going to be okay, that she would move on, even if he didn't really want her to.

Gunfire snapped Chase back to reality. Ty pressed a button on her left shoulder and what had been a missile attachment turned into a long barrel with a sight near her elbow. She expertly targeted the tower at the top of the entrance and took out a pair of snipers in under a minute, and the barrel and sight disappeared as quickly as it had appeared.

Trip motioned for the team to follow and they made their way silently down the concrete stairs and into the facility. Jiminy and Quick remained posted at the bottom of the stairs while Chase and Ty headed down the left corridor and Rock and Trip went right in search of the laboratory and the leader of the mutants.

They hadn't made it very far when Chase and Ty ran into trouble. They were pinned down by a troop of mutant soldiers around the corner from a Plexiglas room that could only be the main lab. Ty rolled to cross the hall and take a shooting position from the opposite side when she was hit. Chase watched it happen; but while everything moved in slow motion, there was nothing he could do as the bullet pierced her side.

They'd already lost Stoic and Tiny – the loss was real, even if he hadn't really known them. But Ty he knew; Ty he trusted; and Ty was someone he couldn't bear to lose, not when he'd already lost so much. Seeing her bleeding and hearing her cry of pain, he went on a rampage. Chase yelled as he jumped out in front of her in the hall, firing shots in every direction, each connecting with another soldier until the hall was clear. He grabbed Ty by the shoulders and started to drag her back toward the position Jiminy and Quick were holding at the entrance. Her body was limp, but her heartbeat was strong and Chase figured she was in shock.

Jiminy heard them approaching and hurried to help Chase get Ty to safety. "What happened?"

"Lucky shot. But the bastard's dead now, and so are the rest of them. I think we located the lab." Chase was still focused on Ty as Quick pulled packing and tape from one of his leg compartments and started to work to stop the bleeding.

Ty groaned when he applied pressure to the entry wound. "Jiminy, go on with the kid," Quick ordered, not looking up. "She's going to be alright, but only if we finish the mission and get the hell out of here soon."

Both men nodded their assent and got to their feet before setting off at a sprint. Their footsteps echoed through the facility as they raced back down the hall to where Ty had been injured. Jiminy's jaw nearly hit the floor when he saw nearly a dozen mutant bodies lying near the Plexiglas doors.

"You guys take most of these out before she got shot?" He looked over at Chase who was also in awe at the number of dead.

"Umm... nope... When she got shot, I just kinda went crazy on them... I had no idea there were so many..." Chase was motionless staring at the bodies, suddenly realizing that he was capable of killing people. He didn't know whether he should feel pride or horror, and instead just mostly felt stomach sick.

"Good for you, kid. Now come on, let's get what we came here for." Jiminy pressed his back to the wall and quickly moved to the entrance of the lab with Chase at his heels.

They entered through the doors into a room that had been divided in half by more Plexiglas. The first room was filled with a large number of computers while the second was set up like Chase's high school chemistry lab, complete with Bunsen burners.

One wall of the computer room looked like a super computer that would have been featured in an old movie, numerous panels with rows of green and red lights and a small screen with a DOS layout. Chase immediately walked over to the device and started looking for a USB port to plug in his arm enhancement.

"I got it. Cover me, Jiminy, there is a lot of information in here." Chase closed his eyes and the download started. After a few minutes, he felt a wash of cold come over him, as though he was going to pass out. "I don't know if I can get all this, man. There are so many files here."

"You can do it, Chase. Just take your time, but we have to get it all. Can't take the chance that the one thing we leave behind is the missing piece that will put an end to all of this."

Chase closed his eyes again. It was almost like he was reading every file as it entered his memory bank, like he was more of a computer than a man. The download finished after what seemed like an eternity and Chase collapsed, exhausted. He heard rapid knocking and realized it was more mutants heading in their direction. He forced himself to his feet. "They must have detected the download," he gasped.

After a quick check of their immediate area, they hustled down the hall and back to where they had left Quick and Ty. Trip and Rock were also waiting for them when they arrived and the REMERS made a swift exit. Rock and Quick carried Ty from the facility and they stopped just outside the bottleneck to allow them to rest.

"We got all the information, but what about the leader? Did you guys take him out?" Chase whispered although they were well out of earshot of the mutants.

"He wasn't there. The last information opened on his computer showed some target on the east coast. They're planning to test their method in a small town in New York."

Chase moved in front of Trip and grabbed him by the shoulders. "I'm from a small town in New York. Do you know where?" The sick feeling in his stomach had returned, stronger this time.

"Some place with only a couple of thousand people. Stoneville or something." Trip watched as Chase fell to his knees.

"N-n-no... it can't be. You have to be wrong."

Suddenly Rock was also beside him. "Afraid not. It was definitely Stoneville and we have about three days to decode the information you have stored up there," he tapped Chase on the head, "and save those people. So, get on your feet; we have to get back to the evac point."

The aircraft that had dropped them off was called to meet them just ten kilometers from the facility. Rock and Trip labored as they carried Ty and threw her onboard before the rest of the remaining REMERS entered. Chase heard a loud bang and glanced back at the facility just as it erupted in a wash of flames. It had been destroyed.

It seemed like only minutes until they arrived back at the base. Chase rushed to the computer lab to download the information he had retrieved from the mutant facility.

Within hours, the army technologists had managed to crack the code and find the information they needed. If they could create the anti-virus, it would have to be administered before or within the first few hours of contact to prevent the mutations from becoming permanent.

The REMERS were gathered in the classroom where Chase had first learned about the Russian experiment before gearing up to try to prevent the release of the virus in his hometown. He was on the edge of his seat during the briefing, tapping his feet in anticipation of the mission to follow. Chase tried to concentrate on the information they were being fed, but his mind was once again drifting to Shaun. More than anything, he couldn't let these monsters hurt her.

"Alright, fellas, that's it. Chase, you and I will carry the anti-virus to their drop zone in case they've already made the drop by the time we arrive. Ty and Quick will be at the centre of town supervising the distribution to those who have not been infected; and Rock and Jiminy, you're responsible for the north end of town, so crowd control and orderly distribution." Trip stood from his seat at the front of the room as he gave the directions.

"You have two hours to collect what you need and rest before we meet on airstrip one. And Chase, do get some rest." Trip tousled his hair and smiled before heading to the barracks.

Chase did try, but he couldn't even close his eyes as images of mutated versions of his friends and family invaded his thoughts whenever he did. It seemed as though only a few minutes had passed when he heard a voice in his head reminding him that there was only fifteen minutes before departure.

Chase barely spoke a word on the flight, focused on what he had to do and hoping and praying that he would be able to catch a glimpse of Shaun. Just seeing her face, even if it was from a distance, even if she didn't know he was there, would be enough. His face flushed red with anger when he thought about the plan the mutants had to destroy his home.

When they touched down outside of town, Chase started at a run for the mutant position. Satellite imagery showed the mutants had landed six kilometers from their position. Trip had chosen Chase for this part of the mission because of his familiarity with the surroundings. Chase had grown up playing in the woods near the town and knew every hiding place and every sheltered area for miles.

As he ran through the trees, Chase swore he saw his six-year-old friends playing Cowboys and Indians, hiding behind the trees. But there were no heartbeats, and nothing to tell him they were getting closer to the mutants either. Chase moved like a man possessed, brushing trees out of the way and ignoring Trip as he struggled to keep up in the unfamiliar place. He was going to find them, and he was going to kill them before they got a chance to complete their plan.

He stopped dead in his tracks. "Trip, you hear that?"

Trip stopped behind him, struggling to catch his breath. "I hear it alright. Any guess as to how many could be ahead?"

Chase craned his neck forward and strained to define one rapid beat from another. "I can't be sure. At least half a dozen."

"That could be great news. If there are still a large number here, they probably haven't left for town." As Trip touched the left side of his head to radio the remaining REMERS, out of the corner of his eye he saw Chase move forward to a large oak tree.

Chase could see some of the mutants from his position and after a couple of deep breaths, he stepped out from behind his cover and expertly killed the three standing closest to him before performing a tuck and roll behind the tree on the opposite side of the path. He held his breath and stepped out firing again, this time taking out two more and pulling back behind the old oak where he started.

Chase felt like he was rushing the line on a football field as he ploughed forward, shooting at everything that moved. He saw Trip coming up behind him, also firing at the mutant base. Chase was moving faster than he ever had, and once again, things around him were slowed, almost to a standstill.

He watched as a bullet left the barrel of his gun and penetrated a mutant standing at the door of the plane. He saw the creature's eyes roll back and his muscles relax as he crumpled to the ground. Chase stopped a few feet away from the body. The only heartbeat now audible was a familiar one. Trip stopped beside him, struggling to catch his breath.

"I have never seen anyone move that fast. I have good news and bad news, however."

Chase held his breath in preparation. "Well, let's have it then."

"It seems that all the mutants that landed here are dead, but we were too late, they already released the virus. They were headed out of town when we caught up with them here."

Chase gasped. "What about the people? Did we get to them in time?"

"That's the good news, it looks like. The rest of the guys are working to distribute the vaccine right now." Trip smiled. "Breath normally, kid. They're all going to be okay."

Chase sighed in relief. "And they won't be trying anything like this for some time, I imagine. That is, if any of them survived."

Trip laughed. "Just in case, cover me, kid. I'm going to make sure that whatever got off the lab on the plane is never discovered or able to be used again."

After a couple of minutes, Trip came running toward Chase. "Come on, you aren't going to want to be around here in a few minutes. We are going to go see if there's anything we can do to help with handing out the vaccine."

Chase could hear the very faint noise of a timer counting down the seconds and knew immediately that Trip had attached an explosive device to the fuselage of the plane.

They were no more than a few hundred yards away when the bomb went off. Chase paused and looked back at the debris that had been thrown skyward. He could see the flames pushing up through the trees and the smoke billowing out toward the town. It appeared to be following them, and he quickened his pace to stay ahead of it.

Chase ran all the way to the centre of town where the medical station was set up. He had planned to stay out of sight, but now that he was here, he knew he had to try to see Shaun again. He scanned the crowd, wishing there were fewer people so he could focus on his memory of her heartbeat and track her down.

He vividly remembered how each beat sounded when he would hold her body close and press his face to her chest. As if conjuring up her memory had called her to him, she appeared, just metres away, but with half of the town separating them in the square.

Her eyes glistened, filling with tears as they connected with his. Shaun fell to her knees, trembling, but she couldn't look away. It was like looking into the eyes of a ghost. She buried her face in her hands and started rocking back and forth, crying loudly now.

Chase was watching her face as he pushed his way through the crowd to reach her. For him, it was a dream come true to even see her face again. He struggled against the mob of people between them. He had to be cautious not to hurt any of the civilians, or allow them to come into contact with any of the buttons that controlled his enhancements.

We just weren't designed to interact in large groups like this. Guess I won't have to deal with any riots at least, Chase thought to himself as he inched closer and closer to where Shaun had collapsed. His heart rate was steadily increasing and now he could only hear hers pounding in his ears.

After what seemed an eternity, he found a break in the crowd and ran to her side. Chase knelt beside her and wrapped his arms around her as he had done so many times before. It felt strange and he recoiled, realizing that his arms were no longer his own.

Shaun didn't pull away, only slowly dropped her arms to her sides, than reached out, running her fingers along the metal that was once his muscular chest, touched the enhancements that now covered his forearms and then pressed her palm to the flesh of his jaw.

"I thought... I thought you were dead..." Shaun's voice sounded like music to Chase. She stared up at him, tears still streamed down her cheeks.

"I know and I'm so sorry you had to go through all this." Chase was crying now as well. He fought the urge to sob as he spoke, tried to keep his voice as steady and calm as possible. "I wasn't allowed to contact you. You aren't supposed to know that I am alive, even now."

"Are you staying... now that I do know?" she choked on the words. "These last few months have been agony. I don't know if I can go through that – I mean, I don't think I can lose you again..." Her voice trailed off and she finally broke his gaze.

"I can't stay here, baby." Chase sniffed and cleared his throat. He knew he had to be strong for her. "I belong with the team now. You know I would give anything to be here with you, but I owe them my life." Chase placed his hand over hers that still rested against his face.

"So, what about me? I'm just supposed to stay here and try to go on with my life?" She lifted her head to again look into his eyes, pulling her hand away. "I've been trying to do that. Trying to move on for months, Chase, really, I have. But it's just not that easy. I can't get you out of my mind, I can't stop thinking about what would have been, the things we would have done if the explosion had never happened."

Chase wiped the tears from her cheeks and then his own. "I had so many plans for us. So many dreams about our future together, and I would give anything in this world to be able to stay here and live that life, or take you with me. I just don't think the military would agree to either of it."

"I went to your grave every day. I would talk to you and tell you about my day, that I made it through another one without you, but that I would always love you and I didn't know how many more I could suffer. Now you're here! You're right here, I can see your face, touch you and hold you and you're going to walk away again."

Chase lifted his chin and looked to the sky with the sound of familiar static that preceded a transmission entered his ears. It was Trip's voice. "Time to move out, guys. Our ride is expected to touch down in t-minus six minutes.

Chase glanced around to find the people of Stoneville were no longer crowded in the square and the medical supplies the REMERS had been distributing were now packed into plastic crates and ready to go. *We did it. We actually did it.* Chase smiled a little at the thought. The feeling reminded him of the moment they had won the state finals, but he pushed the aching feelings of loss down and held on to the pride he felt. The threat to the town was over and now that they had produced a vaccine, it would be a long time before the mutants posed any kind of a threat like this again.

When he turned to look back at Shaun, he saw his father coming toward them. "Come on, son, we have to take off." General Davies gave them a little distance. He knew the decision to keep his son alive was the right one, but he did regret making him give up everything in the process.

Chase pulled Shaun close to him. "Wait right here," he whispered in her ear and stood to approach his father.

"I can't go, Dad." He looked over his shoulder at Shaun, still sobbing. "I can't leave her again. I love her too much to walk away." Chase hung his head and brushed away a tear from his face.

"I know you do. I'd love to be able to tell you that you can stay here and live out your lives together if that's what you want to do, but you'll just have to look at the positive side of things, son. At least this time, you'll have a chance to say goodbye."

Chase didn't move, only lifted his head to meet his father eye to eye. "I'm not going without her."

Trip and Ty were now standing beside him and had

heard the conversation between the two Davies men. Ty placed her hand on Chase's shoulder.

"With all do respect, General, the girl is already compromised. I don't see any harm in taking her along."

"Well..." General Davies paused. "I'll see what we can do. But either way, we can't take her with us now. You still have to go to the debriefing." He turned and stepped a few feet away, pulling out his walkie-talkie.

Ty grasped Chase's shoulder tighter to comfort him. "It's going to be alright. With the threat level down, I'm sure the General will do everything in his power to make it happen for you. After all, you are his son."

Chase looked back at Shaun again. She had managed to get to her feet. She had a look of anticipation and questioning, but he could only half smile and shrug his shoulders. Shaun tried to force a smile in return, knowing that this could be the last time she saw his face.

She studied his features, looking beyond the metal that was now covering much of the boy she remembered. She barely noticed the difference and didn't care that his physical appearance had changed. Shaun stared at him for what might have been an eternity before she looked up at the footsteps coming back toward them.

"Here's the deal." General Davies was clipping his communicator back on his belt as he returned to the group. "After the debrief, Shaun will be allowed to join you if she wants. But there are conditions."

Chase practically jumped into his father's arms. "I don't care about conditions, Dad."

"I should warn you, however, if the mutant activity ramps up again, she will have to be taken away to a secluded area for her own safety."

"Fine, fine, that's perfectly fine." Chase was almost skipping as he made his way back to Shaun.

He stopped suddenly, a few steps from her and listened as her heartbeat started to race. She was still working to fight back the tears and expecting the worst. A large smile exploded across his face and he could see the relief in hers. He finally continued forward and grasped her hands in his.

"I have to go right now, baby. But I'm coming back for you. I swear it."

Shaun grabbed him and pressed her face to his chest. He didn't smell the same way he used to, but strangely, she could still make out motor oil... "I know you will," she said, her words pressing into him. She held him, trying to make up for lost time, but he soon pulled away. She looked up into his face, just as she remembered it, and found a smile wavering on her face. Finding the strength she needed to send him on his way, she said, "Just don't take too long, huh? A girl might think that you abandoned her or something and start looking for a new guy to replace you." At his grin at her words, she finally released his hands and just stood in place, watching as he joined the rest of the REMERS and headed for their plane.

Shaun smiled and waved while Chase looked back until she was out of sight. When he finally disappeared from her view, she collapsed on the curb, unable to stop grinning. "I know you'll be back for me. I know it in my heart that we're meant to be."

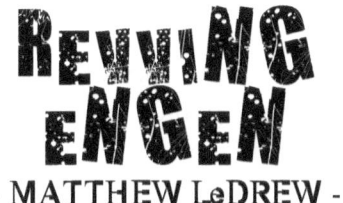

- MATTHEW LeDREW -

Coral Beach, Maine

Tash leaned back on the wire-mesh chair she'd found at the supermarket, her cell phone pressed tightly to her ear and her coffee slowly getting cooler in front of her, bleeding steam into the cool September air.

There was a table with an umbrella sticking up from its centre that was almost exactly like the other ten that surrounded it, differenced only by the placement of the freckles of rust that decorated them. The balcony that surrounded the top floor of the supermarket on all sides was rarely used to the point that most people had forgotten it was there. They stopped and stared at her now as though she were some alien being as they shuffled past, their plastic bags of groceries cutting deep gouges into their fingers on their way to their cars. She smiled and nodded at each one that looked at her. Some smiled back, most looked away quickly.

"Small towns," she mumbled softly to herself, then sat up. Her voice became louder and clearer as she spoke into the phone. "No, sorry. Yeah. Yeah, I have it here in front of me."

She reached for the paper she'd bought while in line for her coffee (which tasted for the world like motor oil). It was a *Star* weekly, the type of tabloid that could be found in any checkout across the country. It had bold headlines like MY BABY'S DADDY IS FROM DIMENSION X and ELVIS IS LIVING IN MY BASEMENT accompanied by horribly photoshopped photographs.

"You know, that might be worth checking out. If Elvis is still alive after all this time..." she stopped, turning to the second page. There was a one-column piece there about the LUCKIEST MAN ALIVE, without the benefit of pictures. "I'm just saying, it would be great. I'd switch it up so that you get the kids and I get the adults, and I'd reenact King Creole every Saturday. You're sure? Damn shame. I'm reading it."

She grabbed her paper cup around its cardboard sleeve and brought it to her scant lips. They were a small bow in the middle of her pointed chin, amidst the faded freckles that dotted her otherwise smooth complexion. She took a long sip as her eyes scanned their way down the article, their brows climbing a notch with every paragraph.

"Wow. This seems like it could be legit." She stopped, listening to the person on the other end of the line for a moment as she finished the article and laid it back down on the table. A second later her coffee was laid down too, and she pried her phone out from between her head and shoulder, rubbing the spot where it had been tenderly. "That's a lot of cash. He could just be good, you know. Despite what he used to say, sometimes a cigar is just a cigar. Be careful. Kid's twenty-one and sitting on that much cash, he's going to be jumpy. Maybe."

Her brow furrowed, and she took another sip of her drink now that both hands were free.

"Back to the Future?" she asked quizzically, her mouth curling up in a smile. After a moment, the smile went away and she rolled her eyes, her voice taking on a frustrated tone. "Back to the Future *Part Two*, then? Yeah. Uh-Huh. Do you think it's anything like that? ...Alright, well, be careful. I'm here, but I don't know how I'm going to find anything in this place. I really hate Maine. Read too many Stephen King novels and now I'm scared of every shadow in every small town it's got. And this one's weird. It's small enough that it barely shows up on the map and doesn't show up online at all, but here it is. It's actually bigger than most towns; it's almost a city. And the people here are cagey... I think it's going to be hard getting anything out of them without looking suspicious."

She stopped talking long enough for the person on the other end to respond, a concerned look flashing over her dark eyes. "Okay, well be careful. I miss you... Out."

She pulled the phone back from her ear and watched as the connection went dead, then laughed and shook her head as she placed it back into her pocket. "Who the hell says out to end a conversation?"

She pushed the weekly Star to the far side of the table and picked up another paper from the seat next to her, the *Beach News Daily*.

∞

Sara Johnson forced her locker door closed, putting all her weight behind her shoulder as she forced the metal door flush with all the others that lined the hallway. Her tongue was sticking out of the corner of her mouth a little as she did so, the pink of it just different enough from the pink of her lips to be noticed.

She heard the mechanism inside it click, then smiled and stepped back from it.

It groaned for a moment, then snapped back open, spilling books and papers out across the hall in a V-shape spreading out from the door.

"Fuck!" she huffed, stamping one foot before dropping to her knees and shoving all the loose sheets of paper into a pile. She had a brief memory of her father teaching her how to play fifty-two pickup as a child, but it left as quickly as it had arrived.

"You know, that wouldn't happen so much if you didn't have your whole life in there." Nick said, leaning against the locker next to her.

She looked up at him even as she continued to gather her books together, having to crane her head back to the point of pain to do so.

He was tall, several inches above any other male in his grade. His brown hair was spiked and gelled up and make him look even taller, monstrous even. It was something he'd been teased about in elementary school but in recent years had become one of his defining attributes, along with his pale blue eyes. Sometimes in the sun, his eyes almost looked white. His height, along with his speed while dribbling and passing, had made him a force to be reckoned with on the school basketball team.

She didn't know how long he'd been standing there, but she assumed that it was long enough that she had made a fool of herself at least once. She gave him a little smile, the right corner of her lip curling just enough to make her irresistible as she fixed her top to make sure he couldn't see down it. There were fishnet stockings wrapped around her hands that had rips along the wrists from where they'd become caught in her large hoop earrings. There were at least two rings on each of her fingers, silver rings on the left hand and gold rings on the right. The gold ones had been polished recently and sparkled in the fluorescent lights of the hallway, while the silver ones were dull and faded.

"I wouldn't know what to do with myself if everything wasn't at arm's length," she said, shoving a hardcover geology text into the locker with such force that the spine creased.

"Come on, take a lesson from Tom Petty."

She raised an eyebrow at him.

"You don't have to live like a refugee."

She rolled her eyes as she continued to shove books and papers into the locker without any concern for their state or the creases created.

He sighed, then bent down and started to help her. He recognized a math book from seventh grade, a hardcover text with a bear juggling beach balls. The bear was smiling stupidly at the fourth wall and reminded him of the bears from the Coca Cola commercials every time he thought of long division. Most people had sold theirs to the next crop of grade seven students during the first week of grade eight, but here was Sara's copy, still occupying the bottom of her locker just in case she ever forgot how to use cosign and needed a quick reminder.

"It's like you're a damn nomad," he sighed, flipping through an array of used notebooks with coiled metal spines.

"A what?"

"Nomad." He smiled. "A person who moves from place to place."

"Always got to be ready for the next big thing," she said, shoving the last of her belongings into the locker and slamming the door shut again. "Can you get this?"

He nodded, then braced his feet against the tile floor and shoved against the door as hard as he could with both palms. There were odd scuttling sounds as the items inside shifted under the weight of the door before finally finding a comfortable position as the lock clicked into place with a solid, metallic tone.

"Thanks," she chirped.

"No problem."

She motioned toward the hall as she started to walk toward the front entrance. He nodded and stepped up beside her, hoisting his book-bag onto his shoulder and jogging the first few steps to catch up.

He stopped after a moment and looked around, a confused look coming over him. "Where's Xander?"

"Out with Grendel. Apparently there was some special kind of speaker he needed for his party on Friday, but he didn't know what kind... so he called on the Nerd Patrol to come help him pick it out."

"Frightening."

"What is?"

"Grendel doesn't have the time of day for him most days, but he needs him for something and: bam. Let's hang out after school."

She stopped and turned to face him, squinting her eyes and tilting her head slightly to one side. "You're not coming to Grendel's party this Friday, are you?"

Nick rolled his eyes. "What was your first clue?"

She frowned, and they continued walking. After a few paces, her tongue clicked against the roof of her mouth (as it always did when she was about to try and convince someone of something) and she continued, "You really should come, you know. It's going to be the social event of the season."

"Why're you talking like that?"

"It's fun."

"It bugs me."

"That's what makes it fun." She smiled. "Anyway, everyone's going to be there... maybe even Teresa Conway..."

He turned and looked at her, her voice having gained a musical tone as she said the girl's name. "Isn't she with Jamie Dawkins?"

"I have it on good authority that she'll be in need of some male companionship before too long."

He sighed. "I'm not coming to the party. I don't like Julian Grendel even under the best of circumstances, I'm certainly not going to pretend to just so I can sit next to Teresa Conway while she downs Cuba Libres until she pukes."

She shot him a look. "You're testy today, aren't you?"

He paused. "Sorry. Rough class."

"That's okay. What're you doing now?"

"Right now I am walking down the hall with you."

She shot him a look.

"Oh, you mean later? Later, I'm doing nothing."

"You want to come to the Factory? ...could be fun. I think Jamie's going to be there if you wanted to play pool."

He smiled. "I'll think about it."

∞

A crack filled the air of the Factory as Nick sent the cue ball crashing into the assembled balls at the other side of the table, the sharp sound echoing off the walls until it seemed to be coming from everywhere.

The Factory was a local arcade, club and dance hall where almost every teen in Coral Beach went when there was nothing else to do, which was almost all of the time. It jutted up from the otherwise calm landscape that had been named 'downtown' even though it was only a small distance from the city centre or even from the outskirts of town, and was always loud and exciting and neon.

Nick leaned back from the table and watched as the billiards began to dance about, ricocheting off each other and the torn green fabric that lined the sides until finally coming to a stop. They were scattered nicely, with the one ball teetering very close to the corner pocket at his right and a small cluster of balls still remaining at the far end of the table. Nothing had been sunk.

"Your decision," he said to Jamie Dawkins, motioning to him with his stick.

Jamie frowned, observing the table. "It's not much of a decision." He leaned over the table, raising an eyebrow as he tried to figure out his shot. His leather sports jacket crumpled and scrunched noisily every time he moved, forcing him to push up the sleeves over and over again. His brother had worn that jacket when he was captain of the Coral Beach Cougars, and his father before that. Now that he was finally captain, it barely ever left his back. Some even said he showered with it on. He squat down to make his eye line level with the path between the cue and the one, finding that it was blocked by the eight. He sighed.

"You could always bank it," Nick offered.

Jamie shot him a look.

Nick shrugged. "Just saying." He turned toward the bar just as Sara was shaking her head at him. She had a tall glass of soda in her hand that was so cold there was fog coming off of it, bathing her neck and chin in chilly, cool condensation that was like fresh morning dew on the leaves outside his house. Julie Peterson was next to her, finishing off the last few bites of a local burger called the Slaughterhouse that dripped sauce and grease onto the paper plate she had strategically placed on her lap. Randy Owchar was there too, his eyes shifting back and forth between the pool table and Julie's exposed tailbone.

"Good break," Sara said, taking a long gulp of her drink and then using it to salute him in a 'cheers' motion, even though he didn't have a drink himself. "But you shouldn't make fun of him like that."

"Like what?"

"The 'your decision' thing?"

He smiled. "Come on... it's that old basketball-football competition."

"Be nice, Lardo," Julie smiled, nudging Sara in what

both girls would often refer to as 'her fat'. "It's fun watching them play like this. It's like watching the apes on Animal Planet."

"You have never in your life watched Animal Planet," Sara replied, moving away from her.

"Have so."

"Oh, yeah? When?"

Julie was silent for a long moment, then eventually let her shoulders slump. "Sometimes you can be a real bitch."

Sara smiled, then turned back to Nick. He wasn't watching them and he wasn't watching the game, even though Jamie had made his shot on the one and missed, leaving the choice of balls in Nick's hands again. He was staring past the both of them into the null space at the other end of the bar. It was a place where nobody typically sat, and was usually occupied by stacks of cola bottles and unopened milk cartons. She turned to follow his line of sight, her hair getting caught on her lip balm as she did.

There was a woman sitting on the furthest seat of the bar.

She was wearing a dark blue hooded sweatshirt that disguised most of her features and even hid her eyes in shadow, but there was a femininity to that slant, triangular nature of the lower half of her face that made her gender impossible to hide. Her lips were small and bright red, and Sara guessed that they had been what had first drawn Nick's attention... they looked too red to be real, standing out bright and vibrant against the comparatively sepia-toned color of the Factory wall. It was as if someone photoshopped crimson lips into an old black and white photo.

She was sipping tea in long mouthfuls from a cup that was so hot that steam poured out of it without the slightest pause, yet she seemed to have no trouble taking it in. Her hands were soft and delicate, the nails on the end of each painted to match her lips.

Sara caught herself staring much in the way that Nick had, finally forcing herself to turn around. She scrunched up her face in an exaggerated scowl and rolled her eyes. "Skank alert."

Nick shook his head, then met her eye again and smiled. "What?"

"Skank alert," she repeated, motioning toward the end on the bar with her head. "As in, be alerted to the presence of skanks. I really didn't think it needed any more explanation."

Nick wrung the edge of his pool stick, turned to look at the table and then back to the stranger. "What makes you think she's a skank?"

"What would you call a thirty-something year old man that came into here, sat in the shadows and watched us while sipping on tea?"

"A pedophile."

"And what would you call a female pedophile?"

"...A skank."

"Hence the skank alert."

He watched the woman for a moment longer. The steam from her drink seemed to dance up from her mug and caress her chin, hugging against the flesh without even touching it and continuing up over her head and out into the atmosphere.

He turned away from her and bent over the table, making his own shot at the one and sinking it effortlessly. It slammed against the back of the pocket with a loud crack before finding its home in the soft leather net below it.

"I'm low," he said, moving to the side of the table without taking his eyes off the balls. They moved for him in his mind like atoms, each one coming into clear focus for a moment while the rest faded into his peripheral vision until each had been examined and reexamined into the equation that was this pool table.

He bent over and made a shot at the five, sending it into the far side pocket with another loud smack that made Julie and Sara both jump, even though they'd been watching as the action unfolded. The cue rolled back until it was almost touching the two, and Nick quickly made his way around to the other side of the table and gave it the final tap needed to send it into the side pocket.

Jamie huffed, wringing his stick but leaning against the pillar closest to the table and getting comfortable.

Nick continued around the table again, finally coming across a clear line between the cue and the six. He pulled his stick back hard and nailed it, leaving a dent of blue chalk in the side of the cue as it rocketed across the table and collided with the six, bouncing off it and sending it into the corner pocket.

He glanced up at Sara and smiled, winking at her. She smiled back, but he couldn't help but notice the woman behind her was still watching them... had even stood up a little to see over the edge of the bar. Although that small, rosy mouth of hers was still held in the exact same expression, he couldn't help but think that there was a smile building across the edge of it somehow.

He turned back to the table and moved around it again, with each step his eyes continuing to flutter back and forth over the balls so fast that the blues of them almost looked white, zipping about in their sockets so quickly that even the irises took on a grayish tone. He found a clear shot at the three and took it, making another shot at the seven before either ball had even stopped moving and sinking both.

Sara smiled and took another sip of her drink. She had the same calculating expression on her face that he did, although she wasn't measuring distance and force. Julie noticed her and smiled, poking her in the side again.

"What?" Sara laughed.

"Leave something for the rest of us, why don't you?"

"The big lion gets the most food," she smirked. "Deal with it."

Nick waited for the cue to stop rolling and finally lined up his shot with the four, cracking the cue into it so hard that it would have been bruised if it hadn't already been purple. He stood up and surveyed the table again. There were seven high balls still scattered around it with three still in a small cluster where they had been since they'd been racked, and the black eight ball sitting alone along one side.

He smirked at Jamie, then bent over and made his shot at the eight. He did not slam it as he had almost every other shot, instead tapping it as gently as he could and letting the two balls collide before sending the second one rolling smoothly toward the top corner pocket. It was like watching it in slow motion compared to the rest of the game, and as all the other eyes in the room (including the stranger's) watched the ball roll its way across the felt, Nick made his way around the table until he was in front of Jamie, his hand out in front of him.

"Pay up," he said, just as the eight sunk into the pocket and clicked against the balls already waiting there.

Jamie peeked up over his shoulder to make sure the ball had actually sunk, frowned, then shoved his hand deep into his pocket and produced a wrinkled and crumpled five dollar bill. He held it up between them for a moment, then slammed it down into Nick's waiting palm. "Next time," he said, meeting his eye with mock contempt.

"I've heard that before," Nick smiled, laying his stick down and making his way over to the bar. He sat down on a stool away from the others and waited for Roxanne to come over and take his order, seeing her shadow move in the back of the house as she tried in vain to clean the grease off the deep fryer.

Sara came over and leaned over the bar next to him, her hair falling down around her. Her arms were crossed across her chest and it pushed her breasts up until they were almost escaping her shirt. He hated himself for noticing, it was one of the things he despised most about Julian Grendel - the obviousness with which he ogled most of the girls in their school - but he simply couldn't help it. The more he tried not to notice them, the more conspicuous they became.

"That was pretty impressive," she said, looking from him to the five he'd won and then back again.

"Thanks," he smiled. It *had* been impressive, he knew,

but it was something he'd become accustomed to and almost had to remind himself that it wasn't normal from time to time.

"Any chance I can play the winner?"

He smiled at her. "I get the feeling you've been playing the winner since grade eight."

Her smile spread and she laughed, not outright but the strange, subdued little hum that was her typical way of expressing herself.

There was an arcade game playing against the far wall behind her, flashing lights and strobe effects every few seconds to try and entice patrons into shoveling quarters into it. The lights were caught in her straight blonde hair and made it glow around her like a halo, first red then green and blue and then back to red again. Her eyes remained the same though, that same sparkle of light that had always been there present even now. She was beautiful, and he found his throat getting dryer and dryer the closer he got to her until the five dollar bill in his hand felt like a pitcher of water at the end of a long walk across a desert highway.

Her lips were pink with lip balm, shimmering in whatever light source had made her eyes sparkle.

He felt himself inching his head closer to hers, and it was as though his body were maneuvering on autopilot without his control. Her eyes fluttered from his to his lips again and again, watching as events seemed to happen in that same slow motion that had made the sinking of the eight ball so dramatic.

"Is this okay?" he heard himself whisper, though he wasn't entirely sure why. He'd seen men try to make unwanted moves on Sara Johnson before, and it typically ended with them getting kneed somewhere very unpleasant.

"Mmm," she said, with that same sort of hum she'd used to respond to him a moment before. Her mouth opened, and he could again see the pink of her tongue against the pink of her lips. Could feel the heat of her breath on his. "I've been waiting for you to kiss me since I noticed those eyes in eighth grade."

He stopped, suddenly in control of his body again. Their lips were almost touching, to the point that a bead of condensation on either's lip would have been felt by the other. They hung like that for a moment before he took a step back.

"What?" she asked, hurt filling her eyes almost immediately.

He swallowed back hard, then cleared his throat.

"What is it?" she repeated, taking him by the arm and forcing him to face her.

"It's nothing," he said, his voice almost breaking as he did so. "Really. Just, ah... just feel like sitting this one out is all."

"Oh."

"Yeah. Maybe I'll play next game. I think Jamie's ready to play now, if you still wanted too."

"Yeah." She nodded, then pushed away from the bar and took a step backward towards the others. "Are you sure you're okay?"

Nick nodded, swallowing back hard again.

Her brow furrowed in worry, but she did not ask again. She turned away and walked back to the pool table, picking up a short pool stick off the wall rack along the way.

He stared at the cash register against the wall from him, the rest of his vision becoming hazy and mossy as he focused in on it. There were thirty-two buttons on it, five of which had cracks in their plastic casings. Two had their labels peeled off, and one number (the seven) was upside-down. It had a thick layer of dust on it despite the fact that Roxanne cleaned it weekly and used it often, and was the same colour of faded pears that seemed to have adorned all mid-nineties technology.

He let out a long sigh and dropped his head, bringing the wood grain of the bar into focus instead. His hands found his way into his hair despite the fact that he knew Julie and Randy might well have been watching him right now and he fought the urge to simply curl into a ball and start to cry.

"That was quite a show," came a smooth, silky voice. For a moment he thought it was Sara. The voice had that same smooth, summery feel to it... as though warmth was a sound that could be heard rather than merely felt.

He turned and saw that it was the stranger, just gliding into the seat beside him. She wasn't looking at him, was instead examining the cash register in much the same way he had been. It was only now that he could see how taut her skin was... it clung to the bone around it for dear life, the muscle of her profiled face pulled tight and ready at all times. Her lips looked like a sideways heart from this angle, but were still that same deep red that he'd noticed before.

Skank alert, he caught himself thinking, but dared not

say it aloud.

"Not really," he said finally, standing on his toes to try and see if Roxanne was coming yet. "I didn't even get to do any bank shots. Usually they're the hard ones. The balls just went in the right places."

"Not the pool," she smiled, laying her cup down on the counter in front of her. "The *girl*."

He turned and looked at her, narrowing his eyes until they were just tiny white slits in his head. "What do you want?"

She smiled. "I think the more appropriate question would be: what do you want?"

He looked at her for a long moment, his tongue massaging the top of his mouth.

"I want to show you something," she said finally, moving just a little bit closer to him. The arm of her sweater grazed against his leg and he felt shivers run up and down his spine like gooseflesh.

"I don't - -"

"*Please*," she said, leaning forward until the light off the counter caught her face. Her skin was smooth and milky white, with just the slightest tint of yellow around each cheek. Her nose was petit and straight, and made her already impressive eyes look large. She reached into her pocket and returned clasping a small metal gadget. It had holes for each of her slender fingers and seemed to make been made specifically to fit her hand. There was a small red dial at the top where her thumb could get at it that was switched to off at the moment, but she lingered near it, ready to turn it on at a moment's hesitation.

He stared at it, taking in every groove and pivot of it.

"What is that?"

"I can't show you in here," she whispered, in that voice like the sun. "Please, just step outside with me for a moment... you'll see."

He frowned. Roxanne finally came out from the back and noticed the two of them, eyeing the pair suspiciously. He turned back to his friends and saw that Julie and Randy had stepped aside to play a pinball game, Randy standing close behind Julie and helping her work the buttons on either side of the machine. Sara was leaning on the pool table with her stick in one hand while the other gripped Jamie Dawkins's back, her nails digging into the smooth leather of his captain's jacket. His hands were cupping her hips in the same place Julie had been poking, and their lips were moving back and forth against each other. Her hair, previously straight, was now one big curl across the top of her head.

Nick stopped, his mouth again going dry. He became aware again of the bill in his hand and clasped it until it became hot as he watched the both of them. She finally dropped the pool stick, letting it fall to the floor with a loud clang.

"Thought he was with Teresa," Roxanne said, scrubbing the grease off her thumb with an old rag.

"Past tense," he replied, then turned back toward the stranger.

She was gone. All that remained of her was the cup of tea she'd been holding, which was still billowing out steam at such an alarming rate that even now, almost empty, he dared not touch it. Out of the corner of his eye, he caught the motion of the door closing, and turned just in time to see the blue arm of her sweatshirt disappear behind it.

He turned back to the pool table where Sara and Jamie still stood with their lips locked together as he hoisted her up until she was sitting on the table, then sighed and turned to follow the stranger out the door.

Sara opened her eyes as Jamie began to kiss the side of her fragile neck and watched as Nick left the Factory. She bit her lip, a look of concern coming over her as she closed her eyes again.

∞

The Factory opened up into a large gravel parking lot that eventually tapered off into grass before becoming the street again. There were no lines or guides in the front lot to let you know where to park, only the occasional divot where the weight of multiple cars had dug ditches into the ground and made guidelines for the next parker to follow. When Nick came out of the Factory, there were no cars parked in the entire lot, nor were there any cars on the road. The closest light he could see was Derek Smith's house across the way, both of its upstairs lights and one of its downstairs lights on and shining brightly at him.

He turned around, finding himself panting even though he wasn't exhausted at all. His tongue felt dry and desolate inside his mouth, and he thought that if he tried to talk it might spread to his teeth and turn them into sand they way they always did on cartoons when the characters went to the dentist. The Factory door had already shut tight behind him, locking all the neon flashing strobe lights of the place inside. It couldn't even be heard from out here, years of complaining neighbors resulting in some of the best soundproofing a very small amount of money could buy.

There was a small sliver of an alley alongside the east wall of the building that led to nowhere. It had once been null space between it and the storage building next door but had since been bricked over on one side to create an area devoid of wind and drifting snow that could be used for a smoking section or garbage disposal, even though neither building did anymore.

He paused and watched the small, dark space for a moment as if expecting it to do something. He could see every inch of it even though there was very little light... every crack or crevice in the brick, every dent on the plaster, every bit of garbage pilled up alongside it.

Slowly, tentatively, he stepped toward it. With each step, his view of it became more and more fixed and narrow, until almost all he could see was the black absence of light that it made. Even he had a hard time seeing into it, the moon above providing little to no aid.

Finally he entered the mouth of the alley and stood there, staring into the darkness and waiting for his eyes to adjust.

She was standing halfway down the alley, almost exactly in its centre. Her hood was still up and the light caught off the fabric on her head and shoulders, draping her face in the same darkness that surrounded her. It made her look like the Grim Reaper, a thought that made Nick turn back toward the Factory's door. He took a step back out into the open, an act that made him feel safer without actually making him safer.

She reached into her pocket without a word, again producing the same small device. She wasn't wearing it now, only cupping it in the palm of her hand. She bobbed it twice, then tossed it into the air and let it come down on the alley floor between the two of them, kicking up clouds of dust and dirt as it landed.

He stared at it again, looking from it to her and then back.

She nodded at him, then took a step back from the device.

Licking his lips, he threw one last glance toward the door of the Factory, then stepped into the dark of the alley. He took one step at a time, always careful to hold his eye on the stranger with every movement he made. Just like with the pool table, his every move altered his perception of her and the way he evaluated her threat... each movement bringing him more and more information.

When he got close enough, he bent down and reached out, caressing one of the slots on the device with his index finger and pulling it toward him until it was close enough that he could clasp it. He stood up immediately and held it in the palm of his hand, examining one side and then flipping it over to examine the other before starting again.

She reached inside her hood, past her head to the area between her shoulder blades.

He looked from the device to her, and was about to ask her what it was again, when she pulled a small blade from the darkness of her hood. It was like it came right out of her face, a reverse of the sword-eaters he'd seen as a child. He dropped the device to the floor again, splashing more dirt onto his jeans as he took a step backward.

She raised the blade high, moving it between her

fingers until it came to a comfortable position and then stopped, the tip of the blade in line with his neck.

"Hey," came a harsh voice. It was stern and hard like he would have expected hers to be. He turned to the end of the alley and saw Tash standing there, her fists clenched at either side. Her face was slender and shadowed by the moon behind it, her eyes blazing white and her face curled up in a snarl. "How about you just fuck off?" she finished, thrusting a finger out toward the stranger.

The stranger tilted her head as Nick began to pant again, turning from one to the other. Slowly, the stranger reached up with her free hand and clasped the nub of fabric at the cusp of her hood and pulled it down, revealing her full face. She was Asian; that thin face finally seen fully with almond-shaped eyes. The skin just over each of them was the same yellowed tint he'd noticed on her cheeks a few moments ago, and bled up into a long mane of jet black hair that went far down her back a disappeared somewhere behind her. When the rest of the sweatshirt hit the ground, he saw that she was athletic, dressed in a red jumpsuit with black edges all the way down it. The handles of twin katana blades protruding from sheaths on her back, the straps crossing her chest in a giant X. She put her knife away and drew one of the blades, again moving it around her fingers until it became comfortable and then readying it to strike. It had four gold spikes coming off the handle, making the legs of a spider, with two red rubies making up the body and the head.

Tash stared at her for a moment, her head tilting slightly to one side. "Swords," she said finally, clicking her tongue against the roof of her mouth. "Sure, why wouldn't it be swords?"

The stranger crouched, moving from side to side like a spider swaying on its web in a spring breeze, her hair remaining perfectly still as her eyes shifted from Nick to Tash and then back to Nick again. A wry smile spread over her lips as she took a step forward, bringing her sword up high.

"No!" Tash shouted, taking her first step forward even as the stranger brought down her blade toward Nick.

Nick wanted to close his eyes but couldn't, could only watch as the blade moved up to the highest point of its arc and caught the moonlight in its path, sparkled briefly, then started its descent back down toward his head. It seemed to be moving slow even though he knew it couldn't be, and he swallowed back hard as it became almost invisible, its sharp thin edge lined perfectly with the area between his eyes. It occurred to him that if he followed it the entire way down, he would be cross-eyed when it struck and that that would likely be how his parents found him: a boy with two heads cross-eyed. As the blade came closer and closer to him, he turned his head and rolled out of the way, diving with such force that his head rammed into the brick wall and split open.

The sword clanged against the concrete and the stranger sneered at Nick, surprised that he wasn't where he had been when she'd struck. The entire passage had taken less than a second to happen, even though it had seemed like an eternity.

"Hey!" Tash yelled, grabbing the stranger by the collar and slamming her against the wall opposite Nick. The stranger tried to raise her sword, but Tash brought up her knee and slammed it into her wrist, pinning it between her bone and the wall. The sword fell from her fingers onto the ground.

"Jesus," Nick gasped, trying hard to catch his breath. "Jesus."

"I think the next time I tell you to back off, you're going to," Tash continued, their foreheads almost touching as she locked eyes with the strange woman.

The stranger pushed her back, making Tash stumble and almost trip over Nick. She pulled back and punched Tash in the side of her neck with such force that she felt her molars rattle. She coughed once, tasting blood as it erupted up from her mouth, then spun back to face the stranger.

"I didn't care for that," she said, hauling back and hitting the woman in the face. The stranger fell back and slammed the back of her head against the brick wall, then fell forward against the ground and spit up a heaping mouthful of blood herself.

"Come on!" Tash yelled, hoisting Nick up under one arm and running with him toward the mouth of the alley.

"Will that stop her?" Nick asked as he turned briefly to stare at the woman from over his shoulder.

"It might slow her down," Tash replied, turning around the corner and breaking into an all-out run.

Sara stared at herself in the bathroom mirror of the Factory. It was cracked and dirty despite Roxanne's best efforts to keep it clean. Coupled with the gray walls around it, it looked depressing when she saw her reflection in it even on the best of days. Tonight it seemed especially dismal.

She tilted her head to one side and pulled her hair away from her neck to reveal a large red spot that Jamie had put there while she had sat on the pool table. She tisked, then reached into her purse and took out a small pad of makeup and started the task of covering it up. When her finger touched it, the memory of watching Nick leave the Factory came back to her, and she let out a deep sigh.

There had been a look on his face that she'd seen before... a loneliness and a heartbreak that she knew she'd caused in some of the other men in her life - one in particular. She'd wrestled long and hard with the responsibility of that, and had held firm to the belief that some people just were that way... that if they hadn't been pining over her they would have been pining over somebody else. But now she'd brought it out in Nick... someone who up until this point had always been strong and kind and happy.

She sniffed as her hand trembled against her neck, and she forced herself to steady it.

"You okay in there?" Julie called, knocking on the door twice.

"I'm fine," she lied, then turned back to the mirror and slathered on some more foundation.

Nick gasped for air as his lungs threatened to burst, each one a hot ball of fire within his chest. Tash ducked the both of them into the shadow of a house and tried to catch her breath, still clutching onto the loose flesh between his neck and shoulder.

"What the hell was that?" he asked, squirming out of her grip and standing a few feet from her. He tried to stand up straight but couldn't, bending over and resting his hands on his knees.

"If we live, I'll be sure to tell you," she replied, pressing her head flush against the wall of the house and looking around its corner. There was nobody coming up the street from where they'd come from, nor was there any sign of movement in the street at all... it was more disturbing to her than if there had been three of that woman bearing down on them with swords drawn. She'd spent most of her adult life in America's cities, and for any street to be this vacant was like looking into the soul of a ghost town. "Is it usually this quiet here?"

"Ah," he started, standing up and squinting at a nearby street sign. "We're close to Laird Street, more the residential area. So yes, people don't tend to stay out late here unless they have a curfew."

"Right," she nodded, glancing over the street once more.

-click-.

He stared at her for a long moment, then shook his head. Sweat dripped off it when he did. "Who the hell are you?" he said finally.

"My name's Natasha. You can call me Tash, most do. And, don't take this the wrong way... but I think I'm here for you."

-click-.

"Me? Me? I'm sorry, how am I not supposed to take that the wrong way?"

"It's a long, crappy story, kid," she frowned, touching

her face where she'd been hit gingerly. She winced once, then pressed harder. "The point of it right now is, I'm here to help. If you don't want my help, that's fine too... it's your call."

Nick stared at her even though she hadn't so much as glanced at him since they'd stopped.

-click-.

"I'm still not sure what you're -"

"Shh," Tash hushed, raising a hand to silence him.

"What?"

"Shh!"

They both paused, each standing as still and as quietly as they could as the cool September air blew around them.

-click-.

"There," she said, raising one finger into the wind. "Right there."

"What is it?" Nick asked, his voice hushed.

"Metal scraping... probably against the concrete."

"Is it her?"

She paused again, her eyes fluttering over the horizon line. "No," she said finally, standing up straight again. "No, it's coming from the wrong direction."

-click-.

"What should we do?"

She frowned, scanning the area from one side to the other. "Let's get the hell out of here."

There was a deli on fifth street that was famous around town for two major accomplishments: they had the worst meat products of any place that served meat products in

Coral Beach, and the best coffee of any place that served coffee in Coral Beach. They even topped Dunkin' Donuts, as hard as it was for anyone from out of town to believe - until they actually tried a cup.

There was one booth in the entire deli that still seemed like it was new, and it attracted the most patrons. Every other cushion had holes and rips in it and springs that struck out in uncomfortable places, but these two adjacent seats had somehow managed to escape the fracas and were comfortable at the same time. Nick sat in one and stared down at his coffee as Tash sipped on hers regularly, pain shooting up the bruise alongside her skull with every sip she took. The gash on his head had stopped bleeding, but it hadn't been hard for the cashier to tell that they'd both seen trouble recently. To his credit, he hadn't asked about it.

"So that's it, huh?" Nick asked, still staring down into his untouched coffee.

"Pretty much," she smiled. It was a warm smile that hurt her lips, but she couldn't help it. He looked sad and cute all at the same time, and her heart went out to him... like a little lost puppy. "Point of it all is, the world's going to hell. In more ways than one... it's been on a tipping scale for quite some time, and now some bastard has come along and decided to give it a little nudge, like someone always does every few decades."

"What does any of that have to do with me?" he asked, almost pleading.

She frowned. "Absolutely nothing," she said honestly, reaching out and taking his hand. "In truth, I don't think much of this does... not really. But I've got a friend who's trying to make it better. And I really think he could... but we figured out a while back that we can't do it alone. We're going to need help."

Nick twitched. "You're talking about me?"

She paused. "... No. No, not you. Maybe someday, but for now, you're too young. It's just not fair. But there are people out there that don't care how fair it is or how young you are. You met one of them here tonight. I think if we'd stuck around, you would've met a second."

Nick turned around and looked out the big windows that lined the deli into the darkness beyond. "They're still out there, aren't they?"

Tash nodded.

"And when you leave... they're going to kill me."

She let out a long sigh. "Probably."

He stared out into the dark for a long moment. "Why me?"

She smiled. "Don't tell me you haven't figured that one out yet."

He turned to her and scrunched up his face.

"I've met a few people with your kind of talent in my time, kid... hell, my friend's tracking one down right now that might have passed his whole life if it hadn't been for a lucky tabloid reporter... but you're not one of them. It's a good mask, I'll give you that, but not to my eye."

His face changed, as though it wasn't sure whether to be hurt of scared or angry or all three.

"Why don't you take out the contacts?"

He swallowed hard, then reached up carefully and touched his eyes lightly with his thumb and index finger. When he withdrew them a coloured contact lens was sticking to each, and when he looked at her again, his eyes were pure, irisless eggshell white. He felt them fill up with tears but forced them back.

Tash got up and moved over to his side of the table, and he immediately broke down and buried his head into her shoulder and started to cry.

"I didn't ask for this," he said after a moment staring out into the darkness beyond the window. He wasn't sure, but he thought he saw something moving in the shadows... like two figures dancing against the night sky.

Tash's face became sallow as the stroked his hair around his ears. "Nobody ever does," she said softly.

Sara forced her locker door closed, pinning her History textbook beneath her arm as she put all of her weight into her shoulder. She forced the metal door flush with all the others that lined the hallway, her tongue sticking out the corner of her mouth a little as she did so, the pink of it just different enough from the pink of her lips to be noticed.

"Christ," she sighed, snarling at the sticky feeling under her arms and knowing that she'd have to feel that uncomfortable, muggy feeling the entire walk home now. She turned to see that Nick had been standing beside her locker, and almost jumped. There was a vacant look in his eyes that she'd never seen there before, and it took her a moment to remember the events of the previous night. She resisted the urge to cover her hickey with her hand. "Hey," she said, as soothingly as possible.

"Hey," he replied solemnly. He looked as though he was about to cry, but didn't. There was unshaven scruff on his cheeks; that was news to her, as she hadn't been aware until now that Nick had even needed to shave. There were bags under his eyes and he was wearing his good coat even though it was still far too warm outside for it. The book bag slung over his shoulder looked full.

She shot his a wry look, then smiled. "What's with the hobo look? Is there a new trend I'm not aware of?"

He did not respond, his lips pursed until they were white.

Her smile faded. "Look, if this is about last night..."

"It isn't," he assured her, waving his hand to one side. He locked eyes with her again. He took a deep breath, then reached up and took her chin in his hand. Her skin was soft and warm. He leaned in and their lips met, hers warm and wet and pink against his. She seemed surprised at first, then pushed up on her toes to get closer to him. He put his arms around her waist and held her like that for a long moment before finally breaking it off and letting her back down.

Her eyes were wide and she didn't seem to be looking at him, blinking several times. "Wow."

He smiled, but somehow he still looked sad. He touched her face again, stroked her cheek with his thumb, and almost leaned in for another kiss... but he didn't. He knew that if he did, he wouldn't be able to do what he needed to next.

"I'm going to be gone for a while," he said finally, almost having to force the words out. "My parents are sending me to school down south."

"What?" Sara asked, shaking her head and coming back to reality. "Then don't go."

"Kind of have to," he said, sighing. "I just... can't be a nomad anymore, I guess."

She stared at him for a long moment, then nodded.

"But you stay here, okay? You stay... you. As long as you're here, there'll be a home in Coral Beach for me to come back to."

Her stroked her cheek one last time, then pushed himself off from the locker and walked down the hall and out of the school without looking back once.

She watched him go until he was long out of sight, still feeling his kiss on her lips and the jolt it had given her... there had been something in his eyes that had been different than any other time she'd seen him, and she felt like she never had gotten the kiss from the boy Nick Carry that she'd been wanting ever since eighth grade, but that maybe she'd been the first person to ever lay eyes on Nick Carry the man.

She smiled a little at that, although she wasn't sure why, then turned to the boy standing at the locker next to her.

"So, you going to Julian Grendel's party on Friday?" she asked him, paying little attention to his response or even if he gave one.

THE TOURNIQUET REVIVAL

- ELLEN CURTIS -

"That'll be 5£, Miss Jones," the store clerk said. His lined face creased into a smile as Ashby fumbled in her pocket for the correct change.

"Here, I've got some on me too," her companion, a thin nineteen-year-old girl with a short bottle-blonde pixie cut, interjected.

"Thanks, Kat."

Though Ashby was her senior by one year, it was always the younger girl who bailed them out of any tough situation. It was also Kat who people went to for advice. Sometimes it seemed like she was the poster child of wisdom and prodigy.

Ashby was typical Irish, her features giving her heritage away the instant anyone glanced her way. She brushed her long red hair out of her bright green eyes, feeling just a bit stupid for forgetting the money.

In the split second it had taken Ashby to fix her hair, Kat had thrown the money on the counter, grabbed up the bag of Halloween candy, and had raced out the door.

"Race ya home!"

Ashby sped after her, catching up to her easily at the street corner.

Kat slowed down so they could talk, still breathless. "We better hurry up and get home," she panted. "The trick-or-treaters will be around soon."

Ashby nodded in agreement. Her cheeks were almost as red as her hair now, courtesy of the autumn chill hanging like death in the air.

They walked a bit further when Kat stopped, her slender fingers fluttering over her abdomen as she let out a breath.

Ashby bumped into her, bringing her attention back to reality. "What's wrong?" she asked, a look of concern spreading across her features.

"Pro'lly nothing." Kat looked hesitant a moment, then replied, "Just feeling a bit stomach sick, you know? More likely it's just those taquitos we had for lunch." The look on Kat's face told Ashby otherwise, however.

"Well then, let's get home quick. I'm not going to be the one holding your *lack* of hair away from you face while you vomit into a pail," Ashby half-joked, trying to lighten the tension she knew Kat was trying desperately to fight back. Kat shot her a queasy looking smile.

The girls were almost at their driveway now, but Kat seemed to be getting sicker by the second. She was becoming unusually pale when the sound of approaching footsteps struck fear into Ashby's heart. An odd chill came over her and she felt a burning in the back of her skull, a paranoia overcoming her and making her feel as though she was being watched.

She turned around and her eyes met those of a tall hooded figure that stepped toward them. He was draped in a long black cloak with red trim that seemed to flow against the breeze, traveling whichever way it pleased. The top half of his face was shrouded in shadow, but his angular chin and large, sneering smile were all too visible. He held something in his hand she couldn't see, but it glinted in the fading sunlight brilliantly.

Terror held her lungs shut, banning her from issuing even a single cry for help. If only she had just kept walking. Maybe then the eerie figure wouldn't have been the first nightmare she encountered upon awakening.

Kat blinked, swimming in the fine lines between her conscience self and her dark, deep unconscious. She felt dreadful, and her head was pounding. She finally found the strength to open her eyes, but when she did, she shut them quickly, wishing the images away. Vibrantly rich crimson drapes surrounded an equally crimson armchair, illuminated by dripping candles. The sight of the man's corpse, whitened and presumably bloodless given his slit throat, was enough to paralyze anyone. She willed away the urge to vomit, though all she wanted to do was purge herself, and the world for that matter, of the lifeless tragedy. The pallid figure couldn't have even been her father's age, yet there he sat, silent evermore.

"Kat?" Ashby's slurred voice came through the candlelit den.

"I'm here," Kat whispered, finding her voice and the courage to open her eyes once more.

Kat and Ashby sat up, side by side on a lumpy, velvet swathed bed sitting in the center of a possibly perfectly square room. They were surrounded entirely by three matching red velvet couches and four armchairs. All ten of their occupants were dead. All ten, ranging in age from a girl in pigtails who might have been twelve, to the middle-aged man Kat had first seen, were clothed in black leather and satins. All ten appeared to have exsanguinated.

"Oh God. Kat, we have to get out of here," Ashby cringed, her words barely a whisper.

"That won't be necessary, Miss Jones," a voice writhing with malicious content drawled. "You and my darling Miss Smith, however, are. It is vital you stay, and it would be most pleasant if you cooperate to the fullest."

The door had opened, allowing a tall willowy man to enter, his reddish brown hair hanging in neat waves all the way to his shoulders. He was dressed like the corpses, but was more elegant, refined. What really struck both girls about him was not his speech, but his thunder grey eyes, which seemed to pierce each girl so completely that it chained them to their spots. They sat in stunned silence for a moment, until Kat found her courage and spoke.

"Who are you and what do you want with us?" The sentence came out jumbled into one breath.

"My name isn't rightly pronounced by the slithering muscles in your mouths," he smirked, looking down at himself. "But *this one* used to be called Gavin."

He locked eyes with Kat, holding it for a long moment until she squirmed uncomfortably.

"To put it simply for your friend here, I am the corporeal embodiment of the demon prince. I was re-incarnated mere months ago when the pitiful entity who inhabited this form jumped off a bridge, committing suicide. It's a shame you humans have such a disregard for death." The man paused before continuing, "You, Miss Smith, will soon be transformed into my princess."

Kat's mouth dropped open, but she shut it firmly again. She glanced over at Ashby and noticed how pale she had gotten. "What about Ashby?" she asked.

Gavin smiled mirthlessly. "That depends on how fast she can run and how good she is at evading my pets. You have two minutes, Miss Jones. I suggest you use them to their full extent." He motioned to the door. Numbly, Ashby got up and moved towards it, almost like she was sleepwalking. Just as she passed Gavin, he hit her square on the jaw, and she began to run. Kat lunged at him.

"Leave her alone, you filthy b-" she screeched before he caught her up and held a hand over her mouth.

"Now, now, sweetness, there's no use in trying to fight it. One way or another, come midnight, the rest of your life will belong to me. One way or another, you will be part of my darkness," he crowed, caressing Kat's cheek. She bit his hand causing him to draw back, letting her slip out of the room to go find Ashby. He smiled at one of the corpses knowingly. "I hope she's aware I'm a man of my word."

Ashby turned the corner again. After what seemed like a lifetime of mindless hallways, finally she found a staircase down. Just as she touched the rail, a familiar hand with chipped black nail polish closed around her wrist.

"It's me, Ashby. We've gotta get out of here. He thinks this is all a game. He's enjoying this," whispered the voice to which the hand belonged.

"Kat, thank God you're all right," Ashby whispered in response. Kat noticed a large purple bruise was already spreading up over her cheek. "This house is like a maze."

"Well. Let's find our way out. Down these?" Kat answered, nodding her head toward the stairs. At that moment, a voice rang through the halls.

"One minute," came Gavin's eerie giggle.

Both girls raced down the stairs, almost tripping on a rug at the bottom. "What way now?" Ashby breathed.

"Left. Trust me; I don't have a good feeling about the right," Kat replied. Both girls raced off again. At the end of the hallway there was a large door. The girls began to walk toward it, glancing cautiously behind them.

"Time's up, ladies. Go get 'em boys!" rang Gavin's voice once more. A thundering crash echoed from somewhere unseen just as Kat's hand reached the doorknob. She turned it quickly, only to reveal another staircase up.

"What now?" Kat whispered - both girls hesitating. She turned around, looking back down the long corridor they had just emerged from.

Two men came around the corner, their dark hair long and matted, covering the eyes and making their expressions impossible to determine. The lower halves of their faces were covered in leather masks that appeared to be fixed there permanently, with only a small grate in the front allowing them to breathe. Their shoulders were pinned back by the black jackets they wore, their arms flapping about wildly as they hobbled toward the girls, buckles from the jackets clattering against the walls with each and every step.

"Up!" Ashby shrieked, Kat already bolting up the stairs ahead of her. She reached the door at the top first, prying it open and pushing Kat inside. She felt her world come out from beneath her as something grabbed her by the ankle and yanked hard. Her head slammed against the floor as she started down the stairs, the door slamming shut behind her.

Kat was alone in the tiny attic. She turned and stared at the door for a long moment, its metal frame mocking her silently. All thoughts were erased from her mind but one: save Ashby, whatever the cost may be. She ran her fingers through her hair and she looked around: furniture, paintings, chests, and dust. She would have to look harder for a weapon. She knelt down next to a small wooden box and opened it.

The contents of the box were dusty and old. There were medical supplies that she didn't think had been in use at any point in the last century. Small glass vials that still contained liquid but were also crusted over and foggy. She huffed long and loud, picking up the shelf by either side and tossing it aside, its contents breaking over the floor.

The level below it wasn't as dusty. It contained small darts and several needles that appeared to have blood on their ends which she decided to avoid... and two guns, sitting there amongst the rest. They seemed out of place, like two elephants on a subway. She picked them up and checked their slides, breathing a sigh of relief when she found that they were loaded.

She closed her eyes and counted to ten to compose herself, then headed for the door, careful to avoid the broken glass.

Pressing her ear to the door, she strained to hear the sounds of her pursuers. Two separate breathing patterns.

Her next decision would haunt her for years to come.

∞

As fast as she could, Kat opened the door, aimed, and took two shots. Neither missed their targets, and both men fell to the floor. Kat let a bit of shock sweep over her. She would need it to suppress her guilt until later.

She raced down the hall again, this time going right where they had gone left. As relief and fear washed over her, she almost wished she hadn't.

The room was filled with the more of the masked men, all surrounding a large rack in the middle of the room. It was made of plywood and tilted up for all to see, someone in the back tightening its gears every few moments to make the ropes binding its occupant in place grow tighter and tighter.

Strapped onto the rack was Ashby, the ropes burning into her wrists and ankles.

Tightening the gears of the rack, back on to Kat, was Gavin.

"'That we are *true* lovers run into strange capers: but as all is mortal in love in nature so is all in nature in love mortal in folly,'" he stated, turning to face Kat, an ugly smirk playing across his lips. "Shakespeare's *As You Like It*. And we *are* true lovers, you and I. You can feel it. I *know* you can."

Kat paused, considering. She hoped she was a good liar. "And if I do, what will happen?" she flirted, eyes meeting his for the first time. Inside it burned her, however she concealed it seamlessly.

"Then you would come to me and surrender yourself."

"Haven't I already? You can let Ashby go when I come to you, and then, not only will I have surrendered, but I'll be yours... fully." Kat played out the last word carefully, grasping for time and at any chance of escape.

Gavin cocked his head to the side and the appearance of a hungry wolf slid over his features, his eyes glowing, almost, as he spoke. "Agreed, but we do it to my... taste."

Kat hesitated again, more fearful, but aware she needed to play her cards carefully.

"Deal," she whispered, dropping the guns to the floor and taking a tentative step toward him. He held his hand up to stop her. The crowd seemed to take a collective sharp breath.

"On all fours. Crawl to me," Gavin said with a cold snicker.

Kat was livid. "I am *not* a dog. At your insistence, I am to be your princess. I have two feet which I will walk on." She struggled to refrain from spitting it at him. To her surprise, Gavin smiled.

"Eric, Brandon, since my lady does not wish to crawl, kindly carry her to me. Handle her gently if you would," he drawled.

Two men stepped forward, hoisting Kat up and almost, but not quite, throwing her at Gavin's knees. He gave a merciless laugh. "Get up, darling."

Kat dragged herself to her feet. Ashby was now only inches away and, seeming to sense Kat's plan, stopped struggling. Kat could only be glad Gavin seemed to be oblivious. She looked him in the eye. "Now let her go free so we may proceed with your plans."

"As you wish," Gavin replied, turning to face Ashby again. He reached into his pocket, searching, for something. Relief swept over Ashby. He must be searching for a key to the locks. She saw the glint of silver just as Gavin pulled his out of his pocket. It was only when Gavin raised his hand that Kat and Ashby fully realized the situation, and by then it was too late. The 'key' stabbed into Ashby's chest, blood spattering onto Kat and Gavin, staining both her hair and his smile with gore. Neither girl had a chance to cry out. As Gavin withdrew the small, thin blade from Ashby's increasingly motionless body, Kat sank to her knees, closing her eyes to shut out the reality and the tears.

"Now, who wants to be next?" Gavin called into the crowd. He bent down next to her to whisper, "I kept my promise, she has been released. From this life at least." The sweet, consoling tone, that of which you might use to comfort a two year old, only sickened Kat further. Her eyes still shut, she felt Gavin move in closer to her and kiss her on the cheek. She felt like lashing out and striking him, but the shock froze her. It was then that she lost herself into the commotion of the sick-minded crowd clamoring to be the next sacrifice.

∞

For the next twenty minutes or more, the smell of blood further consumed the room, and though it felt like an eternity to her, she still didn't open her eyes. The sounds told her enough. It was only when the screams subsided into echoes in her mind that she dared to open her eyes.

It was to her great surprise that she found Gavin kneeling next to her. "It's time," he stated, his haunting eyes dancing over a large wooden table that had been placed in the middle of the room. On it lay a circular stone basin filled with blood, presumably that of the people who had just died. Looking around, Kat saw only five people remaining, other than herself and Gavin.

He helped her to her feet and led her to the table. Kat didn't really hear what he was saying. The drone of his voice only penetrated her at two points: the words 'dying' and 'reborn'. She wouldn't let it happen. Almost at the table, she shoved Gavin hard, his fingers flailing wildly to try and catch her. He grabbed her hair and pulled as he fell forward onto the table.

She twisted, letting it rip out and raced over to where the guns remained. Without thinking, she shot the rest of the cult followers dead, cursing herself for missing three shots, and for regretting missing the shots. Then she turned to Gavin.

"You don't want to shoot me, Kat. It's not too late to finish the ritual," he murmured, almost fearfully.

"Bloody Hell! You are CRAZY, understand?!? CRAZY!" Kat yelled, finally snapping. "You killed the only real friend I've ever had and you just expect me to comply?!" she screamed, motioning to that which she had not yet acknowledged, Ashby's still form. Kat was in tears now.

She aimed and fired.

The bullet hit Gavin in the stomach and he curled into himself, folding into a ball.

She ran to Ashby. She was still clinging to life. Kat felt her heart soar at the discovery. "I'm gonna get you out of here," she murmured into Ashby's hair as she picked her up and cradled her gently in her arms. Leaving the room, she ignored Gavin's pleas for help. He was still alive when she managed her way out of the house, maybe even still alive when she set the house ablaze. He was not still alive however, as she carried Ashby's body toward the approaching ambulance, toward their salvation, and toward the dawn of a new day.

AT MIDNIGHT, THE DAWN

- ELLEN CURTIS -

She took the mug gladly. It was cracked in places, but still managed to hold the warm liquid adequately, even with its blue varnish fading and chipping. Breathing in the steam, she smiled up at Alexi in thanks.

It had been like this between them ever since they had met, mere weeks ago. He had started caring for her, and it was the first time since she had run away that she hadn't been relying only on herself. She took a sip.

"How is it?" He smiled at her as she gulped down the tea.

"Warm," Cassidy replied thankfully, clear blue eyes flashing and dancing as the heat woke her up again. She giggled a bit as he blushed.

"So, any word from Romulus on our next job?" The tense words spilled from Alexi's lips in a jumble, and his eyes gave away his nervousness.

She responded with eyes twinkling as she watched her friend squirm. "Have you heard about the abandoned convent down by the docks?"

"You mean the one kids keep disappearing from?" Alexi balked, startled.

When Alexi had first come here two months ago, he had gotten off the plane in Helsinki with two of his friends, and in a matter of minutes they had been separated. He had searched for them, tried their phones, until finally someone picked up, days later. The voice was shaky and unfamiliar, though her screams and sobbing had convinced him that there would be no hope in finding his friends alive. She had convinced him in that moment that the most he could do to not end up like them was to stay the hell away from the docks where they had died. Sometimes, Cassidy reminded him of that girl.

"That's the one," Cassidy said, coy smile lighting her features. "Apparently Romulus heard about some guy named Scorpio taking it over and brainwashing all the girlsies and boysies trapped there. He wants us to take him downtown, get Scorpio on his side. Should be fun right?"

Alexi's voice caught in his throat. "Should be fun."

Cassidy shook out her matted blonde hair, bending over the sink and washing out the street dirt. She couldn't count the number of times she had done this at various coffee shops, fast food joints, and other public venues. Still, they had to look the part, and today they needed not to be messed with. It would be a difficult task, especially when dealing with a guy who had appeared out of nowhere and single-handedly gotten a snaky reputation in less than a week.

"Alexi, hand me some paper towel," she huffed, finishing up with her hair. She took a large wad from him and wrung out the excess water, turning to the hand dryer on the wall to finish the task. Alexi still hadn't spoken much, and she had begun to wonder if he'd be up to the job ahead.

Hurrying now, she quickly washed herself down, removing the smell of sweat off her skin, then changed into a black woolen sweater she had stolen the day before, pairing it with a skirt Romulus had lent her for the job. She smeared on bright red lipstick taken from the store they were in, then turned to face Alexi.

He couldn't help but smile at the stunning transformation.

Walking out of the store, the duo didn't glance up to meet the eyes of the store clerk. Out of the corner of his eye, Alexi could see he regarded them with suspicion: the street girl transformed into a deadly butterfly accompanied by a well off looking boy.

Outside he hailed them a cab, opening the door for Cassidy when it arrived before climbing in himself. "The docks please. We're headed for the convent," he said, trying to exude a confidence he was in fact having a difficult time finding.

The driver looked back, startled, as Alexi passed him a bill and motioned him onward.

The taxi sped along, giving Alexi the feeling that the driver wanted them gone as fast as possible. When he looked at Cassidy he saw she was smirking at the erratic driving. She turned to him and laughed when she saw that his jaw was clenched and firm, flooding his face with tension. Suddenly, they lurched to a screeching halt. Alexi flicked another bill at the driver, then got out wordlessly.

Cassidy strode toward the small wooden door nestled in a stone exterior and gave it a heave, expecting it to be jammed.

It flew open effortlessly.

"Odd," she murmured, glancing back at Alexi.

"Trouble?"

She paused, looking queasy, and nodded.

It had the Hallmark of a classic horror movie.

First it was their effortless entry, and now the musty odor of a dank, damp basement. Their breath hung in the air in front of them, the winter chill reaching inside what must once have been a thriving convent.

Times had changed though, and the nuns who had lived here had either died or gone to live at someplace else. Once, visitors and perhaps relatives would have entered here, but the entryway now seemed to hold only ghosts. A reception desk lay untouched to their right, save for being adorned with a bronze cross that the new residents had turned upside down. The light was minimal, but in the dimness of the entrance hallway the filth of their surroundings was visible. More visible, however, was a light coming from under a door near the end of the hall.

Alexi cringed.

"Shall we?" Cassidy whispered.

He nodded in reply.

Sticking close together, they crept toward the door quietly. The stone floor was covered in dirt and masked their footsteps well, but when they tried the door, there was a loud groan before the hinges gave.

The couple cringed, and a voice rang clear through the convent. "Miss me, darlings?"

It was like listening to velvet, or perhaps drowning in it.

He could barely breathe. He could see his breath was coming out in shorter bits, as the clouds in the cold air were becoming smaller and less frequent. He could hear Cassidy's voice somewhere next to him, shouting something like: "Don't do this to me," but the world went black before he could tell for sure.

The smell of vomit assaulted his nostrils as he woke. The lumpy mattress under him seemed to be wet, seeping through his shirt and chilling his skin. He blinked his eyes open, and was startled to come face to face with a white-blonde, blue eyed version of himself. This version seemed slightly taller, thinner, paler and even more out-there than he was. And cocky. This version seemed cocky.

Trying to sit up, Alexi's head immediately started to swim. He only got a few inches off the mattress before a combination of dizziness and handcuffs pulled him back down to the bed. "Where's Cassidy?" he slurred, the words coming out more like, "Whars Cashity?" His brow furrowed in frustration at the tongue that had seemingly gotten heavier in his mouth while he slept.

"Hold on, boy," Scorpio snickered. "Cassidy is fine; she'll be with us in a little while. We just need some... alone time first."

"And why do we need alone time?" he replied, slurring slightly less. The furrowed brow had turned quizzical as he waited for the response.

"Well, Alexi Hunter, it seems I have the bodies of at least two of your friends lying around, and even though my girl warned you not to come here, you came anyway. That's admirable, I suppose, but also a bit stupid. After all, the two of them together didn't make it out of here alive. What makes you think you can, with my girl?"

Alexi's jaw dropped. "Cassidy is…"

"Mine. Yes, that's a hitch in your plans, isn't it?" He chuckled, and Alexi was dimly aware of a cold glint permeating his eyes. "Sure, she appears to be on Romulus' side and yours too, and maybe she is… but first and foremost, she is loyal to me. Fear is a good tool against those who would defy you."

"What are we really here for then?" Alexi asked gravely.

"You are here to negotiate a deal. You play on my team, or I let the brainwashed maniacs loose on the city, a few at a time, night by night, until they've got the whole place overrun. They're contagious, you know. If you agree, I'll give them parts of the cure, bit by bit, as you do my bidding." Scorpio continued to smile. "If you're not good, I might even feed our precious Cassidy to them, though that would be a shame, don't you think?"

Alexi's face grew dark. "How do I know they're really infectious? What work would I be doing for you?"

"As for your first question, I could answer that by letting them loose in the city, but that wouldn't be very nice of me, so let's avoid that. The other option, which I do believe is the one you'd prefer, involves me going to fetch one of our little infectees and simply showing you how delightfully rabid and dangerous they are."

Alexi winced at his words.

A jubilant expression to crossed Scorpio's features when he saw that, like a man on his wedding day.

"And the answer to my second question?" Alexi asked, eyes narrowing. Scorpio's expression became nauseously close to pure delight.

"You'd take care of Romulus. For good. Cleverly, mind you. It wouldn't be some simple hit. I want to completely neutralize both him and his whole silly cell. Of course, he will have to be killed, but first I need to make sure that there will be no repercussions, and no one to take his place." Scorpio's business-like smile slid back into place. "It shouldn't be too hard for you, should it?"

Alexi regarded him with a long stare before replying, "No, it shouldn't. Just why do you think I'm the right one for the job though?"

His grin faded as he got up and left the room. He paused at the door, turning back over his shoulder to regard Alexi. "Let's just say I've fallen out of mother-dearest's favour, and the only one I feel like I can trust is my brother."

For a long time, Alexi debated the validity of what Scorpio had said. Yes, he had been adopted, so it was possible to have siblings, theoretically. Yes, he did see a resemblance. Yes, also to the probability of finding family in this city. That was what he had come to Helsinki for in the first place, but after the disappearance of Rochelle and Thomas, his focus had turned more to proving his independence... and to some extent, revenge.

He had purposely lost all contact with his Canadian adoptive parents after finding out that they had lied to him for the first twenty years of his life. They were rich, conservative and absent from much of his childhood. In some ways, finding out he was adopted had made him feel like he was abandoned twice.

"Alexi?" Cassidy whispered tentatively, poking her head around the corner of the door. Only now did he look up from his reverie, fully taking in his surroundings for the first time.

The vomit stained mattress matched the stone floor, which was caked in bile and blood. Another bed was pushed against the opposite wall, giving the room the same feeling as a cell. It didn't help that he was still chained down.

"Are you okay? Scorpio wouldn't tell me where you were," Alexi's asked, his expression worried upon seeing his companion. It didn't matter that she had lied to him. They were in this together.

"Am I okay? Alexi, you're the one covered in puke and chained to a bed!" She threw her arms in the air, exasperated.

She crossed the small space between them and took a set of keys out of her pocket. Looking up at his face, she answered the question that resided there. "He gave me them to free you with. I'm supposed to get you cleaned up and to your real room. The only reason you're in here is because you apparently wouldn't stop puking. Or that's what he says anyway. He's had me distributing parts of the cure to all his science projects since you passed out yesterday."

The locked handcuffs clicked open as she jiggled the key.

"So they really are all infected with something?" he asked, sitting up and rubbing his wrists.

Cassidy looked at him uncomfortably. "I don't know if it's that they're infected as much as I think they might have died… and come back to life."

The two friends wandered down a narrow corridor in silence. Alexi hadn't said a word since Cassidy had dropped the crazy bombshell on him. Finally though, his head was swirling too much not to ask.

"What do you mean you think they died? People can't die and come back to life just like that. And certainly not a whole roomful of them," he whispered, really coming closer to a hiss. The idea was so insane, yet he could tell Cassidy had been serious. "What makes you think that anyway?"

"Alexi, they're half rotted. It's not gangrene, or some flesh eating disease. He's experimenting on corpses, making them come back to life. I saw one of them, submersed for two days in a tank of water. *Two days*. Do you have any idea what a bloated corpse looks like?"

He shook his head, brow furrowing.

"Well soon you'll get to see one talking. Now mind you, they don't say much that's overly pleasant to listen to. Mostly stuff about how they'd like to eat me when

Scorpio's not looking."

"What do you mean, 'When he's not looking?' He can't be around all the time, and I haven't seen any cameras."

Cassidy stopped walking and turned to face him. "It doesn't matter if he's here or not. There are no cameras, but trust me, he's always watching and he always knows." Her voice had gotten quite quiet, and fear had sprung into her eyes.

"Then what will happen if he knows I know that they're all..." He searched for the word. "...undead?"

"Who says he doesn't want you to know?" Cassidy began walking again.

She came to a door and Alexi was surprised to see that it had a number pad next to it. Cassidy quickly punched in six numbers, and the door opened.

It was dark inside at first, until Cassidy flicked on a light switch. It was then Alexi realized he hadn't seen any windows since he had woken up. "Are we underground?" he asked.

She nodded curtly.

He looked around and did a double take. They were in a lab, or perhaps a mortuary. A cold stainless steel operating table was in the middle of the room, and various desks, shelves, and workbenches lined most of the room.

Cassidy led him through that room though, and down into a wide hall. It was pitch black, and only when he heard a feral growl did he realize they were walking past cells.

"Casssidyy. We're sssoo hungryy. Why don't youu come over closer and let us have a look at youu?"

"Whooosee the new one? Food? Is he the food?

Massster wouldn't let us have any todays."

The voices followed them down the hall.

"Stick close and don't pay any attention to them," Cassidy muttered. She pushed open another door, and suddenly they stepped into the light again.

They were in a communal shower.

"Hurry up and get clean. There's a change of clothes waiting for you by the sink. I'll guard the door." Cassidy had taken on a brusque, prison guard type persona; and for a brief moment Alexi wondered if he could really trust her.

Still, he did as he was told. There wasn't much sense arguing when Scorpio might be watching. Alexi shuddered, remembering. They were in a shower, for god's sake. Wasn't anything sacred anymore? With that in mind, he shed his ruined clothes in a hurry, not caring when icy water hit his bare skin, and caring even less that he still didn't really feel clean when he turned the water off. He toweled himself off quickly, practically running toward the pile of clothes, which to his relief, actually fit quite well. "Where are we headed now?"

Cassidy glanced up. She had had her ear to the door, listening, and motioned for him to be silent. After a moment like this, she finally straightened up and regarded him at last. "You've made them restless. Seems they think you're dinner. Through the next door, if you please." She pointed to another door, leading on from the showers.

Alexi regarded her for a moment, trying to see what had gotten in to her before he went on. He realized it was fear.

She led him through the tunnel into his room. She hated doing this to him. It was bad enough Scorpio had made her take him here. She hated dealing with demigods; mind you, Alexi wasn't bad. She guessed that had to do with the fact that he still didn't know. In her opinion, it was better not to.

They crossed the threshold into his room, and once again she felt his eyes on her. It was different than when Scorpio looked at her, that was for sure. When Alexi looked at her, she wasn't just a piece of meat. Not that that could ever mean anything though. She couldn't let it, and she knew he never would either, not if he found out who he was.

"So you can sleep here. No one will pester you. Scorpio will come for you when he needs you. I'm in the room down the hall, knock if you need anything. We've got internet down here, so you can search up stuff if you want, but he's got something done to the machines that won't let you access chat sites or anything where you can upload data. Basically, he's got nothing enabled on there that will let you go running for help. Not that we'd get any anyway. We're too far below ground, and the tunnel system is like a labyrinth. I'll let you get some privacy now."

Alexi couldn't find the words to say to her before she turned and left. He was taken aback by her mood swings. Leading him all over the place, she had seemed like some crazy headmistress, and now she was turning into a timid servant, like the kind his 'parents' had employed. It was a weird feeling.

Pacing the room, which was slightly larger and much comfier than the previous rooms had been, Alexi felt cold. This 'brother' of his most certainly was not normal, and he intended to find out what his deal was. He wanted answers. Following a hunch, he whispered into the silence, "Scorpio, if you really are all seeing like Cassidy said, come here. I want the truth."

Nothing.

He waited for a minute. "Lousy bugger. I knew it couldn't be true."

"Well I beg to differ, little brother. Now what is it you want so desperately from me that you decided to talk into the night like a madman?" Scorpio other worldly voice floated to Alexi's ears. He spun around to face him.

"How'd you do that?" Alexi yelled crossly. He scowled at Scorpio with contempt, willing answers to flow out of him.

Scorpio just laughed. "I did that, just as you could too, if you bothered to try. All you need to do is open yourself to the possibilities, and they become wide open to you. If Mother hadn't sent you off, maybe you would know that."

Alexi cringed. He hadn't expected the last part. "And why would Mother have sent me away? To avoid becoming like you?" he asked, his voice shaky and defiant.

"Maybe," he winked. "Maybe she just wanted you growing up with a human perspective, so you'd identify with them. Unlike me, who she outcast for my 'un-godly' behaviour."

Alexi's jaw dropped as he began to put two-and-two together. "Wait. Ungodly? Do you mean…?"

"We're demi-gods, brother. And Mother seems to think that I'm the bad child." His eyes were literally sparkling as he watched his brother taking-it-in in amazement.

"So where do we stand? What good is telling me this going to do? What if I find the ability to overthrow you? Where does Cassidy fit into this?" Alexi was shaking as he asked this, voice raised.

From the next room, muffled voices assaulted Cassidy's peace and quiet. So he finally knew. There was no hope now. He would find the power, just like his brother's, and his fate would be sealed. Two demi-gods residing on the same planet, let alone in the same city, would certainly be disastrous. She listened harder, catching her name.

"Well, my little Alexi, Cassidy, as you know, is human. She is therefore expendable. Perhaps not to you, though I do believe you will begin to see things my way, but she is expendable to me. Furthermore, she is of little use, so don't count on her to get you out of this. Remember, I have the upper hand. That's something she knows, and something those friends of yours, Rochelle and Thomas, knew all too well. A little consolation though, you could save them eventually, if you do enough work for me that would get them the full cure. That's your choice though. Even then, they might not be to your liking."

Scorpio's words hit her like bricks. Expendable. That's all she was to him. Even after all she had done, after he had handpicked her, she was still just a pawn in his crazy game of chess. What was worse, she knew he was right. Some day, Alexi would see her that way too. Her last chance was to help his friends. They had been the bait, but all a 'cure' would provide them was a return to death.

Cassidy knew too well that once one of Scorpio's projects died, they were nothing more than a corpse, even if they could walk and talk. It was nothing more than a synthetic existence.

She heard Alexi's door close, and footsteps retreating down the hall toward Scorpio's room. There was a chance, albeit a small one, that together she and Alexi could take out Scorpio. He would be too powerful for the two of them alone though. They needed help, and getting it would be difficult. She peeked her head out the door and checked if the coast was clear.

That Scorpio was omniscient was actually a bit of an over-cautious lie. He could tune in to conversations, yes, but he couldn't be everywhere at once. Her plan would require the best of timing. Hurriedly, she dashed towards Alexi's door, flinging it open, then shutting it tight behind her again.

"Alexi, you have to listen. I have a plan."

It was a clear outline, with little room for error. Cassidy would do her part, and Alexi his. Then, they would rendezvous back in time for the 'big finale'. Neither of them could know if any of it was actually possible. They had to have hope though, Alexi thought. Without it, what chance did they have? Cassidy took one long look at him. He wouldn't have agreed to the last part anyway, so it was better to trust her instincts. She had for most of her life, and right now, they told her to forget her love for him, and concentrate on saving him, and possibly the rest of the good world. "I'll be right back, 'kay? This shouldn't take too long. If it does though, start without me. You're the last hope." She fought back tears, smiling almost convincingly.

He leaned over and kissed her cheek sadly. "You better come back." He said it as though he knew she wouldn't, holding her gaze and filling her with his sorrow. Already in her eyes, he had taken on a sort of glow, and she knew she had been wrong about him turning out like Scorpio. When she could take his gaze no more, she tore from the room.

Through the tunnels she ran, through the showers, and straight into the holding cells, locking the door firmly behind her. She flicked on the light, and simultaneously hit another set of switches. The glass of the holding cells opened, as did the door to the lab. She was now the bait, but hopefully it would be enough.

Scorpio sat up in bed, screaming in rage. It was an unearthly noise. He dreamt of her always, his pet Cassidy, and now she was doing this to him. To them even. Feeding herself to his experiments and trashing his lab. She must have snapped. He had heard a lack of sunlight sometimes did that to humans. Nevertheless, she was his. He propelled his mind towards her and materialized amongst chaos.

Alexi touched the part of his mind he now knew had been kept dormant. The part his true mother had made sure only love could unlock. He could now get there. Into the darkness, he whispered, "I need you now," and a pair of bright white wings exploded from his back as the room burned in a white light.

"Mother. I need you now. Your son continues to stray."

An ethereal being stepped forward. "Then you've found it in yourself what needs to be done?" Alexi nodded. "And you've made your choice?" Again, he inclined his head. "Then I will give you my help."

Another light blinded his eyes, and he was released back to Earth.

The corpses fell, as pristine and composed as they had been when they were first killed. Cassidy lay in a heap on the floor, no longer attacked by undead animals tearing at her flesh. Blood caked the room, but strangely, it touched neither her, nor one of them. The only evidence in the room of the epic struggle that had taken place was the charred skeleton standing statuesque over the girl, skeletal wings attempting to shield her from the onslaught of dozens of brilliant souls being freed into the sky. In another room, just down the hall, a new demi-god awoke. He was not the hardened and blackened soul that had been sent to Earth as a lesson to himself, but rather he was the one who had been sent to teach love, through adversity in the hardest situations, to himself and others.

Alexi floated through the tunnels, nearing his destination. He glided through the doors that had been blasted open until he came to her. Entering the room, the skeletal angel crumbled into ash, blown away by an unexplained wind. He then went to her, broken on the floor. Gently cradling her in his arms, her eyes flittered open. "How are we even here? I thought I was going to die," she forced out the words in a whisper, weak.

"We're here because I chose you."

FALLING INTO FIRE

- ELLEN CURTIS -

There was nowhere left to go. It was as if the Earth had shattered and left us all standing there, in the stain that had become our existence. I remember the feeling perfectly. It was like falling into fire and ice all at once, and then realizing that every fiber of your body was about to explode. That was how it felt on the day that he left us.

The staccato crash of running pierced the hall, annihilating any silence that had previously existed there.

The figures emerged from the smoke, gasping for air and getting nothing but burning, smoldering smoke. They held their sleeves up to their faces and pressed on, plummeting toward the end of the hall.

There were three of them, one man and two girls – one no older than five. Their eyes stung and watered feverishly, sending floods of water down their cheeks and making it impossible to see.

Blonde hair escaping from her braid, the older girl

bolted ahead of the others and reached for the doorknob. She let out a shrill shriek and withdrew her hand, now sizzling and covered in pustules of raw skin. The smell of burnt flesh mingled with the odor of chemicals and her eyes began to water even more from pain and the stench.

"Damn it, Lil!" the man hissed, pushing his glasses up before helping her to her feet. "I told you they would burn the labs, too. They don't want it to survive. They never have."

The small girl sobbed, golden tears falling down her flushed cheeks.

"Aisli, stop blubbering and start running!" he ordered, pushing Lillian and Aisli back down the hall and toward a smoky stairwell they'd emerged from. It wasn't long before they were once more gagging on the thick black cloud that made its way throughout the facility and into their lungs. Lillian pulled Aisli behind her, trying to see through tears and smoke, all while fighting the throbbing pain that had become her right hand. Eyes burning and almost blacking out as she attempted to climb the stairs, she neared the point of breaking. "Robert, I can't do this anymore, we need a way out now!" she screamed, pulling as much oxygen in as she could from the smoky interior before starting into a fresh coughing fit.

Robert turned to glare at her over his shoulder for a moment, then pulled them both into his arms and continued up the stairs and into the smoke.

"We can't get out this way," she said, struggling to find the breath for each word. "You're going to get us killed."

The child's eyes widened, and more tears came.

"The only way we can go is up into the smoke," he

said, not bothering to stop or even look at her when he spoke. "Down would mean going through sector D, which should be filled with flames. The only way out is up through the smoke, through a window or an exit."

If Lillian still questioned this, she did not say so out loud.

Robert did though, although he tried his best not to show it. He'd seen the effects of fire on human flesh before and did not want to experience that for even an instant; but he'd also seen the bodies of people who'd died from asphyxiation, their lungs drowning when there was no water in sight and burning when there were no flames near. It wasn't much of a choice either way, and certainly not one Robert liked to make. Despite the fact that the man seemed to be indifferent to the suffering of his companions, Robert had worked at this facility since its first walls had been put up. It was his entire life, and now that life was quite literally in danger of being ended. Maybe if things hadn't gone the way they did, maybe if he hadn't been so adamant on completing the project even once they realized it was a failure, the building wouldn't be burning and they could have started over from the beginning.

But it was too late for that now though.

After what seemed like stumbling through poison forever, they reached an unlocked door. Robert noted that Lillian's wheezing had all but stopped and that Aisli had ceased sobbing. Lillian's breath had become harsh and ragged, and was becoming fainter by the second. He flung the door open and dashed inside without bothering to check where exactly they were heading. As long as it meant breathable air, he didn't care.

He eased the girls to the floor, then shut the door behind them in a vain attempt to lock the smoke out. As the door latched, they were plunged into darkness. The soft plinking of water on tiles filled his ears, and his smoke filled nostrils were suddenly alerted to a sickening scent that the recesses of his mind quickly identified.

"Activate lighting system," he whispered, and like magic the room was bathed in an eerie violet glow. He swore softly under his breath as he took in the surroundings.

The mess hall was filled with bodies. Dozens of people lay dead, spread across tables and strewn over counters, some face down in overflowing wash basins. The bulletproof glass that had once stood between the service area and the space for lineups lay shattered on the ground and driven into a teller's body. Blood was spattered onto the white walls of the room like lipstick on a mirror, reflecting the devastation that had taken place. Without realizing, Robert sank to his knees in a pool of half-congealed blood, soaking his already soiled lab coat in a fresh layer of filth. Until now, it hadn't even occurred to him that the violence had struck during the mid-day break.

"Robbie, why aren't we moving?" came a soft whimper from behind him.

Startled back from his reverie, Robert turned to face Aisli. She was clambering to her feet to see around the room better. The child's lilac eyes stood out against her pale skin, startling and foreign looking on an otherwise normal face. That is, if a child with such striking features was normal. Her high cheekbones and wispy body gave her the appearance of a faerie changeling, and her small red lips made her appear Geisha-like. The combination had been blinding to Robert when he had first seen her, and still was.

"We need to get Lil breathing again," he muttered; then speaking up, "Aisli, I need you to help me. Lil's not breathing because of the smoke. I'm going to need you to find me an oxygen canister. There should be one in the emergency stash; you know where it is, in the kitchen."

She nodded and dashed off, darting between bodies as if she were simply walking through a crowded room and not a graveyard.

When she returned, Lillian was barely conscious. She dragged several canisters of oxygen and masks behind her. Wordlessly, she attached a mask to a canister and placed it over Lillian's nose and mouth. Ever so slowly, Lillian's eyes fluttered open as she began to fill her weakened lungs.

Robert watched her until he was sure she would be okay, then turned to Aisli and attached a mask to her face as well, and then one to his. Within minutes, the trio was set to continue.

Getting up carefully, Lillian picked up Aisli and following Robert to the door, she threw him a wary glance. "Where's the closest exit?" she whispered, her voice hoarse as if she had been screaming. Condensation formed around the plastic lip of her mask with every word she spoke, then faded again before the next. "We have to make it out of here alive, even if it's just for everyone else's sake. No one deserves what's happened here."

Robert's brow furrowed, but Lillian couldn't tell if it

was in disapproval or thought.

Slowly forcing out the words as if they were covered in glue, Robert answered her. "There's an exit by the elevator that takes you straight into sector H. It's the least likely to be closed off or guarded." His bloodshot eyes couldn't meet hers as he placed a hand on the door handle and yanked it open. She couldn't know, he wouldn't tell her. Only hours before they had been laughing together as they came out of this same room. Only hours before, the station had been intact, and no one had been killed. Nobody had been hunting them down and he couldn't bear to tell her that the one person outside of the station that they had trusted was the one that had murdered the life they had led here.

They ran back out into the smoke, continuing up the stairwell. The further up the stairs they got, the less smoke they encountered, until finally they reached a door labeled *Sector H: Exploration Unit*. A thin beam of light peeked out through the dimness of the hall, and Lillian recognized the small beacon to be the light coming from a control panel.

"Robbie, do we have clearance to get in here?" came the soft lilt of Aisli's voice from the dead silence.

He pivoted to see the girl, clutching on to Lillian's shoulder and looking back at him, pale face covered in a layer of dirt.

Before he could speak, a loud crash echoed through the facility, the sound of metal grating metal piercing their ears. Quickly, Lillian slid Aisli off her shoulder and with her uninjured hand she punched a twelve number access code into the lockbox just above the knob.

The door began to open shakily, sticking as the power

flickered. The gap was just wide enough that they could squeeze through single file to the other side.

The glass hallway that had once been the window to the hundreds of government researchers housed within the facility was shattered. Test tubes and vials were overturned, workbenches were smashed, and blood was splattered across every visible surface. There was not a single body was in sight, but the air smelled of acids and the decomposition of flesh.

Lillian wretched and fell to her knees. As Robert bent to help her, he noticed Aisli seemed rather unaffected by the whole ordeal. She didn't even exhibit any signs of being in shock, as if the tears she had shed earlier were simply for show. It puzzled him that such a young child, previously unexposed to violence, would not cower in fear at their present situation; however, he hardly had the chance to ponder this observation further as the sound of gunfire rang clear, amplified by the sheer volume of shattered glass. Lillian's head shot up, eyes wide, and in a split second she had managed to place herself in front of Aisli, shielding the girl from any bullets. Cursing to himself, Robert raced toward them, lifting them up and carting them toward the exit.

Before they were even halfway to safety, he felt a bullet splice through his upper thigh. Warm blood flooded down in a torrent as he raced with the girls toward their freedom. He stumbled then, tumbling behind an overturned table that only barely provided them any cover.

Silent tears marred Lillian's face as she attempted to stifle the blood that was flowing from Robert and leaving him without life. Glasses askew across his nose, he attempted to push them up, but only left a streak of blood on their surface. Managing a weak smile, he caught her eye and spoke his last words. "Get Aisli out, love. I don't want to see you for a while yet on the other side." Eyelids fluttering, his head drooped and his body went limp, leaving Aisli and Lillian alone against an undetermined number of pursuers.

"Lil, we have to go now. Leave Robbie here, it's what he wanted," Aisli whispered, voice level, as if she were reciting the alphabet.

Lillian looked up into Aisli's eyes and nodded, picking the girl up and peeking around the corner of the table. Bullets still flew in their direction, but as Lillian darted out of the protection of the table, they seemed to dance around the pair.

They were just feet from the exit when the door swung open. "Cease fire, troops!" was the order issued by a stern masculine voice.

Lillian froze, clutching Aisli to her chest, mesmerized by the familiar voice that had once played to happier dialogue. It couldn't be him; he would never harm anyone this way, especially not her or Aisli. Stepping into view, however, was Lillian's worst fear realized.

He was tall and greying, with short wavy hair falling into his sharp blue eyes. They had once smiled at her, wrinkling in a welcoming way that lent the knowledge he had earned in his years. There was no smile present now though, simply a thin line painted across a stubbly face. The long blue-grey coat he had worn every other time she had seen him was replaced with dark green fatigues. Lillian only felt despair as she looked upon the face of her mentor, realizing that he too had been swallowed up by the bureaucracy that they had fought against.

"Lillian, sweetheart," he said, his voice as easy and as soothing as it had ever been. It made her want to throw up. "I really would hate to have to kill you for the experiment, but if you can't hand it over, I'm going to have to. The old man has a taste for traitors being served to him on a silver platter, and I'd rather be able to tell him you cooperated to the fullest. What do you say to that? A life for yours?" He smiled, and it was so like the way he used to smile that she realized it must have been an act all along. He reached his hand toward her, keeping constant and hypnotic contact between their eyes.

"A life for a life, Colonel? Is that what you call killing thousands of people, just so you can terminate an experiment that evolved into more than we could ever dream?" Lillian spat, wrapping her arms around Aisli more snuggly. "There is no way in hell that makes sense."

He laughed at her and took another step forward. "Sweetheart, you're holding onto that abomination as if it actually has some place in this world. Hand it over, and you won't have to die. You can start again, with a new position in a new center. There's no reason for you to lose your life over a failed project." His words felt cold as they lodged themselves into Lillian's ears, hardening her to his cause.

"You were like a father to me," Lillian whispered shakily. "I thought I knew you, but I see now what you really are. You have no right to call me sweetheart, and Aisli deserves better than for you to call her an abomination.

She is living, breathing, thinking, and just as human as I am, and certainly more human than you are!" She was shaking in rage, but Aisli seemed quite content to remain in her arms, and gave no signs that she was upset by the Colonel's words.

"Lil, could you please put me down for a moment? There's something I'd like to show your friend," Aisli asked calmly, her fist cradling some hidden object.

Lillian and the Colonel stood for a moment, shocked that Aisli had spoken. He glanced at his firing squad, and then at the two girls.

"Troops don't shoot. Lillian, put it down and we won't harm it. You have my word," he barked.

"Like that means anything."

"Please."

Lillian couldn't tell if it was a ploy to get Aisli, or a moment of sheer stupidity on his part, but she could tell that Aisli had something up her sleeve.

Literally.

Hesitating for a moment, she gently placed Aisli on the ground and let the girl waddle over to the Colonel. His curiosity getting the better of him, he bent down as Aisli approached so as that he could be eye-level with the child.

Slowly, she extended her closed fist toward him and then opened it, palm up.

Lillian strained her neck to see, but only caught a glimpse of the Colonel's puzzled reaction before Aisli blew on her palm. The room, and seemingly the whole world, exploded in a blinding light.

She had been intended as a simple experiment. Nothing more, nothing less. But in the instant that it had taken to create her, something of magic was born.

For every one project we have, there are a dozen side projects. Most never accomplish anything and were never meant to, but every so often something amazing comes out of one of those accidents of science. Like penicillin.

There was a particular genome that kept going astray in the main project. Something that kept appearing in each and every test subject and making life horrible... so we removed it. But for scientists, that's rarely enough. It's not enough to fix something; they have to know why it was broken in the first place. So, a new sub-group was formed to study it.

Some had joked that the genome had been God himself trying to tamper in our affairs. That he'd reached down and put a wrench in our gears to try and stop us. That was how it got the nickname 'The God Gene'.

Aisli was born by chance, after many failed experiments, when there was no hope left for the project. With an upsweep of interest, government funding had been acquired easily and the project had taken off. Two brilliant students were selected to care for the experiment, Lillian Harper (2329347) and Robert Strong (9704986).

Both students excelled in their studies, and their understanding of the mind. Aisli started out as a one year assignment for the duo, on the recommendation of their professor. As Aisli grew, so did the mutual love between the child and her guardians. But as love grew, so did interest in the young creation, and when the interest began to wane, there was hell to pay.

When the project was terminated, Aisli was permitted to live as Lillian and Robert's foster child; however her abilities began to multiply. Some, for the better, but some were too strange and foreign, and therefore dangerous. The Colonel advised Robert and Lillian to lessen their attachment to the girl, whom they began to refer to as their daughter, and he also began to advise others. I began to see the danger in keeping Aisli alive, now that funding was abolished, so they began to construct a plan to silence the unfortunate experiment once and for all. Little did they know, it could put up a fight.

With every experiment there are risks, and rewards. Though Aisli did not prove a viable source of research or revenue, the things we learned from her continue to aid us today. This project is therefore being filed as a success, though it is being closed until further notice.

The old man reached for his glass again and brought it to his lips, finding it empty. He frowned and then placed it aside. He closed the folder in front of him and tossed his pen back into the mug on the edge of his desk before turning and opening the drawer beside him.

He rummaged around it for a moment before finding what he was looking for, withdrawing a large rubber stamp and pressing it down against the top of the folder. When he lifted it, the bright red letters proclaimed their message proudly:

Engen filename - Compendium - CLOSED.

ENGEN TIMELINE

With over twenty novels spread over three different series by many different authors, the Engen Universe of titles is growing every day and into genres we couldn't have imagined! From the original ten book *Coral Beach Casefiles* thriller series, its crime novel sequel series *Xander Drew*, our flagship adventure title *Infinity*, or single-novels like *Jacobi Street* or *light|dark*, there's something in the Engen Universe for everyone with more books by more authors on the way soon!

...But how do the events relate to one another, chronologically? While some astute readers have guessed at the potential timeline (some accurately, some not), we're going to finally set the question of the Engen Timeline to rest.

Turn the page for an up-to-date guide of the ever-widening world of Engen, featuring the works of Ellen Curtis, Andrea Hackett, Sarah Thompson, Jay Paulin, and Matthew LeDrew!

In the 10 Years Prior Black September

"Reptilia" by Matthew LeDrew
published in *light | dark*.
Danger descends on a small secluded town in the form of a deadly virus with fantastic and terrible side-effects. Can a small group of doctors escape alive?

Compendium by Ellen Curtis
Three short stories forming the basis for the Engen Universe's ties to suspense, genetic engeneering, and the supernatural. Features the stories "The Tourniquet Revival," "Falling into Fire" and "At Midnight, the Dawn."

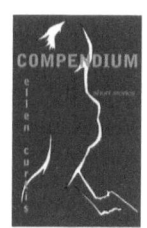

"The Theogony" by Matthew LeDrew
published in *light | dark*.
A tale of young Theo Flaherty of the *Infinity* series and his time admitted against his will to the Black Springs hospital, where he learns to paint, and seeks out his father.

Black September

"Revving Engen" by Matthew LeDrew
published in *light | dark*.
A direct lead-in to both *Infinity* and *Black Womb*, Tasha travels to Coral Beach, Maine on a hot tip about a recently discovered young man with incredible abilities.

Infinity by Ellen Curtis & Matthew LeDrew
Faced with a destiny he's uncertain of, the enigmatic Victor must bring together four unique people with very special abilities... or face the tasks ahead alone. Guaranteed to excite!

Black Womb by Matthew LeDrew
Fifteen years ago, something happened in Coral Beach, Maine that resulted in the present death of a seventeen-year-old boy. Now four high-school students must try to solve the mystery... before the killer picks them off.

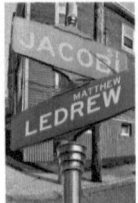

Jacobi Street by Matthew LeDrew
When a mysterious painting shows up at an art gallery he works at, Bob must work with Eddie and Sloan to track down its sinister origins and convince the people living on Jacobi Street of them, before its too late!

Transformations in Pain by Matthew LeDrew
When two girls are assaulted and one is hospitalized, the residents of Coral Beach must put their shared tragedies behind them and stop the man responsible, as well as unlock the secrets behind the true nature of the Womb...

Year One: October

Smoke and Mirrors by Matthew LeDrew
The approaching trial of Genblade brings closure to the people of Coral Beach, until people start showing up dead in the same manner they did when he was at large.

"Scarlett" by Andrea Hackett
published in *light | dark*.
Introducing Scarlett, the slightly damaged hunter on a mission to save others from the monsters from her past.

"The Inevitable" by Ali House
published in *The Lightbulb Forest*
A young woman must contend with the
emergence of a frightening new power alongside
the emotional high of a first date.

The Tourniquet Reprisal by Curtis & LeDrew
A man lives in Atlanta, Georgia that people
don't talk about, but everyone knows he's there.
He arrived a year ago and turned a gaggle
of uneducated youth into something new,
something to fear.

Roulette by Matthew LeDrew
As the teen suicide rate in Coral Beach starts to
climb astronomically fast, Xander travels to Los
Angeles to fight his most terrifying adversary
yet… and learns that the only thing worse than
looking for release… is finding it.

Year One: November

Exodus of Angels by Curtis & LeDrew
Victor's enigmatic past is illuminated when
Jaycee accompanies him to visit a new friend
in the paliative care ward of the Black Springs
hospital, where Theo also happens to be
searching for a cure for Leigh.

Ghosts of the Past by Matthew LeDrew
Coral Beach faces its most awesome threat when
one of Engen's past mistakes is unleashed upon
the unsuspecting populous. Friends and enemies
unite to fight a common enemy… but will even
that be enough?

Touch Your Nose by Matthew LeDrew
Simon Monk must infiltrate the San Fransico branch of Shane Industries, a massive company with deep ties to the Engen Universe. Where do his true loyalties lie? And can he get out without causing harm?

Ignorance is Bliss by Matthew LeDrew
After being set through the ringer one too many times, Xander decides that his life with Julie needs a little more attention… which is bad news because a new villain has come to town with his sights set on Adam Genblade.

"Gristle While You Work" by Jay Paulin published in *light | dark*.
A short story centering around the rise of a new, and possibly cannibalistic, serial killer in the Engen Universe.

Becoming by Matthew LeDrew
For months Xander Drew has been doing his level best to keep the streets of Coral Beach clean, which means it's time for the forces of darkness to strike back… all at once.

Inner Child by Matthew LeDrew
Julie is hospitalized with life-threatening wounds to both body and soul. But the real threat comes from the hospital walls themselves, as a demonic presence makes itself known to Xander and his friends.

End of Year One

Gang War by Matthew LeDrew
The Tees, a homicidal gang of evil men, has finally been taken down by Xander Drew. But his victory is short lived, as retired Tees are mysteriously killed. With a town of suspects, anyone can be the culprit… including one of their own.

Chains by Matthew LeDrew
Sociopath Derek Smith has been freed from prison and is praying on the weak; and none are weaker than August Styles: a pregnant girl with Down Syndrome who has run away from home.

"Omega" by Ellen Curtis
published in *light|dark*.
A sinister division of Engen begins a series of experiments on pregnant women in a fashion eerily similar to those that created the original Black Womb project.

The Long Road by Matthew LeDrew
Xander meets the American people — and realizes that the world is harsh and wicked, but can also be soft and gentle, even loving. Xander Drew comes of age on the road, and sets his new direction.

Year Two

Cinders by Matthew LeDrew
Detective Horton enters a violent and dangerous world he didn't know existed beneath the veneer of order and structure that he has based his entire deductive method around.

Sinister Intent by Matthew LeDrew
One of the killers Detective Horton could not catch has resurfaced: a serial killer who flaunts his sinister intent in front of the Los Angeles Police Department, making it so that no one is safe.

Faith by Matthew LeDrew
Xander's mysterious and troublesome past returns to haunt him on the streets of Los Angeles; a place where even more people can get caught in the crossfire of the games of death and deceit that makes up his life.

Flickers in the Night by Matthew LeDrew
Lisa Rowdan is hunted by her haunting -- and powerful -- ex-boyfriend Ryan through a lonely city street. Can she escape him?
One of over twenty great sprine-tingling short stories!

Family Values by Matthew LeDrew
Xander and his new friends Crowley, Lisa, and Tim investigate a series of kidnappings and murders that stretch back decades, all of which have the same similar twist: victims being found after years of being missing.

The Future

Fate's Shadow by Matthew LeDrew
When one of Xander's old cases comes up for trial, Megan Greene returns with it. The former friends are led into conflict regarding her client's innocence. However, they put their difference aside when they both become targets of the vigilante known as Shiro Gilbert.

about the authors

Ellen Curtis is a writer and web tv personality born and raised in St. John's, Newfoundland; whose aptitude for the written word began at a young age, when she began writing short stories, poetry, lyrics and novellas.

She was 'discovered' at a Sci-Fi on the Rock writing panel in 2008, and her first collection of stories, *Compendium*, was published just over a year later in October 2009.

Since then she has risen to become one of Engen's lead authors, working on high-profile projects such as the *Infinity* series of adventure novels, as well as continuing her own endeavours.

She has written three novels for the Infinity series, a book of short stories, and is co-editor of the *Sci-Fi from the Rock* series.

In her spare time she enjoys reading, art, music and spending time near the ocean.

Matthew LeDrew holds an Honours Degree in English from the Memorial University of Newfoundland with a minor in Anthropology, and studied Journalism at College of the North Atlantic in Stephenville, Newfoundland. He was honoured to be a jury member of the 2018 NLBA awards.

He has written twenty novels for Engen Books: the ten book *Coral Beach Casefiles* series, *The Long Road, Cinders, Sinister Intent, Faith, Family Values, Jacobi Street, Touch Your Nose, Infinity, The Tourniquet Reprisal,* and *Exodus of Angels* the latter three of which with co-author Ellen Curtis. He lives in St. Johns, Newfoundland.

Andrea Hackett has always been told she had a wild imagination. It was only natural that as soon as she learned to write sentences she started to put her imagination onto paper and share them with others. She currently resides in Outer Cove with her sons, step daughter, and husband.

Since launching the Ink'd Well Comics line in late 2009, **Jay Paulin** has been busy. He is best known for co-creating the annual charity anthology *What the Wild Things Read* that shines a spotlight on up-and-coming creators, many from the Maritimes.

Sarah Thompson was born and raised in Grand Falls-Windsor, Newfoundland and graduated from the journalism program at the College of the North Atlantic in Stephenville. She has spent eleven years as a broadcast journalist in Newfoundland and Labrador, as well as for Fort McMurray, Alberta.

www.ingramcontent.com/pod-product-compliance
Lightning Source LLC
Chambersburg PA
CBHW051942240626
47153CB00005B/1600